SEA
STRIKE

SEA
STRIKE

James H. Cobb

G. P. PUTNAM'S SONS
NEW YORK

G. P. Putnam's Sons
Publishers Since 1838
a member of
Penguin Putnam Inc.
200 Madison Avenue
New York, NY 10016

Library of Congress Cataloging-in-Publication Data

Cobb, James H.
    Sea strike / by James H. Cobb.
        p.   cm.
    ISBN 0-399-14324-6 (acid-free paper)
    I. Title.
    PS3553.0178S4   1997   97-23466 CIP
    813'.54—dc21

Printed in the United States of America

10   9   8   7   6   5   4   3   2   1

This book is printed on acid-free paper. ∞

Book design by June Lee
Map by Jeffrey L. Ward

Dedicated to Amanda's three "grandfathers":
Chief Petty Officer Marshall R. Havemann, U.S.N.
Machinist Mate 1st James Vincent Cobb, U.S.N.
1st Lieutenant Woodrow Carlson, Idaho National Guard

CHINA, TAIWAN, AND VICINITY

MONGOLIA

RUSSIA

45°N

Beijing •

NORTH KOREA

40°N

Sea of Japan

• Seoul

CHINA

SOUTH KOREA

Tokyo •

Hiroshima Kobe

35°N

Yellow
Sea

Shanghai   Nagasaki   JAPAN

Yangtze River

INSET
AREA

Hangzhou

30°N

East
China Sea

RYUKYU ISLANDS

Pacific Ocean

FUJIAN
PROVINCE

Formosa Strait

Chilung

T'aipei

25°N

Miyako Shima

Hong Kong •

TAIWAN

South
China Sea

Philippine
Sea

20°N

Shanghai and
Yangtze River Estuary

15°N

• Manila

CHONGMING
DAO

Yangtze River

Sandbar

PHILIPPINES

CHANGXING DAO

HENG
SHA

Yangtze

River

10°N

Shanghai

Approaches

0 Kilometers   400

0 Kilometers   20

0 Miles   400

0 Miles   20

MALAYSIA

5°N

5°N

120°E   125°E   130°E   135°E   140°E

© 1997 Jeffrey L. Ward

SEA
STRIKE

☆ Over the Formosa Strait
0245 Hours Zone Time; July 16, 2006

Moondog 505 cruised at 20,000 feet, a geometric crossbreed of shark and manta ray skimming effortlessly over a misty seafloor of gray starlit clouds. Under the canopy of the big F/A-22 Sea Raptor, her pilot and systems operator slouched in their ejector seats in matching postures of slack-muscled semialertness. The night's mission was a milk run, one that left them both with plenty of brainpower to spare, enough to allow them to take a bookmark out of an old topic of discussion.

"Daggone it! You're a woman, you ought to be able to give me some kind of a handle on this thing."

"Dig, indeed I am a woman. I am also a rational adult human being. Your wife, on the other hand, is a certifiable dingdong with the mentality of a five-year-old."

"That's cutting it a bit thick, Bub."

"Hey, I'm not the one driving you crazy. Coming up on Waypoint Echo in ten seconds. Come left to zero one zero true on my mark. Three . . . two . . . one . . . Mark."

"GPU confirmation on Waypoint Echo. Steering zero one zero true on base leg for Waypoint Foxtrot. The thing is that she says that it's fine with her if I want to do another hitch."

Lieutenant Alan "Digger" Graves was a sandy-haired Georgia expatriate who was fighting a losing battle to hold a troubled marriage together. His backseater, Lieutenant (j.g.) Beverly "Bubbles" Zellerman, was an Oregon-born brunette who was fighting a battle of her own to stay inside the Navy's prescribed weight-to-height parameters. They had been flying together for almost two years now. Long enough to pass through both professionalism and friendship to become a blood- and instinct-bonded team.

Once, during a rather depressed and alcohol-intensive leave in Singapore, they had even slept together. Afterward, they had agreed that it had not been a cosmic experience for either of them. They had fallen back into their professional and friendly roles with a sigh of relief, the only lingering aftereffect of their encounter being an exceptional openness to one another's frailties.

"Dig, she can say any damn thing she wants, but you darn well know that every time you bring up the subject, she turns into the psycho-bitch from hell for the next week."

"Then what in the sweet damn-all does she want?"

"She wants you out of the Navy, and she wants you to take the blame for it. Five years from now, when you're moaning and pissing about throwing over your career, she wants to be able to give you that smug little smile and say, "Well, it was your decision.""

Graves sighed. "Yeah, I can buy that scenario, knowing her."

As he spoke, he shifted the pressure on his rudder pads and rocked his side-stick controller, slaloming the swing fighter through a lazy scissoring maneuver. Twisting in his harness, he peered aft, trying to pick out the dark silhouette of any pursuing aircraft against the lighter cloud deck.

He did not expect to see anything back there. His threat boards were clear and the Sea Raptor was state-of-the-art in stealth technology, theoretically immune to detection by any of the local air-defense nets. However, milk run or not, "checking six" was a wise man's precaution, especially when there was a war raging off your left wingtip.

It was a remarkably little-known struggle for one taking place in the telecommunications age, especially when one considered that in scope and in the sheer cost in human life, it was rapidly developing into a major conflict.

There were few news bites devoted to it on the global infonets. There were no carefully earnest young video journalists broadcasting live from the battlefields. Articles on it were rare outside of those professional publications devoted to international policy and the military sciences.

It didn't even have a recognized name yet in the historical sense, although a number of possibilities were being bandied about. In fact, the only point generally agreed upon was that it had begun at a place called Tiananmen Square.

It had been slow to grow. The first hint to the outside world occurred when the People's Republic of China started to close off certain provinces to foreign visitation. The explanation was "a program of civil reorganization."

Then came the carefully worded press releases from Beijing concerning the suppression of "bandits" and "counterrevolutionaries."

The satellites knew the truth, however. Arcing high over Asia on their global sentry, the reconsats of the other major powers monitored the villages burning each night and the growing number of dead in the streets of the cities. By the summer of 2006, it had become obvious to the world that its last major Communist empire was tearing itself apart.

It would not be an easy breakup. The old men in the Forbidden City had watched the disintegration of the Warsaw Pact and the Soviet Union, and had learned from it. They had prepared for this last stand and they lashed back ruthlessly with all of the resources available to them. The casualty count of the second Chinese civil war might surpass that of World War II. Possibly it already had. Not even the involved combatants knew for sure.

Moondog 505's task this night was to peek over the wall of silence and give the West a look into the heart of this conflict.

Digger and Bubbles had launched off their home carrier, the USS *Enterprise*, an hour before and five hundred miles to the southeast. Making landfall off Shantau, they had turned northward into the Formosa Strait, that narrow band of sea that separated the Chinese mainland and the island of Taiwan.

Paralleling the coast, roughly twenty miles offshore, they commenced their reconnaissance run. Five Oh Five was carrying Elint (Electronic Intelligence) and Sigint (Signal Intelligence) pallets in her internal weapons bays, and antenna pods clipped to her underwing hardpoints. So equipped, she could perform a multitude of tasks ranging from the location and identification of radio- and radar-transmission sites to gauging telephone net communications loads and electric-power-plant outputs.

Upon returning to the carrier, data would be downloaded and relayed to a number of different destinations—the Office of Naval Intelligence, the Defense Intelligence Agency, the CIA—all to be processed and correlated with the rest of the information stream flowing in on the crisis. Another piece to be used in assembling the great puzzle of China.

"So, what am I going to do about it, Bub?"

"So, admit you've got a losing situation and get the hell out of Dodge while you can. Don't wait till a kid comes along and complicates the situation."

"Aw, shit!"

"My feelings exactly!"

There was a minute's worth of silence as Graves stared out into the night beyond the canopy.

"The problem is that I still kind of love her."

"I kind of love butterscotch sundaes too, pal, but I'm trying not to let 'em dictate to me." Bubbles's voice softened. "Dig, it's just not working anymore."

Zellerman was about to add to that thought when, abruptly, she leaned forward, peering into one of her console screens.

Graves caught her move in his rearview mirrors. "What's up?" he asked, going taut.

"I don't know." Her fingers danced on a keypad, calling up a replay from the plane's Forward Looking Infrared Scanner.

"I think we just overflew a cruise missile stream."

"You sure?"

"Pretty. Three thermal plumes . . . looks like small turbojet plants . . . running nose-to-tail at wave-top altitude at about one-mile intervals. Speed about six hundred knots . . . Damn, there's another one! Four bogeys this time. Running east to west, just like the last batch."

"Who's shooting at whom?" Graves demanded.

"I don't know. It's got to be the Chinese, but as for which side, I don't know. I can't imagine why either the Rebels, or the Reds, would be firing in on the mainland from way out here. Whoa! Aircraft contact!"

"Where away?" Graves instinctively rocked the side-stick forward, plunging 505 into the overcast like a crash-diving submarine.

"Down on the deck again. Two groups of four in loose-deuce formation. Twin-engined fighter types. Can't ID the model. Airspeed five-fifty, east to west. That's an air strike, Digger!"

"Who are these guys? I don't think either the Reds or the Rebs have night-capable strike aircraft."

"Well, somebody does!" Zellerman's hands were flying across her console now, trying to keep pace with the accelerating data flow from the sensor packs. "Fire-control radars are coming up all along the coast! Multiple sources, gun and SAM systems!"

"Anyone painting us?"

"Negative, negative! We're clear so far. But we've also got some airborne cascade jammers lighting off to the east. Four or five of 'em. Big suckers!"

Up in the forward cockpit, a warning tone sounded. "I'm getting something on the threat boards now," Digger exclaimed.

"I've got it. No lockup. We're still below valid return thresholds. It looks like we're being scanned by an Airborne Early Warning aircraft of some kind. . . . It's way the hell off to the east of us, too. . . . Might be an E2D, but I don't think it's one of ours."

"What are you getting along the mainland now?"

"The side-scan FLIRs are picking up heavy thermal flares around Hsiamen and the Signal Intelligence monitors are reading defense-suppression jamming from what looks like NATO-standard ECM. Somebody's doing some bombing out there. I'm also seeing a formation of surface ships out in the Strait. Man, I wish we could use the radar for a second!"

"Have you gone certifiable?" Graves snapped. "Somebody's just declared World War Three out there! If we radiate, we're hamburger. Hang on, I'm reversing us out of this."

"Wait a minute!" Zellerman protested. "We don't know what's going on yet."

"We don't have to know what's going on! We just have to stay alive long enough to tell somebody about it."

"Let's at least get a look at this surface group. Come on, Dig, this is hot stuff going down!"

". . . All right. One look and then we're history."

Graves throttled back and flared the Sea Raptor's air brakes, letting her sink through the cloud cover. As they descended, Zellerman called out the clearing image feeding into her displays from the infrared scanners.

"It looks like a convoy . . . two parallel ship columns in the center. . . . Three medium-sized contacts and one large in each, with the big guys trailing . . . They're being screened by four, no, make that six, small escorts with another medium-sized guy out on point."

"Okay," Graves said, arming the chaff and flare launchers. "Threat boards are clear on tactical ranges. Do you confirm?"

"Confirm surface targets are full EMCON."

"Here's how we'll do it. We'll break through the overcast about six miles out from the target and at two thousand feet. We'll come around to the east, make one pass down the side of the formation, then we turn away and evade to the south. Get it all now, because we ain't gonna be back."

"Aye, aye. Gun cameras enabled and slaved to the FLIR. Recorders are running."

"We're doing it."

They punched down and out of the clouds, and the powerful thermographic imagers of the camera system cut through the darkness and the residual murk.

It was indeed a convoy. A flotilla of fast missile patrol boats guarded the flanks of half a dozen tank-landing ships and a pair of huge, Seagoing Barge Carrier–class superfreighters.

And leading the force as it steamed westward was the unmistakable cowbarn-over-speedboat silhouette of an Oliver Hazard Perry–class frigate.

Staring into his targeting screen, Graves wondered for one bewildered moment why his nation had conspired to launch a surprise attack against the People's Republic of China. Then he recalled that the U.S. Navy wasn't the only fleet in these waters that had Perrys in commission.

"Sweet Jesus! Chiang Kai-shek should have lived to see this," he murmured in awe, forgetting his resolution to pitch out and flee the area. "They're doing it. At long damn last, they're really doing it!"

"Who's doing what?" Zellerman demanded.

"That's part of an invasion fleet, Bub. A Taiwanese invasion fleet. After sixty damn years, the Nationalists are going home!"

☆ The Beaches at Chinchiang, China
0331 Hours Zone Time; July 16, 2006

Thunder rolled across the beaches of China and flame rained from the skies. The Nationalists had carried the multiple rocket-launcher batteries of their artillery regiments on the weather decks of their landing ships. Now those batteries were in action, raining an intermittent barrage of high explosives and white phosphorus in on the Communist beach defenses.

Under these conditions, absolute precision and accuracy were impossible. Given, though, that each launcher could shred an area larger than a city block with each salvo, precision and accuracy were also irrelevant.

Tears of rage and frustration streaked the face of Colonel Yuan Kai of the People's Liberation Army. Peering through the observation slits of his command bunker, one-half mile back from the beach line, he watched a personal nightmare become reality.

He had warned them. He had warned them all that the running dogs of the Kuomintang were still the true greatest enemy. They had not listened to him. The generals had become too focused on their fight with that bandit rabble in the south. They had drained the coastal commands of manpower and equipment, leaving nothing but the dregs behind to protect the sea frontiers. And the Nationalists had been watching, and waiting.

The running dogs had turned to leap at China's throat once more.

"Lieutenant!" Kai snarled over his shoulder. "Have you gotten me a line through to Regional Defense Headquarters yet?"

"No, Comrade Colonel. The telephone links appear to be down, sir." Kai's aide, a tall and stoic young officer in field combat gear, stood across the room, close beside the two signalman specialists manning the radio set and switchboard.

"Then what about the radio?"

"Heavy jamming, sir. All channels are blocked."

"Damnation! Keep trying! Get me through!"

Hissing an epithet under his breath, Kai turned back to the observation slit. Lifting his night glasses once more, he swept them across his regiment's defense sector, trying to get a firmer grasp on the extent of the developing catastrophe.

There had been no warning of an attack, just the cruise missiles that had killed his radar and the antiaircraft emplacements, kicking the door open for the strike aircraft that had followed.

As his men had poured out of their barracks bunkers to dash to the fighting emplacements along the beach, they had been mowed down by cluster bombs and incinerated by napalm. The scattered handfuls that had reached the dubious protection of the blockhouses now cowered under the merciless hammering of the naval bombardment.

There were other forces at work in the night as well.

The ground shuddered. Parallel to and just beyond the low surf line, a row of towering water plumes lifted into the air. Each plume had marked one of the beach obstacles. The row of concrete-and-steel blocks intended to deter the approach of landing craft had just been destroyed, no doubt by demolition charges laid by skin divers or ROVs.

They would be coming very soon now.

"Lieutenant! Have you gotten through to anyone yet?"

"No, sir," the aide replied calmly. "All communications are still down."

"Then send a runner! Have him take the headquarters' company truck, if it's still intact. Have him take a message to Regional Defense Headquarters. Inform them that we have a major landing under way in zone twelve. We need assistance immediately! The situation is critical!"

His aide gave an acknowledging nod. Going to the mouth of the bunker, he passed a hastily scribbled note and a quiet order to the two sentries stationed there. In moments, the soldiers were dashing away down the communications trench.

Suddenly, the generalized scream and roar of the rocket barrage abated. The abrupt silence was as disconcerting in its own way as had been the uproar of the bombardment. Kai refocused his attention into the night.

They were coming now. Low, angular forms were moving in from the sea. Like a pack of crocodiles, a flotilla of troop-carrying amphibious tractors was steadily churning closer to the beach.

From one of the surviving blockhouses, a machine gun chattered a feeble challenge. The savage crack-*wham* of a powerful naval rifle answered. Another, larger shadow was moving closer to the beach as well, a guardian frigate of the Nationalist Navy. If the ballistic rocket barrage had been a shotgun, the warship's flat-shooting five-inch guns were sniper's rifles, primed to take out the last vestiges of beachside resistance.

The devil take the PLA high command. Where was the air cover he had been promised in the case of a landing? Where was the artillery? Where were the torpedo boats?

The first rank of landing tracks was holding just off the surf line. Rocket launchers flared on their broad, armored backs and projectiles arced up and across the beach, each trailing a heavy line behind it. Kai recognized the technology at work. Those lines were hoses. Hoses that were even now pressurizing and filling with a liquid high-explosive. When fired, the hoses would burn through the beach minefield, the concussion triggering sympathetic detonations amid the mines buried there, clearing a path.

The Nationalist combat engineers keyed their firing switches. Bluewhite chain lightning laced the beach, each bolt flanked by lesser, sandy explosions. Thin though it might have been, the last barrier was down.

The lead Nationalist Amtrac, a massive, American-built LVTP-7, heaved out of the surf. Transitioning from its propellers to tank treads, it gingerly began to pick its way up one of the blast-cleared channels.

Kai prayed that he would see the flash of one of his own missile launchers, that the tractor would stumble to a halt spewing flame.

It did not, and a second followed it up out of the sea, and a third.

The Nationalist frigate was firing over the Amtracs now—deliberate hammering bursts from its main turret, each carefully targeted at the beach fortifications.

Kai bitterly considered how the one good thing about his dearth of troops was that he was able to disperse what he did have out among a large number of fortifications. Chiang's bastard sons would be expending a lot of their time and ammunition demolishing empty bunkers.

Then, abruptly, Kai realized something, something that made the cold hand of a corpse close around his heart.

The Nationalist frigate was keeping to a very deliberate fire-control template. Probably operating under GPU guidance, it was systematically picking off a series of the beach defense emplacements.

And it was targeting only those emplacements that had men assigned to them.

"Treason!" he whispered.

The Nationalists must have gained such knowledge of his troop deployments from within his own headquarters company.

"Treason!" he choked.

"Sir?"

Kai pounded his fist against the frame of the observation slit. "The damned Nationalists have infiltrated us, Lieutenant! That's how they know our defense deployments so well! Some filthy traitor inside our own regiment has sold us out!"

"No, sir," his aide replied quietly. "There are no traitors here."

"By all that is sacred, there are! They knew that this was a weak point on the coast! They knew the positioning of our beach obstacles. They even know our troop deployments. There is a traitor, Lieutenant, and if we get out of this alive, I will see him hunted down and hanged!"

There was no answer, except for the sound of a rifle bolt being drawn back.

Kai started to turn away from the observation slit, his hand instinctively going for the pistol holstered at his belt. Before he could complete either move, however, something smashed him down from the concrete observation step. Colonel Yuan Kai had only time enough to acknowledge an instant of pain and a momentary chaotic image of his aide standing in the bunker doorway, raking the room with gunfire.

As Kai fell, the aide pivoted, his short-barreled Type 56 assault rifle still clamped to his hip and hammering terror. The two signals specialists tried to get to their feet, one clawing for his own weapon, the other attempting to lift his hands in surrender.

The Lieutenant slashed his fire stream across them, sending them both to the floor. Lifting his aim, the aide used the last few 7.62mm rounds in the clip to destroy the bunker's communications console.

Ejecting the empty magazine, he swiftly reloaded, watching the bunker doorway for anyone investigating the gunfire.

No one came. The chaos out in the night had blanketed this little pocket of killing. The aide took a single deep, deliberate breath.

"No, my colonel," he said almost apologetically to the blood-streaked room. "There are no traitors here tonight. Only patriots."

Ducking out through the low doorway of the bunker, the aide headed down the communications trench. His work here was finished. However, the regimental Political Officer and the Chief of Staff still had to be dealt with down at the auxiliary command post.

☆ USS *Cunningham*, DDG-79

1332 Hours Zone Time; July 15, 2006

Commander Amanda Lee Garrett peered over the shoulder of her chief engineer, watching the blocks of red and yellow play across the schematics on the computer flatscreens. Each told a tale of catastrophic damage and systems failure. The enemy missile strike had hurt the USS *Cunningham*—badly. "Mr. McKelsie? Stealth systems status?"

"Everything's off line except for the chaff launchers. The hit's taken out both the transformers and the envelope processor stack."

The Duke's lean and acerbic stealth systems officer had his khaki shirt unbuttoned in the heat. They'd lost air-conditioning early on in the engagement and the ventilators had been dogged down to seal out the smoke that was rapidly saturating the ship's internal spaces. The temperature in the Combat Information Center was skyrocketing as a result. Uniform protocols had been abandoned. He ran a hand back through his damp, thinning red hair and continued the litany of disaster.

"We've also taken skin damage, and these fires are going to start cooking the RAM off the hull in pretty short order. As of right now, we are bare-ass naked."

"Damn, damn, damn! Dix, tac situation?"

Lieutenant Dixon Lovejoy Beltrain, the Duke's tactical action officer, leaned in over his console, stripped to the waist, his quarterback's torso slick with sweat.

"Hostile strike flight has disengaged," he reported. "All other incoming rounds have been foxed or intercepted. Board is clearing."

Miraculously, the great SPY-2A arrays of the destroyer's Aegis radar system were still functional and feeding their images onto the Large Screen Display that dominated the forward bulkhead of the Combat Information Center.

"That's something, anyway," Amanda muttered. They were being granted a little time. Maybe enough to make repairs and escape.

"Raven's Roost, do we have a weapons ID yet?"

"Raven's Roost" was the Duke's Electronic Intelligence–gathering section, one of the four subsystem bays that angled off from the octagonal CIC compartment. A boyishly slender figure appeared at the bay mouth a moment later.

"An Otomat Mark Three, Boss Ma'am," Lieutenant Christine Rendino replied. "One round. Air launched."

Again, a little plus. The Italian-built Otomat used a jet-propulsion system. Honest flame from burning kerosene and no chunks of unconsumed rocket fuel sprayed around to complicate fire and damage control.

Christine took another step or two into the central compartment. "How bad are we?"

The little Intel officer's reaction to the temperature had been to knot the shirt of her work khakis up under her breasts and to bind a sweatband around her short ash-blond hair.

"Real bad. We took the hit right in Power Room Three. Main Engine Control was taken out as well, and we've got fires all over the place back there."

Perspiration stung Amanda's eyes, and impatiently she swiped it away with the back of her hand. She was feeling the heat as intensely as her subordinates were, but captain's dignity had limited her to rolling up her sleeves and pony tailing her own thick sorrel-colored mane with a rubber band stolen from a chart table.

"Captain!" It was the rating stationed at the CIC's helm station. "All rudder and engine control has just gone down. The ship is losing way and is no longer responding to the helm."

"Damn, damn, damn!" Amanda spun back to the damage-control panels.

Chief Thomson was dialing down through the hull schematics to the lower deck levels. By another small miracle, the craggy lieutenant commander had been off station, outside of Main Engine Control, when the missile had hit.

"We've lost both primary cable trunks. The portside was cut by the initial explosion, and we just had a burnthrough into the starboard. The Halon flood didn't hold it. We've lost too much compartment integrity."

The *Cunningham's* spinal cord had just been severed.

"What about the hangar bay?"

"No direct involvement yet, but they have a major fire right under their deck plates. The big problem is going to be the aviation-fuel bunker and the helo-armaments magazine. They're right down there in the affected frames."

"Do we still have deluge control in those spaces?"

"So far."

"Arm the systems and stand by to flood on my command."

"Aye, aye, Captain."

The aft compartment hatch swung open, giving entrance to both a gas-masked sailor and a billowing cloud of white smoke. Amanda slammed the door back against its gaskets and twisted the dogging handle as the seaman tore off his breathing gear.

"Report from DC Alpha Delta," he reported breathlessly. "All engineering watch officers are dead or missing, ma'am. They were all either in Power Three or Main Engine Control when we took the hit. Chief Nelson reports that we're holding the fire at frame nineteen, but we're not getting it pushed back."

"How bad's the hull damage?" Amanda demanded.

"One hole on the port side at frame twenty, ma'am. 'Bout six by four. Just above the waterline."

"How are they doing on the farside of the fire?"

"No contact with Delta Fox. We can tell they're workin' it, but no commo."

Amanda internalized another savage curse. With the intercom and sound-powered nets down, she knew more about what was happening two hundred miles away than she did inside the bulkheads of her own ship.

"Captain!" Thomson yelled from the DC panels. "We got a high-temperature warning in the helo-ordnance magazine!"

"Execute the flood."

"That extra weight aft could put the impact hole under the waterline, Captain. With our internal integrity shot, we could lose the entire block to uncontrolled flooding."

"I'm counting on it. A little water won't kill us, Chief, but this fire just might."

"Captain," the seaman runner spoke up. "Chief Nelson still has rescue parties aft of the bulkheads looking for survivors."

"Hold the flood!" Amanda stabbed a finger at the runner. "Get back down to Chief Nelson and tell him that he has . . ." *Think, Amanda, how long can that weaponry take exposure to direct flame before destabilizing? Three minutes?* ". . . two minutes to pull his teams back behind the bulkheads and get things buttoned up. Then get topside and go aft over the weather decks. Inform the Delta Fox leader of the same thing. Got it? Go!"

"Aye, aye!" He pulled on his gas mask again and plunged back out into the almost solid wall of smoke beyond the hatchway.

The atmosphere inside the CIC was also rapidly becoming contaminated. Soon the duty watch would be needing their smoke masks as well.

Amanda ignored the thickening air and returned her attention to the damage-control screens.

She had to get her ship moving again. Thankfully, that task might not be too insurmountable. The Cunningham-class destroyer utilized an integrated electric drive. Her main motors were carried outside of the hull in twin pylon-mounted propulsor pods similar to the engines of a dirigible airship. There were no shaft alleys to flood. No boiler to explode. No reduction gears to strip. One just had to get the power from point A to point B.

She drew a fingertip across the primary display. "We've got to run a set of jumpers from the transformer bay of Generator Room Two, here, to the primary propulsor junction box back at frame twenty-two. Then a second set of power cables and a new control linkage back to the steering engine room."

"Shouldn't be any problem except for the junction box," Thomson replied. "It butts right up against that transverse bulkhead there. We got fire just on the other side of it now, and there's going to be water in a minute. God knows what kind of shape it's in. I'd better get back there and have a look at it."

"I'll take care of that, Chief," Amanda said. "Notify Commander Hiro on the bridge that he has the con."

"Begging your pardon, ma'am, but I'm not sure that's such a good idea."

"Chief, you're the last of the senior engineering staff we have left. I need you here, so that leaves me. I helped work on the design of the Duke's drives; I should be able to figure out what's busted, and what's not. Anyway, I need to take a look around and see what kind of shape we're in."

"As you say, ma'am."

"I'll send a runner back with word of what's going on in the stern. Initiate that magazine flood now. And get the internal communications back on line! Carry on."

She removed a smoke mask from its locker beside the hatch. Popping the plastic caps off its filters, she strapped it on. Taking a battle lantern from its rack, she opened the watertight door and plunged out into the vapor-filled passageway.

Throughout the entire explosion of activity within the CIC, two of the naval officers present had taken no active part in the operations. A full captain and a lieutenant commander, they had stood by, silently observing as the men and women of the duty watch had dealt with the developing disaster. Now, still unspeaking, the senior of the pair donned his own breathing mask and followed Amanda.

The battle lantern had been an act of futility. The smoke killed the beam in only a couple of feet. This wasn't as critical as it might have been, however. Amanda Garrett knew the Duke's interior spaces like the back of her hand.

Surrounding her in the murk, handy-billy motors roared, wood slammed into metal as shoring timbers were hammered into place, and the men and women of the DC teams blasphemed their way through their procedures.

She hesitated for a second in the passageway, then turned to the ladder that led one level up.

The *Cunningham's* wardroom had been converted into a casualty receiving station. Its limited deck space was jammed now with loaded stretchers and cluttered with discarded medical-stores packaging. The *Cunningham's* chief hospital corpsman, Bonnie Robinson, was working her way around the compartment running triage on the moaning injured for Doc Golden.

Lieutenant Commander Daniel "Doc" Golden was the latest addition to the Duke's company. It wasn't a common thing for a Navy doctor to be assigned aboard a destroyer. Normally, small surface combatants had to make do with only a corpsman and the hope for a fast medivac out to a carrier or tender.

However, the *Cunningham* had been designed for independent operations, and Amanda had recently made herself insufferable in certain quarters until she had acquired Golden. She had lost a crewman on her last cruise because she hadn't had a physician aboard ship. She would not let that happen again.

"How are we doing on the wounded, Doc?" Amanda asked, lifting her smoke mask.

"We don't have nearly enough of them," Golden replied, working over an IV set. "We've got a whole lot of Missing in Actions down in the engineering spaces." Golden moved with a youthful swiftness that seemed incompatible with a head balding toward middle age. His usual air of studied casualness had been transformed into a focused professionalism.

"What's the status of the ones we have been able to get to?"

"What you'd expect. Flash burns and concussion injuries. We're getting a lot of smoke inhalation now."

As if in response to his words the passageway hatch swung open, admitting another billow of smoke and a pair of DC hands carrying a third limp form between them.

"Smoke?"

"Yes, sir. Mask failure."

"Set her down in the corner and get some O_2 into her. Robinson, we've got another customer!"

"Aye, sir."

Golden glanced back at his CO. "And while we're on the subject, Captain, this place is beginning to remind me of a Ramada Inn I stayed at in Miami Beach once. The air-conditioning doesn't work, and you can't open the windows. Request permission to start evacuating the wounded out onto the weather decks. These people need uncontaminated air."

Amanda considered for a few moments. "Negative. We're still in a combat situation here. We may have to start launching missiles again at any time. I don't want unprotected personnel topside if it can be avoided."

"Captain . . ."

"Hold out here for as long as you can. If evacuation becomes absolutely imperative, notify me. That's all, Doc."

"As you say, Captain."

Amanda Garrett resealed her mask and left the wardroom. The four-striper who had been shadowing her, and who had been observing silently throughout her dialog with Doc Golden, followed suit.

Amanda dropped back down one deck and headed aft, moving through the smoke-saturated passageways with an ease and a swiftness that was almost supernatural. She stepped over unseen hoses and cables and around gaping access panels simply because she projected that they would be there in this given situation.

Passing through another watertight door, she sensed she was entering into a comparatively large open space, the *Cunningham's* belowdecks helicopter hangar. Turning to her left, she stepped ten paces off to starboard, station-keeping by brushing her fingertips along the bulkhead. The form that she knew should be there loomed before her.

"Arkady?"

"Right here, Captain."

Amanda could make him out only as a hazy outline in the smoke, but she knew he would be clad in his inevitable gray Nomex flight suit. She also knew that he was only a few inches taller then her own five feet seven, and that the eyes behind the faceplate of his smoke mask were an exceptionally clear and penetrating blue. In short, she knew Lieutenant Vince Arkady as well as she did the decks of her own ship.

"What's the bay status?"

"We've got a hot deck situation, Captain. No breakthroughs reported, but we're keeping things hosed down."

"Okay, we're going to be rigging a bypass to get power through to the motors and steering gear. Get set for it and have your people stand by to assist the cable teams."

"Will do."

"And we've got to ventilate these spaces. Drop the helipad elevator and get some of this smoke out of here."

"Tried it, Captain. No power. We're trying to get the circuits reenergized now."

"That's no good. We've got to ventilate now. Pop the safety latches with a crowbar and bleed the pressure out of the hydraulics reservoirs. That should bring it down. If it doesn't, get a couple of jacks from the DC locker and force it."

"Aye, aye."

He gripped her shoulder for a second, then he was gone, yelling commands to his unseen hangar crew.

Amanda continued to follow the bulkhead around, squeezing past the parked bulk of Retainer Zero One, one of the pair of SAH-66 Sea Comanche helos assigned to the *Cunningham's* aviation section. Ahead, a man-sized oval of dull yellowish light became visible, and a moment later, she emerged through the open hatchway into the clean air of the small well deck right aft.

Peeling off the mask, she granted herself the luxury of a single unforced breath. The sea breeze blowing across her perspiration-dampened clothing produced a delicious chill, but she couldn't enjoy it for long. Ignoring the somber-featured man who had followed her out of the hangar bay, she circled the aft Oto Melara turret and descended through another deck hatch.

The atmosphere was considerably cleaner in the stern spaces, leaving only the belowdecks darkness to contend with. It took Amanda a matter of moments to locate the aft DC site leader and her team three levels down.

"We're tight, ma'am," the Chief Petty Officer reported in the glow of the battle lanterns. "The bulkheads at frame twenty-three are holding with no burnthroughs. The steering engine is okay and I've had hands down to check both access tunnels into the propulsor pods. No damage to the main motors. We just need the juice to bring everything back up."

"You'll get it. The jumper teams are coming in right behind me."

"Okay! Hey, Wheeler! Get the access hatches open on the main junction box. Reichsbower, you do the same for the steering engine space. The rest of you guys fan out and start checking breaker panels. We got power coming in. Let's go!"

"Hey, Chief!" The voice of the man the site leader had sent to the junction box echoed in the passageway. "Come here, quick!"

Amanda followed the CPO as she hurried toward the call.

Seaman Wheeler was kneeling beside an open knee-level access panel in the side of the passageway. He had his flashlight aimed at a double X of blue tape stuck to the inside of the hatch.

"Ah, shit!" the Chief exploded. "Water damage!"

Amanda nodded grimly. "Cracked bulkhead or seal failure, they'll call it. I should have figured they wouldn't make it this easy. Okay, new game plan. We'll have to run a second jump back from Power Room One. We'll feed the starboard propulsor from One, the port from Two, jacking directly into the feeder cables at the head of the access tunnels. We'll control the motor RPMs directly with the generator outputs."

She started back for the 'tween-decks ladder. "I'm going forward to get 'em moving on the new setup. Have your people get the access tunnels open again and stand by to splice into the main power busses—"

"Hold it, Captain Garrett. No sense in wasting any more of your time, or ours." The officer who had been trailing behind her stepped into the beam of her battle lantern. "I think we can terminate this thing now."

Amanda took a deep, deliberate breath. "Aye, aye, sir," she replied, reaching for one of the "dead" interphones on the bulkhead.

"Bridge."

"Bridge, aye." The voice of her exec, Lieutenant Commander Kenneth Hiro, came back crisply over the circuit.

"This is the Captain, Ken. It's all over. Secure the conflagration drill. Well done to all hands."

The 1-MC speakers took up the call a few moments later.

"Secure the conflagration drill. I repeat, all decks, secure the conflagration drill. Main Engine Control, energize all circuits. Damage-control teams, shut down all smoke generators and commence stand-down. Set condition X-Ray in all spaces and ventilate the ship. All hands, the Lady says well done."

The overhead lighting blazed on with a glare that momentarily made the eyes ache. The ventilator blowers came on stream as well, producing the soft roar of moving air that was the underdeck sound signature of a healthy man-of-war. The smoke haze began to flow toward the intake grilles.

"I hope I wasn't being premature in issuing that 'well done' comment, Captain Johannson," Amanda continued, recradling the phone.

"Not in the least," the Fleet readiness officer replied. "Of course, I'll have to run a formal evaluation with the rest of my inspection team, but since your crew performed today the way they've been doing all week, I don't foresee any problems."

He extended his hand to Amanda. "Congratulations, Captain. You've got yourself a four-oh ship. I'd say that you're cleared for deployment."

From down the corridor, some covert listener produced a muffled whoop. In seconds, the word that the Duke had made it would be spreading along the scuttlebutt line from bow to stern.

☆   ☆   ☆

Amanda made her way topside again, past the damage-control hands, who were starting to clean and rerack their gear. This time when she emerged onto the well deck, she could take the time to savor the clean Pacific trade winds.

The USS *Cunningham* lay at anchor in Pearl Harbor's East Loch. There, for the past week, she had been deeply involved in the process of winning back her spurs.

The big guided-missile destroyer was just out of the repair yards following a long and difficult combat deployment in the South Atlantic, having been the sole American naval vessel to see action during the recent military confrontation with Argentina.

Despite this, and despite the fact that the *Cunningham* had emerged from the Antarctic campaign with numerous battle honors, including the Presidential Unit Citation, the Duke had to re-prove her readiness to return to sea.

For the past month, she and her crew had been involved in a grinding ritual of tests and drills: gunnery requalification, engineering requalification, aviation and ASW requalification.

The climax had been the weeklong mass-conflagration and damage-control exercise. With this last hurdle cleared, the ship and crew were rated as ready to depart on their scheduled duty deployment to the western Pacific.

Looking forward, Amanda could see that the helipad elevator was down as per her orders and that a few last wisps of the odorless, nontoxic smoke from the exercise generators were issuing from the open well, like steam from the crater of an inactive volcano.

Just forward of that, fared into the trailing end of the streamlined superstructure, the towering fin of the *Cunningham's* freestanding mast array stabbed upward. It was shaped like the raked back blade of some gigantic tanto fighting dagger, and the slight roll of the ship made its tip carve a delicate invisible pattern in the vivid blue of the Hawaiian sky.

Here and there, small clusters of sweat-soaked but jubilant crew personnel were emerging topside through the destroyer's weather-deck hatches, including some of Doc Golden's erstwhile "patients." They still had a good job's worth of cleanup and reordering to deal with, but for the moment the men and women of the Duke could take a breather and feel proud.

Up on the rim of the helipad, Vince Arkady appeared. She caught the flash of his grin as he spotted her on the well deck. Moving deliberately, he lifted his arms and clasped his hands overhead in a boxer's declaration of victory.

Amanda smiled as well, and replied in kind. Reaching back, she snapped the rubber band that confined her ponytail. Shaking her hair down around her shoulders, she leaned against the deck railing and took a deep breath.

☆ The White House, Washington, D.C.
2032 Hours Zone Time; July 15, 2006

It was the most pleasant part of the day in Washington. Evening was just taking the edge off the sauna bath heat, leaving a mellow glow that would hold well into the night. Secretary of State Harrison Van Lynden didn't have the time to enjoy it, however. His town car swept through the security checkpoint at the gate and wheeled up the curving drive to the south portico of the White House.

Ahead, brake lights flared, marking the arrival of another member of the crisis team. As his own vehicle drew up and came to a halt, Van Lynden recognized Lane Ashley, director of the National Security Agency, disembarking from the limousine ahead. Briefcase in hand, she paused for a moment, waiting for him.

"Good luck, sir," his Secret Service driver said. "On whatever it is this time."

"Go watch CNN, Frank. They probably know more about it than we do."

"Where did they catch you this morning?" Ashley inquired as they hurried down the quiet, carpeted corridors of the presidential residence.

"Preparing for a very long day with the Belgian Prime Minister. Possibly one of the ten most boring men in Western Europe."

"You were lucky," the tall, graying blonde sighed. "Brian and I were about to fly out to the West Coast for our son's wedding."

"None of us are lucky today, Lane. God, what a can of worms!"

They broke off their brief conversation as they approached the security team that flanked the access elevator to the White House briefing room. Even though he had made this passage scores of times during this administration, the Secret Service men carefully compared Van Lynden's spare, Yankee features with the photograph on his identity badge.

Then, with suitably respectful suspicion, they touched an ID wand to the badge's magnetic tab. The resulting electronic chirp verified that the Secretary of State was indeed who he said he was. The process was repeated with the NSA director, then they were cleared through into the elevator and down into the White House's secured underground level.

"Were you able to get something put together?" Ashley inquired as they began to descend.

"Something. But the Boss still isn't going to be happy."

Benton Childress was a middle-aged black man, solidly built and tending toward portliness. His predilection for rather hairy tweed suits and gold-framed glasses gave the classic impression of a college history teacher. Not surprisingly so, for he had once been one. He had also been a Rhodes scholar, the mayor of a major midwestern city, and a lieutenant colonel in the Missouri Air National Guard. Currently, he was the forty-fourth president of the United States.

He was looking over the golden frames of those glasses now, regarding the three members of his assembled crisis team much as he must have a group of recalcitrant students.

"Miss Lane, gentlemen," he said. "How in the hell was this allowed to get past us?"

Like another ex–Missouri National Guardsman who had sat in the Oval Office, President Childress had a decided propensity for plain speaking.

"Too many tasking assignments and not enough assets," Lane Ashley replied, levelly meeting the President's gaze. Having battered her way up through the old boys' network within the CIA, she was well capable of doing some plain speaking of her own.

"Most of the resources we've had deployed on the western Pacific Rim have been focused on what's been happening inside mainland China. We simply weren't looking back over our shoulder at Taiwan."

The current incarnation of the presidential briefing room was done in dark cherrywood, the wall paneling and the massive conference table and chairs surrounding it. Its carpeting was blue, and the only diversions from the room's Edwardian elegance was the discreet systems workstation in one corner and the single large flatscreen display inset into each wall. The superb air-conditioning and temperature control didn't even hint at the fact they were twenty feet underground.

"There's another aspect to that as well, sir," Van Lynden added. "When the Chinese civil war went hot, the Taiwanese went on a heightened state of military alert. Then, over the past six months, their government has been reporting a series of provocative actions taken by the Reds. Aggressive jamming of communications and early-warning radar. Patrol boats and aircraft fired on. That kind of thing.

"In response, they instituted a partial mobilization of reserves and tied on a series of major readiness exercises and war games. Given the unsettled state of affairs in their neighborhood, these appeared to be reasonable precautions. No doubt they buried a lot of their invasion preparations inside all of this other military activity."

"That was pretty goddamned convenient for certain people," Sam Hanson said.

With a ramrod spine and a steel-gray brush cut, Presidential Security Adviser Sam Hanson still looked and sounded very much the marine he had been for thirty years. With the advent of the Childress administration, he had stepped directly across from the chairmanship of the Joint Chiefs of Staff to this slot on the President's cabinet.

"We might want to go back and have another look at some of those 'provocative actions.'"

"I don't think that would accomplish very much, Sam," Ashley said. "We know that many elements of the People's Liberation Army have rebel sympathizers operating within them. It would have been easy enough to arrange incidents from the inside."

"Or they could have been genuine," Van Lynden interjected. "The Red Chinese have a history of attempting to intimidate the Taiwanese. Maybe they were trying to bluff the Nationalists out of an involvement in the war, and it backfired. Either way, I don't think it makes all that much difference now."

"Good point, Harry," Childress said. "I guess Monday-morning quarterbacking isn't going to gain us much ground. Let's see what's going on now, then we can decide what we're going to do about it. Director Ashley, I believe you have a situational update for us.

"Yes, sir."

The NSA woman nodded to the systems operator seated at the workstation. "First image, please."

The conference room's indirect lighting dimmed. The Large Screen Display at the far end of the room activated, filling with a computer graphics map of mainland China and its environs.

Along the coast south from Shantau to the Vietnamese border and inland to Szechwan Province, the map glowed yellow. Manchuria and north-central China were marked in solid red, as was the major offshore island of Hainan. The western provinces were a swirled mottling of both colors.

"This is our current best estimate of the situation in China as of July fourteenth. We know that the rebels—or United Democratic Forces of China, as they refer to themselves—hold the southeast, with their core power base being the Canton–Hong Kong area. The Communists maintain control of Beijing and the northeast."

"The old cultural dividing line between the bread eaters and the rice eaters," Van Lynden commented.

"Essentially so," Ashley agreed. "In the western provinces, things are more complicated. What has been a more or less straightforward civil war in the east has collapsed into a mass of localized conflicts and insurgencies between a large number of different ethnic factions, political groups, and plain, old-fashioned warlords. Most voice allegiance to one side or the other, but most also are operating with their own agenda.

"We don't think that even the Chinese know what all's going on out there. In the Trans-Gobi region, contact has been completely lost with some provinces. Since we're talking about hundreds of thousands of square miles here, it might take years to get communications reestablished. When we do, we might find we have some entirely new nations to deal with."

"The ones that we have are more than enough for the moment." President Childress grunted. "Continue, Ms. Ashley."

"The overt phase of the Chinese civil war began approximately two years ago with an outbreak of large-scale civil protests in the Canton–Hong Kong area. The point of contention being both the replacement of locally born administrators with northern Chinese and the increasing bleed-off of profits from the Canton Special Economic Zone by the Beijing government.

"When the PLA Local Force units were ordered to suppress the rioting, there was a mass mutiny within the district command, a 'revolt of the colonels' that led to most of the troops siding with the rioters. The leadership of the United Democratic Forces of China surfaced shortly thereafter to serve as the ad hoc government of the area in rebellion.

"The revolt spread from there. Most of the Main Force divisions have apparently sided with the Beijing government, as have the majority of the surviving air force and naval units, and the Armed People's Police. The PLA Local Force elements and the People's Militia have generally sided with the rebels.

"This has led to a kind of strategic stalemate, with the UDFC's greater numbers being counterbalanced by the Communists' superior mobility and firepower. As a result, the battle lines in the eastern provinces have been essentially static for the past six months. That changed last night. First overlay, please."

The map graphics altered. Now, on the eastern Chinese coast, opposite Taiwan, there was a patch of orange notched into the red zone like an inflamed wound.

"I believe Mr. Hanson has the operational end for us."

Hanson nodded an acknowledgment and picked up the thread of the briefing.

"The show started during the early-morning hours with multiple air and cruise missile strikes. It was a classic tasking template, laying fire in on airfields, air-defense sites, command-and-control nodes. We've got something here that will show how things went down. The recon footage, please."

A second screen lit off and filled with an almost supernaturally clear video overview of a low, hilly farmland, taken from what looked like about a thousand-foot altitude.

Van Lynden recognized the feel of the area as coastal Asia.

"How was this imaged, Sam?" he inquired.

"Through a microwave link with one of our Aurora strategic reconnaissance aircraft. We're flying a relay of them out of Tonopah to supplement our reconsat coverage. At the time this was taken, this flyboy was over Fujian Province at about a hundred and twenty thousand feet. He's going to be taking a look at the military air base at Fuzhou here in a second."

The video image panned around smoothly as the aircraft banked and came in on target. Hanson removed a laser pointer from his inside suit pocket. As they began to "drag the line" down the main runway at Fuzhou, he utilized the bright star projected by the pointer to catalog the destruction.

"See those pale streaks running across the runways and taxiways, the places where it looks like the ground's boiled up? Runway breaker submunitions dropped from aircraft-mounted scatter packs did that. Bet there are some air-dropped land mines in there, too. . . . Over there, 'long side the runway, that's a bomb crater . . . now. At one time, though, from the look of the wreckage around it, it was an antiaircraft emplacement. Hangars gone . . . tower and admin buildings gone . . . Those aircraft revetments didn't do much good. Bam, bam, bam, a whole squadron of F-8 Finbacks blown away. . . . Probably fragmentation airbursts steered in over target by laser guidance."

"Night delivery, CBUs, and precision-guided munitions," President Childress commented. "That's all state of the art."

"Yes, sir. High speed and low drag all across the board. We're identifying late-model ordnance from all over the world. Israeli, Brazilian, South African, as well as some home-brewed Taiwanese stuff we've never even seen before."

"None of those ready-alert fighters looked like they even had the chance to start their engines."

"They didn't, Mr. President. Far as we can tell, the PLA's entire sector air-defense net crashed just as the first Nationalist strike wave crossed the beach. Massive internal sabotage. They had this thing *organized!*"

The video run ended and the screen returned to the map image.

"At any rate," the Security Adviser continued, "by first light, the Nationalists had achieved tactical air supremacy over the province. They followed up by putting a full marine division ashore here, at Chinchiang, supported by a series of battalion-scale airborne and airmobile landings and Special Forces paradrops in the Communist rear areas.

"Follow-up waves are going in across the beach now, with the primary axis of assault trending southward. My guess is that they're going for the port facilities at Amoy."

"What were the Reds doing while all of this was going on?"

"They were being taken very by surprise. Fujian was supposed to be a secure rear area for them."

Ben Childress frowned as he digested the data block.

"What about the rebel factions?" he said abruptly. "How are they involved in this?"

"It's obvious that the United Democratic Forces and the Nationalists are working hand in glove," Lane Ashley replied. "Concurrent with the invasion, there was a whole wave of sabotage and guerrilla attacks throughout the province, plus evidence of a number of major defections from within the local Communist defense forces.

"Also, the landing was coordinated with a major UDF ground offensive out of their Hunan stronghold area. They must have been planning and working together on this operation for a long time."

Van Lynden hadn't been looking forward to this moment. President Childress shifted in his chair to face the Secretary of State. "What about this, Harry? Every word that's come across my desk from State has indicated no major connections between Taiwan and the rebels. Supposedly, the UDFC was almost as distrustful of the Nationalists as of the Communists, and the Taiwanese government was losing interest in a mainland involvement. What happened?"

"We were false-flagged, sir. Obviously, the Nationalists and the UDFC have a covert support and planning network in place, one that we never even had a suspicion of. Also, obviously, they've developed a mutually compatible political agenda and a close alliance.

"I accept responsibility for this failure within State. I can offer no excuse except for the fact that the Nationalists have probably been putting this structure in place, bit by bit, for the past fifty years, and they've done a damn good job of it. As Sam pointed out, they had this thing organized."

Childress nodded and took off his glasses. Removing a folded white handkerchief from his coat pocket, he began to polish the lenses with great deliberation. Everyone on the staff recognized the action as one of the President's favorite "thinking stalls." Finally, he redonned them with a crisp, precise movement.

"Well, people," he said. "Let's face it. They whipped our ass, and they whipped it damn good. However, I don't think that recriminations, self or otherwise, will accomplish all that much. We need to shift focus to what's going to happen next and what's to be done about it. Any projections?"

"Nothing beyond a major destabilization of the situation," Lane Ashley sighed. "As we have seen, the Nationalist military is both well trained and well equipped with state-of-the-art armaments technology. While numerically not as large as the forces fielded by either the Communists or the UDFC, they will provide the rebels with the mechanized ground units and the air and sea power they lack. That, plus a guaranteed source for logistics and high-tech weaponry. I have to say that this definitely tilts the odds against the Beijing regime."

"I don't think anyone at this table will expend too many tears at that eventuality," the President said dryly.

Sam Hanson straightened slightly in his chair. "The question is, sir, what the Reds will be willing to do to tilt things back their way."

"What options do they have?"

Sam Hanson answered. "Barring pro-Communist outside intervention, something about as likely as a hailstorm in hell, there's only one. Go nuclear."

The briefing room suddenly became quieter, and somehow cold. In councils such as this, the "N" word was not bandied about lightly.

"General Hanson," Childress said, reverting to his Security Adviser's old rank. "I've read the theoretical studies that were made back during the dissolution of the USSR on the concept of a nuclear civil war. Frankly, I never put much stock in them. I have a hard time visualizing any national leader sanctioning the use of atomic weapons against his own people."

"Sir, we are talking about an Asian culture here. I know that making cultural judgments is considered politically incorrect these days, but this reminds me of a story I heard that came out of the Korean War.

"It seems that some members of the Red Chinese government were concerned about the possibility that the United States might use the atomic bomb against them. When the question was put to the high command of the People's Liberation Army, one of the generals just shrugged his shoulders and said, 'So, we lose a few million. What of it?' That could be the kind of mentality we may be facing here."

"But, damn it all, they'd be blasting their own nation into a radioactive wasteland. What would be the gain?"

"It wouldn't be a matter of gain, Mr. President," Van Lynden cut in. "It would be a matter of loss. The most basic premise of international statesmanship since 1947 has been that you never back a nuclear power into a corner that they can't get out of. That may be happening here."

"How so, Harry?"

"In a civil war situation, you have everything to lose, and nothing to lose. The Red leadership knows that if the rebels come out on top, they have nothing to look forward to, except for exile at best, or a war crimes trial at worst. They could very easily decide that half a country is better than none."

"God damn."

This time Childress didn't bother with his glasses as he paused to contemplate this thought.

"We must assume," he said finally, "that the Nationalists would have worked this out as well. Knowing the risks, why would they be so willing to go to the wall? They have the options. Why court that kind of obliteration?"

"Maybe they figure they have a kicker," Hanson replied.

"The only cards strong enough to count in that kind of game would be megatonnage and throw weight," Van Lynden said. "MAD—mutual assured destruction."

Childress shifted his attention to the NSA director. "What about this, Ms. Ashley. Could the Nationalists or the UDFC have nuclear capacity?"

"The exact nuclear status of any of these involved parties is open for debate, Mr. President," she replied. "Of course, the PRC was a nuclear power long before its civil war. However, we are not certain how much of that arsenal remains in their control, or is operational. For example, we know that all three of Red China's Xia-class fleet ballistic-missile submarines were laid up last year, apparently for lack of resources to maintain them.

"We also know that on at least two occasions, the UDFC expended considerable effort in trying to seize a portion of the remaining Red atomic arsenal. Major land battles were fought over the PRC's strategic missile bases at Tongdao and Luoning."

"What was the outcome?"

"We aren't certain. We do know that in both instances, the PLA blew up the facilities before retreating and that neither is operational at this time. Our best sit-guess is that if the UDFC has managed to seize atomic arms, they'll probably be in the form of low-yield tactical weapons: artillery shells and mines, free-fall bombs, and warheads for FROG and Scud-type battlefield missiles. Not strategic arms, but big enough to make a considerable mess."

"What about the third side of the equation, the Nationalists?"

At this question from the President, the three advisers exchanged sober glances. "That's a very good question, sir," the NSA woman said. "One we've been trying to get an answer on for some time."

"I don't need that kind of ambiguity, people."

"That's all we can give," Van Lynden replied. "The status of Taiwan as a nuclear power has been one of the great question marks in the arms-control field since at least the late seventies."

"That's right, sir," Hanson added. "They've had the reactors, they've had the tech, and, God knows, they've had the motivation. They've also maintained a low-key but very active R-and-D exchange program with Israel and South Africa, both states with known atomic capability. For example, we know that the Nationalists have fielded and used domestically produced variants of the Israeli Jericho battlefield SRBM and Masada cruise missile—both of which, by the way, are nuclear-capable delivery systems."

"And yet Taiwan has signed the nuclear nonproliferation treaty and has stated repeatedly, both to us and to the U.N., that they do not have nuclear arms. Do you believe they're lying?"

"I believe that they may be guilty of a polite political sophistry," Van Lynden replied. "Israel has also repeatedly stated that they do not have nuclear weapons, and technically speaking, that's the truth. What they do have are component sets that can be assembled into functional weapons in a matter of hours. That could be the case here."

"Good Christ Almighty," Childress whispered. "Three different fingers on three different buttons and a high desperation level all the way around. And they thought the Cuban missile crisis was bad."

"That's the assessment, sir. The destiny of China for the next century, i.e., for one quarter of the human race, is going to be decided over the next couple of months. Now we need to decide just what part we're going to play in that decision."

"You've saved me from having to state the obvious, Harry. Now, do you have any suggestions about what part we can play?"

Van Lynden nodded. "Yes, sir, I do. We take advantage of the situation."

The Secretary of State lifted his briefcase to the tabletop. Opening it, he removed a thin file folder.

"My proposal paper, sir," he said, placing it in front of President Childress. "I suggest that we take this opportunity to try to initiate a series of crisis-reduction talks with the three primary involved parties. A peace conference to be held on some neutral ground.

"We try to bring in all of the western Pacific Rim states—Japan, the Philippines, Korea, everyone who'd be downwind of a Chinese nuclear exchange. We try to get them to support the peace process by exerting what diplomatic pressure they can on the combatants."

"If I recall correctly," Childress replied, "both the Beijing government and the UDFC have responded with outright truculence to outside interference in their conflict. They claim that it's solely an internal Chinese affair. What makes you think that the Nationalists will be any different, or that anything has changed?"

"Just that the potential for an atomic war is escalating rapidly. Despite Sam's story, I am pleased to say that atomic war still scares the hell out of a lot of people. Maybe that fear will be the crack we can fit the tip of a crowbar into. If we can just get somebody talking . . ."

Van Lynden let his voice trail off.

The President's attention shifted around the table. "Ms. Ashley?"

She placed her ops plan beside the Secretary of State.

"Staying on top of this situation is going to require a massive retasking of our reconnaissance and intelligence-gathering assets, both NSA and military. I'd like State's assistance in getting us permission to forward-deploy TR-2, Darkstar, and RC-10 assets into Korea, the Philippines, and Singapore.

"I'd like to say Taiwan as well, but that might be imprudent under the current situation. To make up for that, I'd like to see if Seventh Fleet could move any of their available Raven platforms into the South and East China Seas."

"Sam, what about a military reaction?"

"Low key for the moment," Hanson replied, sliding his contribution across the table. "Place all of our units in the western Pacific on an increased state of alert. Reenforce the Seventh Fleet with whatever odds and ends we can move out of Pearl. Issue the 366th Composite Wing a flyaway notification for possible deployment to the Far East, and advise CENTCOM that the Chinese theater of operations is now a zone of concern."

Childress nodded in thoughtful agreement.

"One thing further, sir," Hanson continued. "I'd advise we enhance our nuclear-reaction capacity. I'm not saying that we change our DEFCON status yet, but I suggest we have STRATCOM alter the maintenance and servicing schedules for the Minuteman and Trident forces to maximize system availability for the next few months. Also, Air Combat Command should tie on a series of nuclear-ordnance delivery exercises for the strategic bomber groups."

"Are you sure that's necessary, General?"

"Hope it isn't, Mr. President. But, on the other hand, I'd sure as hell hate for us to be the guy who brought a knife to a gunfight."

Childress nodded. "Valid point. Thank you all for your input, and for your rapid response on this situation. I think we have the basis for a plan of action here. Now, there's one thing further you can help me on."

He gestured toward the three operations files before him. "When we go active with this, I'm going to have a lineup of isolationist congressmen outside the Oval Office demanding to know why we're getting involved in another nation's internal catfight halfway around the world. Any suggestions about what I should tell them?"

There was a moment of general silence. Then Van Lynden said, "Maybe you could point out to them that if the Chinese civil war goes nuclear, we can expect to see at least a couple of dozen old-fashioned, dirty-style atomic bombs detonated in the Earth's atmosphere within a very short period of time.

"If that happens, every living thing on this planet is going to be involved."

☆ Pearl Harbor, Hawaii

1930 Hours Zone Time; July 15, 2006

The big ship was quiet, her passageways empty, her crew dispersing to the pleasures of a Honolulu night.

Following the conflagration drill, they had brought the *Cunningham* back to her shoreside moorage at the Pearl Harbor Fleet Base. Today they had finished with the grind of their requalification exercises. Tomorrow, the work of preparing for West Pac would begin. But for this evening, Amanda Garrett had decreed a well-earned stand-down for all hands.

In her cramped sleeping cabin, she admired herself in the small bulkhead mirror as best she could. The ex-pat Hong Kong seamstress she patronized here in the islands had been right. The azure Egyptian cotton did highlight the golden hazel of her eyes.

Sleeveless and slit-skirted, the cheongsam fit as only a tailored garment could, its high collar adding an extra touch to the natural authority of her carriage. Amanda gave an approving nod.

She stepped out into the cabin's office space. Checking the batteries in her cellular phone, she clipped it into place on the end of her purse. Slipping the strap over her shoulder, she picked up her small overnight case and turned for the door.

There were four icons in the *Cunningham's* wardroom. The first was mounted on the forward bulkhead, where it would be the first thing seen by anyone coming through the main entryway. A foot-high capital *E*, done in white-enameled metal, it signified the Pacific Fleet E for Excellence the destroyer had earned the previous year. It denoted that the Duke had scored in the top ten percent during her initial qualification exercises.

Below it was the second icon, an enlargement of a campaign ribbon, the ice blue, frost white, and sea gray of the Antarctic blockade. It was a unique honor. Only the USS *Cunningham* and her crew could wear it.

On a conventional vessel, these badges of accomplishment would have been displayed prominently on the bridge wing. On a stealth hull, however, even a few inches of nonspec paint would have made a difference in the ship's radar cross-section.

To starboard of the entryway, mounted on the redwood-paneled bulkhead, there was a magnificent oil painting of the *Cunningham*. It was a commissioning gift presented to the ship by Amanda's father, Wilson Garrett, retired rear admiral turned noted maritime artist.

And finally, to port was the ship's metaphysical heart, a pair of naval aviator's wings sealed in a small glass case—another commissioning gift presented by another rear admiral, Randy "Duke" Cunningham, the Navy's first supersonic jet ace of the Vietnam era and the destroyer's valorous namesake. This evening, the wardroom also contained a small group of the *Cunningham's* officers. Doc Golden and Dix Beltrain were in whites, obviously preparing to go ashore. Ken Hiro, on the other hand, was still in work khakis. Seated alone at the big mess table, he was at the nexus of a solid fan of ship's paperwork. As Amanda entered the compartment, conversation trailed off and all three men rose to their feet in response to a courtesy older than military tradition.

"Good evening, gentlemen," Amanda said. "Plans being made?"

"That's right, Captain," Beltrain replied genially. "Doc and I here are getting set to tear up the town tonight. It's his first time on the beach in Hawaii."

"Haven't you ever been ashore in Honolulu before, Doc?" Amanda inquired.

"Technically, once, on vacation with my ex-wife, Marilyn. Every expensive boutique and every cheap tourist show on the island, that's what I know."

"Not a very good experience?"

"Let's put it this way." Doc solemnly reached up and tapped his balding brow with a fingertip. "I lost some of this when a genuine, authentic Polynesian fire dancer over at Don Ho's lost control of his tiki torch."

Doc Golden accepted the resulting explosion of laughter with dignity.

Beltrain gave a dubious shake of his head. "Doc, I think we're going to have to put some overtime in on you."

"Just no luaus. It casts a pall over the whole thing if you take someone to a luau who can't eat the pig."

Amanda chuckled again and balanced her overnight case on the edge of the mess table.

"All right, Ken. And what are you doing still aboard?"

"Just taking care of some of the usual, Captain," Hiro replied, looking up distractedly. "By the way, looking good tonight, ma'am."

"Thank you." She smiled. "But that doesn't get around the fact that you've barely seen your family this week. We're going to be off for West Pac in less than a month. If you don't spend some time on the beach with your wife and kids before then, Misa will poison my yakitori next time you have me over for dinner. There's nothing here that can't wait. Go home."

Hiro grinned back sheepishly. "Okay, Captain. Just give me another half hour on the watch lists, then I'm out of here."

"Deal. Half an hour. And I'm holding you to it. Thirty-five minutes from now and the duty security team comes in here with guns drawn to put you over the side."

"I have been warned, ma'am."

"You have, Ken. If anything comes up, I can be contacted through my cellular. Good night, gentlemen. Have an interesting evening, but no broken bones and no felony arrests. We have work to do tomorrow."

Amanda was not cognizant of the prolonged gazes that followed her out of the wardroom. Finally, Doc Golden spoke almost reverently. "I was not aware that the Navy issued commanding officers who looked like that."

"Yup," Dix agreed. "We do not get to see that side of the Skipper too often. Appreciate it while it lasts, Doc."

"Let's just also continue to appreciate that she is the Captain, gentlemen," the Duke's exec added from the mess table.

Hiro picked up his pen once more, then hesitated. "However, I will concede that somewhere on the island of Oahu tonight, there is one extremely lucky son of a bitch."

The fire-and-gold explosion of an island sunset dominated the western sky. Around the massive fleet base, a growing constellation of work lights were flickering on in response to the oncoming tropic evening.

Within the complex, trickles of interior traffic merged into a stream that flowed toward the checkpoint at Nimitz Gate. Civilian day workers going off shift and military personnel on pass, it was a flow that would reverse itself with the coming of the morning hours—the natural, living inhalation and exhalation of the big naval installation.

Out on the pier apron, Amanda looked back for a few moments to admire the sleek lines of her ship.

Because of her outriggerlike propulsor pods and the comparatively delicate RAM jacketing of her hull, the big guided-missile destroyer had to use the "Mediterranean Moor." She was backed in between two piers, her airbag-padded stern butted up against the breakwater and her folding gangway extending down to shoreside. A broad V of spring lines braced her in place and her anchor held her bow out toward open water.

Harbormasters hated to see the Mediterranean Moor used, because a Cunningham took up twice the moorage space of a conventional vessel of her 8,000-ton displacement. Shipmasters hated doing it as well, because it was a damn finicky piece of ship handling.

However, with the rose-tinted gaze of a proud skipper, Amanda was willing to overlook this minor foible of her command.

With the rakish sweep of her finlike mast array, the long open foredeck running almost half the length of her hull, and her low, streamlined superstructure, the *Cunningham* more resembled the creation of some imaginative yacht designer than she did the classic image of a man-of-war. The two small Oto Melara autocannon turrets fore and aft only hinted at the massed firepower concealed by her stark sleekness.

Her exotic design was mandated by the strict parameters of stealth technology. She was the lead vessel of the U.S. Navy's first class of blue-water low-observability surface combatants all but invisible to the probing radar beams of a potential enemy.

This quest for stealth ranged into the visible spectrum as well. The only flash of true color anywhere about the *Cunningham* was the Stars and Stripes flipping lazily at her jackstaff like the tail of a contented cat.

Instead of the conventional Navy gray, she was painted in the dustier low-observability hue used on the latest generation of U.S. carrier aircraft. The name across her stern and the big ID numbers under the flare of her radically raked clipper bow were done in outlined "phantom" letters and numerals.

A darker, tiger-striped pattern was also overlain on the base color: wavering, sooty bands that ran vertically down the length of the hull and horizontally up the height of the mast array. A computer-designed derivative of the First World War's "dazzle" camouflage, it served to confuse electro-optical targeting systems and to break up the Duke's distinctive silhouette, rendering her harder to identify.

Even pierside, the Duke's outline had a tendency to merge into the growing background shadows in odd ways, as if she were a specter preparing to fade into the night.

Much as Amanda was about to do herself.

She smiled wryly and unlocked the door of her leased automobile, releasing a puff of the day's retained heat. A few minutes later she was part of the traffic stream flowing toward the main gate at Pearl.

She headed east along Nimitz Highway, staying with it even after it changed into Kalakaua Avenue and plunged into the heart of downtown

Honolulu. Following the shoreline of Mamala Bay past the tourist kitsch of Waikiki, she circled around to Sans Souci and the other quiet beaches below Diamond Head. It was a moderately long drive from Pearl Harbor, but that was the price that had to be paid for a degree of privacy.

Amanda pulled into the small oceanside restaurant that had the big, leafy hau tree shading the out-of-door tables on its lanai. A Pontiac Banshee sports coupe was already parked in the lot, its driver leaning back against its fender, waiting for her.

A few moments more and Amanda was exchanging her first night's kiss with Vince Arkady.

During the trial by fire of the Antarctic campaign, they had become comrades and confidants. That they would also become lovers had been a given long before they had been able to act upon the possibility.

Amanda had frequently told herself that getting romantically entangled with one of her own junior officers was possibly the single most stupid thing she had ever done. However, she had always received the same answer: that the only thing more stupid might have been not getting involved at all.

☆ Honolulu, Hawaii

2120 Hours Zone Time; July 15, 2006

The Hau Tree Lanai was at the same time both a premier and a pleasantly understated restaurant. American-style prime steaks and seafood were offered, with outdoor seating, a sea breeze, and superb view of both Mamala Bay and the Honolulu beachfront.

It was a wonderful place to lounge with a cool drink on a warm night and watch the lights of the city. Especially in good company.

Amanda took a sip from her after-dinner sherry and soda, lightly pressed Arkady's hand against her thigh beneath the shelter of the table.

"Congratulations," he said.

"Hmmmm? For what?"

"Scuttlebutt has it that we aced our exams today. We keep the E."

"That isn't official by a long shot . . . but I think we did all right." Amanda allowed herself to preen just a little.

"As if there would be any doubt." Arkady grinned at her. Rakishly handsome and with dark hair pushing the Navy's length standards, the helo pilot looked a little more pirate than naval officer tonight. His appearance was enhanced by the casual safari shirt he wore tucked into his brushed denim slacks.

"I never promote overconfidence, Arkady," she replied, "in either myself, or in anyone else. And that brings up something I need to talk to you about."

"Okay, shoot, babe."

Amanda set her glass down and sighed. "It's no big deal, really, but you got a little sloppy on the ship today."

"Sloppy?" He frowned. "Was there a problem with air division?"

"Oh, no." Amanda shook her head emphatically. "The air group was fine. No problems. It's just that when we were talking in the hangar bay during the conflag drill, you got a little familiar. You reached out and patted me on the shoulder. It was just a little deal. And God knows I didn't have a problem with it personally, but I did have an inspection officer on my tail. It wouldn't have been a good thing if he'd seen that."

"Hell, I know that, babe. But we were in zero-zero visibility. Nobody saw anything. I'm sure of it."

"I hope not. But we can't afford to get lax. Especially aboard ship. You know how the Navy feels about relationships inside a chain of command. I could get you in so much trouble over this—"

She was interrupted by a snort of laughter. Arkady bent forward over the table, trying to control his spontaneous explosion of mirth.

"I'm pleased that you find the imminent disintegration of your career so amusing," Amanda said with pointed irony.

"Babe, that's not it at all. It is just that you are so damn predictable in some ways."

She cocked an eyebrow. "Others have told me that on occasion. But what do you mean exactly?"

The aviator lifted her hand to the tabletop and squeezed it gently between his. "It's like this. It takes two to run a romance, and if I remember right, I was the one who wanted to push the point when we first met in Rio.

"For two, the Navy always comes down a lot harder on the senior member of a liaison like this than they do the junior. You're the one who's putting her neck on the line because of me.

"Nonetheless, there you go, dragging all the blame over onto your side of the bed. For God sakes, lady, can't you just sit back and enjoy an illicit love affair without taking the weight of the world on your shoulders?"

Amanda gave the minutest shake of her head. "Nope." It felt very good to laugh with her young lover just then. During some of her introspective moments, Amanda had tried to analyze what Vince Arkady's role was in her life. Possibly it was that he made her remember there was a world beyond the parameters of naval regulations.

That, plus other things. Amanda drew his hand to her face, lightly nuzzling it for a moment. It was a good hand, strong when it needed to be, but likewise gentle, and roughened by honorable service.

"Babe, there's a question I've never asked you before."

"What?"

"What made you decide to become a naval officer?"

That was an interesting question. Amanda reached for her drink and took another thoughtful sip.

"I really couldn't say exactly," she replied. "I can't recall making any kind of concrete decision about it. I've always loved the sea more than just about anything else I can think of. And around our house, you just sort of absorbed Navy through your pores."

"Your dad, the rear admiral?"

"Um-hmm." Amanda nodded. "Thirty years on the line, including the Persian Gulf Tanker Wars and Desert Storm. And then there was my grandpa Marshall. He served aboard just about everything from the China river gunboats to the USS *Missouri*.

"I wish you could have met him, Arkady. Grandpa did Neutrality Patrol duty in the Atlantic before World War Two, the Doolittle Raid, the Aleutians, the Solomons, the Philippines, and Korea. He had seen it all and done it all, and when I was a kid I was sure that he was just one pay grade below God. I would sit and listen to him and Dad yarn for hours.

"Somewhere along the line, I just started knowing that I wanted to be like them. And that someday I wanted a ship of my own."

She looked out across the beach below the restaurant lanai, watching the waves angle along the sand.

"I suppose," she said after a few moments of reminiscent silence, "that it was something of a shock to my father when he found out that his baby girl wanted to be a hairy, smelly sailor, just like he was."

The corner of Arkady's mouth quirked up. "I don't know, it seems to me that he was pretty proud of his 'baby girl' when he pinned the Navy Cross onto her back at Norfolk."

"Yeah." She smiled to herself in the twilight. "I guess he was."

Suddenly, there was a shrill electronic trilling. Diverted, Amanda reached into her shoulder bag and the cellular clipped to it. She had the professionalism back in her voice by the time she had flipped open the phone.

"Garrett here."

"Hey, Boss Ma'am. This is Chris. Sorry to interrupt whatever I'm interrupting, but I think we have a kind of situation developing."

"What's happened, Chris?" Amanda tried to identify the odd murmur of sound she heard behind her intelligence officer's voice.

"Do you have your encryption on?"

Amanda glanced at the switch and the check light of her cellular's security option. "Yes, I'm secure. Go."

"'Kay. Here it is. There has been a major national security event somewhere within the Seventh Fleet zone of operations. Seventh Fleet and naval Special Forces elements are being mobilized, and the Duke can expect an alert-to-deploy notification in the immediate future."

Again that odd burst of noise interrupted Christine.

"Chris, where are you? Aboard the ship?"

"Uh, well, no. Actually, I'm speaking to you from the ladies' john of Haole Joe's Sports Bar."

Amanda knew that Christine Rendino, unconventional though she might be, was not prone to making prank phone calls to a superior officer. Nor was she in the habit of becoming dysfunctionally intoxicated. There would be an explanation, and Amanda waited for it.

"We've got a lot of base people over here watching the night game from stateside. The Mariners are dying in agony in the seventh inning, in case you're interested. . . ."

"I'm not. What's your point, Chris?"

"Anyway, starting about forty-five minutes ago, pagers and cell phones started going off all over the place. Four people from the Seventh Fleet Operations Center, a couple of guys from NAVSPECFORCE, even a couple of civilian ONI analysts, all of 'em scorched out of here like tomcats going over the wall at a neutering clinic.

"Shall we say that this aroused my curiosity. I retired to the ladies' relief facility here and set off a few pagers of my own. I can confirm that this isn't a localized phenomenon. Command and operations personnel are being pulled in from all over the island."

As she followed Christine's words, Amanda gestured across the table to Arkady, motioning him to come around and listen in on the conversation. Swiftly, he circled the table and hunkered down beside her chair, leaning close to listen in.

Christine continued. "Finally, I called a friend of mine who is standing a port watch out aboard the *Yellowstone* tonight. They can see both Seventh Fleet Ops Center and NAVSPECFORCE HQ from their moorage. Both places are lit up like a dance club on Saturday night and have a steady stream of traffic going into their lots. Fa' sure we have an event on."

Amanda nodded slowly. "Is there any chance at all that this could be some kind of readiness exercise?"

"No," Christine responded decisively. "I don't think so, Boss Ma'am. The vibes coming off this are wrong."

Amanda nodded again. Christine's "vibes" were something that she trusted implicitly. She was not only a friend, but she was also one of the rising stars of her field. Behind that carefully cultivated Valley Girl persona, there was a cool and crystal-clear intellect of formidable capacity. A perusal of personnel records would have shown that Christine Rendino had the highest IQ of anyone aboard the *Cunningham*. And that, Amanda had to admit, included the captain.

"What's your best guess on the crisis point?"

"I don't have to guess; I know. I had them switch over to CNN during the seventh-inning stretch. They've just announced that the Nationalists have dealt themselves into the Chinese civil war. Taiwan has launched an invasion of the Chinese mainland."

"You are kidding me!"

"Kidding not. They went across the beach this morning. And fa' sure, this is going to have some people freaking out."

"And you think we're going to get a piece of it?"

"Our new lords and masters over at NAVSPECFORCE are already getting a piece of the action. We're the only stealth hull they have in the Pacific just now, and we've just passed our requals. Add it up, Boss Ma'am."

"I see your point, Chris."

"I just thought you'd like the word. Do you want me to keep digging on this?"

Amanda stared unseeing across the restaurant lanai, her thoughts accelerating. As always, Christine's logic was impeccable. If there was a flare-up looming in the Pacific, the *Cunningham,* as one of the fleet's most capable surface combatants, would be going. She had gained a few hours, possibly a day, on her deployment notice. How to spend it best?

"Negative, Chris. Go on back to your ball game. I'll take it from here."

"Okay, Captain." Christine's voice grew intent again. "I trust that I didn't interrupt anything too critical?"

"No." Amanda suddenly became aware of Arkady's body warmth pressing close. "Not yet."

She signed off. At her side, her Air Division leader rocked back on his heels. "Well, what's the word, Captain?"

"Nothing," she replied thoughtfully. "We're going to let it ride for tonight."

Noting his raised eyebrow, she continued. "Even if we did start pulling the crew back aboard now, we probably couldn't get all that much done before morning. If the Duke is due for a crash deployment within the next couple of days, the best thing we can do is to let our people get a little shore time. It might be their last for a while."

"Makes sense to me." Arkady nodded.

"Right." Amanda crisply snapped the phone shut and returned it to her purse. "Damn, damn, damn! We had a deployment-preparations schedule all roughed out, but that's shot to pieces now. I'm sorry, Arkady, but I'd better get back to the ship and see what I can start piecing together."

"Okay, babe. But before you do, can you do me one favor?"

"Of course. What?" She looked at him inquiringly. He was still kneeling beside her chair, meeting her gaze levelly with a spark of affectionate humor dancing in those damnably blue eyes.

"Would you please repeat all that stuff you said about shore time for the crew and everything. Only this time around, just for fun, substitute 'Amanda Garrett' for 'crew.' I'd just like to hear how it sounds."

In her moment of distracted confusion, she almost started to do it. Then she found herself dissolving into something close to a giggle. She collapsed back into her chair and reached out to caress his cheek. "Vincent Arkady, you are a sin. My sin."

"Like you said, babe. It might be the last time for a while."

"So it might."

☆ Honolulu, Hawaii

0745 Hours Zone Time; July 16, 2006

Again the trilling of Amanda's phone registered on Vince Arkady's consciousness, this time piercing through layers of sleep. There was a silky slithering on the bed beside him, and the pleasant pool of warmth that had been curled against his back was gone.

By the time he had rolled over and opened his eyes, Amanda was up and across the room to answer the call.

"Garrett."

Last night she had drawn open the drapes and the glass balcony door to allow the sea breeze and moonlight into their hotel room. Now she stood backdropped by the morning blue of the bay and the sky, totally unself-conscious in her nudity, completely intent on whomever she was speaking with. To Arkady, just then, she was all things desirable and beautiful.

She stood posed, one hand on her hip, one long dancer's leg carrying her weight, the other relaxed with her knee slightly bent. Her tousled auburn hair flowed down around her tanned shoulders, making the scar across the top of her left collarbone stand out. What had hurt her there? he wondered. That was another one of those things that he hadn't had a chance to ask about yet.

It took him a few moments to focus on her conversation.

"Okay, Ken. Have they given us a fixed sortie time yet? . . . How about a destination?"

He watched as she nodded slowly.

"Okay . . . Anything else? . . . Ten hundred hours? Damn, what time is it now?"

He watched Amanda look around the room for the time. Her old Pusser's Lady Admiral wristwatch, along with her earrings and panty hose, had ended up on the floor beside Arkady's side of the bed. Scooping up the watch, he took it across to her, receiving a quick smile of thanks in return. As she checked the time, he ran his hand down her bare spine in a good-morning caress, receiving a quick brush of her lips in thanks.

"Okay, Ken," she said into the phone. "It's eight-fifteen now. This is how we'll work it. Schedule an Operations Group for all division heads for oh one hundred hours this afternoon. I should be done with the Admiral by then. I'll pass the full word at that time. In the interim, you know the drill. Recall all hands and inform them we are deploying . . . sometime in the near future. Then initiate a full stores and spares replenishment. Get us re-fueled and commence taking aboard our warloads. Also, set a priority list on whatever in-port maintenance we may still need."

"I presume all officers have been notified? Lieutenant Arkady? Haven't you been able to locate him?"

Amanda glanced over her shoulder. "Don't worry about it," she deadpanned perfectly, leaning back against him. "I think I know where he can be located. Is Chris aboard yet? Okay, as soon as she's in, get her working on one of her patented situation briefings on the current Chinese conflict. I want to know what we're going be facing. . . . Very good, then. I'll be back aboard as soon as I'm finished with MacIntyre."

Amanda flipped the phone shut, staring unseeing across the room. "Arkady," she said, "Chris was right. It is China. How soon will Aviation Section be ready to load?"

"Whenever you want it, Captain. We're caught up on all shoreside maintenance. I'm scheduled to run both helos through the RAM calibration range up at Schofield this afternoon. We're set to go."

The conversion was beginning. Naked, with the scent of last night's passion still on their skin, they were already slipping back into their professional personas. Aboard the *Cunningham* there would be room enough only for the Captain and the Lieutenant. It was a reasonable requirement of the careers that they had chosen, but the man and the woman had the right to regret the necessity.

"Time to ride," Amanda said. "I have to be back at the base in about two hours."

"Will you be able to grab some breakfast before you get back to the ship?"

"I think so."

They sank down on the end of the bed. Amanda nestled against him, neither of them quite willing to come back into the real world for another few moments.

"Thank you, Arkady," she murmured.

He slipped his arm around her and gently nuzzled her hair, kissing her forehead just at the part in her soft bangs. "Thank you. It's just till next time, babe."

"'Til next time."

NAVSPECFORCE Headquarters reeked of fresh paint. Naval Special Forces Command was the new kid on the Pearl Harbor block. Accordingly, it had inherited one of the oldest base administration complexes, a sprawling set of single-story cinder-block buildings that dated back to the Vietnam construction boom. A major renovation and rebuild job had been required; civilian contractors could still be found puttering in odd corners of the complex, leisurely applying the finishing touches.

NAVSPECFORCE was a new kid in more ways than one. The successor to the U.S. Navy's old Special Warfare Command, it was an effort to bind all of the Fleet's diverse unconventional warfare and intelligence-gathering assets under one roof: SEALs Marine Force Recon, commando carrier and raven submarines, and the Special Boat, Aviation, Submersible, and Patrol Craft Squadrons.

Thanks to the insistent and effective politicking of Vice Admiral Elliot MacIntyre, the newly appointed CICNAVSPECFORCE, the new command had also acquired all of the Navy's stealth hulls, including the USS *Cunningham*.

It was a controversial move, the controversy emanating from without, as the other Fleet Flags screamed over the loss of ships and assets, and from within, as Special Forces commanders brooded over their loss of independence.

As for Amanda, she was ambivalent. The Annapolis-bred conservative in her was leery of overspecialized cloak-and-dagger outfits. On the other hand, there was a potential challenge about special operations, one that she found very intriguing.

"Morning, Captain," Christine Rendino sang, falling into step beside Amanda as she walked down the entry corridor.

"Good morning, Chris. What are you doing here?"

Like Amanda, Christine was wearing a set of summer Navy whites. Unlike Amanda, however, some minute aspect of attitude and posture downscaled them from a uniform into mere clothing.

This was part of a faint and indefinable air that always seemed to hang around the Duke's intel, one that tended to make some more conventional personnel vaguely uneasy. It was the sensation that hallowed traditions and standards were being acceded to only out of amused indulgence.

"I was called in to be briefed on some totally radical new toys we're going to get to play with," Christine replied.

"Such as?"

"A tactical remote sensor net for littoral operations."

"The hydrophone buoy system?" Amanda had read some of the literature on the system.

"Exactly. A fast SOSUS barrier to go with a side of fries. This will be the first actual tactical deployment. We're getting a whole lot of other neat stuff, too."

"Anything special I should know about?"

"Hmm, just that it means that we're going to be working up close, Boss Ma'am. Up close and personal."

Precisely at ten hundred hours, MacIntyre's aide ushered Amanda into the Admiral's office.

She had served under Vice Admiral Elliot Edward "Eddie Mac" MacIntyre's command a few months prior. He had been Commander in Chief Atlantic Fleet when she had taken the *Cunningham* into the Antarctic campaign. Since then, and since being assigned to NAVSPECFORCE, she had met with MacIntyre aboard ship and on the neutral ground of official functions a number of times.

This, however, was her first meeting with the Admiral on his home turf. As Amanda crossed the dozen steps to his desk, she made a quick, discreet survey of the room, seeking to learn more about the man by his personal environment.

A bold, abstract seascape hung on the inside wall, along with a collection of pen-and-ink prints of American warships. The ones he had served aboard? Possibly.

A stereo cabinet sat in the corner, the hide of some exotic-looking animal, maybe a tree kangaroo, mounted above it. Its music rack was loaded with an eclectic-looking assortment of CDs, cassettes, and even a few frayed LP jackets.

There was also a well-filled bookcase, a wooden model of an Arab sailing dhow placed on its upper shelf. Amanda recognized it as genuine Red Sea craftwork.

Then there were the photographs displayed prominently on one corner of the desk. The two college-age boys and a younger girl, and an older picture of a lovely raven-haired woman.

As for the man himself, Elliot MacIntyre was somewhat more than average height, had broad, square-set shoulders, and a craggy solidity. His brown hair was graying and his face had weathered with long years at sea. Nonetheless, Amanda noted a younger man's vitality in the way he moved, and a youthful intensity in his dark eyes.

"Captain Garrett reporting as ordered, sir," she said, her fingertips snapping to her brow.

"Good morning, Captain," MacIntyre replied, returning her salute. "Please, sit down. Coffee?"

His voice was good as well, steady and deep with no hint of condescension.

"Yes, sir. Thank you," she answered, sinking into one of the chairs facing the desk.

MacIntyre gave his aide a nod, then settled back into his own chair.

"First of all, Captain," he continued, "I'd like to mention that your re-qual scores came across my desk this morning."

Amanda straightened slightly. "Our observer team leader indicated to me that he was satisfied with our performance. I hope that you are as well, sir."

MacIntyre nodded. "To say the least, Captain. The *Cunningham* is hanging on to her E. You hit the upper ten percent in all divisions. Actually, closer to the upper two in most. Exceedingly well done. But then, that's what I've come to expect from the Duke."

Amanda felt herself begin to flush. "Thank you, sir."

"You may not want to thank me after this briefing is over. How soon can the Duke be ready to sortie?"

Oh, Lord, here it comes, Amanda thought feverishly. They needed to get the ship pulled back together again after the conflag exercise. They needed to fully replenish. They needed to deal with at least some of their in-port maintenance backlog. Those of her crew who had dependents in Hawaii needed some kind of time to get them squared away.

But there was also only one answer she could give for the Duke.

"If we can get some help with our loading, sir, we can be under way by sixteen hundred this afternoon."

MacIntyre nodded again and smiled slightly. Amanda guessed that a check had just been made on a positive side of a column.

"Very good, Captain, but things aren't quite that bad. I can give you a little less than forty-eight hours. We need you out of here by oh six hundred the day after tomorrow."

Amanda released a mental sigh of relief. "No problem, sir."

"Good enough. Here's the package. You're being deployed into the East China Sea to act as an independent intelligence-gathering platform. Once on station, you will monitor the developing aspects of the Chinese civil war, via both your ship's systems and the tactical sensor net you will be setting up.

"Specific tasking orders will be issued to you through this command from the Defense Intelligence Agency, as the situation develops."

The Admiral paused as his aide reappeared with a tray bearing two steaming mugs and the appropriate accoutrements, unobtrusively placing it on the desk sideboard.

"Thanks, Simons," he said. "Cream and sugar, Captain?"

"Yes, sir. Both."

MacIntyre served her himself. Amanda noted the touch of courtliness as he did so. It matched the way he had come to his feet when she had entered his office. Amanda, in turn, accepted it as her just due.

Returning to his chair, MacIntyre tilted it back to a comfortable angle.

"The basic mission premise is pretty simple," he continued, following his first sip of coffee. "The tricky aspect is going to be setting up your remote sensors. The Duke will have to work inshore, inside Chinese coastal waters. Just how far inside will be left to your judgment and the tactical situation.

"However, the very bright and very expensive people who designed this paraphernalia seem to indicate the closer the better. Your intelligence officer will be able to outline the exact parameters of the sensor-deployment envelope for you."

MacIntyre set his cup on the desktop. "Your mission profile may also include having to fly projection missions over the mainland with your helos.

There will be some National Security tie-ins on this aspect of the deployment. Your intel will be able to fill you in on this as well."

Her cooling coffee forgotten, Amanda frowned lightly and considered the mission outline he had just given her.

"Once I'm on station, who will I be answering to in theater?" she inquired.

"You'll be working inside Task Force 7.1's modified local operating area. You'll be drawing replenishment from them and, should this thing go to guns for any reason, you'll be under their tactical command. Beyond that eventuality, however, you'll be operating on your own recognizance."

An independent command. The chance to cut loose from a carrier's apron strings and be a captain-under-God again.

"The thing is," MacIntyre continued levelly, "you'll have to develop a good operational relationship out there with Admiral Tallman. I know Jake. He's a good man. But we Flag types can be somewhat short when it comes to having an outsider rambling around in what we perceive as our territory.

"Technically, you may not be under his command, but you sure as hell are going to have to work with him."

"I understand, sir." Amanda nodded. "I'll do my best."

"I'm certain you will, Commander. That's why I'm writing a comparatively junior officer such a massive blank check. Because I think she'll know all the right places to cash it."

It wasn't necessary for him to mention that he was drawing that check on his personal reputation and that of his new command.

Amanda knew that Elliot MacIntyre had antagonized more than a few people in setting NAVSPECFORCE up the way he wanted it. Those people would be more than pleased to see this operation fall flat on its face first crack out of the box.

"The *Cunningham* will not let you down, sir."

"I can't conceive of her doing so, Captain."

"Does this operation have a designation yet?"

MacIntyre gave another nod. "Yes, it has. I chose it myself. Operation Uriah. Remember your Bible?"

She did, and smiled as she made the connection. "Very appropriate, sir.

Uriah the Hittite, sent to the forefront of battle. And I fully expect the *Cunningham* to be far more fortunate in danger than he was, sir."

Amanda gave Christine Rendino a lift back to the ship following their briefing sessions. Lord! She'd have to find time to turn her car in at the leasing agency before they sailed. Just something else to have to worry about.

At least they had forty-eight—no, make that forty-two now—hours to work with. A month's worth of preparation to complete in less than two days. But with her people, just maybe she could make it.

"Interesting night?"

"It certainly was, Chris. Who would have figured the Taiwanese would pull an off-the-wall stunt like this?"

"Ahem, that was a query, not a statement. As in 'Was it an . . .'"

"It was all right," Amanda replied, striving to keep her voice carefully casual. "I just went out to dinner."

"Now, why do I find that hard to believe?" Christine turned in the passenger seat to face Amanda. "Word is that you were wearing your blue China dress last night. You've shown me that outfit, Skipper, and that is not something you'd wear to 'just a dinner.'"

The blond Intel had her large gray-blue eyes locked on Amanda with the fixed intensity she reserved for an exceptionally interesting intelligence challenge.

"Chris, what's this all about?"

"It's not about anything, other than the fact that I'm an incorrigible snoop. Why do you think I chose this career path, anyway? Now, who's the new guy?"

Amanda just managed to keep from squirming uncomfortably behind the steering wheel.

"Chris, you know how I am. My affairs are my affair."

Not exactly true. She and Chris had shared more than one port-of-call story over the years of their acquaintance. But, God, what was she supposed to say now?

"Besides, Lieutenant," Amanda continued, "we've got more important things to worry about at the moment."

Invoking rank wasn't the best save in the world to use with Chris, but it was all she could come up with at short notice.

"As you wish, Captain," Christine replied primly, refocusing her attention outside of the car, the faintest trace of a grin ghosting around her lips.

They came within sight of the Duke's moorage, and Amanda forgot the growing complications of her personal life. Loading operations had commenced, with a row of Navy deuce-and-a-halfs lined up at the foot of the aluminum gangway. Work parties were already hogging a steady stream of crates and cases across the well deck and through one of the watertight doors into the hangar bay.

A final fuel top-off was under way as well. A heavy hose snaked up from a dockside valve head and down through a deck hatch to an internal bunkerage point, carrying a flow of high-density kerosene into the destroyer's tanks.

As Amanda and Christine crossed the sun-softened tarmac from the parking lot to the gangway, they noted a small group of people clustered at the gangway base. Three of them were *Cunningham* hands—the Officer of the Deck and the coverall-clad gangway security team. The other pair of seamen wore standard Navy dungarees and had seabags lying at their feet.

They all snapped smartly to attention at Amanda's approach.

"Good morning, Mr. Selkirk," she said, answering their salute. "What's going on?"

"A couple of new hands reporting aboard, ma'am," the OOD replied.

"Very good." She looked over her new crewmen, reading name tapes and ratings badges and opening a couple of new mental personnel files. "Seaman Kirby . . . Seaman Langdon, I'm Captain Garrett, your CO. You've managed to sign on just as we've caught an emergency deployment order, so we're all going to be a little busy for a while. Check in with the exec, Commander Hiro, for your duty stations and quartering billets. Once we're at sea and we get things lined out, we'll get a chance to talk. Until then, gentlemen, welcome aboard the Duke."

Amanda and her officers continued on up to the deck, leaving the two sets of enlisted hands to eye each other dubiously. Finally, one of the new men said, "Hey, we've never done a cruise with a woman captain before. What's the word?"

The two veteran *Cunningham* ratings exchanged the bored glances of seniors putting up with the new kids in school.

"The Lady's okay," the female half of the team replied, shifting the sling of her snub-barreled riot gun. "She sticks by the crew and she doesn't get in your face over the small stuff. The big thing is that you gotta do your job."

"Yeah," her opposite number added darkly. "You let down the ship, and the Lady'll hand you your cock in a hotdog bun."

☆ Pearl Harbor Approaches, Outbound 0545 Hours Zone Time; July 18, 2006

Clad in a worn set of work khakis, with a *Cunningham* baseball cap tugged low over her French-braided hair, Amanda Garrett lounged back in the bridge captain's chair, one deck shoe braced comfortably against the wheelhouse grab rail. They were exiting out into the deeper waters of Mamala Bay from the gut of Pearl Channel. Already she could note the darkening blue of the surrounding waters. Likewise, she could sense the first tug of the great open-ocean rollers coming in from the Pacific.

"All engines ahead standard. Make turns for twenty knots."

"Aye, aye, ma'am," the lee helm responded from the central bridge console. Dropping a hand down to the lever-studded control pedestal that separated him from the helmsman, he rocked the throttles and power levers forward. The rushing whine of the great turbogenerator sets increased. There was a palpable surge of acceleration as the Duke tacked on speed, the V of snowy foam streaming away from under her forefoot broadening in response.

"All engines answering ahead standard. Making turns for two-zero knots."

Amanda smiled to herself, reveling in the sensation, as a skilled rider might enjoy lifting a thoroughbred stallion into a canter.

Off the starboard bow, one of the big Honolulu tourist schooners lazed along on a breakfast cruise, cheating on the wind with her auxiliary diesels. Her rail became a solid wall of camera and binocular lenses as the big man-of-war swept past, and humbly, the sailing ship dipped her flag in salute.

"Quartermaster, reply with two on the siren, please."

The Duke's air horns blared, echoes returning faintly off the receding shoreline.

The schooner drew away astern, and Amanda shifted her gaze to the row of repeater monitors mounted above the brow of the bridge windscreen. Seeking out the navigational radar, she checked her clearance with the cruise vessel.

Okay, looking good.

"Navicom status, please?"

"We are at initial point, Captain," the duty quartermaster replied from his workstation. "SINS and GPU cross-referenced and verified. Course is on the boards and Navicom is ready to engage."

Another brow telescreen displayed a computer-graphics chart of the Oahu approaches, and a glowing set of departure headings now materialized on it, angling away to the west.

"Very well. Helm, engage autopilot and go to Navicom." The helmsman tapped a pattern into his systems keypad. Smoothly, the Duke's prow began to come around into the rising sun as she hunted for her new course.

"Steering two six five degrees true, Captain. Autopilot tracking on marked headings."

"Very well. Pass the word to all compartments. Stand down from Condition Zebra. Set cruise mode in all spaces as per Plan of the Day."

At that declaration, the bridge crew could allow themselves to relax. They were clear of the harbor, and from here, if necessary, the *Cunningham* could take herself to the rendezvous point ten days away off the coast of China.

Amanda pushed herself out of her chair and stretched. "Okay, Mr. Freeman," she said, addressing the Officer of the Deck. "You've got the con and the start of a beautiful day out here. Enjoy."

She went aft to the hot-water urn in the chart room and made herself a mug of tea from her private stash of Earl Grey. Flying in the face of the purists, she dumped a packet of creamer into the brew along with a couple of sugar cubes. Sipping appreciatively, she went forward again and out onto the starboard bridge wing.

Crossing to the rail, she assumed the traditional Navy slaunchwise lean against it, a few inches down from Ken Hiro. She'd noted that her exec had been lingering out here during most of the departure.

"Misa and the kids weren't dockside this morning," she commented quietly. "Is everything okay?"

Rather guiltily, Ken straightened. He was generally a little stoic, but today Amanda had taken him by surprise.

"Uh, sure, Captain, everything's fine. They never come down to the pier anymore when we haul out this early. Instead, we have this thing that we do. I say my good-byes the night before, then I sneak out of the house the next morning before anyone else is awake. Misa has an alarm set, and after I'm gone, she gets the kids up and they drive out to Keahi Point."

He nodded toward the shoulder of the passage they were sweeping past. "They watch us clear port from there. It's just something that works for us."

"Sounds like as good a way as any," Amanda replied, nodding in sympathetic agreement.

Looking aft along the weather decks, she noted that Ken wasn't the only one drawing out his farewell. Little groups of *Cunningham* sailors were lingering along the rails, watching Oahu disappear into the haze behind them. It was an endemic situation in the New Age Navy. The somewhat older, more career-oriented crews meant more hands with dependents to leave behind. It was the trade-off that had to be made for their experience and professionalism.

Amanda could understand their feelings, but she couldn't say that she shared them. For her, whether she was conning an 8,000-ton man-of-war or a twenty-four-foot cruising sloop, heading out had always been a time of renewal, a chance to shake free of the dirt of the land and find new challenges.

She knew that this mind-set stemmed partially from the fact that she wasn't leaving anything of real import behind her. Early on in her career

Amanda had realized that, if she was to gain a ship of her own, she would have to travel light.

Accordingly, she had organized a life that could be carried in a pair of suitcases or contained in a set of cabin lockers, deliberately avoiding all long-term entanglements, either physical or emotional.

This total independence had worked well for her, and for some time now she had lived as contentedly self-contained as a turtle.

Recently, though, she had begun to wonder if she hadn't been a little too efficient with how she had engineered her world. Generally she managed to brush the thought aside as just a symptom of looming middle age, but, sometimes, looking at Ken and his family, she found herself thinking that maybe having something permanent somewhere to come home to might not be all that bad.

"Captain," the OOD called from the wheelhouse hatchway. "Retainers Zero One and Zero Two are inbound and on rendezvous approach."

Vince Arkady and his wingwoman, Lieutenant (j.g.) Nancy Delany, were coming home to roost.

"Very good, Mr. Freeman," Amanda called back over her shoulder. "Go to flight quarters and bring the helos aboard at your convenience."

"Aye, aye, ma'am."

The vibrant growl of rotors filled the air and the *Cunningham's* pair of SAH-66 Sea Comanches came into view astern. Fenestron-tailed and sleekly hunchbacked, the two small machines bore the slightly odd aerodynamics of stealth technology. A LAMPS variant of the U.S. Army's latest generation of scout helicopters, their low detectability was intended to complement that of their mother ship.

Tucked into a stylishly tight formation, they swept down the Duke's starboard side a meager fifty feet above the wave crests. Maneuvering as if they were chained together, the two helos flared out and dumped speed, station keeping just off the snub wing of the bridge.

Looking across into Retainer Zero One's forward cockpit, Amanda could see Arkady's helmet turn toward her. Even through the tinted visor she could sense that damnable grade-school grin of his. She lifted a hand in greeting, and he gave an acknowledging nod. The noses of the two helos then dipped in unison and they gained speed, pulling ahead of the ship. As

Amanda and Hiro watched, they popped up and into a flashy crossover break around the *Cunningham's* bow, heading back to line up on the helipad.

Amanda took another draw at her tea and contentedly lounged back against the rail. On the other hand, there was still a lot to be said for being able to take everything that was important to you right along with you.

☆ Shanghai, People's Republic of China
2320 Hours Zone Time; July 17, 2006

The fast attack squadron held to the center of the broad Huangpu River channel. Running on displacement with their hydrofoils retracted, their dark blue-gray paint rendered them all but invisible. The air around them was filled with the deep-toned rumble of idling diesels and the peculiar combination of miasmas unique to Shanghai: the wet sewer and seaweed stench rising up from the Yangtze estuary, the waxy, raw petroleum from the great Zhongxing refinery complex, and the dry, choking haze of an uncountable number of small charcoal fires.

To the west, the city itself was spectral, a place where the shadows had been granted free rule after the setting of the sun.

Upstream, in what had been the old Foreign Settlements along the Bunt, dilapidated 1930s-vintage skyscrapers were silhouetted against the sky, dark and jagged like some ruin of the Second World War frozen in time. For all of the city's teeming millions, nowhere could more than a dozen lights be seen in a single sweep of the eye. There was no longer power to spare to illuminate the streets, and even such a simple thing as a lightbulb was now a precious commodity to be carefully husbanded.

Lieutenant Zhou Shan could recall when the night skyglow of Shanghai could be seen from forty miles off the coast. That had been on his cadet cruise only a few short years ago. Now he sometimes wondered if the night would ever be held at bay again.

The Five Nineteen boat was the trailer in the column, and Zhou's helmsman steered by the pale plume of wake produced by the craft ahead. They possessed none of the night-vision equipment available aboard some of the Fleet's larger and more modern vessels, and even their elementary radar was useless in these confined waters.

The Five Nineteen was an old copy of an older design—the venerable Hushuan-class hydrofoil torpedo boat. No point defense beyond the manually operated twin 14mm machine-gun mounts fore and aft. No guided weaponry at all except for the pair of massive 53VA antishipping torpedoes in their twin launching tubes. No extensive sensor suite. No countermeasures. Probably no real chance of survival against a truly state-of-the-art enemy.

Zhou was not unduly concerned about the age of his small command. When one served in the People's armed forces, one learned to make do with less than the latest and the best. What was perturbing was not being able to maintain what he did have in the best condition possible. Beneath his fingers, he could feel where corrosion was eating into the paintless cockpit railing, and he could detect a faint, uneven stammer in the growl of the single engine they had on line.

Their apportionment of sea stores and spare parts, frugal under the best of conditions, had grown almost nonexistent over the past few months. What was worse, ever since the beginning of the war, the squadron had been sitting uselessly in its home base at Changshandau, slowly rusting away, while bandits and counterrevolutionaries tore the heart out of the People's Republic.

When the squadron had been ordered south, Zhou had hoped that at long last they were being committed to battle—possibly even against the gangsters of the Kuomintang who had dared to return from their island kennels.

Instead, they had been directed here to Shanghai, reasons unexplained.

Behind him the young officer heard tools clatter and bosun Hoong swear fervently in his thick North Coast accent. The bosun and two other of Five Nineteen's deck hands were struggling with a frozen bolt at the foot of the hydrofoil's stubby radar mast. That had also been unexplained—why they must be prepared to fold their radio and radar masts down parallel to the deck.

Zhou was estimating that they must soon be coming to the second of the right-handed bends in the river's channel when he suddenly observed a shadowy form materializing out of the darkness, just off his course line.

"Stop engines!" he snapped at his helmsman.

Over the transmission howl, he heard the voice of Captain Li hailing him. His squadron commander was holding the flag boat just off the central channel, one of his deck hands waving the other fast-attack craft past with a red-lensed flashlight.

"Is all well with you, young Shan? No problems with the channel?"

"All well, Comrade Captain. No difficulties."

"Good. We are almost home. The squadron is being dispersed to separate moorages along the eastern side of the river. Stand on upstream until you clear the shipyards, then watch the left shore for a blinking signal light. Your signal will be short, long, short. Turn in toward it and follow the instructions of the guide. Are you ready to lower your masts?"

Zhou looked aft. "Just another few moments, Lieutenant," Hoong grunted from deck level.

"Yes, Comrade Captain. We are prepared."

"Excellent. Carry on, Shan."

Zhou's combination of frustration and curiosity drove him to call out once more. "Comrade Captain, can you tell us what our mission will be here?"

"As it is everywhere, Comrade Lieutenant," Li replied, a faint reproof in his tone, "to serve the will of the people." That left nothing more to be said. Zhou ordered his helmsman to advance his throttle and the Five Nineteen boat gained way once more.

They were coming up on the curve of the river, with Shanghai's Fuxing Dao industrial district to starboard and the Hudong state shipyards to port. Watching the east bank intently, Zhou thought he had spotted his moorage beacon. Then he caught himself just before issuing the command to turn. This flashing light had quite a different source.

Zhou realized he was looking at the rear face of the shipyard's huge covered graving dock. The entryway had been curtained off with a wall of tarpaulins, and light leaked through at one point, the harsh, blue-white flicker of arc welding.

Bringing up his night glasses, Zhou panned them across the yard. As he did so, he began to realize that more was going on within the seemingly dark and deserted facility than was first apparent. Trucks rolled past, running on hooded headlights. Many figures scurried through the shadows, and more light leaks indicated that the lower floors of several of the machine shops and administration buildings were occupied and operating.

The young naval officer knew full well that shipbuilding, like most of China's other heavy industry, had come to a near-complete standstill because of the war. Something very exceptional was taking place over there.

So intriguing was this concentration of stealthy activity that Zhou almost missed the true signal being flashed in their direction.

"Helmsman, come left."

The Five Nineteen boat nosed in toward the bank, and the head of a pier solidified out of the gloom. For a moment, Zhou thought he was to tie up alongside it. Then he saw the guide atop the pier motioning them underneath it.

"Hoong! Lower the masts!"

"At once, Lieutenant."

Zhou observed that the pier's central pilings and underbracing had been cut away, leaving an empty shell. As the hydrofoil's bow slid into the deeper, creosote-scented blackness beneath the decking, her hull squealed against preset fenders and dolphin boards. Moisture pattered on the decks. Reaching up from the cockpit, Zhou's fingertips brushed a sheet of wet canvas suspended horizontally overhead.

He understood. His nation no longer had functional reconnaissance satellites, but their capabilities were well understood. The pier would shelter them from direct visual observation, and the water-soaked tarps would smother their heat signature, rendering them invisible to thermographic scanning.

The torpedo boat's engine grumbled into silence and the ever-efficient Hoong began to direct the line handling in the glow of a single battle lantern.

Zhou remained in the cockpit for a time longer, considering. There was something in the wind here. Something major. Something they were involved in now.

Perhaps he would find his piece of the war after all.

☆ Hotel Manila

Republic of the Philippines

0800 Hours Zone Time; August 6, 2006

"It's eight o'clock, Mr. Secretary."

For a moment, Harrison Van Lynden couldn't remember where he was, a common occupational hazard for those in the profession of jet-age statesmanship. Then his memory came back on line.

Manila. The first day of the crisis-reduction talks.

"Thank you, Frank. I'm awake," he replied, sitting up.

"Breakfast, sir?" the Secret Service man inquired from the bedroom door.

"Yes. My usual in about fifteen minutes."

"It'll be ready, Mr. Secretary. Ms. Sagada will also be up shortly with the morning situation update."

"Thanks again."

The door closed. Van Lynden rose from the bed, stretching out the last kinks of the previous day's long air journey. Crossing to the full-length balcony windows, he pulled aside the gold brocade curtains, revealing the glittering gunmetal blue of Manila Bay.

For security's sake, the Philippine government had elected to house all of the different delegations attending the Chinese crisis-reduction talks at a single location, one that could also serve as the site for those talks. With a profound sense of either irony or history, they had chosen the Hotel Manila.

The sixteen-story grand dame of the Philippines had served many purposes during its long existence. Prior to World War II, it had served as Douglas MacArthur's residence as he had futilely attempted to prepare the old commonwealth for the coming conflict. The hotel had seen an invading Japanese army march in to seize its namesake city, and had served as the headquarters for its conquerors. Surviving, the hotel had seen another army, this one of liberation, storm Manila. Its walls still bore the bullet scars of strafing American fighters.

Now, as he watched the morning traffic build along the waterfront boulevards, he wondered what new chapter would unfold here: the ending of a conflict or the beginning of a holocaust.

The bacon and eggs were excellent, and the atypical side dishes—fried rice, guava, and jackfruit—added piquancy to the meal. Seated in the suite's living room, the Secretary of State divided his attention between his breakfast and the young woman seated on the couch across from him.

Lucena Sagada, his Embassy liaison, had the honey-colored skin and ebon eyes and hair of a Philippine native. Her light summer suit had the cut of the Beltway, however. After serving her State Department internship in Washington, she had returned to the homeland of her grandparents to make the optimum use of her linguistic and cultural heritage.

"We finally have a complete delegation listing, Mr. Secretary," she said, looking up from her open laptop.

"Let's see, that should be Mr. Apayo from the Philippines, Keo Moroboshi from Japan, and Mr. Chung Pak from Korea. Any word on the Russians and Vietnamese?"

"Still no word from Hanoi. I think they can be safely counted out. As for the Russians, we've received official notification that they will not be sending a delegation. They do request, however, that a member of their local embassy staff be permitted to sit in as an observer."

"I don't have any problem with that," Van Lynden replied. "We won't have them in stirring the water, but at the same time, they'll be kept current on the developing situation. Good compromise."

He speared a final neat slice of jackfruit on the tines of his fork. "Now, let's get on to the main show. Who are we meeting from the Chinas?"

"Both delegations arrived yesterday evening, sir. Within an hour of each other."

Ms. Sagada removed a recordable compact disc from her briefcase and snapped it into the input slot of her laptop. Rising, she crossed the room and set the little computer on the coffee table beside Van Lynden's breakfast tray.

"The CIA Station Chief at the Embassy had a video crew out there covering the arrivals," she said, tapping the actuation key. "Here are the Nationalist and the United Democratic Forces representatives arriving. They flew in together from Taipei."

On the flatscreen, Van Lynden observed two individuals descending the stairway of a smart-looking executive jet. "I recognize the first man. Mr. Duan Xing Ho of the Taiwanese Foreign Ministry. I've worked with him a couple of times through the American Institute in Taiwan. He's a good international man. One of their best. I don't recognize this gentleman, though." He indicated the spare, white-haired figure that followed Duan.

"According to the NSA database on the United Democratic Forces of China, he is Professor Djinn Yi. He's a former faculty member of the People's University of Canton, having taught history and political science. Currently, he appears to be serving as a kind of ambassador-at-large for the UDFC."

"What do we have on him?"

"Not very much, Mr. Secretary. Unmarried. Native of Guangdong Province. Considered academically brilliant. At one time, an unimpeachable Party member. However, that wasn't enough to protect him when the Red Guard went on their rampage back in 1966. He and his older brother were among the Chinese intellectuals herded into the reeducation camps during the Cultural Revolution. Professor Djinn was incarcerated for over eighteen months. His brother died, supposedly from a combination of beating and starvation."

"I imagine that could turn just about anyone."

The video zoomed in on Djinn, and Van Lynden studied the man, looking past his age-gaunt features and the stiffness of his movements to the alert glitter of his eyes and the calculating way he studied his surroundings. The Chinese Presidium had made a very bad enemy out of this old man.

The video clip ended and Ms. Sagada reached forward to call up another track.

"Okay. Here we go with the Communist delegation."

Two more men descending another aircraft stairway. One, short, heavy-set, and wearing an old-style Maoist suit. *Haven't seen one of those in a while. What might that indicate, Harry? A throwback of attitude or a statement of policy?* The other was tall, soldierly in bearing, and clad in the uniform of the People's Liberation Army.

"These are the two representatives from the People's Republic," Sagada continued. "Deputy Premier Chang Hui'an and General Ho Chunwa."

"Very heavy metal indeed. I know Chang only by reputation. He's not an international man. I don't think he's ever even been out of the country before. He does carry a lot of Party weight, though.

"As for Ho," Van Lynden continued, "I've met him. It was years ago, before Tiananmen. Very sharp. Very tough. But he thinks. He's open to reason. Who's the senior man of the delegation?"

"That's . . . rather nebulous at the moment, Mr. Secretary. The delegation appears to be under a joint leadership."

Now, that's interesting, Van Lynden thought. *The only time the Communists don't work with linear chain of command is when there's a factional confrontation going on between two near-party power groups. A trust breakdown between the Party and the PLA? Is somebody afraid that somebody else is ready to sell out? Very interesting indeed . . .*

Ms. Sagada snapped off the laptop. "That's about all we have new on the delegations, sir. I also have a prospective conference agenda for your consideration and a request from the press corps for a statement from you concerning the goals of the United States in these talks."

"I'll be pleased to let them know as soon as I'm sure myself." Van Lynden laid his napkin across his plate. "What's the latest military update from the Chinese mainland? The short version."

"Static, but with buildups continuing on all fronts. The Nationalists are continuing to land troops within the Amoy beachhead, while the Communists continue to mass forces to the north and west of the city. Apparently, they're preparing a major counterattack to drive the Nationalists back into the sea before UDFC can break through to them from the south."

The young Embassy liaison shook her head. "Our military attaché says things should blow out there soon. Very soon."

"How that battle goes, so may go this conference."

Van Lynden got to his feet. "Is there a secure terminal here in the hotel?"

"Not yet, sir. The communications rooms for the delegations won't be up and running until sometime this afternoon."

"Then we'll need to go across to the Embassy for a while. Let me see, the opening session isn't scheduled until . . . ten tomorrow morning. Right?"

"Yes, sir."

"Very good. Until then, from, say, noon today on, see if you can dial us in to meet with as many of the other delegates, one on one, as possible. Nobody may be willing to talk substance before the first session, but at least we might be able to feel out some attitudes."

"We, sir?" There was a faint hint of expectancy beyond the professionalism in Luccna Sagada's voice.

Van Lynden paused in donning his suit jacket. "You're my liaison officer, aren't you? Part of your job is keeping Ambassador Dickenson fully apprised on the status of these talks. As far as I can see, the best way to accomplish that is for you to be directly involved in them. Is that amenable to you?"

The young woman's sobriety momentarily disappeared in the bright flash of her smile. "I'd like that very much, sir."

"Fine. Start setting us up. In the meantime, I've got some people to talk to."

Van Lynden started for the elevators, his security team deploying around him with the unobtrusive efficiency of the stage ninjas in a kabuki play.

The Secretary of State was already losing himself in what he had learned that morning, adding the scraps of information he had garnered to the matrix of knowledge, instinct, and intuition he was building around the China crisis.

During his years in the diplomatic service, Van Lynden had developed an entire arsenal of mental mechanisms to help him maintain the clarity of thought and total focus needed for this brand of heavy-gauge statesmanship. One of them was "tagging": applying a descriptive and readily recallable symbol to each of the other involved parties. In those video clips today, he had found his tags for the Chinas: the planes the opposing delegations had arrived aboard.

The Nationalists and UDFC had flown in on a gleaming new Taiwanese Air Force Dassault 9000. Sleek, compact, and efficient, the little executive jet had more resemblance to a model put together by some painstaking hobbyist than it had to a real aircraft.

The Communists had arrived on board an aging Boeing 727, its paint stripped by a myriad of hail- and rainstorms, its tail cone blackened by years of burning low-grade jet propellant. An unmatching aileron and cabin door had indicated where another airframe had been stripped to make this one operational.

That was the dichotomy. The cutting edge of tomorrow, driven by the power of global trade and technology, versus the outworn giant, obsolescent and weary, but not quite ready for the scrap heap.

☆ One Quarter Mile off the Meizhou Wan Peninsula People's Republic of China 0134 Hours Zone Time; August 8, 2006

"Closing on point item, Captain. . . . Closing . . . Closing . . . Closing . . . And mark!"

"Very good, Quartermaster. Lee helm, all stop on main engines. Helmsman, initiate station keeping on hydrojets."

"Aye, aye."

Everyone on the *Cunningham's* bridge kept his or her voice low. All odds were that a normal speaking tone wouldn't have carried across to the shore of the inlet, but their reaction was instinctive to the black, looming presence of the hills that surrounded them on three sides.

Sweat prickled under the combination flak vest and life jacket Amanda wore, and the Kevlar helmet she had donned over her command headset pinched painfully. She ignored the discomfort, and her eyes flicked from repeater to repeater: the sweeping low-light televisions, the passive radar detectors, the radio-frequency scanners. All clear.

"Deployment crew," she spoke into her lip mike. "We are on station. Get it in the water."

Sliding out of the captain's chair, she crossed to the starboard-side bridge doorway and stepped out onto the bridge wing. Below and forward, deck hands worked swiftly in the dim cool glow of light sticks. The VLS's missile-handling crane had been deployed and its cable was now linked to a dark lozenge-shaped object the size of a large hot-water tank.

Now, with the howl of its motor muffled by a blanket, the crane lifted the module from the deck and swung it out over the rail. The winch reel reversed and swiftly the object was lowered into the low, oily swells. A line was yanked and a shackle released, freeing it. It bobbed at the destroyer's side for a few moments as ballast chambers flooded, and then it was gone, sinking from sight.

"Bridge, buoy has been deployed."

"Very well. Secure the deck."

Amanda crossed back into the wheelhouse. "Helm, back us off about fifty yards on the GPU. Hydrojets only."

"Aye, aye, ma'am. Translating astern now."

Impatiently, she waited out the seconds as her ship reversed silently through the shadows.

"Translation complete, Captain."

"Thank you, helm. Resume station keeping. Sonar, this is the captain. We are clear of the buoy. Transmit your test codes. Intelligence section, stand by."

The *Cunningham's* sonar transducers swept the surrounding waters with a low-powered sound beam, a beam that carried a carefully modulated binary message for a certain listener. A hundred and twenty feet down, on the muddy bottom of the inlet, the listener responded.

The maritime reconnaissance buoy uncoupled from its sinker weight and unreeled its mooring line, drifting back toward the surface like an inverted spider on a thread. Just beneath the waves, it halted its rise and extended a waterproof radio antenna.

"Bridge, this is Raven's Roost. We have acquired a test signal. All buoy systems read green. We have a successful deployment."

"Very good, Raven's Roost. Actuate the buoy."

The maritime reconnaissance buoy conversed with its mother station aboard the *Cunningham* for a few microseconds more, then retracted its antenna. Smoothly, it winched itself back down to the midpoint of its tether. A technological first cousin to the naval pressure mine, its anechoic sheathed bulk was packed with hydrophones and signal processors instead of high explosives. From its position within the cove, it would passively monitor the comings and goings of all sea traffic that would come near. The accumulated information would be electronically stored for a schedule of high-speed data dumps over the next few weeks.

Ever since her arrival in-theater, the Duke had been systematically seeding the Chinese coastal waters between Shanghai and Amoy with a network of these remote sensor units. This was the last to go down.

With its successful placing, half of the night's tasking program was complete. The riskier part was still under way. Amanda paced slowly in front of the helm console. Around her, in the dimness, the rest of the bridge crew stood or sat, wire-nerved and sweating.

"CIC, this is the bridge. Is Raven's Roost seeing any change at all in the local signal environment?"

She could have called that same data up on one of the repeaters at her elbow, but at the moment she wanted to hear another human voice.

"Still okay, Captain," Ken Hiro replied reassuringly. "Raven's Roost reports all quiet on all frequencies."

As per their set doctrine, she and Ken traded off positions when the ship was at battle station—one on the bridge, the other in the CIC, or vice versa as required. Thus, no single hit could likely take them both out simultaneously.

"We still have another fifteen minutes before they're due back aboard," her exec continued.

"Yeah." She resumed her pacing, driven by tensions akin to those of a mother whose children were out of reach.

Twenty miles inland, Vince Arkady found this particular insertion sortie getting old fast. The back of his neck was aching from the drag of the heavy night-vision visor mounted on his flight helmet. He was also perforce having to stay totally focused on the Sea Comanche's controls. Retainer Zero One was running in full stealth tonight. The snub wings she usually mounted had been unshipped, and the loss of lift was throwing off his feel for the aircraft.

For the past half hour, he had been snake-dancing the little helicopter along the ridgeline. Hugging each swale and circling each knoll in an airborne version of a combat infantryman's sprint and cover, he had been giving his passenger the opportunity she needed to conduct her survey.

"Hey, sis, leave us not take all night on this thing. Okay?"

"Patience, patience," Christine Rendino murmured back over the intercom. "I know what I'm looking for. It's just not all that easy to find in this neighborhood."

In Zero One's rear cockpit, the Intel used a joystick controller to track the helo's thermographic sight along the road that ran up the valley floor. She needed a good patch of cover right up alongside that road, preferably the west side.

The farms down there had probably been first cleared and divided into fields sometime before the birth of Christ. Since then, God knows how many meager harvests had been worked out of those fields by God knows how many generations of peasants. Even the lower hillsides had been ribbed with growing terraces, eking out every last yard of crop space. All of the wildness had long since been worn off this land, leaving only the stone fences and thin, tired soil.

The search wasn't totally hopeless, however. Many of the fields were overgrown and abandoned. This valley was located dead-on between two opposing armies, and with the ingrained survival instincts of the Chinese peasant, most of the locals had gotten the hell out while the getting was good. The occasional light in the lonely scattering of villages marked where someone was either too old to run or too weary to give a damn.

Christine broke off her line of thought as a darker patch began to scroll across the screen, a large irregular bead strung on the pale thread of the roadway.

"Okay! That's it, boy! At your two o'clock."

"Rog, sis. I see it. Scanning for threats . . . Looks like nobody's around. . . . Goin' in."

Retainer Zero One kicked over into a dive down toward the valley floor.

It had been a woodlot. Its spindly collection of poplar trees had been harvested off almost at ground level sometime in the recent past, leaving only a low tangle of brush behind. The narrow road that ran through it had been oil-paved at one time, indicating a major thoroughfare for this part of the world. Now, though, that paving was breaking down into potholes and muddy gravel.

The road wasn't the primary concern this night, barring its utility as a landmark. The regional main-trunk telephone cable buried beside it was.

To conduct modern-day military operations, rapid and extensive communications are both an absolute necessity and a glaring vulnerability. All radio frequencies can be scanned and monitored, and even the tightest microwave transmissions can leak. Even if all messages are encrypted, an alert Signal Intelligence unit can still learn a great deal from direction-finder bearings and traffic volumes.

Accordingly, as others had before, the Communist military leadership had come to value landline telephone as their only truly secure communications net.

Christine and Arkady were about to prove them to be in error.

Retainer Zero One went into a low hover just off the pavement, her rotor wash whipping the scrub. Arkady scanned his surroundings again through the cool, green glow of his low-light visors, seeking sign of any movement, any covert observer. His ears were attuned to the helo's threat board, ready to react to the first instant of a warning squall.

"Ready to open bay doors?" Christine inquired.

"Yep. Let's get it done, but let's make it fast." Opening the weapons bay would also open a hole in the Sea Comanche's stealth envelope, leaving them vulnerable for a few seconds to a sudden radar sweep.

In the aft cockpit, Christine cradled a remote control box in her lap, a light coaxial cable linking it to the auxiliary systems jack of the dashboard display. As the belly doors snapped open, the sensor unit that was revealed began to react to its environment, projecting its readout onto the oscilloscope display of the control box.

"Yeah! We're hot! This is it!"

She flipped the guards up and off a row of actuator keys and hit them in sequence.

A launching tube swung down from the helicopter's belly, like an insect's ovipositor, aiming vertically at the ground below. A black-powder propulsive charge fired and a metallic spike the length and diameter of a man's arm punched down through the underbrush. Driven into the soil for three-quarters of its length, a protective cap blew off and a slender antenna deployed. On Christine's control box, a green diagnostic light glowed.

In the past, tapping an enemy landline would have been a laborious and risky task performed by a Special Forces team. This method was swifter and placed only two people directly at risk. A hypersensitive induction coil within the sensor they had just planted would read the faint electromagnetic modulations radiating from the telephone cable. Recorded and electronically compressed, they would be stored for later burst transmission to an orbiting NSA satellite.

Until the unit's batteries wore down, or until a human-size object entered the range of its motion sensors, triggering the thermite self-destruct charge, the PLA's phone was effectively bugged.

"Spike's set. Go!"

The launcher retracted and the bay doors slammed shut. Retainer Zero One dipped her nose and regained airspeed, skimming the valley floor and angling away to the east.

"Well, that wasn't such a big deal, now, was it?"

"Repeat that question once we're back on the Duke, sis."

"How are we on time?"

"Right on the edge. If nothing goes Murphy on us, we can just make the rendezvous."

Arkady aimed Zero One upslope toward a shallow saddle in the far ridge. The low, rolling landscape with its lack of tall trees and high-tension lines made for good helicopter country, and the night sky had been comfortingly clear of hostile traffic. If they could just stretch this rollout a little longer . . .

Flying nape of the earth, a bare twenty feet above the ground, Zero One crested the saddle.

"Sheeeit!"

Arkady's right foot smashed down on its rudder pedal, nearly bending the mount. Retainer Zero One flared around like a startled quail, the abrupt g-load forcing a protesting yelp out of his passenger. With weed stalks sweeping her belly, Zero One raced back over the saddle and downslope again.

"Jeez, Arkady! What's going on?"

"It appears, sis, that Mr. Murphy has just bitten us in the ass."

While they had been planting their bug, a solid wall of steel had rolled across their line of retreat.

Arkady dropped south half a click along the ridgeline and gingerly hovered up to an observation position.

"Where the hell did all of these guys come from?" he murmured.

"From the PRC staging ground at Fuzhou," Christine replied grimly. "Fa' sure, that's got to be at least a full armored division down there."

Through the night-vision systems, they could see a steady stream of military vehicles flowing for miles along the valley floor: tanks and armored personnel carriers, interspersed with an occasional truck or fuel transport. They were moving in combat mode, the AFVs running on their own tracks instead of being carried aboard lowboys, cannon out-angled, covering both sides of the roadway.

Cataloging the stream, Christine noted that a majority of the tanks were angular, late-model, Chinese Type 85s. Here and there, however, was the flattened teakettle turret of an older Type 69. At one point, the Intel even thought she spotted the brakeless gun barrel of an ancient Soviet-built T-55.

A shot-up outfit, she decided, brought back to fighting strength with whatever odds and ends could be swept up out of the depots. She panned the video system along the column, storing the images.

Arkady backed the helo below the crestline again.

"We," he said, "are royally screwed. We're going to have to swing wide and circle around these guys, and that's going to flush our time line right down the toilet."

"Any chance of just sneaking through a crack?"

"Nope. The Nationalist Air Force has been giving these guys a hard time lately. You can bet every antiair vehicle and deck machine gun in that column is manned. Stealthed or not, we'd get burned flying over that outfit. We've got to go around."

"Boy, are we gonna get yelled at when we get back, or what?"

Arkady paid Zero One off and headed back upvalley. "Let's just hope that there's somebody still there to yell at us."

"Captain, this is Raven's Roost." It was the voice of Lieutenant (j.g.) Randy Selkirk, the number-two man in Intelligence Division. "I think there may be somebody out there."

A cold, hard hand clinched inside Amanda's guts. Her eyes went to the glowing rows of repeaters again. *Low-light . . . Tactical display . . . ECM . . . Scanners . . .* Nothing.

"I'm not showing anything here, Mr. Selkirk."

"It's on the electromagnetic detection arrays, ma'am. Very, very low gain. Too low for the discriminator circuits of the Aegis system to recognize as a valid contact. We can't even get a clear bearing on it, just that it's somewhere to seaward."

"Any idea what it could be?"

"Looks like systems discharge. Generator static and make-and-break, that kind of stuff. But he's either really small or he's Faraday-screened damn near as good as we are."

A tone of frustration began to creep into Selkirk's voice.

"On the other hand, we could just have a very active thunderstorm over the horizon. I'm sorry, ma'am, just can't call it any closer."

The junior officer was trying, but he had yet to develop Christine Rendino's almost supernatural ability to analyze and extrapolate data.

"No problem, Lieutenant. Keep working the contact and keep me advised."

Amanda rechecked the time hack that glowed in the bottom left corner of each monitor. They were six and a half minutes–plus on the projected recovery time.

Arkady, Chris, where are you!

Something had gone wrong. Arkady would not miss a rendezvous like this unless something had gone seriously wrong.

She crossed to the port side of the bridge and scanned the star-spattered sky above the hills that rimmed the inlet.

No commander should ever be stupid enough to take a friend or a lover. Why the hell couldn't she learn. Why couldn't she be like those other officers, who could maintain that cool, emotionally insulated distance from those they served with.

Because the best ones seem to be the ones who give a damn. The old comment of Arkady's echoed unbidden out of her memory.

Well, she was giving a damn now, for what it was worth. But the only concrete action she could take was to decide how long she dare wait for them here at the recovery point.

All right. Compute to the worst-case scenario. They crashed or were knocked down early on during the insertion mission.

Could they have survived the crash? Were they in PLA custody? *No, dammit! Forget that! Stay focused on the scenario!*

Say the wreck was immediately identified by someone who knew what a LAMPS-variant Sea Comanche was and what kind of range it had. That would give them their search radius for the launching platform. How long would it take for the Red military to initiate a hunt? What kind of assets would they have available?

"Captain!" The strangled urgency in the lookout's voice made Amanda whip around. "Surface contact bearing zero five oh off the starboard bow!"

Instantly, she was at the lookout's side, gazing up into the low-light monitor. On the gray-toned screen, the unmistakable, rakish silhouette of a large warship could be seen rounding the northern headland about a mile offshore.

A second followed in column a few moments later, and then a third, farther out to sea. Angling across the entrance to the inlet, they had just cut off the Duke's only line of escape.

The sudden, soft howl of hydraulics broke the shock paralysis that had settled on the bridge. The forward Oto Melara mount was indexing around to cover the intruders. Farther out along the bow, a scattering of small octagonal hatches popped open on the upper surfaces of the Vertical Launch Systems. Each open hatch revealed the dark mouth of a missile silo.

Down in the CIC, Dix Beltrain was baring the Duke's fangs.

"All stations. Stand easy." Amanda spoke deliberately into her lip mike, keeping her voice low and totally neutral, allowing no inflection that might increase tensions or trigger a premature reaction. "Helmsman, let's go for a reduction in aspect here. Maintain station keeping, but bring our bow around to the mouth of the inlet."

"Aye, aye."

Under the silent impulse of the auxiliary hydrojets, the destroyer's knife-edged bow began to come around. The 76mm turret remained fixed on target, a pivot around which the ship seemed to turn.

"Captain," Ken Hiro's voice sounded in her headphones. "We make them out to be a pair of Red Chinese Block 1B Luda guided-missile destroyers, with a single Jianghu-class frigate screening them to seaward."

"I concur on that, Ken." Amanda had accessed the controls of the Mast Mounted Sighting System, zooming in and panning over the Chinese warships using a trackball controller. To the unaided human eye, there was nothing to be seen out there but black, but to the powerful nite-brite optics of the MMSS, night did not exist.

The Ludas were handsome ships. Built on the hull design of the old Soviet Kotlin class, they had the lean, greyhound sleekness of the old-school steam turbine destroyer. More to the point, however, both vessels still had their gun turrets trained fore and aft and the launching cells of their C-801 antiship missiles hadn't been up-angled into firing position.

A quick call-up on another repeater verified that the Red task group was also running full EMCON, with all search-and-fire control radars down.

Slowly, the hair that was bristling down the back of her neck began to lower. Maybe these people were out hunting for trouble, but they weren't hunting for the Duke.

"I think we're okay, Ken," she said slowly into her headset. "I think that this is just a coincidence. That's a pretty good slice of the surviving Communist surface fleet out there. I doubt they could have gotten it into position this fast just for us."

"Yeah." The tension in Hiro's voice eased down a notch as well. "I wonder what they're up to?"

"Hard to say. Maybe an antishipping sweep or a coastal bombardment run. Those Ludas each pack a couple of 130-millimeter mounts. They could be planning to shoot up a Nationalist supply depot or something as part of this big drive they're building. Whatever it is, I think we'll just lay low and let them go on their way."

The *Cunningham*'s bow was coming around now, tracking on the passing hostile vessels. The tiger-pattern camouflage on her hull merged her into the backdrop of the shore. The earlier-generation Chinese optics would be left with nothing to see except for a narrow break in the white line of the surf.

A short time before, Amanda had been praying for Arkady's return. Now she prayed that he would stay away just for a few minutes more, just until the enemy had disappeared beyond the southern headland.

Maybe that was why the voice that issued from the overhead speaker carried the impact of an exploding bomb.

"Gray Lady, Gray Lady, this is Retainer Zero One. Do you copy?"

She loved him and she had been worried about him, but just for the moment, she could kill him.

"Retainer Zero One," she snarled after dialing into the air operations frequency. "We have hostile surface forces in the area!"

Low Probability of Intercept radio was just that. There was still a chance that they could be detected.

Arkady's reply was unperturbed. "More than you know, Gray Lady. We've just hovered up over the ridgeline about three clicks south of your location. In addition to your Reds, there are three fast-attack craft in the next cove down the coast from you. Chris identifies them as Taiwanese Navy Hai Ou missile boats. Looks like hot times a-coming!"

"Acknowledged. Stand by, Zero One."

Amanda toggled back to the Combat Information Center. "Lieutenant Selkirk, this is the Captain. Could this Red task group be the source of that first EM contact you had?"

"Negative, ma'am," the Intelligence Officer replied emphatically. "The emissions coming off of these guys are burying the needle. That first contact was hardly there at all."

Amanda nodded and gave herself a five count to think. By the time the count was finished, she had her ops plan assembled.

"Lee helm. Bring up your Power Rooms. We're going to be moving."

Keying her headset, she continued. "All stations, this is the bridge. Here's the situation. The Reds are sailing into an ambush. They've got one Nationalist missile boat group stalking them to seaward and another waiting for them down the coast. As soon as they move into the cross fire, I suspect that the Nationalists are going to hit them with everything they've got. I intend to pull us out of here under the cover of the fireworks. Stealth systems . . ."

"Stealth, aye."

"Mr. McKelsie, we'll try to sneak out under passive stealth alone. Keep all active jammers and decoy systems armed and on standby."

"Will do."

"Tactical Officer."

"Here, ma'am."

"Dix, bring up a couple of Standard HARM flights. If anyone gets a radar lock on us, I want you set to send a round right back up the beam."

"Is that Red and Nationalist both, ma'am?"

"Negative. Red only. I guess we can allow that much favoritism."

"Will do."

"Main Engine Control."

"Yo."

"Everything you've got, Chief."

"What else?" There was a faint tinge of surprise in Commander Thomson's voice.

"Air One."

"Air One, aye," Lieutenant Nancy Delany, the Aviation Section's exec, replied from the air operations center at the rear of the superstructure.

"We're going to be making a flying recovery on your boss. Have the helipad prepped and standing by. I want that helo down and belowdecks as fast as possible."

"We'll be ready, ma'am."

Amanda dialed back to the air ops channel.

"Gray Lady to Retainer. You are instructed to hold at your current position and maintain observation of the Nationalist missile boats. Report when they open fire, then proceed up the ridgeline and return to the ship. We will be departing the inlet at high speed and turning to the northeast. I repeat, to the northeast. Follow our wake out and recover immediately. The helipad is standing by to receive you."

"Roger," Arkady came back crisply. "Will comply."

Amanda paced behind the helm station. The duty helmsman already had the maneuvering chart of the inlet dialed up on his console repeater, the water depths outlined in glowing azure computer graphics. His left hand played with the controls of the auxiliary hydrojets, while the fingers of his right curled around the rudder controller.

Beside him, the lee helm leaned in over the center pedestal, one hand on the propeller controls, the other on the master throttles. The power levers had already been firewalled and the glowing bars of the generator-room output displays were dancing at their peak, matched from belowdecks by the whispering howl of the great Rolls Royce gas turbines.

Amanda dropped a hand to the helmsman's shoulder. "Okay. Here's how we'll work it. I'm not going to have a whole lot of time for giving orders, so I'll let you take us out. We've got some shoals around here, so keep us right in the center of the channel. As soon as we get the water for it, we'll be turning away to the northeast. I'll give you the word when. Got it?"

"Yes, ma'am," the young sailor replied tautly.

Then they waited. One minute more . . . two . . .

To the south something like heat lightning played beyond the hills.

"That's it!" Arkady's voice rang over the circuit. "The Nationalists are launching!"

"Move out!" Amanda commanded. "All engines ahead full!" The twin contra-rotating propellers at the head of each propulsor pod spun, the water humping up and boiling along the Duke's stern quarters. In seconds, a rising bow wave was building under the destroyer's stem as she surged ahead.

Out to sea and to the south, a massive mushroom of orange flame sprouted and rose into the sky, the thunder of its growth arriving a few heartbeats later. Raked by a missile salvo, the little Jianghu-class frigate that had been screening the Communist formation disintegrated, the explosion of her own magazines enhancing the destruction.

The lead ship of the Red destroyer column had taken a hit as well, sending flames licking along her aft deck and the gun barrels of her stern turret angling crookedly into the sky.

However, the little Taiwanese-built Hsiung Feng (Male Bee) antiship missile had failed to pierce life-deep through the Luda's thicker skin. Now the wounded warship, along with its undamaged partner, were lashing back at their attackers. Main-battery rifles belched gouts of hellfire and autocannon mounts hosed tracers across the surface of the sea.

With their missile cells empty, the Nationalist fast-attack craft would now be going defensive, hugging the shallows and scurrying away to the south. They wouldn't be a problem, Amanda acknowledged, but the surviving Red ships would likely soon be. They would probably reverse course and head back to the north, this way. And the Duke's reduced radar cross section might just about match that of a fleeing Hai Do.

She glanced at the iron log and silently willed it to climb faster. *Twenty-one knots . . . Twenty-two . . . Twenty-three . . .*

The *Cunningham* cleared the mouth of the inlet, gaining speed with every rev of her screws. Another stab of Amanda's finger called up a navigational readout, and she studied the fall-away of the sea floor from beneath the keel.

"Helm, come left to zero four five."

"Helm answering to zero four five, ma'am!"

"Mr. McKelsie, are we being painted yet?"

"Negative. No scans on this bearing!"

Twenty-five . . . Twenty-six . . . Twenty-seven . . .

"Captain, aircraft contact off the stern, bearing one eight zero degrees."

On the low-light monitors, Retainer Zero One could be seen rapidly overhauling the ship. Churning along a meager ten feet off the deck, her rotor wash flattened the spray of the wake crests. Tonight, Arkady couldn't be concerned with niceties such as wind direction and proper angle of approach.

Swinging slightly wide, the helo porpoised upward, her landing gear extending. Each maneuver flowed into the next as she weaved back in over the destroyer's helipad, Arkady's sure hand steadying her through the superstructure and stack turbulence. Then Zero One was home, touching down delicately in the center of the hangar-bay elevator.

Amanda watched as the rotors spun down and the pad crew moved in to secure the aircraft. The helicopter's canopies swung open and the shadowy form in the forward cockpit lifted and clasped his hands in his familiar proclamation of victory, a gesture aimed directly at the monitor camera and at her.

She turned back to the iron log. *Thirty-six knots . . . Thirty-seven . . .*

That was it, then. No Luda ever built could overtake them now, not even if they had the devil himself and the ghost of Chairman Mao tending the fire rooms.

To the south, the gunfire had ended. Only two light flares remained, the flames that outlined the damaged Communist destroyer and the burning oil slick that marked the grave of the frigate.

A quick check of the emission displays showed that all radars in the area had been shut down again. Nobody back there was looking for a fight anymore.

A twin surge of elation and relief flooded through Amanda. *Foxed you all, you bastards! Catch me if you can!*

She stepped back out onto the starboard bridge wing. Out here, away from the vision systems, the night was the night again. The faint, hazy glow of the Milky Way arced overhead, sharing the sky with uncountable stars. Astern, the dark silhouette of the Chinese coast was already losing form.

She stripped off her life jacket and helmet and let them drop to the deck, and savored the cooling gale generated by her ship's passage. Just for a moment, she wondered how crew discipline would be affected if the Captain let out a whoop of sheer joy.

Amanda looked over her shoulder, from the captain's chair, as Christine and Arkady filed onto the bridge.

Coming up to her side, Arkady said formally, "Captain, I wish to apologize for being unable to meet my appointed time. An unexpected encounter with Communist forces mandated a course deviation to maintain mission security."

Amanda nodded. "All's well that ends well, Lieutenant. We all had some unexpected encounters tonight. How did the deployment go?"

"Spike's in the ground," Christine reported from her left. "It was on target and is working."

"That'll be it for the insertion missions, then, at least until something busts or gets discovered. We'll rendezvous and replenish with the Task Force tomorrow afternoon and then head north to Shanghai to start the next download sweep of the coastal monitors."

"Good enough," the Intel replied. "Begging your pardon, Boss Ma'am, but when can I get clearance to transmit a message? We saw some stuff out there that I really need to pass up the line."

"Well, we're clear of the Chinese twelve-mile limit now. I was planning to stand down out of stealth mode in about another half hour. The radio room is already prepping a sighting report on that shoot-up we witnessed inshore tonight. You could tack your stuff onto that if you like."

"That'll work. I'll do it."

Amanda looked back and forth between her two officers. "Now, how did it go out there?"

Arkady gave a curt shrug. "Barring a couple of detours, pretty much your basic piece of cake."

"Yeah," Christine agreed. "A romantic night out under the stars with a handsome aviator. You ought to try it sometime, Skipper."

There was a humorous edge in her friend's voice, but before Amanda could remark on it, Christine was gone, heading away aft.

Arkady stayed on. Leaning against the side of the captain's chair in a carefully orchestrated posture of nonchalance, he gazed out of the bridge windscreen. After a couple of minutes Amanda inquired again, this time keeping her voice pitched so that only he could hear.

"Now, how did it go?"

"Oh, good for about a level-two set of the shakes. But only a level-two."

"It was about the same here."

She slipped her hand off the armrest of her chair, letting it drop down between them. Shielded by the shadows and by the positioning of their bodies, their fingers touched and they clasped hands tightly in the early-morning darkness.

☆ Hotel Manila

Republic of the Philippines

0841 Hours Zone Time; August 8, 2006

Lucena Sagada was left-handed. It was a useful trait in that she and Van Lynden could share the same legal pad set in the center of the U.S. delegation's table. Now, although her face was impassive, her Parker ballpoint danced impatiently across the yellow facing sheet.

I understand the preference for the oblique approach within Asian diplomacy, but couldn't someone at least give us a hint about what they want!

The Secretary of State let the corner of his mouth quirk up, and he replied with the Bic softpoint he was using.

For the moment, the primary players all have exactly what they want.

?

A test pattern.

???

Vice Premier Chang of the People's Republic had been the first up to the dais that morning. Now, half an hour later, he continued to speak, his voice pitched low, almost hesitant at times. His words, carried through the translator's earphones, carried all of the old hard-line phraseology: "the People's struggle," "capitalist aggression," "Western imperialism."

However, his rambling narrative, beyond a generalized condemnation of the wrongs being done to Communist China, seemed to have no goal, no real objective. That had been the standard for the first two days of the talks.

No one else seemed unduly perturbed over this state of affairs. The other delegations, Japanese, Filipino, Korean, the other Chinese factions, had, each in turn, added their own share to this growing pool of polite neutrality. Spaced around the conference room's perimeter, the Asian statesmen sat listening, emotions carefully disengaged.

It was an environment that the average Western diplomat might find daunting. However, Van Lynden had been here before.

No one has said anything yet because no one yet has anything to say, he continued on the notepad. *Everyone has been establishing and testing their channels of communication. Now they're in a holding pattern, waiting for the cue for the real show to start.*

The big fight building on the mainland?

I suspect that will be it.

Suddenly, their full attention snapped back to the speaker's dais. While the English translation had remained as blank as before, the first faint tinge of true feeling had crept into Premier Chang's voice.

"... I remind those who attend this conference, and the world as a whole, of the triumphs and tragedies of the People's Republic. We have risked all, we have overcome all, and we have defied all! As the other socialist states have lost heart in the struggle, we have persevered! It is our intent to continue to do so ..."

Van Lynden watched the eyes of the small, heavyset man focus around the room, checking off the other delegates, lingering longest on the combined Nationalist/UDFC block. Beyond the neutrality of his features, those eyes glittered coldly.

Better tighten it up, Comrade, the Secretary of State thought. *Your mask is slipping. You really hate everyone else in this room and you're just dying to show it.*

"... in the face of blind-eyed rebellion, in the face of the thugs and gangsters of the Nationalists, in the face of this outside interference in the internal affairs of China. We shall persevere!"

Concluding, Chang turned away from the dais, moving abruptly. At the PRC table, General Ho looked on impassively, the tall soldier's stone-planed features allowing not even a suggestion of what he might be feeling. To date, he had not yet made a presentation at this conference.

Ms. Sagada's pen flashed once more.

At least we know who the lead man of the Red delegation is now.

No!!! Chang's just pushing the line. Ho's the key man. When he starts to talk, we'd better be ready to listen.

Jorge Apayo, the Philippine secretary of state and host/chairman of the conference, assumed the dais and announced that the American representative had requested time to address the conference.

"Well, my turn now," Van Lynden murmured to his assistant. Removing the translator phone from his ear, he got to his feet and crossed to the podium.

He had opened the folder that held his notes and was just taking that first, deep speaker's breath when he noticed something back at his table. Lucena Sagada had been wearing a second earphone, one that linked directly into the U.S. communications center in the hotel. Now she tilted her head and lifted her hand to the ear that held the link. A moment later, she picked up the marker pen that he had been using and scribbled furiously on their legal pad. Reversing it, she flashed Van Lynden the message: *It's happening now!*

The U.S. Secretary of State replied with a minute nod. He took a second, deliberate breath and closed the folder that held the notes he had prepared. Leaning into the dais, he spoke.

"Ladies and gentlemen. People are dying. It is time we get to work. . . ."

☆ 1.5 Kilometers North of the Nationalist Primary Line of Resistance, Fujian Province, China 0841 Hours Zone Time; August 8, 2006

The young Nationalist Army officer lay stretched out on the thin, sour-smelling soil, the handset of the field telephone held tightly to his ear. Its buzzing carrier tone was very important to him at the moment; it direct-linked him not only to the other three launcher vehicles of his unit but back to his battalion headquarters as well.

Very soon, his life was going to depend on that link.

His antitank section had forward deployed to this ambush site just before first light, setting up in the thin cover of a brush line that separated two fields. By necessity it had been a hasty deployment; they'd had to move up during the narrow window of opportunity between the withdrawal of the PLA night patrols and the estimated zero hour of their attack. His vehicles would have to rely on their camouflage nets and the rapidly dissipating morning mist for cover.

His command vehicle was two yards to his rear and two to his right. An open Toyota-clone 4 × 4, it mounted a Taiwanese-made copy of the Israeli-designed Mapats antitank missile launcher. His gunner knelt in the truck bed beside the weapon, peering through the sights of the laser-targeting unit. The loader/driver crouched just behind him, alert and waiting, the fiberglass canister of a reload round cradled in his arms.

Setting the phone down for a moment, the Nationalist officer tilted his helmet and pressed the side of his head to the ground. Now he could hear something else, a deep, rumbling reverberation through the earth.

Readjusting his helmet and reclaiming the handset, he spoke a single sentence.

"They are coming."

And they were. Great lumbering forms plowing through the ground fog. Main battle tanks and armored personnel carriers, deployed in the classic Red-doctrine "wall of steel" battle formation, grinding in toward the Nationalist defenses.

"Stand ready."

The antitank officer had already picked his mark downrange, the rubble of the old stone wall at the far end of the field, maybe a thousand meters out. Still clutching the field phone, he used his free hand to bring his binoculars up to his eyes.

No need to call out targets. His men knew their business. Wait for it. Wait for it. The first rank was driving up and over the wall. For a split second, their gun barrels and optics would be elevated above the horizon and out of firing alignment.

"Shoot!"

Four designation lasers lanced out at the Communist AFVs. Four heavy antitank missiles followed an instant later. Riding plumes of crackling orange fire downrange, three of them found a home.

The big shaped-charge warheads of the Mapats rounds punched cleanly through the forward armor of their targets, incinerating them from the inside out. Deck hatches blew open, and dark clouds of vaporizing flesh and metal boiled into the air. Ammunition exploded and the massive turret of one Type 85 lifted off of its hull on a pad of flame.

Good salvo! Risk a second? Do it!

"Reload!"

Behind him, he heard the hollow *tonk* of the expended round canister ejecting from his vehicle's launcher. He used the shouted cadence of his firing team's reload drill to time his next order.

Out across the field, the Reds began to react. APCs clanked to a halt, dropping their tail ramps and releasing their infantry squads. Tank guns traversed wildly, seeking targets, and tracer streams began to lash the Nationalist positions.

"Shoot!"

Four more rounds blazed across the open ground. Four targets died. The young officer's field glasses happened to focus on a Red YW 534 armored personnel carrier just as it took its hit. The vehicle's tailgate had dropped, but its infantry squad had not yet had a chance to disembark. Now they were expelled from the rear of the vehicle as chunks of shredded humanity intermixed in a white-orange fireball.

He yelled his final order into the handset.

"Fall back!" The exclamation was both a command to the other firing teams of his section and a statement of intent to his own waiting CO.

He yanked the phone handset loose from the landline and scrambled for the passenger seat of his truck. His driver was already behind the wheel, kicking the engine over, as the gunner cast loose the last of the camouflage netting.

There was a whispering rattle overhead. Eighty-one-millimeter rounds began to drop in the Red positions. As per the preset ambush scenario, the battalion mortarmen were laying a barrage of high explosives and white phosphorus in on the Communists. Hopefully, under the cover and confusion of the smoke, the antitank section would be able to successfully disengage.

False hope.

A tank cannon slammed. The easternmost vehicle of the section flipped into the air like a shotgun-blasted beer can, the broken bodies of its driver and gunner spinning away to one side.

The command 4 × 4 lunged forward, crashing through the thin brush screen, breaking line of sight with the enemy. A new sound was coming from the sky now: the deeper wailing howl of heavy howitzer shells. The Nationalist division's 155s were joining in the battle.

As the surviving section vehicles bounced back through the gap in the minefield, proceeding to their battle stations in the battalion line of resistance, the young officer considered the engagement he had just lived through.

It had been a good exchange. One launcher for seven AFVs. That, plus the fact that they had broken the momentum of the Red advance and had stalled them in place long enough for the artillery to tear them up a bit more. A very good exchange.

He could only hope that the families of the men he had just lost would see it that way.

Variants of this first engagement were being repeated scores of times over all across a twenty-mile front. Fifty-five thousand Communist soldiers and eight thousand armored fighting vehicles were rising up out of the mud and hurling themselves headlong at the Nationalist beach-head defenses.

Battle raged on all levels. On the ground, tanks intermixed in a clumsy dance of death, turning, spitting, and dying. Behind the hills and ridgelines, helicopter gunships stalked and sniped at ground targets. In the middle altitudes, squadrons of jets slashed at each other, while in the stratosphere, artillery shells and rockets passed in flight, arcing along their ballistic paths to destruction.

One would almost have to go to the edge of space to find peace. And there, one would also find an observer.

Circling in a lazy racetrack pattern at 75,000 feet was one of the world's oddest-looking aircraft. Described as resembling "a clamshell glued in the middle of a yardstick," the Darkstar reconnaissance drone bore no insignia beyond the distinctive sooty shading of its Ironball Gray stealth paint.

All but immune to ground-based detection, it rode the midnight-blue sky on its slender, straight wings, the systems in its observation bay system-atically recording the holocaust below.

Six hundred miles to the east, over the East China Sea, the Darkstar's command-and-control aircraft also orbited. A converted U.S. Air Force KC-10 tanker, it maintained a continuous DTI datalink with its distant robotic charge, exchanging flight and navigational instructions for a continuing real-time download from the drone's sensors.

From there, the data was relayed through the KC-10's commodious communications suite to half a dozen different destinations within the United States and the Pacific Rim. A great many people were interested in the outcome of this particular battle.

"All right, Major. What's going on out there?"

Sam Hanson and Lane Ashley sat in the darkness of the small Pentagon briefing room. The National Security Adviser and the NSA director were awaiting the latest word on the distant conflict.

Before them, the shadowy form of the duty briefing officer stood beside a computer-graphics map of the Chinese mainland.

"At the moment, sir, the core of the Communist offensive appears to be their Third Guards Tank Army. This is both the PLA's best fire-brigade outfit and their largest available block of mobile reserves."

The briefer indicated the key points on the map, his arm and pointing fingertip a black silhouette across the glowing wall screen.

"They are hitting the Nationalist beach head from the north and west, along three separate lines of advance. Here, from Fuzhou, from Nanping, and from Sha Xian, one divisional strength column along each axis. The Communist objective is obvious. They are attempting to collapse and destroy the Nationalist beach head before the United Democratic Forces can launch their own offensive to break through to and link up with the Nationalists."

"What are their chances of succeeding?" Director Ashley inquired.

"The Reds are going to get their asses blown away . . . begging your pardon, ma'am."

"You sound pretty sure about that, Major."

"We are, ma'am," the briefer replied. "What the Reds have been hoping for is to beat the UDFC to the punch, to destroy the Nationalists before the rebels are set to move. What they don't realize is that they've already lost the race."

"The United Democratic Forces are ready to go?"

"Yes, ma'am. If our intelligence estimates are correct, they've been set for several days. We believe that they've been waiting for the Communist attack."

"Now that the Communists have committed to their offensive, we believe that the UDFC will jump off down here, across the Shantau River line, probably within the next twenty-four hours."

Hanson nodded. "It makes sense, Lane. The Reds are going to be blindsided. Once they've committed to the attack on the Nationalist beach head, they won't have the mobile assets available to react to the UDFC offensive."

"What will happen to the Nationalists?"

"The Reds might be able to gain a few kilometers here and there, but they won't be able to concentrate and follow through with their offensive. They'll be caught in the worst of both worlds."

"Yes, sir," the briefer added. "That will be about the shape of it. We are projecting that the Reds are going to lose the bulk of the Third Guards Tank Army. By this time next week, the Rebels should have broken through down at Shantau and will be driving north to link up with the Nationalists. With all of their theater reserves either burned up or committed, the Reds aren't going to be able to stop them."

The room lights came up and the briefing officer came to a parade rest beside the briefing screen, his Joint Chiefs of Staff identification badge glinting. "We project that the PRC defenses are going to collapse and they are going to lose all of Fujian Province. They probably aren't going to be able to restabilize the front again until somewhere up around the Wenzhou River line."

"And then?" Lane Ashley asked.

"That's still anybody's guess, ma'am. The RAND conflict-simulation teams haven't yet extended their projections beyond that point."

"Then make it your own best educated guess, Major. In your opinion, how serious a setback will this be for the Communists?"

"Very serious, ma'am. This is a critical battle, a nexal point in the course of the war. Something like Gettysburg or Stalingrad. If the Reds lose this one, and the odds are they will, I can't see how they'll be able to recover."

"I'll buy into that assessment," Sam Hanson added. "I think that we're seeing the beginning of the end here."

"I don't like the sound of that phrase," the NSA woman said grimly. "Major, how about the Communist nuclear arsenal? Has there been any change of status reported?"

"We have no new information on that subject at this time, ma'am."

☆ East China Sea
110 Miles North of Chilung, Taiwan
2221 Hours Zone Time; August 8, 2006

"It looks to me like we're seeing it all across the board."

"Yeah. We're still getting a set level of work transitories off the fishing fleet, but fa' sure we're not hearing the engines as much. These guys are falling back on sail and oar power more and more all the time."

"That would indicate to me that the Reds are stepping up their fuel rationing."

"Very possible, Jer, but I don't think we've got a long enough baseline to call it for certain sure yet. It could be that the locals are just taking advantage of a long stretch of favorable coastal winds. We'll cross-reference this tomorrow with the net reports from the past couple of weeks and see what we shall see."

They had been at it in Raven's Roost for over five hours now. Lieutenant (j.g.) Gerald Selkirk's eyes felt as if they were lined with sandpaper and a pulsing headache thudded at the back of his skull. His boss, however, seemed to still be going strong. The only clue she gave to the protracted length of this analysis session was the mound of candy-bar wrappers growing beside her on the workstation console.

That, and the glasses. Christine Rendino donned her glasses only when she had a massive load of close work. Even then, they were rarely actually looked through. Rather, Chris kept them shoved up onto her forehead, an accessory and an adjunct to her high-intensity thinking.

"Okay, Jerry, what's next on the boards?"

Selkirk fumbled for his personal-computer pad. Lieutenant Rendino apparently wasn't ready to call it quits for the night yet. Truth be told, he didn't mind it too much. The Duke's senior intel might look like his kid sister, but watching her work was a continually fascinating and humbling experience.

"Well," he said, "Fleet intelligence is on the lookout for a Red Chinese coastal convoy. Seems they've lost track of one somewhere."

"Whoa, somebody was a Mr. Fumble-fingers. What got lost?"

"A five-ship group," Selkirk replied. "One coaster of about six hundred fifty tons' displacement, two more of about three hundred tons, one two-hundred-tonner, and all escorted by a single Shanghai IV–class patrol boat."

"What dope do we have on 'em?"

"It formed up at the Port of Qingdao. Loading a mixed cargo of military stores, possibly rations, lubricants, and equipment spares, it sailed on the night of the second, heading south. . . ."

As he spoke, Lieutenant Rendino's fingers began to clatter across the terminal keyboard in front of her, calling up a theater map out of the navigational database.

"Satellite recon then spotted the convoy at the ports of Shijiusuo, Lianyungang, and Sheyang sequentially during the daylight hours of the third, fourth, and fifth. The ships only appeared to be laying over. No indication of cargo handling."

The Intel's right hand shifted over to the workstation's mouse, clicking off the location points.

"One night track is listed, off Andongwei Point, between Shijiusuo and Lianyungang. The formation was painted on radar by one of our P3E's flying out of Seoul. Again running south, hugging the coast, at about eight to ten knots."

"Pretty straight so far," Rendino commented. "They were playing bunny rabbit, hedge-hopping down the coast. They'd lay up in a defended anchorage during the day and steam only at night to duck the Nationalists. What next?"

"Track was lost down around Shanghai. According to this, the two medium-size coasters may have shown up down at Hangzhou Wan, but the other units have disappeared. Fleet wants to know what happened to them and to the stores they were carrying. They've queried us as to whether any of our hydrophone buoys may have gotten anything."

"Could be, Jer. Number one is just north of the Yangtze estuary, right on what should have been their course line. Pull the latest downloads for that hummer and let's have a look at them."

Selkirk pushed his chair back the scant foot permitted by the narrow central passage of the intelligence bay and reached over his shoulder to the disc-storage rack. Selecting the appropriate CD case, he rolled into place again. Cycling one of the loading trays, he fed the disc into the system.

"Set," he said, accessing the data from his half of the analysis station.

"Okay, call up the audio tracks from the early morning of the sixth. Time reference . . . about 0200 to 0500 hours. Set your search gates for a package of four medium-speed, single-screw diesels and one high-speed, multiscrew diesel."

"Searching."

The signal processors scanned through the compressed data on the disc, seeking for one specific pattern and, after a few moments, finding it.

Another flatscreen lit off, a cascade display showing a pattern of five passive sonar signals. Five bands of shimmering light flowing from the top of the monitor to the bottom, each band carrying the sound signature generated by a specific ship as it had passed by the listening buoy.

Lieutenant Rendino clicked on the audio feed and ran the volume bar full over.

Now they could hear them: the churning cavitation of propellers, the rumble of power-plant noise, the hiss and slap of hulls butting through the waves. Even without the processing of the cascade display, the trained ears of the two intelligence officers could begin to make out the individuality of the vessels. The clatter of a loose shaft hub, the repetitive chirp of a bent screw blade, an intermittent thud as some poorly secured piece of cargo shifted with the roll of the deck.

As clearly as with their eyes, they could see the convoy slipping through the night.

"Okay," Selkirk reported. "Speed by blade count is between eight and ten knots. No aspect change. They aren't zigzagging. Exact time index is oh three one oh hours."

"Yeah." Christine nodded. "That's just about right. That'd put 'em off the Yangtze estuary at first light. They laid over in Shanghai, and then moved on again. Why'd Fleet miss that?"

"Don't know, Lieutenant."

"Jer, call up the Shanghai data annex. Access maritime and naval activity for the day of the sixth and see if anything's listed that matches up with this outfit."

"Aye, aye." Selkirk's hands played his keyboard, his eyes sweeping across the glowing lines of text that welled up in response. It took him perhaps five minutes to be sure.

"Nothing. No shipping groups that match up. No individual vessels listed in port at the time that could have been part of the convoy. Damn little activity of any kind."

"Well, sca-rew! Where did those guys get to?" Rendino frowned, pondering.

"They might have gone upriver. The Yangtze is deep-hull navigable for better than a thousand miles upstream."

"Maybe, but let's be sure. Load the dump from buoy two. It's just south of the estuary. If the convoy ducked us somehow and continued on down-coast, number two should have 'em."

The disc exchange took only a moment.

"Set."

"Okay, Jerry. Search for the convoy's sound signature, twenty-one ten hours to twenty-four hundred hours."

"Searching . . . nothing. They're not there."

"Well, sca-rew again. Widen the search gates. Full scan of the sixth, the entire twenty-four hours."

This time the search took a little longer. Five familiar traces flowed down the Cascade display.

"Got 'em," Selkirk announced. "The buoy acquired them at time reference oh seven three one."

"What!" Christine Rendino's chair slammed upright as she leaned into the screen. "They bypassed! They bypassed Shanghai altogether and kept running on down the coast in broad daylight!"

"That's a major change in policy."

"It sure is, and given their location, it's a real dumb one . . . as I think these guys are about to find out."

The signature tracks on the display began to broaden and waver slightly.

"Blade count is increasing and we're getting aspect changes. They're tacking on speed and starting to zigzag."

"Fa' sure I'd guess so. This should be interesting."

For a full three minutes they watched the weaving traces. Then one of the five lines abruptly terminated in a spherical blob of greenish luminescence.

"Hold it," Christine snapped. "Backtrack thirty seconds. Replay and bring up the audio."

This time they listened to the desperate hammering of racing propellers as the convoy lumberingly sought to evade, then the hollow reverberating slam, like a giant's fist driving into the side of a fifty-foot oil drum. The lighter, faster beat of the escorting patrol boat's screws ceased. As the reverberations of the blast faded, they heard the thud of secondary explosions and the crack and squeal of tearing metal. The sound of a ship starting to break up.

"Quiz time, dude. What did we just hear?"

"An above-the-waterline hit on a small hull." Selkirk answered promptly, accustomed to this kind of drill from his division officer. "Medium-size warhead. Single detonation. A precision-guided munition of some kind, probably an antishipping missile. Since the buoy wasn't picking up on any other surface or submarine sound sources in the area, it was probably air-launched."

"Very good. Now that they've killed the guy with all the antiaircraft guns, it's playtime." Lieutenant Rendino extended her hand and indicated one of the remaining tracks on the cascade display with her forefinger. "He's next."

As if in response to the tap of her fingernail, the track flared out into another death blossom. The crash of the missile hit echoed from the speaker.

"There went the biggest coaster." Christine squirmed a little in her chair. "God! Watching a real pro at work always makes me hot."

Reaching forward again, she aimed the finger of doom at another track. "Now this guy. In about one minute."

It was ten seconds short of a minute when the first harsh burp of sound issued from the speaker, a baritone snarl like the ripping of canvas.

"Can you call that one, Jer?"

Selkirk shook his head regretfully.

"Cannon fire hitting the water," Christine continued. "They're strafing the smallest coaster."

They listened on as the aerial predators slashed at their prey. The steady thrum of the coaster's propeller began to stagger like the beat of a failing heart . . . and then stopped.

There were no further fireworks, and the screws of the two surviving Communist vessels began to fade in the distance.

Lieutenant Rendino switched off the recording. "You're going to be writing this up for Fleet, Jer. What are you going to say about it?"

Selkirk took a deliberate breath to buy himself a couple of seconds of thinking time. "The Red convoy was engaged south of the Yangtze estuary by a Nationalist Air Force antishipping sweep. Given the position and timing of the engagement, the Nationalist strike presumably consisted of two Ching Kuo fighter-bombers, staging out of their air base at Chilung in northern Taiwan.

"This would match the performance and range envelope of the Ching Kuo operating with a Standard antishipping load-out consisting of one Hsiung Feng II antishipping missile plus drop tanks. The targeting and fire template of the strike itself appears to match this load-out as well.

"Three bogeys were killed—the escort, the six-hundred-and-fifty-ton coaster, and the two-hundred-tonner. The two surviving coasters proceeded on to the anchorage at Hangzhou Wan. All targets accounted for."

Lieutenant Rendino nodded approvingly. "Not bad. But you missed three points that Fleet may be able to make some use of. Point one, the Nationalists were using air-to-air refueling. Yeah, a Ching could reach the engagement point from Chi-lung on one strike load, but just barely. These guys were boogyin' around at low altitude for an extended period of time as if they were running fat on gas.

"Point two." The blond Intel ticked it off on her fingers. "This was a full four-plane flight, not a two-plane element. Again, these guys were hanging around down on the deck, without a care in the world, within a few miles of a major Red air base. This says to me that they had a couple of little buddies up on high, ready to do nasty things to any party crashers."

"Yeah, I can see that now." *Damn, why couldn't I see it before?* "What's the third point?"

"That a real old salty dog was leading this pack. He took his time, eyeballed the tactical situation, and killed the sole immediate threat with his first shot, then apportioned his remaining ordnance out to the maximum amount of damage to the surviving targets. Bet he was at least the squadron exec, maybe even the old man himself."

Selkirk shook his head in wry self-abasement. "Why do I even try. Nobody can touch the master."

Christine Rendino grinned and shrugged. "Hey, what can I say? Being just totally cool comes naturally to me. It's one of those genetic things. Seriously, though, Lieutenant, if you're planning to stick with intelligence work as a career track, you've got to remember one key thing. It's not enough to just go around cataloging what the other guy is doing. You've got to be able to crawl inside his brain and figure out why he's doing it before you've got the whole package."

A thoughtful expression suddenly passed over her face. "Like, for example, why did those poor damn Chinese decide to commit suicide the way they did?"

"You mean by running in daylight?"

"Yeah. Admittedly, darkness isn't as much cover as it once was, but it's still something. That convoy was right outside of Shanghai, the most heavily defended port facility the Reds have. Why didn't they lay over again and wait for nightfall, like they'd been doing along the rest of the coast?"

"They had a delivery deadline to meet?"

The senior Intel shook her head. "No. If they'd had to shave some time by running during the day, they would have done it up north, farther away from the Nationalist bases.

"They must have been ordered to bypass Shanghai for some reason, a big enough one so that the Reds were willing to risk an entire convoy of critical military stores for it. Now, what could be going on in Shanghai to justify something like that?"

Selkirk didn't have an answer for her. He suspected that she wasn't expecting one.

Christine Rendino reached into the paper bag that sat on the deck at her feet and removed another Milky Way. Peeling down the wrapper, she leaned forward onto the console and took a deliberate first bite, taking on a refueling load of sugar and caffeine.

All the while, she stared at the glowing map of the Shanghai approaches with the fixed intensity of a cat in front of a mouse hole.

☆ 200 Miles North of Miyako Shima Island
1041 Hours Zone Time; August 9, 2006

The vista from the climbing helicopter was one Amanda could appreciate. If the *Cunningham* was the cutting edge of the U.S. Navy's presence off China, then this, Fleet Task Force 7.1, was the bulk and the strength of the blade.

Ahead, slotting the horizon at precise ten-degree intervals, were the wakes of the ASW destroyers, foam white against ocean blue as they sanitized a path for the formation. Out on either flank were the two Aegis cruisers tasked with throwing their antiair shield of radar and guided-missile firepower over their comrades.

Looking back, past the Sea Comanche's fenestron, she could make out her own ship nestled close to the Task Force's big Sacramento-class AOE. The Duke and the fast combat support ship were running side by side, their wakes merging behind them into a trailing snowy train. Fuel and cargo-handling lines bridged the meager 150-foot gap between the two vessels as the destroyer executed an UNREP, an under-way replenishment of critically needed supplies.

The centerpiece and justification of it all was just ahead, the great slab-sided form with its unique cubical island structure, a design quirk left over from a radar system that never really worked all that well. It was the grand old lady of the fleet, the USS *Enterprise*, jeweled by the sunfire striking off the canopies of the ranked aircraft on her decks.

"Now, that is a pretty, pretty picture," Arkady breathed into the intercom.

"I agree," Amanda replied. "This is her last West Pac. One of her reactors has already been powered down due to neutron fatigue. When she goes home this time, it's to the breakers yard."

"Yeah." She saw his helmet bob in acknowledgment. "I'll tell you something though, babe. On the day they haul the Big E's flag down, I'm going to take myself out and get me drunk enough to be able to cry."

"You can lend me a shoulder, Arkady. I'll have a few tears to shed myself."

The aviator keyed his radio transmitter.

"Air Boss Seven One Alpha, this is Retainer Zero One cross-decking from USS *Cunningham* to Task Force Flag. Requesting approach and landing clearance."

"Retainer Zero One, we are involved in a fixed-wing recovery at this time. Hold on station off our starboard quarter and stay alert for descending traffic. You are next to land."

"Retainer Zero One. Rog."

Amanda twisted around in the cockpit and scanned astern. A single F/A-18 Super Hornet was in the approach path, riding the invisible beam of the Fresnell lamp down to the carrier's deck. Flying dirty with undercarriage, tail hook, and flaps all fully extended, it seemed to float hesitantly out of the sky, unwilling to surrender the freedom of flight. Then, as the flattop came into the field of vision, the true perspective of the landing became apparent. The last few seconds of the plane's descent became a flashing blur of speed, climaxing with the puff of blue smoke that marked the impact of landing gear on antiskid.

"Retainer Zero One, this is Air Boss Seven One Alpha. You are cleared to complete cross-decking. Be advised you will be positioned on Spot Three. Watch for your deck controller."

"Roger D. *Cunningham* arriving."

As Retainer Zero One sidled across the last thousand-odd yards to the carrier, Arkady switched back to the cockpit interphone. "What's the game plan, babe?" he inquired.

"What do you mean?"

"This is going to be your first face-to-face meeting with Admiral Tall-man. Knowing you, you've got to have a plan."

"Nothing much beyond trying to convince him that we'll stay out of his hair if he'll stay out of ours."

"Watch yourself, though. Trying to convince an admiral that you know more than he does is touchy work."

"I'm going to try it anyhow. You know me, love. I hate being tied down." They found themselves taking pleasure in this use of endearments, taking advantage of this pocket of privacy to let down their guard for a brief moment.

"You sure? We haven't tried it that way yet." Amanda heard the grin in Arkady's voice, and she reached forward over the cockpit divider to administer a quick poke in the shoulder.

The circle-dot-line deck symbol of a vertical landing point grew under the helicopter. Bouncing lightly on her landing gear, the Sea Comanche touched down.

One of the *Enterprise*'s flight-deck hands escorted her on the dash across to the base of the island. A marine orderly was standing by at the hatchway, waiting for her.

"Captain Garrett?" he yelled over the clamor of the flight deck. "Admiral Tallman sends his compliments and requests that I escort you to his day cabin."

"Very well," she yelled back, shedding her flight gear. "Let's go."

Amanda followed him into the island structure. As she passed through the hatchway, she reached out and gave the worn metal near the dogging latches a greeting pat. Shore dwellers have friends, lovers, and relations. Mariners also have ships. Amanda had put a tour in aboard the Big E a few years back. It was good to say hello again.

"Pardon me, Corporal. Before we go topside, I need to freshen up a little. Is there still a women's head on this deck?"

"Yes, ma'am. Two frames aft down this passageway."

Amanda was unzipping her Nomex flight suit as she brushed past the door. Underneath, she was wearing a set of summer khakis, not one of her usual wash sets, but one of her custom tailoreds, ironed out into knife-edged creases. She'd considered wearing her whites but had decided that would be overkill. But she had brought a new set of decoration ribbons.

When one went into the lion's den, one carried what ammunition one could. *Gentlemen, there is one Navy Cross in this room, and neither of you is wearing it.*

A few moments to check the touch of makeup she had donned and another few to comb her hair smooth from the tousling it had received from the rotor wash, and she was ready.

The *Enterprise*'s Flag Quarters were that curious mix of luxury and utility unique to such habitations. Golden oak wall panels and navy-blue carpeting challenged an overhead cluttered with cable clusters and insulated duct work. The large combined office and sitting room was furnished with a comfortably masculine-looking couch-and-chair set done in burgundy leather. The two men occupying the cabin hastily came to their feet as she was ushered in.

"Commander Amanda Lee Garrett reporting on station, sir."

"At ease, Commander, and welcome aboard." Admiral Tallman was a solid man carrying only a little middle-aged weight. His dark hair was thinning and his rather narrow brown eyes shone with a mixture of humor and shrewd intelligence. When he shook her hand after their exchange of salutes, there was a slight bow and touch of old Georgia courtesy to his action. There was also a faint smile on his face. He recognized the meaning behind those neat rows of gleaming ribbons over her left breast and he appeared willing to acknowledge her points on protocol.

"Commander Garrett, this is my chief of staff, Commander Nolan Walker."

Walker was essentially a colorless man, gray eyes and pale skin providing no contrast for his graying blond hair. As Amanda accepted his hand she could feel the adversarial sparks jump between them. She couldn't quite call whether it was because she was a woman or because she had a ship and he didn't. There weren't all that many command slots in the modern Navy, but there were a lot of officers like Walker, a year or two overage in grade and listening to their career clocks ticking down toward zero.

"A pleasure to meet you, Commander Walker," Amanda replied levelly.

Tallman gestured Amanda into one of the cabin's chairs, taking the couch for himself. Walker preferred to stand, leaning back against the cabin's desk.

"I'm glad we've finally got to meet face-to-face, Captain," the Admiral said. "I've heard a lot about you and the Duke."

"I hope it's been favorable, sir," Amanda replied politely.

"It has been from my intelligence people. They say the *Cunningham's* been coming across with some pretty good stuff. This remote sensor net you've been deploying seems to be producing as advertised."

Amanda nodded. "We've had good luck with it so far. Mated up with our onboard Elint and Sigint systems, we seem to have a pretty good package going. I have to give the credit to Lieutenant Rendino, my intelligence officer, and her people. They're the ones who are making it work."

Tallman shrugged. "It's still your watch, Captain. The thing is, you seem to be working in pretty close. From the look of it, you were right up on the beach last night."

Amanda nodded. "That's an aspect of stealth doctrine. You simply can't reduce the radar cross section of a vessel the size of the *Cunningham* to zero. There will just about always be some kind of residual return. If you loiter around in open water, you run the risk of standing out enough to be noticed, like a ball bearing on a beach. If you work in close, you can lose your RCS against the shore clutter."

"And what about land-based radar?" Walker inquired pointedly.

Amanda shrugged. "Fixed systems are easier to avoid than mobile ones. And there's always the hope they'll mistake you for a fishing boat."

Admiral Tallman frowned and gave a brief acknowledging grunt. "About how many more times do you think you'll need to go into Chinese territorial waters?"

So that was the bite. Amanda shifted slightly in the chair. "That's hard to say, sir. As of yesterday, the net's fully deployed. We shouldn't have to do any more work along that line except to replace a malfunctioning or a compromised unit. On the other hand, to react to a possible collection opportunity . . . We'll just have to see how the situation develops."

"We've received the post-action report on this last sensor insertion of yours, Captain," Commander Walker interjected. "Frankly, there are certain aspects of it that concern the hell out of us. You damn near got your ship trapped in the middle of a major firefight out there."

"I agree it was tight, but we were able to successfully disengage. That's been the only really close call we've had so far on this deployment."

" 'So far' is the operative phrase here, Captain. What happens next time?"

"They haven't caught me yet, Commander."

"It is a point of concern, though, Captain," Admiral Tallman said. "We're operating right on the edge of a major shooting war out here. It wouldn't take a whole lot to tip us over that edge."

"I am cognizant of that point, sir," Amanda replied. Like the boss mare of a band of mustangs, she was beginning to scent a trap. Best to bring up a few heavy guns of her own. "And I'm sure my superior officer, Admiral MacIntyre, is aware of it as well."

She saw Tallman's eyes momentarily flick over to his chief of staff. Ah, they were running a 'good cop–bad cop' on her. The loop would be coming soon; she'd better be ready to duck out from under it.

"The problem is that the *Cunningham* isn't the only American naval vessel out here," Walker said, pushing the point, "and the Red Chinese aren't going to worry too much about American chains of command. If you hit the trip wire out there, it could be one of our ships that gets targeted for retaliation."

"That is a valid point, Commander," Amanda replied cautiously. "Do you have any suggestions about how we should address it?"

The "good cop" took over.

"We think we do, Captain," Admiral Tallman said, smoothly picking up the line of the conversation. "Now, Operation Uriah is strictly NAVSPEC-FORCE's baby, but since we're both sharing the same MODLOC out here, I'd like to establish a set of liaison protocols. Our intel people are already working together routinely and doing a good job of it. We ought to be doing the same thing operationally. It just makes good sense for the right hand to know what the left is doing."

There it was. It was very subtly and politely worded, but the literal translation was still: Hey, lady, this is my sandbox and you, by God, better start playing by my rules.

Amanda smiled. "That does seem reasonable, sir. However, I don't think that I have the authority to amend my mission parameters to that extent. I think that the best call would be for you to contact NAVSPECFORCE directly and work up a set of protocols through them."

Literal translation: Fuck off! You're not my boss and we both know it.

Amanda awaited the follow-up. Walker straightened angrily at the desk, but before he could speak, Tallman caught him with a slight shake of his head.

"You're right, Captain Garrett," he replied quietly. "That would be the proper way to handle this. We'll look into it." He rose to his feet and extended his hand. "I expect you'll be wanting to get back to your ship here presently. It was a pleasure meeting you."

Amanda stood up as well and accepted the handshake. "It's the same for me, sir. I appreciate the opportunity to meet the people I'm working with face-to-face."

"It does promote understanding, Captain."

After Amanda Garrett had departed, Admiral Tallman and his chief of staff worked through a well-established ritual. Commander Walker drew two mugs of heavy-caliber Navy coffee setting them on Tallman's desk, while the Admiral unlocked the bottom drawer and removed a contraband bottle. Opening the fifth of bonded Kentucky bourbon, the senior officer poured a carefully metered ounce into each cup.

Recorking the bottle, Tallman restored it to its hiding place and returned his attention to Walker. "Well, what do you think?"

"I think she's a rogue and a glory hound, and I think she's going to be a lot of trouble."

Tallman laughed briefly. "Now, don't hold back on me, Nolan. What's your real opinion?"

"I'm serious, sir. Garrett is a loose cannon, and a loose cannon with an attitude. We do not need that out here just now."

"Yeah, I might buy in on the attitude. But then, that's not necessarily a bad thing." The Admiral took his first experimental sip of his laced coffee. "She's a destroyer driver, and destroyer drivers are like fighter pilots. They're no damn good unless they're just a little bit cocky."

"She's also a risk taker."

"That's also part of the job. Just as long as they're calculated. Let's face it. Maybe she is nosing into our territory, but she's also coming across with some of the best tactical intelligence we're getting off the Chinese coast."

Tallman tilted his chair back. "Eddie Mac MacIntyre seems to think that she's the greatest thing since the invention of the screw propeller, and he does not impress easily. Maybe we should just let it ride."

"Sir, we don't have a handle on this woman!"

"That may not necessarily be such a bad thing, either. If something blows because of her, well, she's NAVSPECFORCE's baby. If we don't have any operational linkage, we can just slough it off on them. If she keeps doing things right, hell, it's going to be happening in our bailiwick, and we'll catch the glow off of it."

Walker frowned and reached for his coffee mug. "I still don't like it, sir."

"Maintain the even strain, son. We'll just give this lady all the rope she wants. She'll either hang herself with it, or she'll bring it back wrapped around something real pretty."

☆ Rizal Park, Manila
2022 Hours Zone Time; August 9, 2006

Rizal Park was the place to be on a warm summer evening in Manila. Young people and families enjoyed the abating of the day's heat, their laughter and the mixed musics of a myriad of radios and disc players drowning out the sounds of the traffic-crowded streets. In much the same manner, the park's gardens and the freshening sea breeze held at bay the ranker aromas of a city in the tropics.

With his tie tugged down a couple of comfortable inches and his suit coat slung over his shoulder, Harrison Van Lynden paced slowly along one of the paved footpaths. Since the beginning of the crisis talks, he had taken advantage of the great park adjacent to the Hotel Manila, this postdinner walk becoming something of a ritual for the Secretary of State. Not only did it work out accumulated tension, but it also gave him the opportunity to mull over the events of the day's session and to plan his next day's strategies.

Absorbed in thought, he didn't notice the figure cutting across the lawn to intercept him.

"A most pleasant evening, is it not, Mr. Secretary?" The voice was from out of the past, but the face was one that he had been seeing daily.

"Not too bad, General. Still a little warm for a man from down east, but I'm getting used to it."

General Ho Chunwa of the People's Republic wore civilian clothing: dark trousers and a short-sleeved white shirt. Only his soldierly bearing remained to remind one of his rank and position. That, and the small cadre of alert and expressionless Chinese who were dispersing out around the area.

Van Lynden was well-acquainted with the phenomenon. His own Secret Service team was maintaining their protective cordon, deployed discreetly beyond easy hearing range. The two groups of agents were now intermingling, studiously ignoring each other and maintaining their watch over their respective charges.

"I have observed you on your walks these past few evenings," General Ho continued. "I, too, enjoy a breath of fresh air at this time of the day. Perhaps we might walk together."

There was an intentness to Ho's expression that belied his bland words. Van Lynden elected to play out the scenario.

"Fine. I'd enjoy the company."

"Very good. Perhaps we can go this way. I have discovered a vista that I think you will find most inspiring."

General Ho's vista was a pleasant enough view of Manila Bay as seen from across the sports field at the west end of the park. The bay could best be observed from the base of one of the larger of the park's many fountains. General Ho seated himself on the eroded concrete bench built into the rim of the fountain's pool

"There," Ho said with satisfaction. "Now we may talk."

"I thought that the old running water gimmick didn't work anymore," Van Lynden commented, dropping down beside the Chinese military man. "They can use a computer filter to separate your voice out of the background noise."

"The secret is to keep the falling water between yourself and the microphones. With the fountain behind us and open ground to our front, I believe we have a degree of privacy."

"I'll have to remember that. Now, General, why are we really here?"

"I need your opinions, Mr. Secretary. Not the diplomatic kind, but the true ones."

"About what?"

"The state of these negotiations. Specifically, if there is any potential flexibility within the stands being taken by the Nationalists and the United Democratic Forces. Any aspect they may not have yet revealed in open negotiations?"

"General, you can't expect me to repeat anything that may have been revealed to me in confidence by any of the other delegates."

"I understand that, Mr. Secretary. I merely ask if the potential exists."

"Well, speaking in all honesty, I suppose I can say that what you see on the table is pretty much what you've got. All three of the involved parties—

yourself, the Nationalists, and the United Democratic Forces—seem to be issuing the same *mise en demeure:* Your collective bottom line seems to be victory or death."

"Indeed."

"The UDFC knows that they've rolled the dice and they have to take it all the way. Speaking bluntly, their leadership is aware that they can expect damn little sympathy from Beijing if they fail. As for the Nationalists, they have a few more options open to them. However, they know that this is their one best shot at regaining influence on the mainland. As for your people, I'm sure you are quite aware of what you have to lose."

"You see no possibilities, then, for a negotiated settlement?"

"There are always possibilities, General. But just now, nobody seems to be giving anyone else any room to maneuver."

Van Lynden suddenly elected to attempt a maneuver of his own. "In fact," he continued, "I'm thinking about pulling out and turning leadership of the U.S. delegation over to our ambassador here. I've got some critical work awaiting my attention back in Washington, and I can't just waste my time spinning my wheels on this."

That was a flagrant untruth. Van Lynden had instigated these talks because his instincts of statesmanship had screamed that this was the single most critical crisis currently confronting the world community. He had no intention of giving up on them while there was even the faintest chance that they could succeed. However, the Chinese soldier's queries had piqued Van Lynden's interest and he was fishing for a reaction.

He received one.

"You must not!" Ho's eyes narrowed and his fist slammed down on the edge of the bench. "It is imperative that you stay, Mr. Secretary."

"Why, General?" Van Lynden demanded quietly.

"That . . . is something that I may not reveal. However, I can say that the status of these talks may alter radically during the next few days. Should that occur, your presence here may be urgently needed. The hours it would take for you to return could prove critical."

"Why me, General? What's so vital about my presence?"

"Because, Mr. Secretary, I may soon be making my first presentation here at this conference. When that storm breaks, there must be someone here who is both distant from the problems that are tearing my nation apart, and yet has influence with both the Nationalists and the United Democratic Forces. There must be someone here who can make them listen!"

"And what about the People's Republic?"

"It must rest upon the others, Mr. Secretary. They are the ones who must listen, for we will not."

There was a third group of agents deployed within Rizal Park that evening, suspected possibly, but unknown to either the American Secretary of State or the Communist General.

They were a sleeper team, long before recruited from within Manila's Chinese ethnic community. Activated specifically to monitor the comings and goings of the diplomatic delegations assigned to the crisis talks, they observed the meeting between Van Lynden and Ho.

Kept at long range by the guard screen, they overheard nothing that was said. However, they could report to their cell contact that the meeting had taken place. Relayed through a series of security breaks, the report did not reach the suite occupied by the combined Taiwanese/UDFC delegation for several hours.

When it did, the recipients were pleased.

☆ 54 Miles East of Xiangshan, China
1201 Hours Zone Time; August 10, 2006

To the ballerina, Borodin is beautiful, yet very challenging. As the closing strains of the "Polovtsian Dances" crashed out, Amanda completed the choreography that she had patterned herself, sinking to one knee and tossing her hair back in exhaustion.

There was no applause. Her only audience was a handful of her crew-people working out on the weight machines across the ship's gymnasium from the exercise mat.

Once, she would have been reticent about dancing where anyone could see her. But now she considered herself rather good for an amateur.

At one time, an involvement in ballet didn't seem appropriate for a female naval officer who wanted to be taken seriously. However, after Drake's Passage, she had become less self-conscious about her hobby. If a Presidential Unit Citation and a Navy Cross weren't adequate professional credentials, then nothing would be. She'd even started to do a little teaching on the side.

Amanda switched off the portable CD deck and leaned back against the bulkhead. "I missed you on toward the end," she said, addressing the small pile of panting, multicolored spandex huddled on the mat beside her.

"That's because I gave it the hell up back around where I was supposed to tie my left leg into a granny knot," Christine Rendino wheezed. "I don't get it. I'm seven years younger than you are, and yet you're the one with the India-rubber muscles and the cardiovascular system of a Clydesdale."

"That's because there's more to my life than a CRT screen and a case of Milky Way IIs," Amanda replied smugly.

"Aaah! Fa' sure, if I wanted to be insulted, I'd get McKelsie to teach me ballet," the blond Intel moaned, rolling over onto her back. "I'm down there in Raven's Roost, twenty-five hours a day, trying to outguess a billion and a quarter moody Chinese, and I'm still underappreciated. Everybody hates me. Nobody loves me. I think I'll go eat worms."

"*Bon appétit!*" Amanda stretched and straightened her leotard-sheathed legs. "Oh, we appreciate you, Chris. According to Admiral Tallman, Fleet Intelligence seems to be very pleased with how Operation Uriah is shaking down. So am I, for that matter. Give yourself an 'Atta girl, first class.'"

"I'd rather have something else."

"Such as?"

Chris rolled back over onto her stomach. "Buy me Shanghai for my birthday, Mommy."

Something in her voice indicated that she had shifted from casual banter to something more serious.

Amanda cocked an eyebrow. "What do you mean?"

"I want a chance to take a look in at Shanghai. A long, close look."

"Have you seen something?"

"It's not so much what I'm seeing as what I'm not seeing," Christine replied, a calculating look coming to her gray-blue eyes. "Something odd has been happening around Shanghai for the past couple of weeks. Can we get secure for a few minutes?"

"Sure," Amanda replied, looping her towel around her shoulders.

They got to their feet and left the gym. Moving forward a few frames, they paused in an empty section of the corridor adjacent to the number-two Vertical Launch System.

"Okay, what have you got?"

Christine shot a quick glance both up and down the passageway, verifying that no one else was within hearing range.

"It's sort of like in those old jungle-adventure movies, Captain," she began. "You know, the ones where the dauntless hero comments about things being too quiet. Well, all of a sudden, the Shanghai Operations Area is getting way too quiet."

"Specifics?"

"Shanghai is the largest transport and communications terminal the Communists have left on the coast," Christine replied, leaning back against the bulkhead. "They've got everything there: dockage, marshaling yards, warehousing. The facilities are fairly up to date, undamaged by the war, and not operating at anywhere near peak capacity. Yet they're channeling troop and supply convoys around the Shanghai terminus.

"Shanghai has the most extensive air-basing complex south of Shenyang, and yet they haven't staged a strike out of there since we arrived off the coast. It's the natural command and logistics center for the campaign against the Nationalist invasion, and yet the Communist Signal Intelligence load out of Shanghai has been dropping steadily. Things that should be happening in Shanghai, aren't. The place is becoming an operational desert."

"Could it be a disbursement? Maybe they're afraid of a Nationalist counterstrike."

"Uh-uh, Boss Ma'am. Shanghai is also one of the most heavily defended positions the Reds have. The Nationalist Air Force hasn't even attempted to penetrate the city's airspace."

Amanda leaned back as well, bracing herself against the corridor grab rail. "All right, what do you think is going on?" she asked, intrigued.

"I think the Communists are overreacting. I think that they're up to something in Shanghai and that they're bending over backwards trying not to attract attention to the area."

"What do you think they're up to?"

"Frankly, I haven't got the faintest idea. But, whatever it is, it has got to be pretty fraggin' big to justify shutting down one of the largest cities in China. That's why I want to take that long, close look."

"What's your definition of long and close?"

"I'd like at least a couple of hours of loiter time right off the minefields at the mouth of the Yangtze estuary. Long enough to get a good cross section of the tactical Elint environment. I'd also like to see if I could tap into the sidelobe of their local telecommunications net. While we're about it, we could also chart those minefield perimeters out a little better."

"The Red Chinese would probably consider our lurking around just off their primary defense line more than a little provocative, Chris."

"Probably," Christine nodded, "but only if they catch us. I've been talking with Fleet meteorology, and they say that a mild storm front will be moving in across the Chinese coast from the south within twenty-four hours. Good stealth weather.

"Also, tomorrow night, there is going to be an unavoidable gap in our theater recon coverage. For several hours during the late evening and early morning, we won't have a satellite in position to cover the Shanghai area. If the Reds are up to something, this would be a natural window of opportunity for them to go about doing their dirty deeds. And if we were right outside listening at the keyhole . . ."

"Yes, I see what you're getting at. Have you bounced this off Fleet Intelligence yet?"

"I've sent in a preliminary situation estimate and I've talked to some of the Flag Intels over on the Big E. They're willing to concede that there might be an atypical pattern developing, but they think that we need to further monitor the situation before making any kind of call on it. Well, that's what I want to do. I want to monitor this real close."

Amanda lightly bit her lower lip in an old habitual reaction to deep thought. If Chris said something was going on in Shanghai, then there was; Amanda had no doubt about that. The question was, would this probe be worth the risk to her ship, her crew, and the crisis situation as a whole?

Of course, there was the easy out. She could put together a situational update and mission proposal and kick it upstairs to NAVSPECFORCE. They could make the judgment call.

But then, the concerns of one comparatively junior intelligence officer might not carry much weight, even with Amanda's strongest endorsement.

On the other hand, she could make the call herself.

She'd wanted an independent command and she'd gotten one. She could interpret this operation as being within the mission parameters she had been given. If something went wrong, though, there would be no one in the whole world to take the blame but herself.

To hell with it. She had bragged about never having been caught. She wanted to dance on the edge one more time.

"Okay, Chris. Let's do it. Draw up a set of mission intents and requirements; we'll run it through an Operations Group this evening."

"Yes!" The Intel lifted her fists in exaltation.

Amanda smiled and reached for the CD player. "This doesn't come for free, though, Chris. In return, I want us to go back to the gym and put at least another half hour in on your modern improvisational before we call it quits for the day."

"Ahh!" Christine moaned and slid limply down the bulkhead to the deck. "Nobody loves me!"

☆ Hotel Manila
Republic of the Philippines
1919 Hours Zone Time; August 10, 2006

Professor Djinn Yi lifted the delicate porcelain cup of green tea from the tray offered to him. As he always did at such moments, he acknowledged the dichotomy of the experience. There was the pain that had been with him since the day a Maoist thug had smashed his knuckles with a steel bar. But then, there was also the gratitude that his hand still worked at all.

He nodded to the silent serving man and joined with Secretary Duan of the Foreign Ministry in taking a first sip of the hot beverage.

"It goes well," the Ministry man said after a moment. "Reports from all fronts indicate success. Our forces continue to hold the beach head stable, while yours have commenced their march north."

"Another inch cut from the dragon's tail," Djinn replied, setting his cup onto the low table that separated the two men.

The two men were in the central sitting room of the combined Taiwanese/United Democratic Forces suite complex. It had been converted into an ad hoc security space for the delegations.

Every inch of the room was swept hourly for bugs, and white noise generators purred in each corner. The curtains were kept tightly drawn and vibrator units had been taped to the windows, ensuring that a laser or radar beam could not be used to "read" any conversation taking place within.

"Quite so," Duan continued. "However, we have also had word from our people in Peking. The Communists are reacting as we had feared. They are initiating their special operation."

"Ah." Djinn lifted his cup once more. "They see their future. They are afraid."

"Speaking truthfully, Professor, so am I."

"We knew that this eventuality would have to be faced sooner or later. The Communists have their plan. We have ours. The one shall block the other."

"In theory." The solidly built Taiwanese diplomat grimaced and set his tea aside. "I must confess that I have my reservations. I still wish we could notify the United States and the other Pacific Rim states."

"No. They would have their suspicions about any pronouncement that we might make. They must make the discovery themselves. Anything less would take the edge off the peril."

"But should they miss the sailing, what then? We may have little time before the Communists act."

"We must trust in the technologies of the Americans to spot the departure. As for the time, that too may work in our favor. We wish for the Americans to act, not to think."

"Trusts and theories," Duan grunted, and sat back in his chair. "We are playing a dangerous game with both your people and mine."

"With all of China," Djinn replied. The former professor from Canton emptied his cup and returned it to the table. A smile crossed his seamed features and he stiffly flexed his fingers once more. "But then, the path to freedom is not necessarily a safe one."

☆ 75 Miles Northeast of Shanghai, China
1854 Hours Zone Time; August 11, 2006

"Yes?"

"It's only Lieutenant Arkady, ma'am."

"Come in."

Amanda wasn't in the office section of her cabin as Arkady entered. He could hear stirring beyond the curtained doorway that led to her sleeping quarters.

"Be out in a second," she called. "Have a seat." Arkady set his flight harness and helmet down on the deck and dropped into the office space's single guest chair. Tilting it back into the corner the couple of inches permissible within the cabin's cramped confines, he braced one foot against the edge of the desk.

Since coming aboard the Duke, he had lounged a lot of hours away in this position. As he always did, he explored the work space with his eyes, seeking for some new fragment of Amanda's essence.

On the bulkhead behind her workstation, a row of sticky notes had been tacked up beneath the small oil painting of Amanda's Cape Cod sloop. The corner of Arkady's mouth quirked up. He had some fond memories of that little sailboat. Especially of a warm evening spent in its cockpit during their last layover in Norfolk.

On this cruise, the painting had been joined by a framed pen-and-ink sketch of a Navy Fleet ocean tug. Another gift from her admiral-turned-artist father, the little vessel, the *Piegan,* had been Amanda's first command.

There was a small stack of books on the edge of the desk. Tilting his chair forward again, Arkady turned them so he could read the titles. Regional reading: a copy of Tuchman's *Stillwell and the American Experience in China* and an English version of Mao's *Red Book.*

He didn't recognize the third volume, a large green-bound paperback titled *Can the Chinese Armed Forces Win the Next War?* Selecting it from the stack, he read the title page and learned that it was a Naval Institute Press translation of a Red Chinese publication.

He was leafing through the first chapter when Amanda Garrett brushed past the door curtain and entered the office. Her usual sober demeanor vanished for a moment in the bright flash of her smile. "Welcome home. How did the recon flight go?"

"No problems. Say, who is this Liu Huaqing guy, anyway?"

"They call him the Chinese Mahan," Amanda replied, slipping into her desk chair and swiveling to face him. Slouching back, she comfortably matched Arkady's posture. "During the 1980s and '90s, Admiral Liu was a major voice for reform and modernization within the Red Chinese armed forces. He was one of the first to call for China to abandon its *jinhai fangyu* naval strategy." She formed the Mandarin phrase carefully.

"That sounds like the Chinese version of an extremely obscene suggestion."

Amanda chuckled. "*Jinhai fangyu* means 'coastal defense.' Historically, the Chinese Navy has always been a small-craft coastal force. They have no tradition of open-ocean operations. Liu felt that for China to truly become a world power, they must develop that tradition and an effective blue-water doctrine to go along with it. Fortunately for us, things fell apart for the Chinese before they could implement many of his proposals."

"Hmm, could I borrow this?"

"Be my guest," she replied. "With the Chinese, we're dealing with a vastly different culture structure. Whether they're enemies or friends, we're going to need to learn how to understand their worldview. Now, what did you find out there?"

"That things were real quiet."

"Unusually so?"

"I dunno, babe. I stayed about thirty miles out and executed four pop-up sweeps above the radar horizon. Nothing on the scope. No guard ship. No shipping traffic. Not even any fishing boats."

"Sub activity?"

"Nobody stuck up a periscope or a snorkel while I had my radar hot. I also ran a line of passive sonobuoys while I was out there without kicking up anything. That isn't saying that there couldn't be somebody lying on the bottom closer in."

"Air? The signal environment?"

"Air ops seem to be just what we've been reading off the Aegis screens. No sign of a BARCAP off the coast. No surface searches up. No standing combat air patrol over the city.

"As for the signal environment, the Reds have a lot of air-search sites radiating around the Shanghai perimeter, but my threat boards reacted to only one surface-search radar. A single low-powered unit out at the mouth of the estuary."

Amanda nodded thoughtfully. "Okay. Those are what your systems said. Now, what did your gut read?"

Arkady grimaced. "Instincts, huh? All right. Vibes-wise, I'm burying the needle. Little Miss Chris is right—something unnatural is going on out there."

She sighed and brushed her copper-brown bangs back from her forehead. "I was hoping that you would say that we silly females were just imagining things."

"No such luck."

"Do your vibes also say whether or not this recon pass tonight is going to be worth it?"

"If the Reds are up to something in Shanghai, it behooves us to find out what."

"And if the Reds are up to something, attempting a probe of the Yangtze estuary now could be the equivalent of sticking our hand right into a hornet's nest." An introspective frown passed across her face.

The aviator had come to recognize the phenomenon. Amanda Garrett seldom ever had any difficulty in intellectually making a decision. Sometimes, however, she had to work a little bit to coerce her heart and soul into line.

Christine Rendino had instructed him in the proper protocol to employ at such times. Listen, and let her talk herself around. Arkady put his own spin on the procedure, however. Encourage the sense of perspective.

"A great philosopher and sage once said, 'He who would count the teeth of the dragon must accept a degree of risk.'"

Amanda cocked an eyebrow. "Who said that?"

"I did. I was sitting right here. You heard me."

That called her smile back up again, along with a low chuckle. "If I was the only one doing the counting, lover, it wouldn't be any big deal. But I have to drag all of you people along with me. That's something I still have a degree of difficulty reconciling myself to."

"It comes with being the Captain. That's why you rate all the cool perks, like these sumptuous quarters. That's why you get saluted. . . . By the way, do you know where the salute really came from?"

"Where?"

"It came from some subordinate reaching up to wipe the sweat off of his forehead because his boss had shown up in time to make the really tough decisions."

He was breaking her down. She was smiling more easily now. "You are not going to be serious here, are you?"

"I'll be as serious as necessary, when necessary, babe. Later tonight, when we're doing the probe, we'll all be as serious as all hell. Especially me, considering I'm going to be Command Officer of the Deck. Because of that, though, I'm not going to prematurely let myself wind up any tighter than I have to."

"Probably a very sound policy."

"I think so. You have dinner yet?"

Amanda shook her head. "No. It's hamburger night down in the wardroom, and I am not going to be able to cope with both this recon run and a government-issue slider at the same time."

"Then where would you like to have dinner?" Arkady prompted.

Amanda started to reply offhand, then caught herself. She recognized the invitation to play the game, and her smile ceased being transitory.

"All right. Let's see. Someplace a little out of the ordinary. No samey-samey."

It was a counterploy to the imposed sterility of their current shipboard existence. Aboard the *Cunningham,* she and Arkady were lovers in an environment where a love affair's traditional expressions—a touch, a kiss, a caress—were all inappropriate, if not professionally hazardous.

However, they were adaptable. The date game was just one of the counters they had developed on this cruise.

"Ever had roast duck?"

"Yes. I like it."

"Good. Then it's the Duck Club at the Monterey Plaza Hotel. It's down there in Steinbeck country, right on Cannery Row. It's the place all of us Monterey boys take our really serious ladies when we want to impress them."

"Sounds interesting. What's it like?"

"Very classy San Francisco. The dining room looks right out over the bay. The sunsets are to kill for, and they have this thing where they have sets of binoculars out on the tables. You can look out and watch the sea otters playing around in the kelp beds."

"How incredibly neat! How should I dress for it?"

Arkady studied her and narrowed his eyes judgmentally.

"We are going to need a little flash here. Red. Definitely red."

Amanda gave her head an emphatic shake. "That doesn't work, love. I can't wear that."

"Sure you can. That 'redheads can't wear red' line was thought up by some brunette who wanted to hog a good thing. Every pretty lady should own at least one little red dress and one pair of red high heels, because she always looks great in them."

"We'll see."

"I'll prove the point. I'll pick you up a couple of hours early and I'll take you shopping. . . ."

☆ Yangtze Estuary Approaches
2331 Hours Zone Time; August 11, 2006

It is one of the great rivers of the world. Born on a windswept mountain plateau deep in the Himalayas, it snakes its way down across the central plain of Asia to end in the East China Sea.

Along the way, it collects the story and the essence that is China. Merging into it is the ice melt of ancient glaciers and the rain of ten thousand storms, the fine-worn silt of the tired fields, and the sweat and tears of one quarter of the human race. It is one of the few things that can even briefly challenge the might of the World Ocean. A hundred miles out beyond its mouth, the waves are still stained brown, the smell of the land dominating that of the sea.

☆   ☆   ☆

"Stealth protocols are fully closed up. Full EMCON is in effect. All radios and radars are secure and all Faraday screens are engaged."

"Very good, Mr. Hiro. Quartermaster, systems and positioning check, please."

"GPUs and SINs cross-check and verify to within a ten-meter circle of error. Qiantan Island is now bearing zero five degrees relative off the bow at nine thousand yards."

Amanda refreshed her situational awareness with a glance at the graphics of the navigational display. The Duke was coming in from the northeast at a shallow angle. In a few minutes, they would turn south past the broad island-studded mouth of the Yangtze, running just outside the mine-defense barriers deployed by the Chinese Communists.

Outside in the darkness, a fine rain sluiced across the bridge windscreen, while within, the light of the instruments and readout screens had been turned down to their lowest settings. Amanda could sense rather than see the others of the bridge crew around her. Likewise, she could sense their tensions grow as the range closed with the Chinese coast.

"Bridge to CIC."

"CIC, aye."

"Okay, Chris. How do you want to work this thing?"

"I'd like to make one slow pass down the perimeter of the outer minefield to chart the entrance and egress channels. That'll also give us enough time to run a full cross-spectrum analysis of the local EM environment."

"Very well. However, I will not take us inside the three-mile limit at any point. That means we'll have to reverse out to the northeast when we approach the Maan Liedao group."

"No problem, Boss Ma'am. If the bad guys are up to anything naughty, we'll know about it by then."

The Intel went off line and Amanda twisted around in the captain's chair to face the shadow that was her first officer.

"Ken, I'm going to keep the con on the navigation bridge tonight. I'd like you to take the CIC."

"Aye, aye."

"And Ken, keep an eye on what's going on in Raven's Roost. Chris might need the help of an Asian-languages expert."

"Captain, I'm barely conversational in Japanese and Mandarin. I'm a long way from being an expert in either one."

"You're the closest we've got. Good luck, Ken."

"Good luck to you, too, Skipper." Hiro moved off into the passageway leading aft.

There was another shadowy figure behind the central helm console, one foot braced on the throttle pedestal and faintly silhouetted in the back glow of the instrumentation.

"Officer of the Deck, how's it going?"

"Pretty good, ma'am. I just can't find the pitch and cyclic on this thing."

"You'll manage, Mr. Arkady. It does an Airedale good to stand a deck watch now and again, just to remind you what the real Navy is all about."

"I'll take your word for it, Captain."

"You'd better. Now, bring her left to one eight three degrees. Hold our speed at ten knots and maintain a parallel course to the three-mile limit at a one-hundred-yard separation by the GPUs."

"Aye, aye."

That dealt with, Amanda slipped out of the captain's chair and stepped through the hatchway onto the starboard bridge wing. From here, by day, she knew that she could have seen the hills of China, but now there were only the varying textures of darkness apparent to the night-sensitive eye.

Back in the wheelhouse, she knew that she could have supplemented her sight with the *Cunningham*'s low-light television systems. However, she wasn't ready yet to fall back on such artifices. Instead, she leaned against the rail and tried to push her own senses and intuitions out into the night.

Her grandfather had sailed these waters once, back in the days of the old Yangtze Patrol. Now, as the warm, misting rain dampened her hair she sought his counsel.

Some eight miles to the south, the Five Nineteen boat tugged fitfully at the end of a too-short anchor cable. They were the southernmost boat of the squadron, deployed in a picket line just seaward of the Yangtze mine barrier. With engines off and all systems powered down, they had been on station for over two hours, the continuing drizzle saturating all hands above decks.

For the hundredth time, Lieutenant Zhou Shan tried to clear the lenses of his night glasses with a bit of sopping cloth. "I can't understand what they expect us to accomplish out here tonight," he grumbled. "Without using the radar, we won't be able to see a thing."

"Perhaps we will accomplish nothing, Lieutenant," Bosun Hoong replied placidly, "but still, here is where they expect us to remain."

Down in the *Cunningham*'s Combat Information Center, Commander Ken Hiro sat in the captain's chair in the central cluster of command stations; Dix Beltrain was manning the tactical officer's console at his right elbow. Now the TACCO glanced across at the Cunningham's exec.

"Commander, GPU fix indicates we're closing with the mine barrier. It might be advisable to bring up the thirty-two, sir."

"I concur. Make it happen."

Beltrain shifted his attention to one of the secondary workstations lining the CIC bulkhead. "Okay, DeVega, lower your dome and light her up. Set your sweep arc for zero degrees relative off the bow to ninety degrees to starboard."

Long before the keel of the *Cunningham* had ever been laid, it was realized that she would be operating in a new kind of military environment, that of littoral warfare. She would have to work in close to potentially hostile third-world coastlines. Accordingly, in addition to her powerful SQQ-89 antisubmarine sonar suite, she mounted an SQQ-32 mine-hunter set as well.

"SQQ-32 is on line, sir. Initiating antimine sweep."

Hiro and Beltrain moved in unison, dialing up the sonar imaging on their workstation repeaters. In moments, a dark spherical mass materialized and began to drift slowly across the flatscreen, a computer-generated simulacrum of the system's echo return.

"Mine contact, sir. Bearing zero eight five relative. Range eight hundred yards. Range is constant. Target is treading aft. System data annex identifies target as a moored contact mine consistent with standard Red Chinese marks."

The old horned horror. The basic design was more than a century old, and yet was still almost as deadly as the day it was conceived.

Its sheer, iron-age crudity was its greatest advantage. Unlike more sophisticated ordnance, it could not be foxed, fooled, or neutralized from a distance. It merely bobbled sullenly at the end of its tether and exploded if anything as much as brushed against it. Disposing of them required the use of a cumbersome and dangerous mechanical sweeping process only slightly less archaic than the mines themselves, or the time-consuming and dangerous task of countermining and detonating them one at a time, using divers or ROVs.

The tactical officer produced the briefest of whistles. "Yeah, glad we didn't let that go for much longer."

"It's good to know your place in the world, Mr. Beltrain."

Hiro keyed his headset microphone. "Bridge, we have contact with the Chinese mine barrier."

"Acknowledged, Ken," Captain Garrett's voice sounded in his earphone. "We see them on our repeaters. We'll hold at about this range from the barrier facing. If you people spot anything that we miss, don't hesitate to override our helm control."

Topside, the rain grew heavier. Like the rest of the watch, Amanda had donned helmet and combat vest. She had come in from the bridge wing, and now prowled slowly along the line of glowing monitor screens, her eyes flicking from readout to readout.

"Captain," one of the lookouts said quietly, "it's getting pretty murky out there. We're losing visual definition on the low-light television."

"Very well. Switch to FLIR."

Throughout the bridge, vision systems were toggled over from standard to thermographic imaging.

Utilizing heat radiation rather than visual-spectrum light, the Forward Looking Infrared Scanners should have easily been able to cope with the deteriorating visibility. However, out in the night, an unusual convergence of environmental phenomena was taking place.

As the low-grade tropical storm saturated the environment with heat and humidity, an exceptionally dense concentration of water vapor was accumulating in the atmosphere—water vapor that absorbed infrared energy.

Concurrently, the heavy, blood-temperature rain and quiet, windless sea allowed a thin layer of warmer fresh water to form atop the ocean's surface, reducing the contrast between the sea and air temperatures.

As these curves of absorption and ambience closed with each other, the *Cunningham's* FLIR scanners began to lose efficiency.

The effect was subtle. With no specific object within immediate visual range, the bridge lookouts observed no change on their softly glowing screens. They had no comprehension that their ship was slowly going blind.

"Anything, Tina?"

"No, ma'am. If the locals are doing any communicating, they're sending Candygrams."

Christine Rendino hovered over the shoulder of the scanner operator as the young enlisted woman systematically swept across the electromagnetic spectrum.

"Nothing at all?"

"I'm hearing what sounds like an elementary police radio dispatch net and a couple of AM radio channels full of music to kill capitalists by. The only military traffic of any kind is some very limited air-traffic-control stuff. The Reds are being real quiet out there."

"Okay. Stay on it."

They were twenty minutes into the recon pass and things were crawling under Christine's skin. This wasn't right. This was so not right that the Intel's finely drawn nervous system was resonating to it like a plucked violin string.

Unable to be still, she stepped from the confines of the intelligence systems bay and into the central space of the Combat Information Center. Pausing for a moment behind the cluster of central command stations, she peered over Dix Beltrain's shoulder at the big Alpha screen on the forward bulkhead.

The side-scan sonar was sketching out the perimeter of the estuary minefield, hacking each mine detected with a GPU position fix that would be stored in the navigational database. At least that was working out right.

Moving on, she crossed over to the stealth systems bay.

Normally, for her this would be enemy territory. But now, with an operation on, her perpetual feud with Frank McKelsie was in abeyance.

"Are you guys getting anything here that we might be missing over in Raven's Roost?"

The stealth boss was hovering over the backs of his own systems operators, much as she had been doing. He didn't take his eyes from the shimmering banks of oscilloscopes even for an instant as he replied.

"Nothing but what's on the program, Rendino. Air-search stuff and one surface-search unit out on the southern tip of Jiuduan Sha. Low powered, probably a Fin Curve. I'd say navigational-assistance radar."

"Any return risk?"

A tinge of contempt crept into McKelsie's voice. "That sucker's practically tube technology, Rendino. They'd have a better chance of spotting us by standing out on the beach with a flashlight."

Starboard side forward in the central cluster of command workstations, the Aegis systems manager methodically ran the *Cunningham*'s primary radar though a repetitive series of readiness checks. The mighty SPY-2A emitter arrays that belted the destroyer's superstructure were powered down while running in stealth mode, but the receptors were active, stealth and intelligence divisions both accessing them for data input on the local signals environment.

The systems operator had just initiated a frequency-scan sequence into the system when he hesitated. He had had a test display dialed up on one of his repeaters and, just for a second, a series of faint ghost targets seemed to dance across the screen. The radar specialist frowned. That sure as hell was not supposed to happen when they were not radiating. He started to troubleshoot.

It didn't occur to him that, for that instant, the operating frequencies of the *Cunningham*'s radar receiver had exactly matched that of the Red Chinese Fin Curve transmitter. If it had, the operator would have paid considerably more attention. He was aware of the phenomenon of UAF reflection: the receiving of a return produced by someone else's radar wave.

☆　　☆　　☆

They were thirty-five minutes into the run. "Raven's Roost. This is the bridge. How is it coming, Chris?"

"The mine charting is going good," came the cautious reply, "but the Elint scan hasn't developed too much. We're still working it."

"Let's not take all night about it, Lieutenant. We can't hang around out here forever."

Rain sheeted across the bridge windscreen now. Multiple windshield wipers slashed at it futilely, while along the inside curve, blowers rumbled, struggling to keep the humidity haze at bay. The bridge air-conditioning was losing the fight against the sauna bath exterior environment.

Moving around to the bridge-wing door again, Amanda popped the latch and slid back the pocket panel. Inhaling deeply, she strove for one real breath amid the growing oppression.

Out in the night, the Five Fifteen boat of the Red Chinese hydrofoil squadron rocked deeply at its mooring. Her skipper peered over the side and frowned. That had almost felt like a wake effect. For a long minute he peered out into the rain-swept darkness, then shrugged the thought away.

Lieutenant (j.g.) Charles Foster appeared at the entrance of Raven's Roost. "Hey, Lieutenant, you want to come over to Sonar Alley for a second? We might have something for you."

"Right with you." Christine Rendino hurriedly followed the junior officer.

Sonar Alley was one of the four subsystem bays that angled off the Combat Information Center. It was located portside forward, diagonally across from the Intelligence center.

"Okay, Chuck, give me a thrill. Whatcha got?"

The sonarman adjusted his glasses in a quick nervous gesture. With brush haircut and a perennial air of boyish earnestness, Foster was a submariner doing a tour in the surface forces as part of the branch officer exchange program. Currently, he held sway over the Duke's extensive ASW suite.

"We're not exactly sure, ma'am," he replied. "We've started picking up a group of sound contacts on the passive arrays. Multiple sources somewhere up the river, sounds like it might be a convoy forming up. You asked to be notified if we detected anything unusual, and I was wondering if this would count."

"Could be. Let's give it a listen."

They crowded in around one of the systems operators. Unjacking their headsets from their belt interphone units, they plugged into the console's audio access points. Silently, they listened for a moment.

"Hear 'em?"

"Yeah." Christine nodded. "How would you call it?"

"Several single and twin medium-speed screws. Maybe minesweeps or some other kind of small auxiliary. But there are three or four big, slow-turning wheels in there too."

"Do you have a blade count yet? Plant noises?"

Foster shook his head. "Not so far. The contact is ducting weird, a lot of fading and distortion. I think these guys might be coming down that smaller river that leads directly into Shanghai. What d'you call it, the Huangpu? I think we'll get a cleaner listen at them when they actually get out into the main Yangtze estuary."

"Okay, Chuck. Fa' sure, keep working it."

"Think we might have something here?"

"We'll see."

On the Five Nineteen boat Bosun Hoong looked out from beneath the scrap of tarpaulin he had been using for a storm shelter. "Looks like the raindragon is passing, Lieutenant."

On the *Cunningham's* bridge, a mental load-bearing relay within Amanda Garrett's subconscious tripped: *It's time to go. Now! Get out of here!*

She keyed her interphone mike. "Raven's Roost, this is the bridge. Chris, I need a sitrep. Are you onto anything positive yet?"

"Nothing to write home about, Boss Ma'am," the reluctant reply came back. "I'd like to push it a little longer if we could."

"Negative. I'm not going to keep the ship at risk for a dry hole. We're sheering off."

Amanda glanced over her shoulder at Vince Arkady's dark outline behind the helm stations. "Officer of the Deck, we'll be opening the range from the coast. Stand by to come left."

"Very good, Captain. Helm and lee helm stations, stand by to alter heading."

Amanda turned back to the navigational display, selecting a departure course on the glowing coastal chart. She had formed the order in her mind and was about to issue it when Christine Rendino's voice crackled over the interphone.

"Captain! Hold it! We've got something here!"

The rain was easing, fading back into a hazy drizzle again. Lieutenant Zhou Shan looked up sharply. Bosun Hoong as well. He had heard it too. Now that the hissing beat of the rain on the wave crests had passed, a new sound had become audible on the deck of the Five Nineteen boat: the unmistakable whispering whine of a gas turbine power plant.

"Stay with me, Captain," Christine pleaded into her mike as she dashed across the confined internal space of the CIC to Sonar Alley.

"Okay, Foster, what's going down?"

The sonar boss looked up from his panels, excitement and concern vying for control of his expression. "That group of sound contacts have exited out into the estuary. Their signature has clarified and we have a blade count! We've got three big targets up there, each running on a single, large, seven-bladed screw!"

"Are you sure!"

"Positive! We're still running 'em through the data annex for a positive hull ID, but they just tacked on some extra speed, and I swear to God, I heard a series of reactor flow valves pop!"

"Ahhh, Foster. I love you and I want to have your children!"

Christine tilted the stunned jg's face up and planted an enthusiastic kiss full on his lips, then she was gone, scrambling back out into the central CIC space.

"Captain, I need permission to drop EMCON!"

"What!"

"For one second! I need to use the SPY-2A arrays to conduct a single, full-power sweep upriver. That's all. The odds are that any Red monitoring station will record it as just a transitory glitch of some kind. Captain, I don't have time to explain, but this is what we came here for!"

There was a moment's hesitation. The other members of the CIC team, drawn in by Christine's exclamation, waited with her for the reply.

Then it came. "Very well."

Amanda's voice shifted from the interphone to the overhead loudspeakers.

"Mr. Hiro, execute a single surface-search sweep to the west with the Aegis arrays. Minimum duration. Full output."

Aboard the Five Nineteen boat, the turbine howl was growing louder, intermixed with the boiling hiss of a hull cutting water. In the wet darkness, it was hard to get a bearing on the sound.

"Hoong?" Lieutenant Zhou ordered. "Get forward and raise the anchor. Helmsman, prepare to start engines. Radio operator, open the channel to the Flag boat. . . ."

"Scan complete, Lieutenant," the Aegis systems operator reported. "Securing primary emitters."

"Imaging in storage?"

"Acknowledged, ma'am."

"Yes!"

"Lieutenant Rendino, what's going on?" Ken Hiro demanded.

"Some very-heavy-caliber shit, sir," Christine replied. Her ebullience was fading now, as she began to analyze and project the potential of what she had just discovered. "Some very-heavy-caliber shit indeed."

Aboard the Five Nineteen boat, Lieutenant Zhou lifted the radio mike to his lips.

In the *Cunningham's* Combat Information Center, all hands jumped as a tense, staccato voice suddenly issued from a speaker in the intelligence bay. Of the duty watch, only Ken Hiro understood what was being said.

"Five Nineteen boat to squadron command! Contact report . . ."

☆　　☆　　☆

Topside, Christine's voice crackled urgently out of the squawk box. "Bridge, this is Raven's Roost! Somebody's just lit off a radio transmitter out there."

"Where away!" Amanda demanded.

"Close! Real close! Too close to get a bearing!"

It would have taken a superhuman not to glance up, just for an instant.

"I repeat, Five Nineteen boat to squadron command. Contact report . . ."

The words choked off in Zhou Shan's throat. He saw a flash of white in the darkness, a broad, low-riding **V** of foam at wave-top level. A bow wave. Then a ship's stem materialized out of the night, sharp edged and radically raked, impossibly close and towering over the hydrofoil.

Zhou was the Five Nineteen's captain. He knew it was his responsibility to save his ship and crew. But he found that he had no miracles to spend.

Vince Arkady shifted his eyes back to the FLIR monitor just in time to see a shadowy form disappearing under the outline of the *Cunningham's* prow. There was no opportunity to order a course change, no chance to make any kind of formal sighting call.

"Watch it!" he yelled. Lunging down over the lee-helm controls, he slammed the throttles closed and threw the propeller controls into neutral.

The *Cunningham's* cutwater touched the port flank of the Five Nineteen boat.

Fire blazed under the flare of the destroyer's bow and all hands on the bridge were thrown forward. It wasn't an impact as much as it was an abrupt deceleration as the Duke drove through the disintegrating hulk of the Chinese fast-attack craft.

"Stop all engines!" Amanda yelled, dragging herself back to her feet.

"All engines answering stop, Captain!" Arkady replied, disentangling himself from the lee-helm pedestal.

"Bridge," the intercom speaker blared. "What's going on up there?"

"We've just PT-109ed a Red patrol boat," the aviator responded into his headset mike. "Stand by, CIC."

Amanda scrambled out onto the port wing of the bridge and peered down over the side. The Chinese hydrofoil had been torn completely in two and its bow section was rolling down the destroyer's side, rasping and scraping along her waterline. Above the crumpling-oil-can noises of the breakup came the sound of a human voice screaming.

Instinctively, Amanda reached back over the aft bridge rail. Flipping open a cover plate, she revealed a small T-grip handle. Giving it a twist, she yanked the handle outward, then socked it back in.

An access panel in the superstructure swung open and a twelve-man life-raft capsule ejected into the sea.

As the Duke continued to forge ahead under her residual momentum, Amanda watched the raft and the wreckage swirl away aft to be lost in the darkness.

Don't foul the props, she thought feverishly. *We can live with anything else, just don't foul the props.*

"Main engine control!" she snapped into her headset.

"Main engines, aye," Chief Thomson's steady voice came back.

"Execute full clearance and alignment check on both propulsor pods. Expedite!"

"Will do. I think we're okay, Captain. I think you got her shut down in time."

"Damage control, report!"

"All boards still read green, Captain. Preliminary reports from DC team Alpha Alpha indicate no leakage and no buckling in the forward frames."

In the encounter between the Duke's reenforced bow and the Red Chinese FAC, the destroyer had won cleanly.

"Main Engine Control to Captain."

"Go, Chief."

"Clearance and alignment checks completed. Propellers are clear. Ready to answer bells."

Thank God. Thank God. Now to get out of here, granted the Reds would let them.

That would be an act easier said than done. Down in the stealth systems bay, Frank McKelsie and his team watched aghast as their threat boards blazed. Surface-search and fire-control radars were lighting off all around the mouth of the estuary. Powerful mobile and fixed emitters were intently beginning to probe the night. A series of weaker, but closer, seaborne units had also appeared, extending off to the north of their position.

"We're screwed," one of the systems operators whispered.

"Screwed, hell!" McKelsie snarled back. "We're so far beyond screwed, they're wheeling us into the delivery room. Stand by your jammers and decoys. We're going to need 'em."

Another outline for potential disaster was unfolding in the central CIC work space. A new voice issued from the speaker tuned to the Communist command frequency, demanding and repetitive. Again, Ken Hiro was the only one to fathom its meaning.

"Five Nineteen boat, respond! Squadron Flag calling Five Nineteen boat. Do you receive? State your contact . . ."

Abruptly, the *Cunningham's* exec levered himself out of the captain's chair. "Put a transmitter on that frequency," he roared, charging into the radio shack.

After a moment's fumbling, one of the sparks extended a hand mike. "You're up, sir."

Accepting the microphone, Hiro began to speak into it urgently in Chinese. *"Five Nineteen boat to Squadron Flag. An unidentified naval vessel has just made a pass near our location. We are proceeding to investigate."*

Releasing the mike button, Hiro yelled over his shoulder. "For Crissake, somebody get on the horn to the Captain! Tell her to get the ship moving to the east!"

On the Duke's bridge, Dix Beltrain's voice issued from the overhead speaker. "Captain, Mr. Hiro says to get the ship moving to the east. He's on the radio with the Chinese, and I think he's trying to run some kind of a substitution play on them."

Amanda picked up on her executive officer's stratagem almost instantly. Even fully stealthed, the *Cunningham* would produce a return on a high-powered military radar at close ranges, especially during low sea states such as they were experiencing now. However, that return would not be much different in size than that of the small craft they had just sent to the bottom.

On their screens, the Reds would be tracking only a single target, *which they would think was their own picket boat.*

Amanda blessed Ken Hiro, then she blessed herself for never trying to suppress the personal initiative of her officers.

"Officer of the Deck, come left to zero nine zero," she commanded. "All engines ahead full. Make turns for thirty knots."

Tightly gripping the ready mike, Ken Hiro leaned in over the communications console, totally focused on the speaker. The command team in the Combat Information Center had reconfigured to deal with the situation. Dixon Beltrain covered both the tactical officer's and the captain's stations while Christine Rendino hovered at Hiro's elbow, ready to relay status reports or instructions as needed.

"Flag boat to all squadron elements, initiate surface-search sweep to the east. Flag boat to Five Nineteen. We do not show any uncoordinated targets on our screen. Can you verify your contact?"

Hiro's mind raced.

"Five Nineteen to Squadron Flag. We believe that the target was an American . . ." Jesus God! What was the Mandarin word for "stealth"? *". . . low-observability warship. Target has broken contact at this time. We are endeavoring to relocate visually."*

"What's going down, sir?" Christine Rendino whispered.

"The Reds were wondering why they weren't picking up any bogeys on their radar. I explained it away by saying we were in pursuit of a Cunningham-class stealth destroyer."

"Too radical! We're chasing ourselves out here."

The Duke raced away from the mouth of the estuary, holding pace with the search line of Communist fast-attack boats, an elephant using technological guile to merge in with a herd of gazelles. Vince Arkady maintained his overwatch position behind the helm station. Looking ahead, he saw Amanda silhouetted against the glow of the repeater banks, studying the tactical displays with a fierce intensity.

"CIC to bridge. Mr. Hiro reports that the Reds are increasing speed to thirty-five knots and are going up on their hydrofoils."

"Acknowledged," Amanda curtly replied to the speaker call. "Mr. Arkady, make turns for thirty-five knots. Stealth systems, bring a blip enhancer on line. Increase apparent RCS and return strength by fifty percent."

Arkady quietly relayed the engine command to the lee helmsman. Just as the radar cross section of the Communist fast-attack craft would increase as they became foil-borne, so would the *Cunningham* as she bent on speed. Their masquerade would hold a while longer.

Arkady circled the helm station and moved up alongside Amanda at the repeater bank. Leaning forward as if to study the displays, he let his forearm brush lightly against hers for a moment.

"I've blown it, Arkady," she whispered. "I've blown it big time."

"Keep rolling the dice, babe. We've still got money on the table."

"Five Nineteen boat, shore stations have detected a radio distress beacon near your initial sighting location. Do you have further information on this?"

"They're asking about a transponder signal," Hiro reported. "It must be the one off the raft we dropped."

"If in doubt, play stupid, sir," Christine said.

"Yeah. *Five Nineteen to Squadron Flag. We have no information on this."*

"Five Nineteen boat, can you yet confirm your sighting report?"

"Five Nineteen boat to Squadron Flag. We have not reacquired contact. Continuing to the east."

Even through the filtering effect of the radio circuit, the Duke's exec could detect the growing suspicion in the tone of the speaker at the far end.

"Five Nineteen boat, are you positive on your target identification?"

"Acknowledged, Squadron Flag."

"I think this guy suspects something's screwy," Hiro growled.

"Just watch it if he starts asking about who won the Chinese World Series, sir."

"Five Nineteen boat, let me speak to Lieutenant Kang."

"Ah, hell. *The Lieutenant is on deck and unavailable at this time, sir."*

There was a decisive click over the loudspeaker.

"We've lost the carrier, sir," the radioman reported. "The Reds have started to jump frequencies."

"That's it," Hiro said, straightening. "They've burned us."

☆　　☆　　☆

"The penny just dropped with a loud, resounding clang, Skipper," Christine Rendino reported regretfully. "They've figured out that we've been faking them."

"Acknowledge. Kill the blip enhancer. Resume full stealth."

Amanda gazed down into the bridge tactical display. A repeater of the big Alpha screen down in CIC, it provided her with a full visualization of the tactical environment. Even though the Duke was currently running radar silent, her direction-finder arrays were providing the next-best thing, the range and bearing on every Chinese energy emitter radiating in the area.

On that display, Amanda could see the Chinese fast-attack craft peeling off of their search line like fighter planes, angling south toward them.

"Officer of the Deck, come right to one three five degrees. All engines ahead flank."

"Engines answering all ahead flank, ma'am. Steering one three five degrees."

There were damn few ships in the world, large or small, with legs long enough to overtake the *Cunningham* when she was running flat out. Unfortunately, a Huchuan-class hydrofoil was one of those that could. More unfortunately still, so could the big Type 53 homing torpedoes they carried.

Amanda had ordered the turn to the southeast in an effort to gain distance on her enemies. However, even as she watched, the Red hydrofoils matched the course change and continued to close the range.

A touch of the repeater's keypad and the call-up of a set of radar return strengths verified what she suspected. The *Cunningham* was well below the return minimums of the comparatively primitive "Skin Head" surface-search systems aboard the fast-attack craft. The hydrofoils were being vectored in by the more powerful Communist shore-based radars. Soon they'd have a solid enough bearing to start launching fish.

And there was absolutely nothing Amanda Lee Garrett could do about it.

She was constrained by the Fleet's current operational Rules of Engagement, the ones that stated in effect, "Thou shalt not return fire until fired upon."

Violating ROE was a sure way for a naval officer to guarantee a court-martial. But, then again, what kind of career did she have left? She had just initiated a world-class international incident. All that remained now was the Duke and the safety of her crew.

Amanda smiled in cold self-irony and spoke into her headset mike. "Tactical Officer, bring up your HARM flights. We're going to be killing some radars here in a second."

Down in the CIC, Dix Beltrain made his ordnance-load selections, heating up the missile rounds and listening as the system-support operators verbally verified the opening of the cell doors in the Vertical Launch Arrays. As he prepared his birds to fly, he also prepared his own mind-set.

Dix had badly fumbled the first live-fire engagement in which he had ever taken part. By self-admission, it had been due to a combination of fear and buck fever. Since then, though, he had developed his own method of overcoming himself.

It was the same kind of mental conditioning he had used in college when he was quarterbacking for Alabama's Crimson Tide: Take up all of your fears, one at a time—the fear of death or injury, the fear of making a mistake, the fear of failure. Study each one until you are sure you recognize it for what it is. Then put it into a little box in the back of your brain, and don't take it out again until after the crunch is over.

It worked for him.

Dix had just finished locking the lid down when the threat boards on his console lit up.

"Coastal Square Tie radars shifting from search to target-acquisition mode," Frank McKelsie announced from the stealth bay. "We are being painted. HY-2 batteries preparing to fire."

Damn, Beltrain puzzled. How had the Lady been able to figure just when the Reds were about to open up?

"We see it, CIC," Captain Garrett's voice came back over the squawk box. "Secure EMCON! Bring up all radars and initiate full-spectrum ECM! All point defenses to Armageddon mode! I say again, all point defenses to Armageddon mode!"

Damn again, but if the Lady had balls they'd likely be solid brass and a yard wide. She actually sounded relieved about the fight being on.

☆   ☆   ☆

A rain-sodden Chinese beach suddenly lit to a smoky orange glare. An HY-2 heavy antishipping missile lifted off of its launching trailer on a jagged plume of fire. Kicked into the sky by its solid-fuel booster rocket, it climbed up and out over the sea.

More commonly known in the West by its NATO code name of "Silkworm," the HY-2 was another elderly weapon. A Chinese-produced derivative of the Soviet SSN-2 Styx, it was one of the first of its ship-killing kind. Literally a small pilotless airplane, delta-winged and turbojet-powered, it was designed as a robotic kamikaze, hunting down its target under radar guidance and diving headlong into it in a moment of mutual annihilation.

Despite its comparative crudity, its half-ton warhead could still deliver a shattering punch, granted it was allowed to hit.

The *Cunningham* herself answered to the threat. As her SPY-2A planar radar arrays detected the launch, a speed-of-light warning was flashed to the network of onboard computers that made up her Aegis battle-management system. Possibly the closest thing to a true artificial intelligence yet devised by man coolly analyzed the threat and considered its options for a few microseconds. Her crew had enabled her to "Armageddon" mode, freeing her to act in her own defense as well as their own. Thus, she counterfired without waiting for human intervention.

Matching performance envelopes against intercept potentials, the Duke took another microsecond to make an ordnance selection from her arsenal. She chose an Enhanced Sea Sparrow Missile, one of a quad pack of such weapons carried in a single cell of her forwardmost Vertical Launch System.

Relays closed and a charge of inert, high-pressure gas hurled the slender, twelve-foot-long projectile out of its cell and clear of the deck. Its own rocket motor ignited and it arced into the sky. The gathering beams of the destroyer's fire-control radar acquired the Sea Sparrow and gave it guidance, hurling it toward the oncoming threat.

Two miles offshore, missile and antimissile met. The HY-2 had just leveled off from its climb when the smaller, triple-sonic interceptor converged on it. There was a blue-white flare in the darkened sky and a smear of flame trailed down to the sea.

"Vampire down! Vampire down! Initial point defense intercept successful. HY-2 is no longer a factor."

"I don't want them to get another try at us, Dix," Amanda snapped. "HARM that battery radar."

She dropped her eyes to the tactical display again and gauged threats and distances. The lead Chinese hydrofoil had closed to a three-mile range, close enough for both a possible radar return and a solid torpedo shot.

"Second target. Lay a Standard in on the lead Communist FAC as well."

"On the way, ma'am."

There was a soft thud from the cold-fire system and a pale, pencil-slender shape lanced out of a VLS cell. It seemed to hover over the foredeck for an instant, then an eye-searing dagger of flame stabbed downward from its exhaust nozzle. For an instant, ship and sea were illuminated as if by a gigantic arc light, then the fifteen-foot missile was away and accelerating toward the coast. The second round followed the first within half a dozen heartbeats, arcing back "over the shoulder" at the *Cunningham*'s pursuers.

The Standard SM-2 had begun its life as a medium-range antiaircraft weapon back in the late 1960s. Soon, however, it had developed a parallel service career as a HARM, a Homing Anti-Radiation Missile. So used, it could be launched against an electromagnetic-emissions source, be it a radio transmitter or radar set, would ride in on the emitter's beam, seeking it out and destroying it—a sharp stick stabbed into the eye of the enemy.

The Red coastal artillerymen were quite aware of the existence of HARM technology. As their air-defense systems detected the *Cunningham*'s missile launch, a warning was flashed across their net and radar operators slammed hands down on kill switches, powering down their transmitters.

Too late. The Standard has a superb memory.

Running on its last fixed range and bearing, the HARM blazed in across the beach. Just short of its goal, its proximity fuses triggered, detonating its 214-pound fragmentation warhead. The resulting shotgun blast of tungsten-steel shrapnel shredded the HY-2 battery's Square Tie radar van and antenna array.

Fortunately for the artillerymen, they had a wise battery commander. He had sited his transmitter well clear of his deployment area, operating it by remote link. As a result, he took only a couple of wounded among his launcher personnel.

The same could not be said for the crew of the lead hydrofoil. The second Standard exploded directly over the small craft, the hail of hypervelocity metal sweeping all life from its cockpit and weather decks in an instant. With no one at its blood-spattered helm, the boat circled wildly for a minute or two until one of the two surviving enginemen belowdecks realized the totality of the carnage and closed the throttles.

"Bridge," Lieutenant McKelsie reported from the stealth bay. "All Red radars have powered down. We are no longer being painted."

"Very good, Mr. McKelsie. Fire a full decoy pattern from the RBOCS. CIC, down all radars! Cease radiating and resume full EMCON. Officer of the Deck, come left to zero four five."

The *Cunningham* began to list outward as she came about at high speed. As she did, stealthed hatches swung open on her foredeck and superstructure and launcher tubes hurled rocket-propelled grenades into the sky. Seeded out over a wide area, the fireworks-like bursts produced by the Rapid Blooming Overhead Chaff System spewed out clouds of highly reflective metal foil.

If the Red radars came up again during the next few minutes, their operators would have to sort through a large number of false targets before they could hope to locate the true return of the fleeing destroyer.

Amanda had no intention of making it any easier for them either. They had been running to the southeast, with the pursuing Red fast-attack craft strung out in a line behind them. Now, by veering away to the northwest, she intended to put that line of small craft between herself and the more immediate threat of the mainland shore batteries.

"Mr. McKelsie, do you verify that the Communist radars are still down?"

"So far, Captain. I think we put the fear of God into 'em."

"Let's hope it holds. Tactical Officer, if you get so much as a flicker, lay another round in on them. Don't wait for my orders, Dix."

"Got my thumb on the button, ma'am."

Two minutes crept by. Three. The main squall line was rolling away to the north and a faint flicker of lightning haunted the horizon. The rain was beginning to slack off, and the quartermaster secured the bridge wind-screen wipers and blowers. The sudden silence was unnerving.

Four minutes. The range from the coast continued to open. Amanda felt a tightness in her chest and realized that she had literally forgotten to breathe. The FLIR systems were coming back on line as the atmosphere cleared, and they momentarily caught the wake of one of the Chinese hydrofoils, streaming away to the southeast. A little longer and the Duke would be clear.

"Square Tie going active on the mainland!" McKelsie's exclamation exploded from the 1-MC speaker like a bomb. "Search sweep . . . going to target-acquisition mode! He's trying for a snap shot!"

"We have bearing on the battery radar," Dix Beltrain counterpointed. "Firing on bearing. HARM going out!"

Blue-white fire glared beyond the windscreen, overilluminating every square inch of the bridge interior. The watchstanders recoiled slightly from the crackling roar of the rocket ignition.

"Vampire! Vampire! We have an active HY-2 seeker head!"

"Light off all radars," Amanda snapped. "Bring up point defenses and initiate full-spectrum ECM."

"Hold it, Captain!" McKelsie interjected. "We are not being targeted!"

"Belay last orders. Maintain full stealth. Are you sure, McKelsie?"

"Positive, Captain! This is sidelobe only. We are not being targeted. We're still clean."

"Who's he targeting, then?"

"I have no idea, Captain. It's just not us. . . . Stand by . . . HY-2 seeker head has just gone inactive. HY-2 is no longer a factor."

One of the lookouts spoke up from his monitor. "Visual event bearing two two zero degrees relative off the port quarter. Appeared to be a detonation flash on the surface, Captain. Now showing a continuous thermal flare on that bearing."

"I think the Reds just had a friendly-fire incident, Captain," Arkady said slowly. "I think Wyatt Earp out there just blew away one of his own boats."

"But that's not how they're going to tell it in the press releases."

Suddenly the weight of her helmet was unbearable. Reaching up, Amanda tugged at her chin-strap release and lifted it off. A freed droplet of perspiration trickled down and burned into her eyes. Reaching up again, she swiped it away with the back of her hand.

"Come right to zero nine zero, Arkady. Maintain all engines ahead full. God, let's just get out of here."

The Day-Glo-yellow life raft rode lightly on the slack sea. Linked to it by a tether, its combination rescue light and watertight radio beacon bobbed beside it. Bosun Hoong used the once-per-second flash of its strobe as a guide as he towed in the limp form of Lieutenant Zhou.

The bosun rolled over the low, inflated sidewall of the raft, dragging the unconscious man in after him with a modest degree of difficulty. Positioning Zhou as comfortably as he could, Hoong began methodically investigating the pouches of survival gear that lined the raft's interior.

A chemical light stick was discovered, and Hoong broke its interior capsule and shook it into life. Using its pale-green glow, he examined his commanding officer's injuries. The younger man was breathing easily and the abrasion at his temple was only oozing a thin trickle of blood. He would likely enough live.

The bosun wrapped Zhou in a Mylar survival blanket taken from another pouch, taking a second one for himself. He was just settling down at the far end of the raft when he heard Zhou moan and start to stir.

"We are well, Lieutenant," he said.

"Hoong, what has happened?" Zhou exclaimed weakly, trying to pull himself upright.

"Rest quietly, sir. There is nothing to be done. The boat has been sunk and we are in a life raft."

"A life raft?"

"Yes, sir. It was dropped by the ship that ran us down. They were Yankees, I think."

The bosun gestured off into the hazy darkness. "There is also a fight going on out there somewhere. I've heard missile launches, and just before we reached this raft, I felt an explosion through the water. No telling who is winning."

"The crew! What about the crew?"

"Dead," Hoong replied, grabbing a bar of hard tropic chocolate from a ration pack. "We were broken in two, and the stern sank almost at once. Enginemen Chang and Waiu and Gunner Zhong went down with it.

"Helmsman Shi, Radioman Feng, and Torpedoman Liau were all crushed in the cockpit by the impact. Gunner Gang was up forward with me, but the young fool had taken off his life jacket." The bosun peeled back the wrapper on the bar. "He drowned, I think."

"The whole crew gone," Zhou whispered. "How could that happen and we still live?"

Hoong took a judgmental bite of the chocolate. "Because it was not yet our time to die, Lieutenant," he replied.

The *Cunningham* continued her run to the east, all hands still at their battle stations but with her engines slowed to ahead standard. They had crossed back over the Chinese twelve-mile limit and the threat boards remained clear. They had successfully disengaged. The fire flash of the crisis had passed. Now the shadow of the aftermath loomed.

On the bridge, Vince Arkady glanced over at the captain's chair. Amanda was seated in it, outlined against the glow of the telescreens, staring out into the darkness, silent and unmoving.

Arkady had known that on this cruise he would be faced with temptation. However, he had primarily been concerned with the physical variety. He hadn't expected to encounter this deeper, more urgent desire—that of wanting to cross over to his lady in front of God and everybody, and to cradle her in his arms, and to whisper that somehow, everything would be all right.

The overhead speaker cut in, breaking the stillness.

"Captain, this is Raven's Roost." Christine Rendino's voice was a total contrast to his own mood. The Intel didn't sound in the least subdued. In fact, she sounded positively ebullient. "When you get a second, could you come down here? You've just got to see this!"

☆ Pearl Harbor, Hawaii
0752 Hours Zone Time; August 13, 2006

Bright island sunlight flooded the combination kitchen and breakfast nook of Elliot MacIntyre's flag quarters.

"But, Dad . . ."

The Admiral grinned to himself as he listened to the classic agonized cry of the American teenager. It was a sound he hadn't had a chance to hear often enough in his life.

"Look, Judy," he said in an equitable manner. "I know that all the kids go over to that nude beach at Waimanalo. I'm also certain that you're mature enough to cope with it. Unfortunately, I'm not. Forget it."

His daughter, fifteen and growing swiftly into the same kind of midnight-haired beauty that her mother had possessed, sighed dramatically and turned back to the kitchen range. MacIntyre grinned outright and returned his attention to the morning paper.

As with anyone doing duty in the services, his career responsibilities had kept him away from his family far more than he had liked. With Judy, his youngest child, and the only one still living at home, he was enjoying his last opportunity at fatherhood.

Breakfast had become an unspoken pact between father and daughter, an atonement for their many separations. Come hell or high water, they would try to sit down at the same table and eat together as a family at least once each day.

"Then can I at least go over to Kim's this afternoon?" Judy went on, deftly popping slices of Canadian bacon into a hot pan.

"Is everybody going to have their clothes on?"

"Father!"

"Be my guest."

The phone rang, and MacIntyre pushed his chair back from the table. "I'll get it."

"Okay. How do you want 'em, scrambled or fried?"

"Scrambled. Two."

He crossed over into the living room with its split-bamboo paneling and comfortable, eclectic collection of furnishings. The telephone deck was located on a reading table at the end of the couch.

"MacIntyre," he said crisply into the handset.

"Admiral, this is Commander Doyle over in Operations." MacIntyre recognized the voice and the name of his morning duty officer. He also recognized the formalized urgency in the man's speaking demeanor. "This communication will require a secure line, sir."

MacIntyre reached down and keyed the tap nullifier and scrambler on the phone's security unit, pausing a second to verify that the check lights came on.

"We're secure, Commander. Go ahead."

"There has been a problem with Operation Uriah, Admiral." The watch officer's voice now carried the slight stammering buzz of a digitally encrypted telecommunication line. "The *Cunningham* has been involved in a live-fire incident off the Chinese mainland."

MacIntyre's jaw tightened and he felt his heart rate begin to climb. "Specifics?"

"A missile exchange with Red coastal batteries. Also with their light forces. Two, possibly three, FAC engaged and sunk."

"How about the Duke? Has she taken damage?"

"No damage or casualties reported. Captain Garrett has apparently successfully disengaged and is clearing the area now. She is requesting to talk with you, sir."

"Right. Inform CINCPAC and Seventh Fleet. I'll be down in five minutes."

MacIntyre hung up the phone and reached for his uniform cap sitting atop the living-room bookcase.

Out in the kitchen, Judy had overheard MacIntyre's end of the conversation. Swiftly, she stacked half of the bacon between two slices of toast and had the ad hoc sandwich wrapped in a paper towel, ready for her father as he passed through en route to the garage. He accepted it and gave her a quick hug in return before striding on.

"Sorry, honey. I have to go."

"I understand."

She did. She was an admiral's daughter.

Truth be told, MacIntyre wheeled his elderly Porsche Targa into his parking slot behind the administration complex within four minutes of his hanging up. He gritted his teeth at the sentry post, begrudging his own orders that made an active security check mandatory for everyone entering NAVSPECFORCE headquarters, including himself.

A minute more, and he was in the operations center. It was a cramped facility, a double row of workstations shoehorned into a smallish room that had at one time served as an enlisted men's cafeteria. Its walls were lined with glowing Large Screen Display telepanels, and the interior lighting was kept low.

The watch officer looked up as MacIntyre entered. "Glad to see you, sir. I think we may have something of a situation developing here."

MacIntyre joined Doyle in front of the graphics display of the Chinese coast. "What's the latest?" he demanded. "NSA is recording a major spike in the Red Chinese command-and-control nets. Their coastal-defense zones have gone on hot alert. Both Task Force 7.1's duty Hawkeye and the Air Force's AWACS patrol, out on Empire North station, are recording multiple aircraft launches from air bases in the Shanghai region. Intent unknown."

"Has Admiral Tallman been made aware of what is happening?"

"Yes, sir. Task Force 7.1 has closed up to general quarters. As yet, there have been no further live-fire events recorded."

"Okay . . . Where's the *Cunningham* now?"

The watch officer indicated a point on the flatscreen. "About twenty-five miles off the coast, proceeding east. They're still clear. The Reds have not reacquired."

MacIntyre allowed himself to feel a degree of relief. His people were out of it for the moment. God knows what might happen next, but they had some time to sort things out.

"Get me a channel to Captain Garrett. And get me a copy of their current ops profile."

"Aye, aye, sir."

There was a headset waiting for him in the adjacent communications room and a personal-computer pad loaded with the pertinent information.

"Milstar link established, Admiral. *Cunningham* acknowledging."

"Put me through," the Admiral replied distractedly. He speed-read the single-page summary of the tasking outline, refreshing himself on what the Duke had been attempting out there.

"You're up, sir."

"Thanks, son." MacIntyre keyed the lip mike. "Captain Garrett? This is Elliot MacIntyre. What have you got?"

Amanda Garrett sounded weary beyond the radio channel's encryption jitter, but she also sounded focused. "A major strategic development, sir."

"That's an understatement, Captain. You seem to have kicked somebody's puppy. We're seeing a heavy reaction from the Red coastal defenses and we're reading you in at only twenty-five miles off the mainland. Are you sure you are secure enough to be dropping EMCON?"

"No choice, sir. I have a priority sighting report and I need instructions. My intel's premise about Shanghai was correct."

MacIntyre glanced at the computer pad again. "You mean about the Reds having a major project there?"

"Yes, sir. We are datalinking our findings now." Across the communications room, a printer began to spit out hard copy. MacIntyre pointed and snapped his fingers, sending a radioman scrambling to retrieve the pages.

"I'm sorry about the mess, sir," Amanda continued stiffly. "I accept full responsibility for the events in the Shanghai approaches. I'm afraid that I've failed your confidence."

"As far as responsibility goes, Captain, you were operating under my orders. And as far as failing my confidence, that has yet to be seen. Stand by."

The report was concise. Four pages of terse military phraseology, but the meat of it might have been contained in a single paragraph.

"Captain."

"Yes, sir."

"Continue to open the range from the coast. As soon as you are clear, cross-deck over to the *Enterprise* and make a personal report on this to Admiral Tallman. I suspect that the two of you are going to have some things to talk about."

☆ Over the East China Sea

0436 Hours Zone Time; August 12, 2006

The eastern horizon was giving birth to a molten-gold sunrise. Amanda watched it from the rear cockpit of Retainer Zero One, her head resting against the seat back. She had made a futile attempt at sleep, but had given it up as a bad job.

They had been an hour in the air with another to go before making rendezvous with the carrier. The Sea Comanche had long-range ferry tanks clipped beneath its snub wings, and Arkady held her down low in the shadows just above the wave tops. Looking forward now, she could see the slight, repetitive movements of his flight helmet as his eyes tracked in a pilot's pattern: horizon to horizon—instruments—horizon to horizon—instruments . . .

Arkady had insisted on flying her himself, downing a load of caffeine tablets to burn away some of the night's fatigue. He hadn't said much since taking departure from the *Cunningham,* but then, that was one of the things Amanda had always appreciated about him. He wasn't afraid of the silent times.

She also suspected that he was partially telepathic, or at least, able to feel the pressure of her gaze on him.

"Penny for your thoughts, babe," he said quietly over the interphone.

"I don't know if they're worth that much."

"Then, give 'em away for free."

Amanda let her breath hiss away softly. "Well, I'm thinking that you might be flying a new skipper out to the Duke later this morning."

There was no response for a moment, then the back of the helmet moved in a minute negative shake. "Nah, I'd bet they'd give her to Mr. Hiro."

"I presume that's supposed to make me feel better?"

"It should. He knows the ship and the crew. And you've taught him everything you know about stealth-operations doctrine. The Duke will be a lot better off in his hands than with some black shoe off a conventional can."

In spite of everything that had occurred within the past twelve hours, and what might happen within the next, Amanda found that she could still laugh. "I think we're missing connections here, Arkady."

Again, the back of that gray flight helmet gave a shake. "No. Not really. The thing is, babe, that I know you. I don't think you really want somebody blowing sunshine in your ear just now. We can't control what kind of judgment call the powers that be are going to make about this situation. That's out of our hands. But last night, when you committed us to that recon run, you did it for what you believed were all the right reasons. Right?"

Amanda let her eyes drift back out to the sunrise. "At the time, I thought so."

"Knowing what you do now, pluses and minuses, personal and world-wise, would you do anything different?"

She was pleased to find that the answer came easily.

"No."

"Well, there you go."

Admiral Tallman's fist slammed onto his desktop like a bomb.

"Commander Garrett," he said in a deadly monotone, "this Task Force is now on full war alert. We are at battle stations. Seventy-five miles to the west of here, my combat air patrol is eyeball-to-eyeball with a full squadron of Q-5 attack bombers all armed for maritime strike. I, for one, would like to know how the hell all this came about."

The tension in the Admiral's cabin was thick enough to be physically tangible. Amanda held a parade-rest posture in front of Tallman's desk while his chief of staff paced restlessly. Beyond the bulkheads, the thunder of air operations raged on at an increased tempo.

"All of the essentials were in my after-action report, sir," Amanda replied levelly. "We were executing a reconnaissance pass of the Yangtze estuary and the Shanghai military district, investigating a theory developed by my intelligence officer. She believed that the Communists have been deliberately maintaining a reduced operational level within the Shanghai military district to divert attention away from some high-security project, or activity, they had under way there."

Commander Walker cut in. "I read the report you passed on to our theater intelligence section. We could find no concrete indication of any kind of special project. As far as I can tell, Captain, all you were operating on was a whole lot of nothing."

"Sometimes that is all you have to start with, Commander," Amanda replied quietly. "At any rate, during the course of that pass, we experienced a failure in our thermographic vision systems. Exactly what, we don't yet know. The systems checked out four-oh both before and after the event.

"As a result, we were involved in a collision with a Red Chinese torpedo boat—one of a squadron that was apparently deployed on picket duty ahead of the estuary mine barrier. We were forced to disengage under fire and to suppress both the mainland coastal batteries and pursuing fast-attack craft with Standard HARMS. Following disengagement, we resumed full stealth protocols and cleared the area."

"I'll say this for you, Captain Garrett," Nolan Walker said bitterly. "When you blow it, you blow it big. The Reds are already stating over diplomatic channels that it was a United States naval vessel that violated their coastal waters. They claim to have concrete evidence. I don't suppose you have any idea what that might be?"

"Probably the life raft we dropped to the survivors of the torpedo boat we rammed."

"Oh, Christ!" Walker exploded. "What in the hell possessed you to do that!"

Amanda snapped her head around to stare down the Chief of Staff. "Because there were men in the water, Commander!"

"That's enough!" Tallman cut in. "Okay, I guess that covers what happened. Now, let's see if it was worth it. Admiral MacIntyre has informed me that you've got some material that I should have a look at."

"Yes, sir. Shortly before the collision we detected what sounded like a convoy assembling up the Yangtze on our passive sonar. At the suggestion of my intel, Lieutenant Rendino, we executed a single high-definition surface sweep of the area with our SPY-2A Aegis radar."

Amanda lifted her briefcase to the corner of the desk, popping the latches. "As you know, sir, the SPY-2A has a skin-track silhouette capacity at closer ranges. That is, we have enough definition on the return to actually get an identifiable outline of the target."

She removed a folded strip of hard copy from the briefcase. Opening the first section, she spread it across the desktop before Tallman. Walker moved in and peered over the Admiral's shoulder, intrigued in spite of himself.

"This is a graphics printout of the skin-track," Amanda continued, "computer enhanced for maximum clarity."

Running down the edge of the paper was a single ink-jetted line, the representation of the river's surface. At two points, the line jiggled upward, producing a sketchy, but recognizable, outline of a small vessel.

"The lead craft, we think, is one of the Shanghai pilot launches. The second is definitely a Lienyun-class coastal minesweeper. Now, here it really gets interesting."

Amanda unfolded another series of sheets. Revealed were two neat rectangles extending above the river line, the larger ahead of the smaller. There was no need for commentary. Tallman and Walker both instantly recognized the sail and the upper vertical stabilizer of a nuclear submarine.

"There are three of them, sir," Amanda said. "By measuring the hull length between the sail and fin, we were able to determine that the two leaders are Han-class attack submarines. The trailer is a Block 2 Xia fleet ballistic-missile boat."

Much as she had done when she had been confronted with this revelation, the two male naval officers became very still and very quiet. Mentally, they were running the same equation: one Block 2 Xia equaled sixteen Ju Lang 2 sea-launched intermediate-range ballistic missiles. Sixteen Ju Lang 2 IRBMs, in turn, equaled thirty-two megatons of thermonuclear firepower.

"All of our intelligence indicates that the Reds have not sortied a nuke for over a year," Walker said quietly. "They laid up their fleet because they lacked the resources to keep them operational. Is there any chance that these could be hulks under tow?"

Amanda shook her head. "No." She removed a CD from the briefcase and placed it on the desk. "This is the track we recovered from our passive sonar. Analysis indicates that all three boats were maneuvering independently under reactor power."

She moved back and paced a step or two. "My intel says that several Chinese nuclear submarines were laid up in Shanghai. The Communists must have made an extraordinary effort to put these three back in commission. They waited until there was a hole in our satellite coverage, then they sortied the boomer. The attack subs are probably acting as escorts, and the torpedo boat that I rammed must have been part of a security screen covering the departure."

"I wonder if your busting in on their party might have scared them back into their hole."

Amanda shook her head. "I'd doubt it, sir. The Communists know that if word gets out that they have an operational boomer, the Nationalists will go for it with everything they have. I think they carried through with the sortie. I think this wolfpack is at sea right now."

Admiral Tallman scowled and studied the hard-copy strip as if all the secrets of the universe were encrypted upon it.

"Nolan," he said finally, "get on the horn to the Flag bridge. Have them bring us around and get the Task Group headed north. Then talk to Air Ops and have them initiate a maximum-effort ASW search pattern covering an area . . . well, starting with everything within a hundred-and-fifty-mile radius of the mouth of the Yangtze River.

"I've got a hunch that the Reds are going to be a little bit cranky about any sub hunting that may be tried up that way, so have the air boss tie on some fighter cover for the Vikings. Set up the Bombcats, a Hummer, some tankers, whatever's needed."

"Yes, sir."

"Then inform Captain Williams and the CAG that I'd like them both on the Flag bridge in a half hour for a situation briefing. Have the staff work us up a data dump on everything we have on the Red Chinese nuclear-sub force and the local ASW environment."

"Aye, aye." Walker turned to the interphone on the cabin bulkhead.

With that done, Tallman glanced at Amanda from beneath lowered brows. "You had breakfast yet, Commander?"

Amanda shook her head. "No, sir."

"Well, go down to the wardroom and get yourself something to eat. Then get back up here in time for that briefing. I want you to sit in on it before you head back to your ship."

"Very good, sir." Amanda tightened the lock on her expression, concealing the surge of relief she felt.

The Admiral continued. "An aspect of your orders was that the *Cunningham* would revert to the tactical command of Task Force 7.1 should we get into a conflict situation out here. As of right now, Captain, I'm activating that clause.

"The Duke is the closest surface platform we have to the primary search zone. I want you to get out there and reacquire that boomer. Then park yourself on his tail until Washington decides what they want to do about it."

"Will do, sir."

Tallman looked up and studied her fully for a moment, maybe for the first time as a subordinate and an asset instead of a question mark.

"You know, Captain Garrett, I think you would have met Napoleon's requirements for becoming a marshal of the French Army."

Amanda caught the reference and smiled back with honest humility. "I know, sir."

Vince Arkady was waiting down corridor from the Flag cabin, out of sight of the Marine sentry posted at the door. He straightened as Amanda appeared around the corner, searching her face for some clue to what might have happened inside.

"I may lose the Duke, Arkady," she said somberly. She let the words hang in the air for a moment, then she smiled, "but not today."

Arkady made a show of snapping his fingers. "Oh, well, back to the old advancement-by-assassination plan, then."

"Afraid so," she replied, starting down the passageway ladder to the lower decks. "Let's go hit the officers' mess. All of a sudden, I'm starving."

"Me too. Jesus, what a night!"

"Yes, and I've got a hunch that this is only the beginning."

Amanda Garrett had departed by the time Commander Walker finished re-laying Tallman's orders via the interphone.

"What was that you were saying about Napoleon, sir? I think I missed something."

The Admiral smiled and crossed his arms on the desktop.

"It was just an old story from the Napoleonic Wars. It seems that this French general was in line for promotion to marshal, and Napoleon's staff was busy talking up the man in front of the Little Emperor. They described in considerable detail the man's accomplishments, battle honors, the glow-ing testimonials given to him by his fellow officers, just generally praising him all over the place.

"Napoleon just waved it all off, saying, 'I don't want to know if the man is capable, I want to know if he is lucky!'"

☆ Washington, D.C.

1412 Hours Zone Time; August 13, 2006

It was a standard presidential motorcade. A District of Columbia police cruiser ran point, its flaring light bar clearing a path through the pre–rush-hour traffic flow on New York Avenue. Then came the three identical black Lincoln limousines. Two transported only Secret Service cadre. The third, the "carrier," was positioned randomly in line with the others. A tan Ford Explorer with the heavy-weapons team followed, and another D.C. cruiser brought up the rear.

Inside the President's vehicle, Benton Childress's press secretary shook his head and commented from one of the rearward-facing jump seats. "The Alliance of American Educators isn't going to be to pleased with your address today, sir."

"Unpleasant realities are something that we all have to live with, Brian," Childress replied, perusing his speaker's notes again. "One of them is that everyone, no matter how noble their cause, is going to have to learn to live with a budget. This government is just beginning to regain a degree of fiscal responsibility. My administration is not going to be taking any backward steps on that path. People had better get used to it."

"You do enjoy doing things the hard way, Mr. President." One of the car phones on the forward divider shrilled. The Secret Service team leader who had been riding in the other shotgun seat took the call. He listened for a moment, then held the handset out to Childress. "It's the National Security Adviser, sir, from the Pentagon."

Childress took the phone. "Yes, Sam."

Sam Hanson's voice was level, controlled, and totally emotionless, the voice of a thirty-year professional warrior addressing a superior officer. "Mr. President. You are needed in the War Room immediately, sir."

Childress didn't even consider asking questions.

"I'm on my way."

He handed the phone back to the Secret Service man. "We're diverting to the Pentagon. Let's move."

No questions were asked there either. The Secret Service man keyed his radio, issuing orders. At the head and tail of the column, the sirens of the police cruisers began to warble and the motorcade turned south, heading for the Arlington Memorial Bridge.

The Pentagon was commissioned in 1942 as the world's largest office complex. At the time there was some debate over what was to be done with it following the demands of the Second World War, it being held as inconceivable that such a vast facility would be required by a nation at peace.

In reality, the Pentagon was saturated within five years of its becoming operational in 1945. Expansion had been required, and the only direction to go had been down.

Several annexes, command-and-control facilities, and operations centers had been built into its understructure over the years. The current War Room had at one time been an underground parking garage. Now it was the place where the blood decisions were made.

President Childress had been here often enough before, but now there was an added charge in the air, like the first eddy of a summer thunderstorm rolling in. Looking down from the glass-walled overwatch balcony, he could see the duty crew at their ranked workstations. They were moving with a focused intentness, and there was a tension in the voices that intermittently issued from the balcony intercoms

Sam Hanson was there, as was an angular, graying Air Force four-star, General Morrell Landry, the Chairman of the Joint Chiefs of Staff. At the moment, the General was leaning in over a communications console, speaking into a telephone handset.

Childress's security adviser turned to greet his commander in chief. "Sorry to disrupt your day, Mr. President, but it looks like we have a major problem developing out in China."

"Beyond what we already have?"

"A geometric escalation, sir. Shit plus has just hit the fan."

"What's happened?"

"One of our stealth destroyers was on a recon probe outside of Shanghai when they ran into a covert Red Chinese naval operation. A major live-fire incident has ensued. At this time, we are reporting no casualties on our side and a full briefing is being prepared for you on the event. However, to cut to the chase, we have learned that the Reds have sortied a fleet ballistic-missile submarine. Intentions and destination unknown."

"And we are to presume that this is an unusual event?"

Hanson nodded. "This is the first boomer sailing that they've had in over a year. It's also apparently taken place under extreme security. Given the current situation in China, we can't afford to see this as being a coincidence."

Childress's breath trickled from between his lips in a whispered sigh. He sank down into one of the padded observation seats that looked out across the War Room.

"All right," he said. "Is there any chance at all that we could be reading this wrong? That this could be some kind of routine evolution?"

Hanson shook his head. "Everyone has been running projections on the

China crisis, CIA, DIA, NSA, RAND, everyone. And, for once, everyone is in agreement. They are all stating in no uncertain terms that the Communists are losing the war. Their backs are to the wall and the only option they might have left is to use the bomb . . . soon.

"God Almighty." It wasn't a profanity. It was a prayer.

The Security Adviser relentlessly pushed the point home. "Mr. President, Red China's reactivation of a major nuclear-strike system at this time can have only one meaning."

President Childress shook off the effect. "Where's the Secretary of Defense?"

"Still at the Advanced Joint Services Fighter Trials in St. Louis. I've already had a sitrep relayed out to him. The same to the Vice President. Do you want them recalled, sir?"

Childress nodded slowly. With his elbows resting on the chair arms and his fingers interlaced, he stared into the future. "The SecDef, yes. Immediately. The Vice President, no. In fact, I specifically want Stan to stay put out there in Utah. Do we have an F-4B in at Hill Air Force Base?"

"Yes, sir."

"Good. Then we'll just put an enhanced communications and liaison staff in at his summer place. It might be a good idea to keep the National Command Authority dispersed for a while."

"I concur, sir," Hanson approved. The President was beginning to react to the crisis in much the same way he had to an in-flight emergency aboard one of his old ANG C-130s.

"What about the Secretary of State?" Childress asked. "Has he been advised?"

"I got off link with Secretary Van Lynden just a couple of minutes ago. He wasn't surprised. He indicates that this tracks with certain events that have been developing within the crisis-reduction talks over the past few days. Harry agrees with the assessment and he believes that the potential for a nuclear event does exist. He'll be standing by to confer with you at your convenience, Mr. President."

"Very well." Childress nodded. "Hold a line on standby for me. Now, how about the military end of this thing?"

"General Landry is standing by with the word."

America's senior military officer straightened at Childress's approach, the cluster of aides and advisers he had been in consultation with falling back respectfully.

"Mr. President."

"The short version, Morrell. What do we have?"

The JCS chairman turned and indicated a map display on the repeater console beside him. "I'm certain that the National Security Adviser has already given you the basics, sir. At about oh eight hundred Washington time, the Reds sortied a three-boat wolf pack out of Shanghai. Two Han-class hunter-killers and a late-model Xia missile boat. The NAVSPECFORCE destroyer that made the sighting was able to make a solid ID on all targets. Unfortunately, our ship was also spotted and was driven off under fire, losing the contact."

General Landry indicated a glowing arc line on the graphics display of the East China Sea, Shanghai at its central point.

"Given the performance envelope of the involved classes of submarine, we know they still must be somewhere within this area. This zone of uncertainty grows, of course, for every minute we fail to reacquire contact."

"What are we doing about it?" Childress demanded.

"Admiral Tallman, commanding Task Force 7.1, is currently deploying his forces to sweep for the boomer. CINCPAC has also made this Red wolf pack a priority tasking for our Okinawa- and Korea-based Orion squadrons. The problem is that the high belligerency level of the Red Chinese is probably going to make any kind of inshore ASW operations extremely difficult. Task Force 7.1 is already being sharked by Red air force units." Landry hesitated for a moment, then continued. "In addition, sir, on my own authority, I have ordered Looking Glass One scrambled."

Looking Glass One, the angel of death. The airborne command post that would assume control of America's nuclear-response forces should Washington, D.C., suddenly become an incandescent cloud of radioactive plasma.

Moving slowly and deliberately, Ben Childress removed his glasses. Taking a handkerchief from his suit pocket, he polished the lenses and asked himself for the ten thousandth time why anyone would become a President, or a military officer, or a teacher, or anything else that would place the destiny of another human being in their hands.

He redonned the glasses with a single crisp movement. "All right, General. That's what's been done. What do you advise we do next?"

"The CNO wants to move a second carrier task force into the East China Sea as well as to move additional submarine and land-based ASW assets in-theater. I concur on all three actions. I feel that getting and maintaining a fix on this boomer is an absolute priority.

"In addition," Landry continued, "I suggest we forward-deploy the 336th Composite Strike Wing into our bases in Okinawa and Korea. They're on Flyaway Alert now, and we can probably have the first elements in the air within four hours."

"We're talking about a major escalation here, General."

The JCS chairman nodded. "Yes, sir, it is. Normally, I'd say that if we need to send a message, we use Western Union. However, if we've got somebody out there who's even thinking about taking the nukes out of the box, we had better show them, and the entire world, that we're taking it damn seriously."

"Anything else?"

General Landry and Sam Hanson exchanged glances.

"Nothing more at this time, sir."

"Very well. Proceed on all points."

☆ Over the East China Sea
0901 Hours Zone Time; August 12, 2006

"What do you think, Arkady?"

"About what?"

"Submarine hunting."

"*Mucho divertimento.* Very interesting work if you can get it."

They were heading home, back to the *Cunningham*. Surfing low over the ocean's surface, the Sea Comanche's rotor wash whipped spray up behind her, spinning a rainbow in her wake as the wave crests flickered beneath her. Arkady was again flying with all stealth protocols closed up, seeking to avoid undue attention. Snowy contrails arcing across the blue of the sky marked the passing of other aircraft in the higher reaches, exact identity and intent unknown.

"What's your opinion of the tech we're going to be facing?" Amanda persisted. She knew more than a little about the subject herself, but Vince Arkady was a dedicated LAMPS helo pilot. As such, he was perforce a master of the trade.

The aviator considered for a moment before replying. "Better than first gen, anyway. The Reds are running albacore hulls and single-screw propulsion trains. I'd call the Han attack boats the equivalent of an early mark Permit class or an augmented Russian Victor 1. Early-seventies stuff, maybe with a few systems updated with imported tech."

"How about the missile boat?"

"The same, only more so. Have you ever seen pictures of a surfaced Xia? They have a free-flooding deck casing around their missile tubes. I bet when that sucker maneuvers, it sounds like somebody flushing the john."

"So you don't think finding these guys is going to be a problem?"

Arkady twisted in his harness and peered at her around the seat back. "Finding a sub is always a problem, just, in this case, maybe not an overwhelming one. What I am wondering about is what we're supposed to do with these guys after we do find them."

"That is for wiser heads than us to decide."

Arkady grunted into the interphone. "Yeah, well, in my experience, ASW is sort of like hunting rattlesnakes with an irrigation shovel. If you manage to find one of the damn things, you have about two seconds to kill it. After that it either crawls into a hole and disappears, or it comes after you."

It was an ominously succinct assessment.

An outsider intruded into their conversation. The filtered voice of the *Cunningham*'s air boss sounded in their earphones, feeding them a new intercept bearing out to the ship. Diverted, Arkady acknowledged the call, replying in kind with a GPU fix and an estimated time of arrival.

Amanda's twenty-four-hour lack of sleep suddenly seemed to overtake her. Either that, or a sudden subliminal desire to escape the loom of this new bank of problems. The August sun pouring down through the helicopter's canopy made her skin prickle and burn, and she tried to seek out a fragment of shade in the corner of the cramped cockpit. She closed her eyes.

☆ Hotel Manila, Republic of the Philippines
1523 Hours Zone Time; August 12, 2006

Deputy Premier Chang Hui'an was just completing an impassioned address as Harrison Van Lynden slipped back into his seat in the conference room.

"What have I missed?" he asked quietly, lifting the translator phone to his ear.

"Another round of enthusiastic but unoriginal West-bashing," Lucena Sagada whispered her reply. "He doesn't seem to be finding many buyers, however. The other delegates continue to 'acknowledge with silence.'"

The Secretary of State nodded and replaced his translator phone in his ear. "I've just gotten off the horn with the President concerning the Shanghai incident. How was Chang referring to it?"

"That's it. Just references. They aren't making the big deal out of it I've been expecting. It's almost as if they are preoccupied with something else."

"They are. What do we have next?"

"A change in the schedule, Mr. Secretary. General Ho Chunwa has asked for time to make a general address to the conference."

Van Lynden straightened abruptly as the Red Chinese officer approached the dais. "We'd better look sharp," he whispered to his young associate. "I think this one is going to be critical."

The General's features were totally impassive. His eyes panned across the great U-shaped table array and the seated clusters of statesmen. They seemed to catch Van Lynden's for a moment before lowering to the single page of notes on the speaker's dais.

"In recent days, the situation within the People's Republic of China has grown intolerable due to the ill-advised actions of misled factions within our own populace and the criminal adventurism of other nations. Accordingly, the People's Government has elected to seek an equitable solution to this current crisis.

"We now put forward this proposal to all of the involved factions within this internal conflict. We call for a cease-fire in place. We call for the withdrawal of all Nationalist forces from the Chinese mainland and a cessation of all outside interference in the affairs of the People's Republic. We also call for the rebel elements to lay down their arms and a normalization of the relationships between all of the involved provinces and the central People's Government.

"In return, the People's government will recognize the full independence of the nation of Taiwan and accept the legitimacy of the Nationalist government. We will offer both diplomatic and trade relationships and a formalized nonaggression treaty.

"To the rebel factions of the so-called United Democratic Forces of China, we promise improved economic and political representation, a reevaluation of national policies concerning certain aspects of civil rights, and guarantees of no retribution against the general populace of those provinces involved in the rebellion."

Ho hesitated, a ripple of some emotion momentarily crossing his face.

"Let no one construe this offer as an indication of any weakening of resolve on the part of the People's Government. This proposal is born solely out of the humanitarian concerns of the People's government and their desire to restore peace and tranquillity to the People's Republic.

"Let our enemies be warned: Should these just proposals be rejected, the People's Government may find it necessary to consider extraordinary measures to bring this conflict to a close and to further the People's agenda."

Lucena Sagada's pen flashed across the notepad.

Is he referring to what I think he is?

Van Lynden replied with a brief sketch of a mushroom cloud, underlined three times.

The conference room went very quiet as General Ho retrieved his notes and started back to his seat—so much so that the sound of another chair being shoved back abruptly pulled in all attention.

Duan Xing Ho, headman of the Taiwanese delegation, rose to his feet. He made no attempt to approach the dais; rather, he spoke from where he stood, his fingertips resting on the tabletop in front of him. His words were quiet, but his violation of protocols made them a shout.

"When the peoples of China began their quest for freedom, we were fully cognizant of the extremes to which the brutal and repressive regime that now rules from Beijing might resort. We wish to assure them that we have prepared accordingly. We wish also to state that should 'extraordinary methods' be employed against the forces or territories of either Taiwan or the United Democratic Forces of China, 'extraordinary methods' of retaliation will also be utilized."

"Oh, Christ!" Van Lynden whispered. "They've both got them!"

☆ Taroka Gorge, Taiwan

0845 Hours Zone Time; August 13, 2006

It is a titanic rift in the granite buttress that makes up the eastern side of the island of Formosa, a sheer-walled crevasse worn down through solid stone. The river that had been the instrument of the gorge's creation still boiled along its floor, the white of its foam contrasting with the grays of the stone and the greens of the moss and lichen that sheathed it.

Man had left his mark here as well. A highway had been blasted and chiseled into the south wall of the canyon and a railway roadbed had been carved into the north.

And then there was the door.

It was set in the northern canyon wall, a spur of the rail line feeding into it. The concrete of its framing had long ago exposure-darkened to match the surrounding rock, and the inch-thick armored steel of its panels was streaked with rust.

The mouth of a quarter-mile-long bunker/tunnel, it had been constructed back in the 1950s as a munitions-storage site. Hundreds of such installations had been constructed throughout Formosa in preparation for the final, inevitable showdown with the mainland. Sunk deep into the mountain's underbelly, it had been used for this critical if uninspiring function for decades.

Then, two years ago, its tasking had been changed.

Air horns blared, sending echoes rippling through the canyon. The doors of the bunker parted and slid aside with a howl of hydraulics, allowing the deep-throated rumble of a diesel power plant to escape. A small switching engine rolled out of the tunnel. Moving at a walking pace, it swung out onto the mainline track.

Three rail cars trailed behind it. The central car was a windowless command-and-control van. The first and third each mounted an erector/launcher rail and carried a single, slender, finned form. The upper stage of each white-painted missile flared out into a bulbous, lozenge-shaped warhead.

The launcher crews and site-defense force walked beside the cars as they deployed. The attention of the security men focused out to meet any potential threat, that of the missilemen turned inward toward their deadly charges.

The train braked to a halt, its engine powering down to an idle. The security troopers pivoted and dropped to one knee, assault rifles at the ready. The launcher crews held at parade rest, grimly awaiting the orders that would send them into action.

They would wait in vain for the next fifteen minutes. The air horns blared again. The switching engine revved up to power and, like a crayfish returning to its hide, the missile train reversed slowly back into its cavern.

The last of the launcher crew followed it into the tunnel. The doors closed behind it. The Nationalist nuclear-deterrent force had just executed its first mission.

☆ Rizal Park, Manila
1728 Hours Zone Time; August 13, 2006

"So," General Ho said slowly, "what the Nationalists claim is true. They have nuclear armaments."

"I am authorized to verify that fact," Van Lynden replied. "Between ten and twenty of your major cities and military installations have been targeted. I am also authorized to state that their ballistic missile delivery systems have been hardened and camouflaged to the point that they would be immune to any first strike launched by the People's Republic."

The Red General gazed silently out across the expanse of Manila Bay, his eyes narrowing. The two men had returned to the bench at the base of the fountain where they had met previously. Van Lynden had requested this off-the-boards meeting prior to the start of the day's round of crisis-reduction talks.

"This is madness," the Chinese officer hissed.

"I agree," Van Lynden replied levelly.

"Do the Nationalists think that these bombs of theirs will deter us from using our own?"

"Will they, General?"

"I don't know." Ho covered his face with his hands wearily. "I honestly do not know, Mr. Secretary. As the conflict within my nation has grown, my government has come to look upon our stock of nuclear armaments as the final and ultimate insurance of our survival."

He dropped his hands to his lap and straightened again. "How they would react should that final reed be broken, I cannot say."

"Survival *is* the point here, General," Van Lynden insisted. "We are no longer talking about the survival of a government here. This situation is escalating to the point that we are talking about the survival of your population. We are now looking at a MAD scenario. Mutually Assured Destruction! Neither side can possibly want that outcome!"

Ho did not answer, and Van Lynden groped for another angle of attack.

"Could it be, General, that we have a balance of power established here? Could this provide common cause for both sides to seek a compromise?"

The General shook his head. "Mr. Secretary, compromise would assure our destruction as surely as the Nationalists' bombs. Each day this rebellion is allowed to continue, our control over our people erodes like a handful of sand held under a stream of water. Plurality is not acceptable to the leadership of my government. To accept the Nationalists and the rebels as our equals would be to acknowledge them as our masters."

"Maybe that should be telling you something, General."

Ho paused for a long moment, then nodded. "Perhaps so, Mr. Secretary. But I am not one of those who will make these decisions. Nor will my opinion likely be asked.

"I am a warrior, and I understand the principles of war: the taking and defending of territory, the enforcement of political will. But we are rapidly passing beyond warfare now. We are entering into an area of hatred and revenge and despair that is perhaps even beyond the rule of logic and self-preservation. The Nationalists and the rebels must understand this. As I have said before, they are the ones with the options."

"What if they don't see it that way, General?"

"Then you had best have escape aircraft standing by to evacuate your Embassy personnel, Mr. Secretary. The radioactive fallout here in the Philippines will probably be quite severe."

☆ The White House, Washington, D.C.
1101 Hours Zone Time; August 15, 2006

"We have identified a total of six firing batteries," Lane Ashley reported. "Two missiles each, for a total of twelve rounds."

"Are we certain that's it?" President Childress inquired grimly.

"We think so, sir, at least as far as their IRBM force goes. The National-ists seem to have deliberately let us have a look at them. They ran them out of their concealment points during one of our reconsat overpasses."

"They wanted us to be able to verify that they actually have a nuclear-strike capacity," Harrison Van Lynden added.

The Secretary of State was attending this crisis-group meeting via a telecommunications channel, his image filling a flatscreen display on the in-ner wall.

The President massaged his temples. "All right. Let's define this capacity a little further. Do we have any performance estimates on these things? Throw weight? Megatonnage?"

Sam Hanson nodded from his chair. "What we're seeing here is a deriv-ative of the Israeli-designed Shavit launch system. That, in turn, was a de-rivative of the Israeli Jericho II theater ballistic missile equipped with a second stage. Lift weight to orbit is about three hundred and fifty pounds. Suborbital is still going to be less than half a ton.

"Our nuclear-ordnance people at Sandia Base project a warhead in the Hiroshima range. Ten to twenty kilotons. Not what we would consider a strategic weapon, but drop one in on a city and you'd still make a pretty good mess out of the place."

"Accuracy? Range?"

"In terms of accuracy, like I said, they are probably good for city bust-ing. As for range, we think they can currently target just about any point within Red territory from Taiwan."

"God damn." President Childress slammed his palm down onto his desk. "*God damn!* Where in the *hell* do the Israelis think they can get off selling strategic-strike technology like this!"

"Sir, I've already had my people check into that," Van Lynden replied. "The Nationalists purchased two Shavit prototypes plus the production rights and design schematics for the system during your predecessor's administration. State approved the sale, as did the United Nations inspectors. The Shavit is a recognized satellite launch vehicle and has been used as such by several third-world states."

"Unfortunately, sir, this is a classic example of swing technology," Lane Ashley added. "Just as an insecticide plant can be used to produce nerve gas, a satellite booster can be used to deliver an atomic weapon. It's a fact we have to live with."

"Apparently. Damn, Lane, how did they get the assembly of this system past us?"

The NSA director shrugged her slim shoulders. "Ninety percent of the components were probably lifted stock off of the Nationalists' booster production line. Likely they just listed them as being quality rejects.

"The launchers and launch vehicles were probably modularized and assembled right in the firing bunkers. Until they were rolled out, there wasn't anything for our reconsats to spot. It's the same kind of meticulous planning that we've been seeing from the Nationalists throughout this operation."

Sam Hanson grunted an acknowledgment. "A year or two back, when they first started using the Shavit, the Taiwanese reported a couple of failed satellite launches with the booster. Those might have actually been ranging tests for this IRBM version."

"Okay, then, they not only have the system, but they've proved it as well." Childress rose from behind his desk and paced a few steps across the room's dark-blue carpeting. Abruptly, he looked up and into the videophone monitor. "Harry, is there any chance that this is going to make the Communists pull their horns in a little?"

Twelve thousand miles away, Van Lynden shook his head. "It doesn't look promising, sir. I've talked off the record with one of the senior members of the Red delegation. The indication that I got from him was that the Reds might very well prefer a nuclear exchange rather than to accept a total defeat."

Sam Hanson cut in. "Sir, with the sailing of the Red boomer, I think we can take that as a given. They are planning to use the bomb. Within the next twenty-eight days, there is going to be a nuclear war."

On the videophone, the Secretary of State looked up sharply. "Twenty-eight days? Where does that come from?"

"Submerged duration, Harry," Sam Hanson replied, slouching back in his chair and interlacing his fingers over his stomach. "Our Ohio-class boomers routinely deploy for sixty days and can stretch out to one-twenty, if necessary. A Russian Typhoon or Delta can do thirty with a stretch-out to forty-five. A Xia can stay out thirty days at the most, and it sortied two days ago.

"The Communist naval bases are all within strike range of Taiwan. The Reds have got to know that the Nationalists are bound to go after that sub with everything they've got the second they get a fix on it. That boomer is dead if it goes home again. They're in a 'use it or lose it' scenario. You don't need a computer to figure that one out."

"We're already seeing a major retasking of Taiwanese naval forces," Lane Ashley added. "All of their submarines and the majority of their large surface units appear to be initiating antisubmarine operations within the East China Sea. The Nationalists are going after the Red missile boat with the bulk of their available ASW assets. And, Mr. President, it might solve a lot of problems if they find that submarine too."

"Go on," Childress said.

"We have run model analyses of several different potential scenarios for a Red Chinese nuclear first strike. In every instance, the warheads aboard that Xia SSBN have been the key to an effective strike. Eliminate them, and the scenarios fall apart."

"The Communists have other nuclear arms, Lane," Van Lynden commented from the telescreen.

"Yes, Harry, they do. But not many, and they can't be sure of their delivery systems. The Nationalists have air superiority over their held territory. It's questionable if the Reds could get air-dropped bombs through to any critical targets.

"The Nationalists are also fielding both the Patriot and the Arrow battlefield antimissile systems. That could limit the effectiveness of any strikes launched by the Reds using their short-range, Scud-type artillery rockets.

"Those sea-launched IRBMs with their big one-megaton warheads are absolutely critical for any successful strike template that the Communists might develop against the Nationalists. Without them, the Reds would come way out on the losing side of any exchange. It would be the equivalent of their committing nuclear suicide."

"That course of action can't be discounted, Lane," the Secretary of State said dryly.

"Maybe not, Harry," Ben Childress commented slowly, "but, no matter what, with those city-busters eliminated from the equation, the Reds would be taking a whole lot fewer people with them."

The group of advisers looked on as the President deliberately removed his glasses and polished each lens in turn. He redonned them after a full minute and looked over at his National Security Adviser. "Sam, get on the line to the Chief of Naval Operations. Have him start tasking for a large-scale antisubmarine operation in the western Pacific. If we commit, this will be live fire. Search and destroy."

"Yes, sir."

"At this time, authorization will be under the Presidential War Powers Act over my signature alone. I want this maintained as a black operation at this time. Full security. No public release or acknowledgment. We cannot afford to let the Reds know what we are considering."

"Or the press, for that matter," Hanson grunted. "That would amount to the same thing."

The President glanced at the NSA director. "Ms. Ashley, as of this moment, the United States has no intelligence priority higher than the hunt for this ballistic-missile submarine! I want this boat found!"

"Understood, Mr. President."

Childress then turned toward the wall flatscreen. "Harry, I'll need two things from you before we can consider committing to further action, one being the assurance that we have exhausted all valid diplomatic options in this situation. The other is the consensus of the other Pacific Rim powers and a commitment of support from them."

The Secretary of State nodded thoughtfully. "I believe that I can come across with both of those, sir. In fact, I know a way that the first can provide us with the second."

☆ Hotel Manila, Republic of the Philippines
2034 Hours Zone Time; August 17, 2006

Harrison Van Lynden came to his feet as the Secret Service agent ushered his two guests into the sitting room of his suite.

"Secretary Duan, Professor Djinn, I thank you for coming here this evening."

"It is our pleasure, Mr. Secretary," Ho replied. "How may we be of assistance to you?"

"I hope we may be of assistance to each other. Please, be seated." Van Lynden gestured to the couch that faced him across the low coffee table.

However, it was tea that was brought forward by another silent aide—steaming green tea served in delicate handleless porcelain cups. More than a gesture of hospitality, Van Lynden was invoking an ancient Chinese ritual of negotiation, one that he hoped would stand him in good stead tonight.

The Secretary of State and his two guests shared the first sip, which signaled the beginning.

"I would like to speak about the current state of the crisis-reduction talks," Van Lynden began. "And I have called you here tonight in this rather unconventional manner because, sometimes, that is the best way to circumvent an impasse. And we are at an impasse, a very dangerous one."

"Impasses are sometimes born of commitment, Mr. Secretary," Professor Djinn replied. "I fear that this is the case."

"I understand that, Professor. Unfortunately, I fear that this commitment of yours, Professor, could lead to the world's first nuclear war. That is an option that I know that neither United Democratic Forces, nor the Nationalists, nor the Communists desire. There has got to be some solution here that does not require the death of millions."

"There is," Professor Djinn replied levelly. "The solution is for the Communists to admit their defeat."

"That's not an easy thing for anyone to admit to. But possibly we might be able to get the Communists to admit that it's time for change. I would like to put forward the following proposition tomorrow. A freeze-in-place of all UDF and Red Chinese forces, a cease-fire, and the deployment of a U.N. observer group to monitor the truce."

"Which would resolve nothing, Mr. Secretary."

"It would put this nuclear confrontation on hold! It would give you the chance to initiate direct negotiations with the Communists. They have got to accept the United Democratic Forces as a factor in China's future. Maybe we can broker some kind of power-sharing agreement."

"And what part would the Nationalists have to play in this power sharing?" Secretary Duan inquired.

"As a supportive faction of the UDFC. Speaking frankly, any cease-fire agreement that we might make with the Communists will probably mandate a Nationalist withdrawal from the mainland."

"That is unacceptable, Mr. Secretary," the Nationalist statesman replied flatly.

"Even in exchange for seeing Taipei enveloped in a thermonuclear fireball."

"Yes." Duan deliberately picked up his cup and drank from it. "We have been denied our homeland and our heritage for half a century. We are a patient people, but even we have a limit to our patience. We are going home, Mr. Secretary, even though the path there may have its risks."

"We of the mainland have also waited a long time," Professor Djinn interjected, picking up the line of the discourse. "We have waited for a liberation from tyranny, a liberation from want, a liberation from death."

The elderly man lifted a torment-distorted hand. "We are dying now. We have died slowly for every day of the fifty years that the Communists have ruled us. Why should we fear their bombs? The death that they give us will only be swifter and cleaner."

Duan nodded in agreement. "We have planned a very long time for this moment, Mr. Secretary. It will be another long time before we could bring another such moment about again. We will not be content with half-measures, nor will we permit half of our people to continue to live under the lie of the Communists!

"We have nuclear arms of our own. We will trust in that shield, and in the hope that Beijing will not be foolish enough to commit this last great atrocity."

"You risk much," Van Lynden replied slowly.

"So we understood when we launched this battle."

Secretary Duan lifted and drained his cup with great deliberation. Professor Djinn following suit. The negotiations were over. Their last word on the subject had been spoken.

"I see." Van Lynden left the remainder of his tea unfinished on the table.

The Secretary of State bid good evening to his two guests. After their departure, however, he recrossed the sitting room and entered his sleeping quarters.

Lucena Sagada awaited him there, tending the microphone relay. Also seated in the room in a collection of acquired chairs were the representatives from Japan, Korea, and the Philippines. Each man was removing an earphone as Van Lynden entered.

"Gentlemen," he said, "now it is my turn to apologize to you about my unconventional form of diplomacy. However, I felt that it was imperative that, in the face of the decision that we must make, you all have the opportunity to hear the latest and last word from our friends the Chinese."

Ambassador Moroboshi gave a slight smile. "I daresay, Mr. Secretary, that it won't be the first time matters of statesmanship have been resolved in a bedroom."

"But few, I suspect, quite this grave," Ambassador Chung Pak responded. Counter to the Japanese, the solid, stocky Korean looked grim.

"The fools are truly going to do it, aren't they?" Jorge Apayo, the Philippine representative, said. "They are going to push this thing until they use the bomb."

"So it would appear," Chung replied. "The Analyses Section of our General Staff have completed their review of the projections provided by the United States. While they will not commit to the extent of the American RAND team, they do say that a nuclear exchange is a definite possibility."

"Our Self-Defense Forces people said probably," the Japanese ambassador interjected.

Van Lynden took a seat on the edge of the bed. "I also know that your people have been doing some projections on what we can expect out here if events do go nuclear in China."

"It will be bad," Moroboshi replied. "Very bad for all of us, including the United States. The equivalent of Chernobyl a dozen times over."

The Japanese ambassador accessed his personal-computer pad. "We are projecting between thirty and forty low- to medium-yield nuclear and thermonuclear detonations within a twenty-four-hour period. We can expect extensive fallout and elevated radiation levels throughout the Pacific Rim. Extensive ozone-layer damage. Long-term strontium 90 contamination in water and soil. The possibility of plutonium hot-spotting that could render hundreds or thousands of square miles of land uninhabitable. Trillions will be required for decontamination and medical aid. Damage to the Pacific economic environment will be beyond significant."

"What about casualties?" Lucena Sagada asked softly.

"Within the western Pacific Rim states, we can expect hundreds of thousands of cases of low-grade radiation poisoning. All nations within the Northern Hemisphere may expect a measurable increase in the number of cancer cases to be recorded over the next fifty years. Possibly by as much as twenty to twenty-five percent.

"These figures, of course, cover only the secondary effects on our nations," Moroboshi concluded with irony. "The situation within China itself will be . . . more difficult."

That silenced the room for a moment.

"Gentlemen," Van Lynden said eventually. "I believe that we all agree that this is an unacceptable outcome. Earlier today, each of your governments received an official note from the President of the United States. It proposed that, should no other alternative be available, we consider intervention in the China crisis. At least to the point of seeking out and eliminating the threat posed by the Red Chinese ballistic-missile submarine currently at sea.

"I put to you now that we have no alternative. Can you tell me now what answer we may expect from your governments?"

Ambassador Chung shrugged slightly. "We are the closest to the flame. We have no choice. If the United States is willing to take the lead in this matter, the Republic of Korea will lend both military and diplomatic support."

"As will the Philippines," Minister Apayo added. "We have few military units suitable for such operations, but we can provide air and sea basing and logistical support."

The focus of the room shifted to Ambassador Moroboshi and the decision of Japan. The Ambassador hesitated for a long moment before speaking. "Japan has forsworn aggressive warfare as an aspect of national policy. It would take a very powerful motivation for us to make an exception to this doctrine. However, the threat of nuclear devastation returning to our shores provides just such a motivation. I believe that you may expect the full assistance of my nation in this matter."

Van Lynden nodded. "Gentlemen, on behalf of the United States, I thank you. May our decision be the correct one. And now I believe we all will need to communicate with our respective governments."

"One point further, Mr. Secretary," the Philippine representative said. "What about the Taiwanese? We understand that their fleet is already at sea in pursuit of the Communist submarines. Would the military action we are considering be launched in coordination with theirs?"

"It would seem logical for us to work with them, Mr. Apayo."

"To the Communists, it may appear as if we are now siding openly with the Nationalists in their conflict."

"That's very true, Mr. Apayo. However, it also appears as if neutrality is no longer a valid option."

☆ Shanghai, China
0744 Hours Zone Time; August 18, 2006

The time of secrecy was over. The squadron had been rallied out of their places of concealment and now was moored in the sun. What was left of it.

Lieutenant Zhou Shan leaned against the finger pier railing and considered his new command. The Five Sixteen, what had been the first officer's boat, was his now. Again, what was left of it. The hydrofoil's upper works had been scored and torn by a massive shrapnel burst, and a work crew from the shipyard labored to scrub the bloodstains from the weather decks.

Bosun Hoong was busy as well, simultaneously endeavoring to both coordinate the repair job and to organize the handful of green seamen who would constitute the Five Sixteen boat's new crew. Given the volume and intensity of his language, neither was proving to be an easy task.

The problems that Zhou was confronting would not be easily resolved either. Captain Li and the political officer had perished when the flag boat had been destroyed by a wild shot from the Silkworm battery. The squadron first officer and his exec were dead as well, dying at least at the hands of the enemy.

Zhou still thought of himself as a junior officer, and yet, now, he was the new squadron commander. Fleet Headquarters here in Shanghai seemed to have neither the authorization, interest, or resources to provide a replacement. Nor, with the submarine force away and clear, did they seem to have any orders for the squadron.

They were on their own, an unusual state of affairs for any PLA military unit. Zhou knew what must be done. He must rally the squadron again. He must get them through the trauma of the losses they had taken and he must prepare them for battle again. Most of all, he must find them a worthy mission.

Unbidden, an image filled his mind. An image of the towering bladelike bow of a ghost ship looming out of the haze.

☆ Seventh Fleet Operations Area

0900 Hours Zone Time; August 18, 2006

** FLASH RED FLASH RED FLASH RED FLASH RED FLASH RED **

** SECURITY AUTHENTICATOR; STINGRAY-BRAVO-SIX-SIX-ZERO **

** ACTIVE-SECURE-************CHECK-VERIFY-GO **

** LIVE FIRE ALERT NOTIFICATION **

FROM: CINC-7
TO: ALL 7TH FLEET LAND/AIR/SEA ELEMENTS

ON THE ORDERS OF THE NATIONAL COMMAND AUTHORITY THE FOLLOWING MODIFICATIONS TO 7TH FLEET OPERATIONAL R.O.E. WILL BE PLACED IN EFFECT, AS OF 1200 HOURS ZONE TIME, AUGUST 18, 2006.

1. MAXIMUM PRIORITY WILL BE GIVEN TO THE LOCATION AND IDENTIFICATION OF ANY AND ALL PRC HAN AND XIA CLASS NUCLEAR SUBMARINES CURRENTLY OPERATING IN ASIAN AND PACIFIC WATERS.

2. UPON LOCATION AND POSITIVE IDENTIFICATION, SAID PRC VESSELS ARE TO BE FIRED UPON AND SUNK AT ALL COSTS.

☆ East China Sea

55 Miles West of Kume Shima Island

1247 Hours Zone Time; August 19, 2006

"Letter from your ex-wife, Doc?" Amanda inquired with a half-smile.

"Better," Golden replied with a theatrical sigh. "It's a letter from my ex-wife's lawyer. The dance may be over, but the malady lingers on."

The majority of the *Cunningham's* senior officers relaxed around the wardroom table as the steward served lunch. The exception was Ken Hiro. With the ship closed up to wartime cruising mode, the Duke's exec and C.O. were going on watch down in the Combat Information Center. This meal was Amanda's chance to stand down a little from the load.

The ship's surgeon made a show of refolding the page and tucking it back into his pocket. "Captain, you should be very grateful to Marilyn."

Amanda set down her coffee cup. "How's that, Doctor?"

"Because of her, you get me. If I leave the service and go up on the beach, she can get her claws into me more easily. However, if I stay out at sea, I get a little intermittent peace and quiet. There's no contest!"

A ripple of laughter ran around the table.

"Come on, Doc," Arkady needled. "It couldn't have been all that bad. You married the woman."

"Listen, flyboy," Golden replied synthesizing a Yiddish accent. "When my ex-wife and I first moved in together, she had to get rid of her cat. I'm allergic. If I'd have known then what I know now, I'd have kept the cat and gotten rid of Marilyn! For the cat, I could have taken pills!"

It was a good light moment, but it couldn't last.

"Hey, Captain," Chief Thomson said. "What's the latest on the sub hunt?"

"We're still pretty much where we stood last night," Amanda replied, cutting the first bite from her hot turkey sandwich. "The mission intent is still to keep the Reds from breaking out into the open Pacific."

Amanda found herself sliding back into her briefing mode, the attention of her officers fixing on her. "Just now, all deepwater exits out of the East China Sea are being blockaded by a multinational submarine and surface task group. The Korean Navy is covering the Straits of Korea. The Taiwanese have the Formosa Strait. The Japanese Maritime Self-Defense Force has the northern end of the Ryukyu island chain, and Seventh Fleet has the southern.

"With the perimeter secured, the containment area will be systematically saturated with ASW assets. We find the boomer, fix its location, and then we kill it. By the book."

"Does anyone have any theories about where this sucker is now?" Frank McKelsie asked.

"Look under your chair," Christine Rendino said. "The current sitguess is that the Reds are hiding out here in the deep waters west of the Ryukyus, waiting for the chance to make a bolt for one of the channels."

"Then what are we doing hanging around out here on our own?"

"We're not quite on our own," Amanda replied. "A secondary picket line of surface units is being deployed out along the Ryukyu trench ahead of the main line of containment. Our mission intent is to flush the Red wolfpack back into the shallower waters nearer the China coast.

"It's a mixed bag of units, JSDF and Taiwanese Navy mostly. Since we haven't had the chance to work up as part of Task Force 7.1's regular ASW team, we were the logical contribution from the U.S. force pool." She paused for another sip of coffee. "Or at least that was how it was explained to me."

"Yeah."

The Duke's officers turned to their meal, each striving to ignore an unspoken truth that hovered over the table. The atomic submarine is the ultimate oceanic predator, the deadliest enemy of the surface warship. Hunting for one out in the deepwater jungle is something like being a sapper probing for a hidden land mine. Sometimes "success" takes the form of a sudden terminal explosion.

They were granted time enough to eat. The mess man was just cutting the dessert on the sideboard when the overhead speaker cut in.

"Wardroom, this is the CIC."

Amanda's command headset was lying in its usual place beside her plate.

Snatching the earphones up, she settled them into place. "Wardroom, aye. What's up, Ken?"

"Somebody's initiated an active sonar search off to the southeast. Range unknown, but over the horizon. We think it may be the next picket ship down the line."

"Any sighting report?"

"Not yet. We . . . stand by . . . Sighting report coming in now. Taiwanese Navy frigate *Po Yang* now reporting a possible SSN contact. They are pursuing the target, attempting to identify."

Everyone around the table had their eyes fixed on Amanda, awaiting her word.

"Chris," she whispered off mike. "The *Po Yang*, what do you have?"

"Ex–U.S. Navy Knox-class frigate. Purchased 1995. Systems updated in Taiwanese yards. ASROC ASW launcher forward, two triple sets of torpedo tubes amidships. Facilities for a single Kaman Super Sprite LAMPS helo." A computer might have been using the Intel's voice as she rattled off the list of facts. "SQS-26 hull sonar and an SQR-18 towed array, both with augmentation packages."

Amanda's gaze flicked across to her tactical officer. "Dix, a Knox versus a Han or a Xia. Who has the edge?"

The TACCO shrugged. "If it's one-on-one, ma'am, it'll go to whoever gets off the first shot. On the other hand, if this is one of our bogeys, he may have a couple of swim buddies out there with him."

Vince Arkady shoved his chair back. "Captain, maybe I'd better get out there and have a look."

Amanda caught him with a quick shake of her head. "Hold it. Let's see if this firms up a little more first."

The remnants of lunch forgotten, they waited through the slow crawl of the minutes, sipping their beverages or toying with dessert as a nervous mess man began to clear the table. The overhead speaker clicked again. "Wardroom. Sonar is reported an underwater explosion."

"Ours or theirs?" Someone quietly voiced the question.

Ken Hiro answered a moment later.

"Captain, we are receiving a distress call from the *Po Yang*. They have just been torpedoed. Position, twenty-two miles south-southwest of us."

"Right! Ken, sound general quarters. Close the range with the *Po Yang*. All engines ahead full!"

Amanda continued to snap out her stream of orders against the backdrop of the alarm klaxons. "Communications Room, make signal to the *Po Yang*: 'Hang on. We are coming to assist you with all possible speed.' Then get on line with Seventh Fleet. Repeat the sighting report and inform them of our intent. Ask if they can get us some additional support out here."

"Aye, aye, Captain."

Her officers were poised around the table, awaiting her command. "Mr. Arkady, you're with me for a second. The rest of you, stations! Let's go!"

They scattered. The aviator was on his feet, straining at the leash, ready to move.

"Arkady, given the rate of knots we're going to be turning, our passage noise is going to take our sonar arrays off line. We'll be going in deaf. Get out there with both of the helos, assess the situation, and sterilize the area. Find me that sub!"

"Will do!" He gave her the briefest of nods, then he was gone, heading away to the hangar bay aft.

"Captain, this is the Communications Room. The *Po Yang* has just reported that she has been hit by a second torpedo. She's gone off the air, and we're receiving life-raft transponders on that bearing."

"Acknowledged. I'm on my way down."

In the hangar bay, the helipad elevator descended with a howl of hydraulics and a flare of warning lights.

"Go! Go! Go! Put your shoulders into it!"

Aviation ratings rolled Retainer Zero One forward out of its servicing spot and onto the lift. The Sea Comanche had been undergoing mission maintenance and other AC hands sidled along the helicopter's flanks, securing access panels.

"Gus! Where are you?" Arkady bellowed as he ducked in through the entry hatch.

"Here, Lieutenant!" AC-1 Gregory "Gus" Grestovitch, Arkady's systems operator, was already at his gear locker donning his flight equipment.

"What's the pod status?"

"We've still got the package from this morning. MAD pod and a sonobuoy dispenser. Fifty-fifty mission mix: passive and active."

"Okay. Have 'em upload a Mark 50 and a life raft. Expedite!"

"Aye, aye, sir!" The lanky AC snagged his helmet from the locker and dashed off to confer with the ordnance-handling team. Arkady geared up himself. Moving onto the lift pad, he swung into Zero One's forward cockpit and started his preflight.

He knew full well that his handling crews were working as rapidly as possible, but the Lady was counting on him. Impatiently, he twisted around in his seat and watched as the life-raft pod and the little Barracuda antisubmarine torpedo were trundled into position under the helo's snub wings. The ordnance hands were still shackling them up as the elevator began its rise to deck level.

The skies were clear, their blue paled by the blazing sun of a summer noon. A single cumulus dome rose on the north horizon. Its white color matched the occasional flash of foam on the wave crests and the long plume of wake trailing behind the *Cunningham*.

The Duke moved out. Heat shimmer boiled the air over the exhaust stacks and the decks shuddered as the propeller revs climbed. Amanda was driving her ship hard to reach the distressed crew of the Taiwanese frigate.

She was also stretching her tactical safety envelope right to the limit as well.

Dammit! He was supposed to be out there covering her. "Come on! Let's get this bird off the deck! Let's move!" The rotors were being swung out and locked into position. The ordnance hands were backing away, waving the safety-pin streamers overhead to verify that the stores were cleared to drop.

Grestovitch dropped into the rear cockpit and the canopy was slammed down.

"Gus, what's Zero Two's position within her search quadrant?"

"Lieutenant Delany was way out to the northeast, sir. Air One has got her turned around and headed for the contact now."

"Ah, nuts! Stand by for engine start."

"Set. The word is we're going after a Chinese sub, sir."

"We are, pal."

"Word also is that they've already blown another can away."

"They have." Arkady flipped his throttles to the start detent and energized the starters. "Crank!"

"Captain's in the CIC!"

"Okay, Ken. I've got her."

"Captain has the con!"

Amanda dropped into the command chair and whipped it around to face forward toward the Alpha screen. "What's our status?"

"The ship is at general quarters," Hiro replied crisply from his position at her shoulder. "Steering one nine oh degrees true. All engines ahead full. Making turns for thirty-seven knots."

"Tactical Officer. Ordnance status?"

Dix Beltrain looked up from the master weapons station at Amanda's right. "Port and starboard torpedo bays armed, ma'am. Vertical Launch ASROC flights are hot. The problem is, we don't have a target."

The story was written on the topaz expanse of the Aegis system's Large Screen Display. The position hack of the doomed Nationalist frigate glowed dead ahead along the *Cunningham's* course line. A graphics circle was looped around it, its radius being the maximum range of a Red Chinese Type 53 torpedo. Somewhere inside that line, the hunter-killer boat that had destroyed the *Po Yang* very possibly still lurked, silent and invisible. They would be sharing that space very soon.

A single Y-shaped helicopter symbol marked with a *Cunningham* ID hack hurried southward toward the zone. It would arrive in the target area ahead of the destroyer, but not by much.

"How about the Nationalist LAMPS helo, Dix?"

"It was apparently caught on the deck, Captain. He didn't get off."

"Zero One's status?"

"Air One reports he's arming up now. Arkady should be launching within the next couple of minutes."

"Other available assets."

"A JSDF Orion has been diverted south, and Task Force 7.1 will be launching a Viking as soon as they can get one turned around and refueled. Both units should become factors within the next three quarters of an hour."

"Damn, damn, damn. That's not going to be soon enough." Amanda tapped her fingernail on the arm of the captain's chair. "Ken, before you head up to the bridge, I'd like your assessment of the situation. Yours too, Dix. Are the Reds going to hang around out there waiting for us, or are they going to beat it?"

Her exec shrugged. "That Red wolf pack is trying as hard as it can not to be found. When that Nationalist frigate chanced across them, they killed it. Now their primary concern is going to be to get lost again. They'll go deep and try to clear the area running at good quiet."

"That makes sense, ma'am," Dix Beltrain added. "But on the other hand, they could have left a rear guard behind. One of the two attack boats might have dropped out of the formation. He could be hanging around out there in the surface duct, covering the withdrawal of the other two guys."

Amanda lifted an eyebrow. "Thank you both for sharing that with me, gentlemen."

"Captain," the Aegis systems manager called. "We've just lost the skin track on the Nationalist frigate. She's gone down, ma'am."

Instinctively, the little group of officers looked up at the monitors of the Mast Mounted Sighting System. A heavy smudge of grayish smoke was lined out along the southern horizon.

"CIC, this is Air One. Retainer Zero One now taking departure."

A droning roar came from overhead, and a Sea Comanche helo appeared on the television screens. Nose down and gaining speed, it pulled away toward the dissipating smoke cloud.

"Talk to me, Gus. What do we have out here?"

"Multiple static surface contacts, Lieutenant. They look like life-raft radar reflectors. No transitories. No moving targets. Nothing I'd call a periscope contact. We've also got Zero Two out there at about our nine o'clock."

Looking to port, Arkady caught the strobe flash of the *Cunningham*'s second LAMPS helo. He thumbed the transmitter key on the end of his collective controller. "Zero Two, this is Zero One. We are airborne and inbound to the target area. You got a copy on me, Nancy?"

"I read you, Lieutenant," Lieutenant (j.g.) Nancy Delany replied. "How do you want to play this, sir?"

Even with her recent promotion, the Duke's number-two pilot still couldn't manage to be casual with her Air Group Leader.

"I want to put a four-buoy box around the area. We'll use our last fix on the sunken frigate as our central datum point. I want buoy placement two miles out from the CDP with a four-mile separation. Buoy coding will be clockwise relative, Alpha, Bravo, Charley, Delta. Passive search. Read back."

As his wingwoman repeated the mission outline, Arkady looked ahead, beyond Zero One's nose. He could make out a stain on the vivid blue of the ocean, the dark shimmer of a considerable oil slick. Also, a cluster of Day-Glo specks in its center.

"Okay, Zero Two. That's the mission package. I'll put down buoy Delta, then check out the survivors. You circle the box perimeter and set Alpha, Bravo, and Charley. Do you verify that you have a dunking sonar on board?"

"Roger, Zero One. I verify."

"Okay. Once you get those buoys drilled in, drop another click south and run a deep listening line. I want these suckers kicked out of the brush."

"Acknowledged."

"Better come right to bearing two zero zero to line up on drop point Bravo, Lieutenant," Grestovitch cut in from the rear cockpit.

"Doin' it, Gus."

To the airborne submarine-hunter, the sonobuoy is the equivalent of the fisherman's glass-bottomed bucket. It gives an ASW aircraft the ability to peer beneath the surface of the sea. A miniaturized sonar system sealed in a watertight casing, it is dropped to the surface of the ocean. There, it lowers a sound head into the depths and lifts a radio antenna into the sky, broadcasting its findings back to a mother station aboard a friendly ship or aircraft.

"Buoy Alpha is down. Buoy Bravo is down. We've got positive datalinks."

"Good enough, Gus. Start working 'em. I'm moving in on the survivors."

Arkady had flown a good number of search-and-rescue missions in his time, but he had never before orbited over the grave of a newly killed warship.

Heavy oil and air bubbled steadily to the surface, the black blood of the fallen vessel. The smell of it flooded the cockpit. Wreckage drifted within the slick. Human forms as well, some that moved and some that didn't. Survivors clustered around a scattering of life rafts, staring up at the hovering helicopter as the inmates of hell might stare at an angel.

Arkady sidled his aircraft near a group of weakly struggling men at the edge of the debris drift and dropped the raft pod he carried. It was the only aid he could give. With its narrow fuselage and two-place fore-and-aft cockpit, the Sea Comanche was incapable of doing conventional rescue and recovery work.

"Gray Lady, this is Retainer Zero One. I am holding over sinking site now. It looks like we may have about a hundred and fifty men in the water. Maybe a few more. A lot of wounded."

"Acknowledged, Zero One," Amanda Garrett's filtered voice replied. "We're ten minutes out."

Arkady lifted his eyes and scanned the horizon. The *Cunningham*'s camouflage paint rendered the ship invisible against the distant haze, but her bow wave flashed white against the blue of the sea.

In Sea Comanche's rear cockpit, Gus Grestovitch plied his trade. Of all the skills of the maritime warrior, sub hunting is still infused with the largest share of black magic. The systems operator was now focusing past the cascade display in front of his eyes and the audio input in his earphones and was feeling for the submarine with his soul.

He wasn't having much luck. The sea itself was damaged here. The wreck, trailing away beneath them, was scrambling the local acoustic environment. Escaping air churned upward. Fire-heated metals sizzled and cracked. Fittings tore loose from the hulk and tumbled away into the deepwater night.

Maybe there was even life left inside that hull. Someone who hadn't been able to get clear before the water closed over the decks. Someone whose last seconds of existence were flickering away in the blackness of some lost air pocket.

Grestovitch closed his eyes and shook the image out of his head. He sure as shit didn't need that just now. He tried to refocus on his instrumentation. As he did so, he noticed something on a secondary readout. He shifted the displays on his multimode telepanel, then shifted them again.

"Hey, Lieutenant?"

Arkady glanced back over his shoulder. "Yeah, Gus?"

"We should have a couple of thousand feet of water under us here, right?"

"Yeah?"

"Then how come the wreck of the frigate is still sitting just under the surface?"

"What are you talking about?"

"Check the Magnetic Abnormality Detector. We've got a big hunk of metal right underneath us."

Arkady goggled over the cockpit rail for an instant and then called up the MAD board onto his own screen.

"Ah, shit! Gray Lady! This is Zero One! We've got a Red sub station keeping right under the survivors! It's an ambush!"

"Helm, hard about one hundred and eighty degrees!" Amanda's voice rang in the Combat Information Center. "All engines ahead emergency!"

The duty helmswoman spun her rudder controller and firewalled the throttles and power levers. The engine song rose into a keen and the hull framing groaned. The deck tilted beneath their feet as the Duke began to fight her way into the commanded turn.

"Sonar, how the hell did we miss this guy?" Dix Beltrain demanded from the tactical officer's console.

"His plant noise was masked by the audio clutter from the wreck," Foster called back from Sonar Alley. "Getting transitories on the bearing now. Sounds like he's flooding tubes."

"Shit, he's taking a shot! Captain, we have a firing solution. Ready for a snap shot with the V-ROCs."

"Negative! Check fire!" Amanda shook her head vehemently. "He's holding right under the survivors. We drop a torpedo on him and we could kill dozens of those men in the water."

"Then what do we do, Captain?"

"We run!"

"Fish swim out!" Foster's voice had risen an octave. "Captain, we've got torpedoes coming our way!"

Two decks down, in Main Engine Control, the state of the world was gauged by two parameters. One was the all-pervasive, steady-state howl of the power-room turbogenerator sets. The other was the faint but equally pervasive vibration that radiated up the support pylons from the huge, radial-gap electric motors in the propulsor pods.

The howl was now a scream, and the vibration was beginning to make the coffee mugs dance on the console tops.

Chief Engineer Carl Thomson paced his set path behind the chair backs of his systems operators—thirty feet to port, then thirty feet back to starboard—his eyes flowing from one telepanel to the next.

"Main Engine Control, this is the CIC."

Thomson paused his pacing and lifted one hand to his headset, pressing the earphone tight to cut out the outside sound. "Main Engine, aye."

"Chief, this is the Captain. We have hostile torpedoes inbound and we're trying to outrun them. I need everything you've got. Right now!"

"You'll get it, Captain." There was nothing more to be said on that front. Thomson lifted his voice. "Heads up! We've got a couple of wake chasers coming up behind us. Stand by to put her to the wall!"

"Chief, all mains and auxiliaries are already at one hundred percent output," one of the Motor Macs called back over her shoulder, fear dawning in her eyes. "We're at red-line limits all across the board!"

"That's the problem with this modern generation of marine engineers," Thomson replied, leaning in between two of the operators' seats. "Some damn fool paints a red line on a dial and you kids think it means something. Smith, kill the anticavitation programs. Set blade trim to manual. Swensen, you call up your IPS flow charts. Let's see where we can scavenge some extra juice."

☆   ☆   ☆

"We got fish in the water! Lieutenant, they've fired at the ship. . . . Son of a bitch!"

Gus Grestovitch snatched for the cockpit grab bar as Retainer Zero One's nose dipped toward the ocean. The Sea Comanche's engines shrieked and she accelerated out of her hover with all of the thrust and lift her rotors could produce.

"Lieutenant! Where the hell are we going?" Gus asked.

"Back!" Arkady replied grimly.

"Dix, what about our own torpedoes? Could we try an intercept shot with a Mark 50?"

The TACCO glanced across at his commanding officer. Amanda sat erect in the captain's chair, her fine-boned features set, her eyes level and controlled.

"No good, ma'am," he replied. "To use the Barracuda's antitorpedo program, we'd need to use wire guidance and the main-hull sonar arrays. We'd have to slow way down and turn in to target to acquire it. I don't think we have the sea room."

The tactical situation was being sketched out on the Alpha screen before them. The Cunningham's own sonars had been deafened by the flow noise of her own passage through the water. However, the data flow from the sonobuoy pattern was being used by the Aegis battle-management system to build a display of the tactical situation.

The Duke's position hack was fleeing back down its course line. Closely pursuing it were two overlapping dot-centered-in-cross icons, glowing in red, the mark of an active, hostile torpedo threat. The separation between the ship and weapon symbols was perceptibly shrinking.

"It looks like we'll have to run them out of fuel, then," Amanda said determinedly.

Beltrain didn't reply. The Duke's senior weaponeer was deep into assembling a critical equation on his console repeaters. Calling up time of launch, range estimations, and performance statistics from the torpedo data annex, he was trying to dispel an ominous gut feeling.

"Oh, Jesus, sweet Jesus!"

"Dix, what is it?"

"The Red fish have a range overlap. They got us, Captain! Impact in four minutes!"

Twenty feet off the deck, Retainer Zero One blazed back along the bearing line toward the *Cunningham*.

Unbidden, the story of the Japanese Zero pilot who had dived into the path of a torpedo to save his carrier came to Vince Arkady's mind.

Futilely, he scanned the wave tops for some sign of the passage of the hostile weapons. Nothing. Old-model fish would leave a telltale stream of steam bubbles behind. Modern units left no more wake than a passing shark.

Beyond having Gus's life to consider, he was denied even the Zero pilot's option. They were targeting the ship commanded by his Lady and there was absolutely nothing on God's green earth he could do about it.

"Set LEAD decoys for ten-second activation delay. Stand by to drop."

"LEADs set, Captain."

"Drop LEAD decoys. Helm, ten degrees right rudder."

The Launched Expendable Acoustic Devices rolled off the *Cunningham*'s stern and into her boiling wake. Upon activation, they would produce the simulated sound signature of their launching ship, literally screaming "Hey, I'm a destroyer!" into the face of the oncoming homing torpedoes. Hopefully, their mimicry would be sufficiently convincing. The LEADs were the last technological trick left in the *Cunningham*'s bag.

"Man, I sure hope that'll do it," Beltrain said fervently.

"Even if it doesn't, we're still going to be okay." Christine Rendino had left the intelligence bay and was now standing behind and between the command and tactical officer's stations. Squeezing in beside Beltrain, she was studying the performance graphs on Beltrain's flatscreens.

"What are you talking about, Chris—" Amanda's demand was cut off by a heavy thudding concussion. On the aft-view television monitors, a towering column of white water leaped into the air half a mile astern.

"We got one!" the sonar chief yelled from the sound bay. "The lead fish just killed the decoys. The second torpedo is . . . shit! The second fish is still running hot and tracking. It's still on us, Captain!"

"Stand by, second LEAD set!" Amanda twisted around to face her intelligence officer. "Now, what are you saying?"

"That fish won't reach us." Christine's finger stabbed at the torpedo stats on the flatscreen. "We're right at the edge of the range envelope for a Type 53."

"Yeah, but there is still overlap," Beltrain insisted.

"Not for real, Dix. The analysts frequently dial a fudge-plus factor into the opforce stats listed in our data annexes. The logic is that it's better to overrate enemy weapons performance than it is to underrate it."

"I can't count on that, Chris," Amanda snapped. "Drop LEAD decoy set two! Zero time activation! Helm, ten degrees left rudder!"

The single scarlet cross-dot symbol of the remaining torpedo still crawled up the *Cunningham's* course line like a spider on a thread.

Now the blue square-dot of a decoy marker appeared in the Duke's wake, a barrier between the fleeing ship and its lethal pursuer. Would it hold? All hands in the CIC gave up on breathing until they learned the answer.

Cross-dot and square-dot merged . . . and passed through each other.

"Captain, torpedo has not decoyed! Continuing to close the range! Ninety seconds to impact!"

"Damn, damn, damn!"

"Then here's something you can count on!" Christine continued relentlessly, grabbing for Amanda's shoulder. "The listed range we have for the Type 53 torpedo is for the original weapons design as used by the Russian Navy. The fish that's been fired at us will be a Chinese copy of the simplified export model—what they call a monkey version weapon. There will be a performance degradation! It's not gonna reach us!"

"I hope you're right." Amanda's hand struck the interphone key. "All decks, this is the Captain! Evacuate all compartments below the waterline and all frames aft of amidships! Rig for torpedo impact! Expedite!"

"That's it!" Chief Thomson yelled. "Lock down your breaker boards and get out of here. Move!"

The temperature in Main Engine Control was climbing fast and the atmosphere stank of ozone and burning insulation. The air-conditioners had been powered down to divert every last critical amp into the drive train. A growing constellation of red and yellow indicator lights glowed on the consoles as system after system climbed into overload.

The watchstanders yanked off their headsets and scrambled for the hatchway and the ladder beyond it that led upward to sunlight and safety. The last Motor Mac out paused for a second and looked back. The Chief hadn't moved; he was still leaning in over the master panels.

"Hey, Chief?"

"Get going, son. I'll be along in a second."

He wouldn't be. They both knew it.

The hatch thumped shut on its gaskets and Thomson slid back into the center seat. An arc warning alarm sounded in the starboard propulsor pod, and he hit the key sequence that killed it with a jet of nitrogen gas.

You don't walk out on your watch when things are looking a little rough. Not if you read out of Carl Thomson's book. The digital iron log was flickering at fifty-one knots. Thomson grinned down at it as his fingers closed around the master power levers.

"Okay, old girl, now let's see what you've really got."

The USS *Cunningham* and Retainer Zero One thundered along side by side. The big destroyer was ripping the sea open in her desperate race for survival. Her bow wave, shaved from the ocean's surface by her razor-sharp prow, sheeted up and back cleanly, nearly to the level of her foredeck. Back aft the snowy arc of her rooster tail rose to deck level and above. Every seventh wave she encountered exploded at the touch of her stem, wreathing her in its spray.

This was a moment frozen in the minds of Vince Arkady and Gus Grestovitch. Never would the Duke appear any more beautiful than she would in these last few seconds before her imminent destruction.

"Tracks are merging!" Charles Foster's voice cracked despite the fight he was making for control. On the Large Screen Display, the torpedo graphic was overlying that of the *Cunningham*.

"Sound collision alarm!

The two-toned electronic yelp filled the CIC. All hands grabbed for a solid hold and braced themselves. All except Christine Rendino. The Intel continued to stare forward into the Alpha screen, her arms crossed defiantly.

"Tracks still merging . . ."

Amanda caught sight of a familiar shape out of the corner of her eye. One of the exterior monitors had locked onto Retainer Zero One. Almost of its own volition, her hand went to the camera controls, zooming in on the helicopter's cockpits seeking for the face of the man in the pilot's seat.

"Frequency shift! We have a frequency shift!"

When the executioner's ax is falling, dare you believe in life?

"We have track separation! Torpedo is slowing! Torpedo is slowing. . . . Torpedo has run out of fuel, Captain. Torpedo is no longer a factor."

"All engines ahead standard." Amanda had to force the words out of her throat. The scream of the *Cunningham*'s turbines trailed down into a protracted sigh.

She counted slowly to ten before opening the 1-MC circuit. "All hands. This is the Captain. We had a little trouble there, but we're out of it now. Resume stations. We've got a sub to go after."

All around the Combat Information Center, aching lungs accepted oxygen and the copper taste of fear was swallowed away. A plume of coolness roared out of the air-conditioning ducts, heralding the return of normalcy. Christine Rendino folded over on the console divider between the command and tactical stations, her breath emptying out of her.

Dix Beltrain gestured toward her with his thumb. "One of these days, Captain, this gal has got to be wrong about something."

"Fa' sure," the Intel's muffled voice replied. "But ain't you guys glad today wasn't it!"

☆ East China Sea

37 Miles West of Kume Shima Island

0131 Hours Zone Time; August 19, 2006

The Red Chinese submarine captain leaned against the railing of the periscope pedestal. Around him in the red-lit dimness of the control room, the duty watch sat or stood at their stations, their eyes fixed forward by the iron discipline of the People's military.

He knew where he had made his error. Engaging and killing the Nationalist frigate had been right. That had been part of the mission. Likewise, so had lingering in the target area to await the arrival of the first rescue ship. It was required that they do as much damage to the People's enemies as they could before the end.

But then it had been an American man-of-war that had responded to the sinking. And not just any American man-of-war, but one of the new ghost ships about which so many wild rumors gathered.

He should have taken his shots and then immediately disengaged. He hadn't, however. He had chosen to linger in the shelter of the Nationalist survivors, trusting in the Westerner's perplexing, yet convenient, military compassion to shield him from the lashback of their sophisticated weaponry. He would run after his torpedoes had struck.

Only, his torpedoes had not struck. And now there was no place to run. There were helicopters out there, systematically boxing him up within a growing network of active and passive sonobuoys.

There was something else out there as well. Shortly after outrunning the torpedoes, the propeller beats of the American destroyer had faded into an ominous silence. Now there were only faint traces of sound filtering in from the limits of their hydrophone range. Spectral transitories as soft as a wolf's footsteps in the snow. The American was warily circling back, turning the hunter into the hunted.

☆   ☆   ☆

"That cowardly son of a bitch," Dix Beltrain pronounced each syllable of the epithet with careful venom, "is just hanging out there under those life rafts."

"Not cowardly as much as extremely pragmatic, Dix. He knows we can't get at him without killing some of those men." Amanda raked back her sweat-damp hair and smiled grimly. "I wonder if he's ever read Monsarrat."

"Who, ma'am?"

"Nicholas Monsarrat. He was an English author who served in the Royal Navy during the Second World War. In one of his books, *The Cruel Sea,* a British corvette captain is confronted with a dilemma similar to this one.

"His ship has detected a German U-boat directly beneath a group of sinking survivors, and he is left with a choice. He can drop his depth charges, destroying the U-boat, but also killing the survivors. Or he can hold his fire, allowing the survivors to live, but also allowing the U-boat to escape and sink other Allied vessels and take other Allied lives."

The tactical officer glanced back at the Large Screen Display. Inhaling deeply, he let his breath escape in a short "whoo." "So what did he decide?" he inquired.

"He chose to drop, Dix. Fortunately for us, military tech has changed some since then. We may have some other options."

"Surface transitory. Bearing two four zero." The Red attack-boat captain looked up at the call from his sonar operator. "Surface impact. Possible torpedo drop."

Had the Americans decided to sacrifice the Nationalists?

"Torpedo going active on the bearing."

They had. It was the only militarily sound choice that could be made.

"Torpedo is acquiring! Bearing is constant!"

"Engines ahead full! Come right to three one zero. Five degrees down bubble! Set depth to two hundred meters!"

Futile act. Futile! The American antisubmarine rocket had delivered a Mark 50 Barracuda torpedo as its payload. The deadliest of the deadly. There would be no contest in this duel, but the game must be played out until the end.

The V-ROC round had impacted some distance from the Han's position, giving the attack boat a chance to work up to a fleeing speed. Radical turns to port and starboard followed, creating diversionary knuckles in the submarine's wake. Steep dives to hunt sound-masking thermoclines. High-angle powered ascents to climb out of the seeking weapon's cone of acquisition. The full spectrum of escape and evasion maneuvers available in the subwar lexicon.

The Barracuda had a counter for each move. The Han had neither the sophistication necessary to fox the incoming Mark 50 nor the performance required to open the range and evade.

The Red crew gradually became aware of an intermittent outside irritation—piercing, almost superaudial, and growing in strength. Ultrasonic sound waves were striking the Han's hull, the sonar impulses being produced by the seeker head of the converging torpedo. A hypertech Deathwatch beetle in the submarine's bulkheads ticked off the last minutes.

The spacing between the impulses shortened and they heard a new sound: the hot hiss of a torpedo propulsor. Somewhere within the Han's internal darkness, someone whispered his peace to a God his society forbade him to acknowledge.

The hissing grew in intensity, softly overwhelming, until suddenly it ended in a resounding slam.

But there was no shattering concussion. No rending of metal. No explosive inrush of water. Just the trailing rattle of the dud torpedo frame rolling away along the hull. The crew of the Han exchanged glances and began to wonder if they might yet survive.

"That unarmed fish flushed him out, ma'am," Beltrain reported. "I've gotta read this guy Monsarrat's book."

"Come by my cabin sometime and I'll loan it to you, Dix. What's his position?"

"Bearing three four oh relative off the bow. Range is twelve miles. Heading three hundred and fifty degrees true. Depth three five oh. Speed twenty-six knots."

"Clearance from the life raft group?"

"About six miles to the north of them, ma'am. We have a safety margin."

"Very good." Amanda keyed in to the surface-to-air circuit. "Gray Lady to Retainers. Kill him."

☆ ☆ ☆

"Okay, Gus, you heard the Lady. Spin 'em up. We're rolling in."

"Aye, aye, Lieutenant. We've got good links and locks. Positioning and drop points coming up on the HUD."

They were over clean water again, well clear of the oil slick. As the Sea Comanche's nose came around to the north, luminescent grid patterns and targeting reticles seemed to materialize inside the tinted windscreen, the targeting path that would guide them in to the drop point. In the distance, the repetitive flash of Retainer Zero Two's navigational beacon could also be seen.

"Zero Two, this is Zero One. I've got you to the south. Let's set up a convergence here and whipsaw this son of a bitch between us."

"Roger, Zero One. Coming in."

"Set for snake-acquisition pattern. Set depth for two five oh. Drop at two miles."

"Roger, Zero One."

"I've only got one unit on board, Nance, so you'll have the follow-through. I will disengage to the east. You will overfly to the north and reverse back into the contact to reengage."

"Will comply."

"You got all that, Gus?" Arkady called back into the rear cockpit.

"Got it, sir. The fish is hot. Verifying that warhead and drop safeties are off."

The waves shimmered fifty feet beneath the helo's belly. On the Heads-Up Display the drop hack crawled in under Zero One's nose as she bore down on her release point. Over the radio band Nancy Delany called out her run. Her voice was tightly controlled. Arkady knew that this would be the first time she had ever delivered live ordnance on a living target.

"Coming in on drop point. Three, two, one . . . drop!"

Its weapon released, Zero Two flared upward and climbed.

"Zero Two is out. Zero One is in. Three, two, and one. Torpedo away."

Streaming its drogue chute, Arkady's Mark 50 hit the water in a clean dive, vanishing beneath the surface with a metallic flash.

"Both units running hot, straight, and normal," Grestovitch reported laconically as Zero One turned away.

There was nothing else to be said. The Han was trapped between two converging torpedoes. No matter which way the sub turned, she would be turning into her own death, leaving her absolutely no place to go.

The systems operator pulled the gain bar of the sonar audio output all the way down and waited.

A patch of ocean suddenly went a hazy gray as a million water droplets were shock-bounced off the surface. An instant later, a towering geyser of white foam lifted into the sky.

"Yeah, babe!" Grestovitch heard his pilot exclaim with a quietly fierce satisfaction. "We nailed that sucker!"

Just to make sure, Gus kicked the audio back up.

The reverberation of the blast rang through the local sea environment, but the sonobuoys had already acquired a massive transitory. The unmistakable shriek of high-pressure air boiling into ballast tanks. The death scream of a mortally wounded submarine.

"Confirm that, Lieutenant. Detecting emergency blow. He's coming up!"

"All right." Arkady lifted his hands off the controller grips for a second, clinching his fists at shoulder height in a brief gesture of victory. "Gray Lady! There she blows! She's surfacing!"

"Acknowledged, Zero One." He could hear cheering in the background beyond Amanda's voice. "Keep him covered and keep us advised. We are moving in to pick up the frigate's crew now. Very well done, Retainers!"

Arkady grinned. The queen had bestowed the touch of her hand.

A widening circle of foam formed on the ocean's surface. A wedge of turbulence appeared within it, and a great black ax blade suddenly cut the waves.

"She's on the surface now," Arkady narrated over the open mike, bringing Zero One into a hover just off site. "Looks like damage to the forward hull. Sail damage. One of the clearwater planes is gone. . . . Decks awash now. She doesn't look very stable. They'd better get the crew off that thing fast. . . . She's settling by the bow! She's going down! Oh, jeez! Gus, get the camera on this!"

The inward rush of water through the torpedo gash was winning out over the outward flow from the ballast tanks. The growing weight was radically shifting the Han's center of balance forward, pushing it back into a dive angle, pushing it beyond a dive angle.

The submarine's hull began to pitch into the vertical, the bow and sail sinking while the stern rose. The cruciform tail fins broke water and lifted almost majestically into the sky, the great bronze scimitar blades of the propeller still revolving slowly.

It was both mesmerizing and appalling. Arkady found himself sidling the helo in closer, warily circling the wavering column of steel. As he came around to what had been the deck side of the hull, he noticed movement and a thin trickle of steam.

Just above the waterline, a hatch had swung open. At its mouth, a figure in a mustard-yellow life jacket struggled like a half-crushed insect, billows of white vapor swirling out past him. With a final convulsive lunge, the figure rolled out into the sea. Feebly, he began to swim away from the doomed ship.

There was more movement within the hatchway. Another man was trying to fight his way clear. "Come on," Arkady found himself murmuring. "Come on. Come on!"

This one didn't make it. The hatch rim dipped beneath the surface. Arkady jerked his eyes away, trying to cut off the image of what must be happening in the gut of that hatchway: the choking inrush of the sea, the merciless pressure that pushed away from the light and into the final darkness.

"There she goes, Lieutenant," Gus said.

With a stately deliberation, the submarine's stern was disappearing beneath the sea. Sinking vertically, it was gone in a matter of seconds, leaving nothing behind but a swirl and a flurry of bubbles in the water.

That, and a single figure adrift in a life jacket.

"Gray Lady, this is Zero One. The Han is a goner. I repeat, the Red boat has gone down. We have a single survivor in the water. I am orbiting him at this time."

"Zero One, this is Gray Lady," Amanda replied, an intentness in her voice. "Drop a smoke float and hold station over the survivor until we can get a boat out there. We're going to need to talk to this guy."

☆ 36 Miles West of Kume Shima Island
1404 Hours Zone Time; August 19, 2006

Rescue operations were still in full sway aboard the *Cunningham*. Half-emptied life rafts clustered around the destroyer's flanks, and all three of her missile-handling cranes were deployed and lifting Zodiac boat loads of survivors up to the weather decks.

On those decks, a rescue assembly line had been established. Hospital corpsmen ran triage, separating the wounded and injured from the stunned and shocked. The former were given into the ministrations of Doc Golden, while the latter were moved along to the next phase.

Cunningham hands led the Nationalist sailors belowdecks to the showers. Hot water and gasoline cleared away the clinging residue of the oil slick and fresh clothing was issued. Then they were taken to the crew's lounge and mess deck, there to be given food, hot coffee, and a quiet time to become reacquainted with being alive.

The Nationalist Navy personnel were given something else as well by the men and women of the Duke. A multitude of gentle slaps on the back, acknowledging nods, and quiet words of support, understood even if the language wasn't. If fate had turned just a little bit differently, they all could have been left floating around out there.

"We're going to have to get her down into the hangar bay in a hurry, sir," Zero One's crew chief yelled over the declining whine of the helicopter's turbines. "We've got medevac helos coming in from Seventh."

"Roger, Chief. Carry on," Arkady replied, levering himself up and out of the Sea Comanche. A RADCON (Radiation and Contamination) Team circled the helicopter, waving Geiger-counter probes over the fuselage surfaces, scanning for any radioactive agents that might have escaped from the sinking Chinese nuke.

Arkady was more than a little pleased when the team leader gave him a thumbs-up and pulled his people back.

Standing with one foot still in a fuselage step indent, Arkady peered into the rear cockpit.

"What it is, Mr. Grestovitch, is a successful mission." Their hands came up and met in a ritual palm slap.

"Another day in towards five and out, Lieutenant," the S.O. replied sardonically.

"Still not planning to re-up?"

"I would have to be out of my fucking mind, sir."

Arkady laughed and dropped to the antiskid decking. Across the helipad, Lieutenant (j.g.) Nancy Delany leaned against the crash-containment barrier, almost lost in the bulk of her flight suit and survival vest.

As Arkady crossed over to her, he noted that the quiet-natured brunette was looking even more somber than usual. It was understandable. She had served aboard the Duke throughout the Argentine campaign and had seen some hard duty. What she had never done before was to drop the hammer on another human being.

"Well, Nancy. Paint yourself a sub under your cockpit."

She looked up, and her brown eyes widened. "Me, sir? We both dropped on the sub."

"Yeah, but I got a good look at that boat when it came to the surface. You dropped off her bow, and as far as I could tell, all of the damage was in her forward aspects. My call is that your unit made the kill, and that's how I'm writing it up. Welcome to the history books, Lieutenant."

"What do you mean?"

"I mean that you and your S.O. are the first ASW team to ever make a kill on a nuke. I don't know what kind of decoration authorization is going to be set up for this deal, but you're going to get some kind of a gong out of it. Count on that."

She ran a hand through her short, helmet-matted hair and looked back down at the deck for a moment. "Thank you, sir," she replied softly. "I don't know what I should feel just now. Excited, or just sick to my stomach."

"Either one's valid." Arkady reached over and rested his hand on the younger aviator's shoulder for a second. "Stand down and get some rest. We've still got another couple of bad boys waiting for us out there."

"Aye, sir."

A superstructure hatch swung open and Amanda Garrett, Ken Hiro, and Christine Rendino emerged, hurrying aft along the helideck. Arkady found himself straightening a little as they approached. His first instinct was to go to Amanda and fold her in his arms. Instead, he had to content himself with exchanging the briefest of acknowledging nods.

"Lieutenant Arkady, Lieutenant Delany, very good work, both of you."

"Our pleasure, Captain," Arkady replied. "How did the pickup go with the Red submariner?"

"He's alive, but there are complications. We're going to check it out now. Arkady, you're with us. Let's go." Proceeding toward the stern, they descended the sloping face of the deck brake to the well deck.

A medical isolation point had been established in the lee of the aft Oto Melara turret, a space outlined in yellow tape marked with the red radiation-warning trifoil. A single, blanket-wrapped form lay within the zone in a basket stretcher. Another figure, clad in a disposable plastic anti-contamination suit, was just backing away from the stretcher.

Recrossing the warning line, he stepped clear and allowed a waiting deckhand to sluice him off with a saltwater hose. A second more and Doc Golden was pulling off his perspiration-hazed hood and protective gloves.

"Is he still alive, Doc?" Amanda asked.

"It depends on your exact definition of alive, Captain." There was a tinge of bitterness in Golden's voice. "His heart's going to beat for a while. He's going to breathe. He's going to feel a lot of pain. However, for all intents and purposes, he's dead."

"Radiation poisoning?"

"Putting it mildly." Golden began peeling off the rest of the coverall. "I think this guy was an engineer, and I think they suffered a massive containment failure in their primary-reactor coolant loop. He was wearing one of those old-style film safety badges. The damn thing was jet black from end to end. I have no idea about how many roentgens this man has absorbed, but it's way over any survival limit."

Golden paused for a moment as he stuffed the contamination suit into its disposal bag. "God, Captain. He was breathing that shit!"

Amanda took a quick step forward. "What about the rescue detail? Have they been exposed?"

Golden shook his head. "Our people may have picked up a couple of rads, but nothing bad. We had antiradiation protocols in place. I had 'em hosed off up here, and they're scrubbing down again belowdecks just to make sure. As for the sub guy, he was sloshing around out in the open ocean for better than half an hour. That's about as good a decontamination as you can get."

"Can we talk to him?" Christine Rendino asked, her voice flat.

"You can try. I've checked him out with a Geiger counter and I can't find any active gamma sources on him, only alpha and beta secondary radiation from his internal tissues. Just don't get too close and don't stay too long."

"Were you able to do anything for him, Doc?" Amanda asked.

"Well, I started him on plasma and whole blood. That'll slow things down a little as his red cell count falls and his circulatory system disintegrates. I also gave him a max load of morphine. That might take the edge off the pain for a while."

"Is there anything more they can do for him on the *Enterprise?*"

"Yeah. Give him a bigger dose of morphine."

Dr. Golden went forward to work with those he might actually be able to help.

Christine Rendino and Ken Hiro hunkered down on the deck a yard or so back from the stretcher, the Intelligence Officer readying a small tape recorder. Amanda and Arkady stepped back to the rail, instinctively drawing closer together. Beyond looking on, they would have no role to play in this.

"How do you want to work this, Lieutenant?" Hiro inquired grimly.

"Let's start with the basics," Christine replied, switching on the recorder. "Tell him that he's been rescued. Tell him where he is, and tell him that we'll do everything we can to help him. Then ask him for his name and rank."

"Right." Hiro began to speak in Mandarin. Spacing his words and carefully minding his pronunciation, he tried to reach the consciousness of the dying man. By millimeters, the Red seaman turned his face toward his interrogators, his swollen eyes opening a fraction.

The skin of his steam-scalded face had lifted in a pattern of bursting blisters. However, the real damage was deeper, in the spreading dark network of subcutaneous bleeding. His capillaries were collapsing from radiation damage. His cellular structure had been shattered by the high-velocity storm of heavy atomic particles that had torn through them.

The submariner knew that his life was ending, and although he was in the presence of his enemies, the *Cunningham's* officers sensed that he was glad not to be alone.

"Ask for his name again, sir," Christine prompted with quiet urgency. "Tell him we want to notify his family."

Hiro repeated his query. This time, there was an answer—a whisper barely audible over the backdrop of ship's sounds. The Duke's exec frowned and rocked back on his heels.

"What did he say, Commander?"

"He says that his family already knows that he is dead."

☆ Task Force 7.1

41 Miles East of Miyako Shima Island

1404 Hours Zone Time; August 19, 2006

In the Flag Plot of the USS *Enterprise*, Commander Nolan Walker looked up jubilantly from the communications copy he held.

"Definite confirmation of the kill from the *Cunningham*, sir. A Han-class attack boat. Wreckage and a survivor recovered. No doubt about it!"

The only response was a noncommittal grunt from Admiral Tallman.

"Is there a problem, sir?"

"No, not a problem, Commander. But let's not get too cocky about it, either."

"One boat down barely twenty-four hours after we start the hunt seems pretty good to me, sir."

"Oh, it was. That bunch out on the Duke did good work. The thing is, though, we just hooked one of the trash fish. The keeper is still out there. We've got to get him in the net before we can do any bragging down at the bar."

Tallman turned back to the strategic display on the main chart table. "Notify Seventh Fleet that we have a solid kill. Then let's figure out what we're going to do next."

☆ 65 Miles West of Kume Shima Island
1921 Hours Zone Time; August 19, 2006

The Captain of the Nationalist frigate was the last man aboard the final medevac helo out to the *Enterprise.* The injuries he had suffered during the sinking had been minor. They would heal within a few days. However, the hole blown in his soul and spirit would linger for a far longer time. This morning, Amanda might have guessed that the Chinese officer was close to her own age. Tonight, he looked like an old man.

"I thank you again, Captain Garrett," he said in carefully precise English, "for the rescue of my crew and for the kindness you have shown us. Also, for avenging the loss of my ship."

"I'm just glad we were there, Captain Kuo," Amanda replied, shaking his hand gently. "I hope we can meet again someday, when times are better."

"Perhaps. When times are better." He drew himself up in the borrowed khakis he wore and gave Amanda a parade-ground sharp salute. Then he turned and started for the waiting Oceanhawk. A few minutes later, the helo was off the deck and climbing into the evening sky.

Amanda followed the aircraft with her eyes for a few moments, then headed inboard.

The battle tensions had dissipated in the Combat Information Center. The watch had changed and the new duty crew had settled in at their stations. Dix Beltrain was still on hand, though, shifting his attention between the chart table, the Alpha screen, and a sandwich snatched from a sack of battle rations.

"What's the dope, Mr. Beltrain?"

Dix took a second to force a swallow and to stuff the sandwich back into its bag. "Currently steering two nine oh, Captain. Making turns for eight knots. Helm control is on the bridge. We are continuing to work a quartering search within the initial search zone. No contacts or possibles noted, or on the board."

"Let's see the tactical."

She joined him at the chart table and looked on as the younger officer's fingertips brushed over the computer graphics on the horizontal screen.

"Seventh is working on the assumption that the sub we killed was covering the boomer, and that it and the other escort are somewhere in this immediate neighborhood. The *Enterprise* group has crossed over to the west of the Ryukyu island chain below us. They've established an ASW line and are sweeping slowly north. Range is about thirty-five miles now."

"Who are these guys up north?"

"A Japanese SDF force built around the helicopter cruiser *Shirain*. They've crossed over the island line as well and are working down towards us along the Ryukyu trench. We've got about a fifty-mile separation with them."

Beltrain traced a curve across the screen. "Out here to the east, all the deepwater channels through the Ryukyus are being covered by attack subs. The *Takashio* . . . the *Asheville* . . . and the *Jefferson City*. The shallow channels are being covered by Orion sweeps. The Reds are stuck in a bucket and we're right in there with 'em."

"What kind of direct support do we have?"

"The big E has two Vikings working the area and we've got two of their SH-60s using us as a control node."

"Any nibbles anywhere?"

"Quiet as a graveyard."

Amanda nodded. "Okay, Dix. What do you think the bad guys are up to?"

"They're down to two options, ma'am. One, they've gone deep and are sitting powered down on a thermocline, hoping that we'll just run over the top of them and go away. Two, they're retreating towards the Chinese coast."

Amanda was tired. The postconflict letdown was under way and she was beginning to feel it. Automatically, she took an extra couple of seconds in her decision making to compensate, carefully turning the problem over in her mind, seeking any overlooked facet.

"If they're lying doggo," she said finally, "we'll let the guys with the towed arrays go after them. We're going to work on the assumption that they're running west."

Amanda gauged distances on the screen hex grid. "Let's say they've been moving out at their best good quiet speed ever since the engagement. Six knots?"

"Let's make it eight, ma'am."

"Okay, eight. That would put them out here about sixty miles to the west of us. How are we looking on fuel?"

Beltrain reached up to an overhead repeater and tapped in a data access. "Sixty-four percent remaining on bunkerage."

"Good enough. We'll steer two seven zero at thirty knots until twenty-four hundred hours. Then we'll come about, reduce speed, and start sweeping back. With any luck, we'll sprint right past these guys and turn this bucket into a box."

"Sounds real good to me, Captain."

"Okay. Contact the hunt boss aboard the *Enterprise*. Advise him of our intentions and see if it meets his approval. If so, then advise the bridge and execute."

"What about our helos, Captain? What do you want to do with them?"

Amanda hesitated for another moment. "Keep them on the deck. As long as the carrier's helicopters are covering us, we'll give our people a rest. Hold one of the Retainers on five-minute alert and the other on fifteen.

"Oh, and one other thing, Dix. Once all of this gets set up, turn things over to the duty officer. I want you to get some sleep and a real meal. I can't have my best tactical officer burning out on me."

"Okay, Mom . . . I mean ma'am."

Beltrain's grin saved him from a backlash.

Amanda joined in the joke with a weary smile of her own. "Just you see to it, young man."

She left the CIC again, heading for the 'tween-deck ladders in the passageway aft.

That space was deserted for the moment, filled only with the perennial rumble of air through the ductwork and a wisp of burnt kerosene leaking upward from the power rooms.

It was safe here to briefly let herself stand down. Sinking onto one of the ladder treads, Amanda closed her eyes.

Throughout that afternoon, she had maintained her own personal "Condition Zebra," keeping her emotions carefully compartmentalized and away from her decision-making processes. Now those compartment doors were opening, allowing a backwash of terror, despair, and panic to flow into her consciousness.

They were all secondhand by now: ghost emotions, the lingering record of battle being replayed in her mind. It would pass eventually, leaving just another layer of scar tissue on her warrior's psyche. But for now, there was the sudden reknotting of her stomach, the sheen of cold sweat, and the sensation of treading on the edge of an abyss.

Amanda gritted her teeth and hugged herself against her internal chill, striving to ride through it. She had not managed completely before she heard voices and the clatter of footsteps coming from below.

Swiftly, she got to her feet and scrambled up one level to officers' country. A long-standing sophistry within the armed forces was that commanders were not allowed to exhibit human vulnerability in front of those they led.

There were exceptions, though.

Without conscious decision, Amanda found that she was moving down the passageway toward Vince Arkady's cabin, cursing herself for the weakness and the luxury of what she was about to do.

"Come in." The response came swiftly to her knock.

Arkady was stretched out on his bunk, and now, as she entered, he rolled to his feet in the balanced and coordinated flow of movement that she had come to recognize as part of him.

"What's up?" he asked, alert and concerned. Her coming here was not a usual thing.

Amanda went to him, slipping her arms around his waist. She rested her head on his flight-suited shoulder, listening to the strong beat of his heart as an affirmation of life.

"I almost lost her today, Arkady," she whispered. "I almost lost her today."

"But you didn't." His embrace closed around her, locking out the rest of the world.

Out in the passageway, another figure silently approached the door to Arkady's cabin. As alert and as wary as a snow fox, she paused and listened for a moment, and then moved on.

☆ East China Sea

0600 Hours Zone Time; August 20, 2006

"Captain, we're ready for you on the fantail."

"Very well. I'm on my way."

Amanda returned the interphone to its cradle. Rising from behind her desk, she donned a dark uniform Windcheater and the overseas cap that she scarcely ever wore. She glanced back one final time at the Bible that lay on her desktop, then stepped out into the passageway.

The fiery multicolors of dawn had faded into the vibrant blue of a tropic morning sky. It was blue that matched the sea, a sea unmarked except for the pale etching of the *Cunningham*'s wake as it curved away toward the horizon.

There were twelve others waiting for her aft: Arkady, Christine, Dr. Golden, Chief Hospital Corpsman Bonnie Robinson, and Chief Thomson. There were also the seven enlisted hands of the firing detail, each cradling an M-16 rifle.

Finally, there was the trestle right aft at the stern rail, and the form wrapped in white canvas and the bloodred flag of Communist China. This latter wasn't standard issue in the flag locker of a U.S. Navy man-of-war, but they had improvised.

A strip of yellow plastic radiation-warning ribbon had been looped out on stands around the body of the Chinese submariner, separating the burial party from him in death as culture and ideology had in life.

As she approached, Commander Thomson gave the brim of his cap a short tug. "Good morning, ma'am."

"Are we ready, Chief?"

"Yes, ma'am."

"Carry on."

Thomson nodded and barked out his next command. "Attention on deck!"

There was a brief shifting and scuffling of shoes on RAM tile as all hands hit a brace. Her crewpeople were facing full forward, but still, Amanda could feel their eyes on her. This was a time to think about mortality, their own and others, and a time to seek for answers. Never more than now was she "captain under God."

"We do not know this man," she began after a moment. "We do not know his beliefs, his hopes, or even his name. We do know that he was a mariner, as are we all, that he did his duty to his homeland, as have we all, and that he hoped someday to return to those who loved him, as do we all.

"Though we may stand at war with his nation, our conflicts with this man are past. We are at peace, and we wish him well on his last and greatest voyage. . . . Stop engines!"

"Stop engines!" Chief Thomson echoed her words into his command phone.

The steady pulsebeat of the *Cunningham's* engines stilled. "Salute!"

Hands flicked up with precision, fingers locked. The firing detail turned outboard, rifles coming up to their shoulders, slender barrels angling toward the sky. A rippling crack repeated three times, expended shell casings tinkling down to the deck.

Not requiring a command, Chief Thomson and Vince Arkady broke attention and stepped forward. Ducking under the ribbon line, they took up a position at the head of the trestle and up-angled the plank.

The body slipped back over the rail and down into the sea with that sizzling zip that is so unlike any other sound in the world.

"At ease. Carry on."

The burial detail broke up, and Amanda was just starting to turn back for the deckhouse when the 1-MC speakers rang across the deck. "Captain, please contact the CIC."

Wordlessly, Chief Thomson removed his headset and passed it to her.

"Captain here. What's up?"

"This is Dix Beltrain, Captain. I just thought you might want to know. We just got the word from the hunt boss on the *Enterprise*. We just killed another one."

☆ 35 Miles West Southwest of Yaku Shima Island Northern Ryukyu Island Group 0427 Hours Zone Time; August 19, 2006

Captain Hikaru Ichijo was out of his cabin bunk and heading for the control room even before the intercom could summon him. His ears had popped as the main induction valve had slammed shut, awakening him. Now the diesels had grumbled down into silence and the decks of his ship, the Japanese Self-Defense Forces submarine *Harado,* were angling steeply as she broke off her snorkeling run and dove for the wet dark.

"Report, First Officer," he snapped, ducking through the hatchway.

His executive officer, Lieutenant Hayao Kakizaki, looked forward from his position at the periscope standard. "Passive sonar contact, Captain-*san.* Submarine target, bearing zero five zero degrees off the starboard bow. Estimated range twenty-five thousand meters. Plot has been initiated."

"Status of the boat?"

"Upon verification of the contact, I ordered the battery charge secured and reverted to electric propulsion. Snorkel and communications masts have been retracted and, as per your posted orders, we have commenced an immediate descent to one hundred meters." Rather breathlessly, the junior officer completed his report.

Ichijo gave an approving nod. "Very good, Hayao. Now get her leveled out and let's see who we have out there."

This was what the *Harado* was here for. She was one of half a dozen SDF submarines strung out in a picket line along the Ryukyus, seeking to contain any breakout attempt by the Chinese into the North Pacific. It appeared now as if the deployment had been a wise precaution.

The submarine commander took a step and a half across the cramped confines of the control room to the main chart tank. Lifting a command headset from the rack around its perimeter, he settled the phones over his ears and then looked down into the three-dimensional holographic projection beneath the tank's glass surface.

Off to the east of the SDF sub, sketched in luminous blue hasure lines, was the Aichi Shima seamount. A stillborn island of the Ryukyu chain, it was a great steep-sided ridge of basalt, reaching upward from the ocean floor two thousand feet below to within two hundred of the surface. Off to the west was the green track of a fishing trawler going about its lawful occasions. Almost due south was the plot of the bogey, a glowing yellow dot-V trailing a course line and flanked by a Kanji data blurb: "Course, 010 degrees true. Speed, 12 knots. Depth, 80 meters.

As Ichijo watched, the plot changed from warning yellow to hostile red.

"Sonar Control, this is the Captain. Do you have an identification on the plotted target?"

"Affirmative, Captain-*san*. Blade count and plant noise indicates a single-screw vessel using nuclear propulsion. Matchup with audio signatures library indicates a high probability that the target is a PRC Han-class attack submarine."

"We've got him, Hayao. Sound general quarters, silent mode."

A soft, but urgent, electronic tone sounded within the confines of the Yuushio-class submarine and the overhead lights pulsed in synchronization, sending her crew hurrying to their stations.

"Torpedo room. Tube status?"

"Standard load-out in all tubes, Captain-*san*. GRX-3 dual-role torpedoes in one, two, and three. A decoy pod in number four."

"Very good. Power room."

"*Hai!*"

"What is our battery state?"

"We have not completed recharge. Seventy-three percent available on all banks."

"It will have to do."

First Officer Kakizaki joined him at the chart tank.

"The ship is closed up at general quarters, Captain-*san,* and we are leveled off at one hundred meters. We are steering one eight zero. Speed six knots."

Ichijo nodded and continued to stare down into the display like a monk meditating at a pond. The Chinese Han and his own slower-moving vessel were running on almost diametrically opposed courses that should shortly have them passing abeam of each other at a fairly close range.

Given the Han's rate of speed, its passive sonar had probably failed to detect the *Harado,* even though she had been snorkeling on her diesels. With this tactical situation, it would be a fairly simple thing to drop into the Han's baffles, the kill slot directly behind the Chinese sub. However, Captain Ichijo had larger game in mind.

"Sonar control, is there any indication of a second target?"

"Negative, Captain-*san*. Only the initial contact . . . Wait a moment. . . . Blade count and plant noise levels are dropping. . . . The target is slowing, sir."

Ichijo nodded to himself. The Han was conducting a classic "sprint and drift," entering the area at high speed and then decelerating to listen for potential threats.

Too late, my friend. Now that *Harado* had switched over to battery power, she was as silent as a shadow on the sea floor.

"Hayao, I'll wager you that this fellow is clearing the way for that missile submarine."

The younger officer nodded his agreement. "That would seem logical to me, sir." He tapped the southern edge of the display screen. "He's probably loitering around out here somewhere, waiting for the attack boat to sterilize this sector. Then he'll spring in."

"Precisely. And if we will hold this course and speed, he'll probably come right to us."

Ichijo's grandfather had been at Nagasaki and had died a long, lingering death as a result. The Japanese sub commander found the prospect of killing a boatload of nuclear weapons most satisfying.

"Should we launch a communications buoy with a sighting report?" Kakizaki asked.

Ichijo frowned. It was a reasonable notion, but a buoy launch could produce enough transitory sound to give away their presence.

"Not yet, but program a buoy and have it standing by in the launch tube."

"At once, Captain-*san*."

The two undersea craft ghosted by each other at a meager mile-and-a-half range, the only difference in their passage being that the Han's older-gen machinery produced just barely enough noise to be tracked by the

Harado's sensors. The Japanese boat was now fully rigged for silent running. When it was necessary to speak, her crewmen whispered. When speaking was not necessary, they kept silent. All nonvital systems had been secured, and even the air-conditioning plant had been powered down to bare-minimum life support.

The sub's internal temperature began to climb rapidly as the waste heat radiating from bodies and equipment was trapped within the well-insulated hull. Shutting down the blowers also deprived the crew of that sensation of free air movement, so critical in maintaining the illusion of open space. The lurking specter of claustrophobia that haunts every submarine began to make its presence known.

"Sonar control. Any indication of a new contact?"

"Negative, Captain-*san.*"

Ichijo and Kakizaki met each other's eyes in a silent officer's conference. "The missile boat could be waiting for an all-clear signal from the Han," the First Officer suggested finally.

"At the ranges we're dealing with, that would mean going active with their main sonar. I doubt they'd want to attract that much attention. I'd say they were working some kind of staged relay system. They're taking their time about things, though."

"Our last bathythermograph drop indicates a mild thermocline at about one hundred and twenty-five meters. Maybe he's gone deep and is ducting underneath us?"

"Possibly. Let's find out. Take us down another fifty meters."

Minutes crawled by, accumulating into a fair portion of an hour. As Captain Ichijo looked on with growing tension and concern, his once sound tactical situation began to come apart. Even given the creeping speed of the two boats, the range between them was growing.

The angle-off was increasing as well and soon the Han would be slipping out of the arc of *Harado's* lateral arrays and disappearing into her own baffles. The Chinese attack sub was also drawing closer to the potential shelter of the Aichi Shima seamount, and still there was no sign of the missile boat.

"Sonar, do you have anything yet?"

"Still no contact in all forward arcs."

Damn all certain setups and all fools who believed in them.

"We can't wait any longer. Hayao, reverse course, hard about one hundred eighty degrees. All engines ahead two-thirds."

"We're going after the Han?"

"It's either that or lose him. Weapons Officer, flood all tubes and stand by to open outer doors. This will be a firing sequence."

"*Hai!*"

The deck tilted beneath their feet as the *Harado* swung around to pursue her enemy.

"Open outer doors and set wire guidance for units one and two. Match sonar bearings on the target and give me a firing solution."

"Speed setting, Captain-*san.*"

"Set for high speed. I want a fast kill on this."

"Control room, this is sonar. Changes in blade count and plant noise. The target is increasing speed."

"*Weapons Officer, where's that firing solution!*"

"Control room. Target is going to full power. We are now getting prop warble. The target is turning!"

"He knows we're here," Kakizaki whispered in disbelief. "Somehow the bastard knows we're here!"

"We have a firing solution," the weapons officer announced from his station. "Outer doors open. All units ready to fire."

Too late. Ichijo stared bleakly down into the chart tank. He'd waited too long. He'd let the Chinese attack boat get too close to Aichi Shima Island. Now it was turning eastward, directly into the craggy seamount. Even running at their seventy-knot sprint speed, their torpedoes could not cross the ten-mile gap between the two submarines before the Han pulled up and over the narrow ridge like a hedge-hopping airplane.

With a solid wall of rock between it and the *Harado's* sensors, the Communist vessel could either continue its dash away to safety or it could reverse back over the seamount at the point of its own choosing.

Ichijo knew that in a sneak-and-stealth duel, his diesel electric boat could more than hold its own. But in an open-water dogfight, using active sonar, the speed and maneuverability bestowed by the Han's nuclear-fired turbines would give it the decisive edge.

"Hayao, launch the communications buoy. At least we can get off a sighting report."

"At once, Captain-*san*," Kakizaki replied quietly.

Within the tank, the Han's trace was closing with the Aichi Shima Island's outline, holding its course and depth and accelerating past twenty knots. Beyond his self-incriminating bitterness, Ichijo felt a sudden puzzlement.

"Sonar control, has the target gone active?"

"Negative, sir. Still passive. The target is not pinging."

The Chinese skipper was riding on nerves of steel to run in on a seamount like that. The Reds used a reverse-engineered copy of a French inertial-guidance system that did not have an extremely accurate baseline. Without active sonar, he must have been steering blind.

"How is that bastard navigating?" Kakizaki exclaimed, turning from the communications panel.

"I have no idea, Hayao," Ichijo replied, watching the Han's plot start to merge with the seamount's outline.

"He's going to have to execute an emergency blow to clear that ridge."

"If he is going to clear it."

Ichijo again keyed his headset. "Sonar control. Put your audio input over the control-room speakers."

The control room filled with filtered sound, the thudding rush of a fast-turning propeller. All hands lifted their faces in reflex to listen. The sound continued steadily for a few moments more and then terminated with the deep-toned slamming boom of steel meeting stone.

The sound of the impact drew out, echoing and reverberating into a continuous, bubbling roar of escaping air and buckling metal. The Captain and crew of the *Harado* exchanged bewildered looks as their former enemy began its death slide down the face of the seamount.

☆ East China Sea
0715 Hours Zone Time; August 19, 2006

"That's the shape of it, Captain," Lieutenant Beltrain concluded. "The second Han is history. He saved us the price of a torpedo by busting himself up trying to evade that SDF boat. Two down. One to go."

Amanda nodded slowly. She and her tactical officers were clustered around the chart table in the Combat Information Center, listening as Dix brought them up to speed on the events that had transpired to the north.

"Yeah," Christine Rendino commented. "He must have been trying to break out into the Pacific through the deepwater channel just south of Yaku Shima. He must have figured that we wouldn't be looking quite so hard for him that close to the Japanese home islands. Ballsy move, but it didn't pan out."

Christine looked up and noted the expression on her captain's face.

"You don't look exactly super-pleased about this, Boss Ma'am. Were you looking forward to collecting a matched set?"

"No . . . No. There's just something odd here."

"What's that, Captain?" Arkady asked, his frown coming to match Amanda's.

"Look." Amanda picked up one of the chart table's data wands and touched a point on the graphics display. "Here is where we acquired our Han yesterday afternoon. . . ." She drew a light line across the chart, the numbers of a digital distance hack blurring beside the wand tip as she measured the range. "Here is where the second Han went down. That's a distance of over three hundred miles. The assumption has always been that both Hans and the Xia were operating together as a single unit. A wolf pack with the attack boats covering the boomer.

"Now, if that was the case, could the surviving Han and, presumably, the Xia have crossed this three hundred miles in the sixteen-odd hours between the two sinkings?"

Ken Hiro shrugged. "Three hundred miles? That shouldn't have been a problem for a nuke."

"No, sir," Arkady said. "I see what the skipper is getting at. Crossing that range wouldn't be any problem for a nuke if it was just cruising. But not if he was running at good quiet. He'd have to creep along at dead slow and he'd have had to zigzag to stay under the best thermoclines. He also would have had to swing wide to get around that SDF Task Force that was operating to the north of us. A Han couldn't have crossed between those two points within that time frame and not have escaped detection."

"Exactly." Amanda nodded. "Dix, has the hunt boss indicated any contact with the Xia up near Yaku Shima?"

"Not so far. Search assets are being retasked to increase coverage in the area."

Amanda nodded again. "I'm willing to wager that they're not going to find anything. Since the start of this operation, we've been assuming that the Red subs have been acting together as a unit. Well, that's wrong. They dispersed after clearing Shanghai. They're acting independently."

Amanda lightly bit her lower lip in thought. "I wonder," she said after a moment, "what else we might be wrong about."

☆ East China Sea

1800 Hours Zone Time; August 19, 2006

. . . Ship closed up to war cruising mode. ASW sweep operations continuing. Search zone expanded at 1200. No contacts. No comments.

Garrett, Commanding

☆ East China Sea
1440 Hours Zone Time; August 20, 2006

The wardroom was empty except for Christine Rendino and a discordant blast of noise. There were heavy metallic overtones to it, a creaking and groaning of tortured steel like a protracted avalanche in a wrecking yard. Intermixed was a continuous bubbling roar and a series of irregular thudding explosions like distant artillery fire. Although she couldn't identify the sound mixture immediately, there was something about it that made Amanda shudder. The discordance was issuing from the wardroom stereo system; Chris was sitting cross-legged on the carpeted deck, directly at the focus of the speakers. Totally intent, she gave no notice that she had visitors.

Arkady, who was accompanying Amanda, came up behind the blond Intel. "Heavy-metal revival?" he inquired with a raised voice.

"Close, but no free game," Christine replied. Leaning forward, she switched off the player. "This," she said, tapping the first disc slot, "was made aboard the Duke down in Sonar Alley. It's the death dive of the Han-class attack boat we killed, as recorded off the sonobuoy net."

Amanda nodded to herself. No wonder she had shuddered.

"Now, this," Christine continued, her finger moving across to the player's second disc slot, "is a download from the Fleet Intelligence net. It's a copy of a recording made aboard the Japanese SDF sub that monitored the sinking of the second Han. Pull up a couple of chairs, guys. I'd like you to hear them both."

The first recording ran approximately five minutes, from the final sinking of the sub to the distant crash of the hulk pile-driving into the marl of the sea floor a mile below.

"Okay, here's the sinking of the second Han. You'll pick up some extra background noise here because the wreck is sliding down the face of an undersea cliff. That's not what you're listening for."

Another few minutes of steely clamor.

"Okay, what was the difference?"

Amanda and Arkady exchanged glances. "Okay, sis," Arkady said finally, "I plead abject ignorance. What are we supposed to be hearing?"

"It's what you aren't hearing. Let me play a section of this first disc once again."

She reset the player and again the cacophony issued from the speakers: the creaking and wailing of buckling steel, the bubbling roar, and, again, that ragged series of echoing booms.

"Those detonations," Amanda said suddenly. "There weren't any on the second recording."

"Bingo!"

"What are they?"

"Those are watertight compartments imploding as the sub sinks below crush depth."

Amanda suppressed another shudder and silently cursed the fact that she had an imagination. When she had been attached to the David W. Taylor Naval Research & Development Center she had seen photographs that had been taken inside a depth-killed sub by a mini-ROV. Physics played weird tricks down in the wet dark. Surrounded by cubic miles of water, the trapped crewmen had died in flames.

As the bulkheads had collapsed and the steel-hard walls of hyperpressure water had burst into the compartments, they had produced atmospheric shock waves that in turn had generated a searing heat pulse. In the microsecond before the compartments had fully filled, everything within them had been incinerated.

"I'm sure that someone around here will be very happy to make me feel stupid for saying this, but so what?" Arkady said.

"What it means is that the second Han wasn't maintaining watertight integrity," Amanda replied slowly. "He was running with his watertight doors open."

"Exactly!" Christine gave a sober nod. "He was wide open. When he hit that seamount he flooded completely from bow to stern in seconds."

"I'm not saying it again." Arkady sighed as he got up and started for the coffee urn.

"Well, think about it," Amanda said a little impatiently. "The SDF sub skipper who was trailing the second Han reported that he thought the Chinese boat had veered off toward Aichi Shima seamount in an effort to break contact."

"Wait a minute." Arkady paused with his mug under the urn's spout. "If they were taking evasive action, they would have closed up to general quarters."

"Uh-huh, and if they had been at general quarters they would have had all their watertight doors and hatches closed and secured." Chris tapped the face of the CD player emphatically. "This is another one of those failed assumptions the Captain was talking about the other day. We assumed this sub loss was due to the result of a fumbled combat maneuver. Uh-uh. This was an operational accident. These guys had no idea that they were being shadowed. They were just chuggin' along, fat, dumb, and happy, and they sailed right into the side of that seamount."

"Son of a bitch," Arkady mused. "You're right. That's pretty good detective work, sis."

"Yeah, thanks," Christine replied noncommittally, continuing to stare at the disc player.

"Now, what's wrong?"

"I'm not sure. I mean, accidents do happen. But these guys were supposed to be good! Theoretically, the best the Red navy had left. Yet they pull this kind of total blooper on the most radically important mission their Fleet's ever launched. I'm getting weird vibrations off this one. We're missing something."

Someone else in the room silently agreed. Neither the Intel nor the aviator noticed that Amanda had also started to regard the disc player with an intent and unwavering interest.

☆ East China Sea

1805 Hours Zone Time; August 21, 2006

. . . Successfully completed under-way replenishment from USS *Sacramento*. Have resumed ASW sweep operations. Ship continues in war cruise mode. No contacts. No comments.

Garrett, Commanding

☆ East China Sea

0919 Hours Zone Time; August 22, 2006

"Retainer Zero One. This is Yancy Five Niner Bravo. We've got him boxed! We've got him boxed!"

In the distance, the S-3 Viking pivoted on its wingtip like a hunting hawk and cut across the nose of the Sea Comanche.

Going to hover, Lieutenant Vince Arkady snapped an order to his S.O. "Down dome!"

"Deploying sound head," Gus Grestovitch replied, keying the command into his systems

"Do we have a tactical?"

"Yes, sir. Receiving data from Yancy Five Niner's buoy pattern. They have two passive buoy lines down and they have a contact. Single submerged target, depth two hundred meters. Course 190 degrees true. Estimated speed sixteen knots. Bearing to target zero four five relative."

"Do we have positive target ID?"

"Positive submarine contact. Blade count indicating a single seven-bladed screw. No plant noise registering. The data annex can't provide a class identification. She's real quiet, Lieutenant . . . so quiet I can just barely keep her acquired."

Arkady frowned deeply, the skin of his forehead tugging at the sweatbands of his helmet. "That doesn't sound right. Not for a Chinese boat turning that rate of speed."

He thumbed his transmitter key. "Yancy Five Niner, do you guys have a positive target ID?"

"Negative, Zero One!" an excited voice replied. "It's got to be one of the Red boats, though. We have verified through Hunt Boss that none of our boats are out here. We have bays open and we have fish spinning for drop."

This kid was eager. His crew wanted a kill hack under their cockpit window.

"Yancy Five Niner, uh, stand by. There's something screwy here. This guy seems too quiet. Advise you verify ID before you engage."

"We have ID, Zero One," the Viking's S.O. insisted. "This guy must be running under a thermocline. We have adequate targeting to drop. We are rolling in now!"

"Hey, Gus," Arkady asked quietly, "did you check the bathythermograph before we left the Duke?"

"Yeah. On the last set of readings there were no appreciable thermoclines above three hundred meters."

"Down dome! Full extension! Two hundred and fifty meters!"

"Dome deploying, sir!"

"Yancy Five Niner, this is Retainer Zero One. Advise you wave off until we verify this bogey. There's something wrong here!"

"Retainer, the bogey is approaching the box perimeter. If we don't drop now we could lose our firing solution! We are dropping!"

The sun gleamed off the windscreen of the ASW jet as it circled back to set up its approach.

"Lieutenant," Grestovitch interjected. "We have full extension. Bathythermograph does not record a thermocline. We have no variance in the target's sound level."

"Aw, Jesus! Gus, go active on the sonar! Full power! Attack ranging!"

"Yes, sir!"

"And override Yancy Five Niner's control on the sonobuoy lines! Bring them active too. All of them!"

"Aye, aye!"

In an instant, the submarine sound environment exploded. A dozen different sonar transponders snapped on, lashing half a hundred square sea miles with interlocking waves of ultrasonic energy. The inhabitants of those sea miles, natural and manmade, panicked.

"Retainer Zero One!" the Viking's S.O. roared. "What in the *hell* are you doing?"

"Saving your ass, Yancy. Stand by!"

"Target is accelerating," Gus reported. "Aspect change, target is turning. . . . Target is diving! Audio spike on passive channels. Data annex now identifying target as a Block II Akula attack submarine. Russian Pacific Fleet. I say again, the target is Russian!"

"Son of a bitch," a shaken voice whispered over the radio link.

"Roger that, Yancy. I advise you remember that we aren't the only kids playing on this block."

"Losing target through the thermocline, Lieutenant," Grestovitch reported. "He's really taking off. I think we scared him."

"Not only him, ol' buddy." Arkady closed his eyes for a moment and emptied his lungs in a sigh of relief.

☆ East China Sea

1800 Hours Zone Time; August 22, 2006

. . . ASW sweep operations continue. En route to new patrol sector. Maintaining war cruise mode. As before, no contacts. No comments.

Garrett, Commanding

☆ East China Sea

0049 Hours Zone Time; August 23, 2006

There was so little there, just the faintest widening in one frequency band of the cascade display. And just the faintest, the very faintest of whispers beyond the sea sounds in the audio output coming over the speakers. God! Was it really there at all?

For the thousandth time, Lieutenant Charles Foster wondered if he was making a fool of himself. The *Cunningham* had been working this frustrating almost-contact for the past two hours, and for the past one, Foster had been riding the main console in Sonar Alley himself. Again, he reached out and tapped in the "Target Identification Analysis" command into the sonar array data annex.

★★NO I.D. INSUFFICIENT DATA GATE FOR ANALYSIS★★

"Shit!"

"Easy, Lieutenant. Like they used to say out this way, 'Softly, softly, catchee monkey.'"

Captain Garrett had been standing at his shoulder for the past hour as well, silent for the most part, observing, waiting, disregarding her own loss of rest and time.

"Any change in aspect?" she inquired quietly.

"No, it's still just hanging out there in the surface sound duct. Bearing between oh ninety-five and one hundred degrees true. Can't narrow it down beyond that. There's just not enough to pinpoint."

"Any new thoughts on range?"

"No, he could be somebody running just ahead of us at good quiet, or he could be some distance away hauling ass. There is just no way of telling."

"Well, we've got an Orion quartering out ahead of us now. We'll keep running down this bearing towards the contact until we hear what he has to say."

Foster nodded, his throat suddenly dry. He swallowed twice and forced the words out, speaking to the slim silhouette beside him in the semidarkness of the CIC.

"Captain, I'm sorry, but I think that this is a dead end."

"Oh?"

"Yes, ma'am. The contact has remained consistently in the surface duct. The contact has not appreciably shifted bearing; it's either not moving or moving very slowly. The contact is intermittent and transitory. I haven't been able to pick up a repetitive mechanical pattern off it like a blade count."

The sonarman swallowed again and finished. "I'm really sorry, but I think I've had us chasing a biological, maybe a pack of dolphins or something."

His captain nodded slowly. "I agree, this is probably a biological. It's shown every sign of it for the past half hour. But I'm not absolutely sure yet. Are you?"

"No, not absolutely, ma'am."

"Then let's stay on it until we are sure."

Foster felt a small, strong hand rest on his shoulder for a moment. "We don't have anything better to be doing just now."

☆ Nationalist Primary Line of Resistance Fujian Province, China 1137 Hours Zone Time; August 23, 2006

The Mapats launcher had twelve kill rings painted around its stubby, charred barrel. The counterpoint was that it was the last surviving firing unit of the antitank section. The young Nationalist army officer didn't feel young. He felt as old as the land itself. The land that had claimed the hopes and dreams of his people and that had now claimed three-quarters of his men.

"Activity on the front!" The call was relayed down the line of raw-earth battalion emplacements. Weary soldiers slid back down into foxholes and bunkers, nestling close to rifle stocks. Machine-gun bolts ratcheted back and slammed forward. Breathing grew ragged.

Automatonlike, the survivors of his crew dragged themselves into position on the dug-in launcher vehicle. Sprawling down at the lip of the emplacement, the Nationalist officer lifted his battered binoculars to his eyes once more.

"All positions, fire only on order!" Another relay came down the line. "Only on order! Watch for the yellow!"

Maybe this time it would be different. Maybe today would be the day. There had been gunfire out along the front all morning, but not aimed inward at the beach-head perimeter.

For the past hour, though, all had been silent.

"Lieutenant, I see smoke. Two o'clock," the gunner reported hoarsely from the launcher station.

The officer shifted his glasses. A plume of yellow smoke was rising from beyond a paddy dike, growing rapidly in volume.

A second plume from a second marker grenade, a third.

"Hold your fire!" The command came down the line more emphatically, striving to overcome the instincts ingrained into the battle-battered Nationalist troops over the last grim weeks.

There was movement on the road that snaked in toward the Nationalist position. Men, soldiers as weary-looking as the Nationalists, clad in a patchwork of PLA uniform parts and civilian clothing. An assault rifle or a grenade launcher held at the ready, each had a strip of yellow cloth bound around his forehead, their sole touch of true uniformity.

They did not look like men who were about to make history.

The Nationalist officer watched as the column drew closer. Then he was on his feet, scrambling out of the emplacement and striding down toward the road. He couldn't say why.

At the point of the UDFC column there was a man of the Nationalist officer's age, if such a thing as age could be assessed anymore. The burned-out eyes were the same, though, and the rebel warrior also had lieutenant's bars stitched to the collar of his combat jacket.

"We have been waiting for a long time," the Nationalist heard himself saying.

The UDFC officer nodded gravely. "It was a long journey here."

And then their arms were locked around each other in a man's embrace.

In a growing roar of voices, more Nationalists swarmed out of their emplacements and down to the road to meet with their countrymen-to-be.

There was a third army nearby as well, or the wreckage of one. The PLA had failed in its desperate effort to prevent the linkup between the Nationalists and the United Democratic Forces. Now its remnants stumbled northward, seeking the vague promise of shelter offered by the Wenzhou River line.

The Red Army bled even as it retreated, however. Again and again, the lash of Nationalist airpower fell upon its back. The skies had been emptied of Communist jets, and even the surviving antiaircraft guns were burned out and low on ammunition.

And there was another, subtler kind of hemorrhage going on as well.

Singularly, and in small groups, PLA soldiers slipped away from the retreating columns. Some concealed themselves and waited for the UDF to overtake them, seeking to switch allegiances. Others simply tossed their weapons into the ditch and started the walk home. A few were caught by their officers, or by the Armed People's Police, and executed for desertion.

Not many, however. Most military and police officials simply didn't care anymore.

The Communist Party's propaganda machine hoarsely bellowed about a new "Long March" into the north, where the People's Revolution would rally once more and arise resurgent. Few listened. It is difficult to produce effective propaganda when the people promoting it no longer believe it themselves.

"Harry, have you got the latest?" Lane Ashley's voice issued from the phone's conference speaker.

"About the UDFC breaking through to the Nationalist beach head? Yes, we've got the word here."

Despite his suite's air-conditioning, Harrison Van Lynden's shirt was damp with perspiration. The printing on the situation report he had been trying to study kept turning incomprehensible as he forced his tired brain to stay awake just a little while longer.

"No," the NSA director replied. "I mean what's happening with Hainan Island. It's just coming off the net now."

Van Lynden swore under his breath and tossed the hard copy down on the coffee table in front of him.

"No, I don't have anything on Hainan. What's happened?"

"The Red garrison there has mutinied. The senior officer cadre is either dead, or in custody, and a committee of colonels and captains is running the show now. They've opted for the rebellion. The entire Hainan Military District has gone over to the UDFC."

"Damn, Lane. I wish I could consider that good news."

"I know," Ashley agreed grimly. "The Reds are starting to come apart. Remember how our conflict-simulation projections were estimating that the Communists could hold out for another eight to ten months? Well, that's recently been derated to six to eight. And personally, I think that's generous."

"How long do you think the Reds have?"

"As long as it will take the UDFC and the Nationalists to refit and re-orient for the march north. I don't think that the Communists are going to be able to establish a valid defense."

"Except for the bombs."

Van Lynden looked out of the suite's windows across the velvet darkness of Manila Bay. He smelled the sour scent of his own weariness, and all at once, he felt old.

"Lane, is there anything new on the Reds' ballistic-missile sub? Anything at all?"

"We only know that it's out there, Harry. All ASW and intelligence assets on the Pacific Rim have been committed to the search, but there is just . . . nothing."

Van Lynden rubbed his hand across his face and wished that he had the energy to go to the hotel bar for a drink. "We're organizing a low-profile evacuation of Embassy dependents and other American nationals out of the Philippines. If we start to get heavy fallout here, things could get pretty nasty in a hurry. What would your best guess be on how long we have before the Communists launch?"

"To tell you the truth, Harry, I think that somebody is taking a last deep breath before they reach for the button."

☆ Philippine Sea

Fifty-five Miles Northwest of Daitō Shima Island

2330 Hours Zone Time; August 23, 2006

"There you've got it," Arkady said, tossing the hard copy onto Amanda's desk. "I can maintain our current expenditure rate on sonobuoys for another twenty-four hours, then we're tapped."

"Will that leave us with a reserve to work possible solid contacts?"

"That'll leave us with nothing but empty racks. If you want to keep any kind of decent reserve, I need to radio Zero Two right now and tell them to stop dropping. I can't wait for our next UNREP, Skipper. If I'm going to stay in this ball game, I need reloads right now."

"I don't know where I'm going to get them from," Amanda replied. "Task Force 7.1 and Seventh Fleet are both in about the same shape we are. The Orion squadrons are eating buoys like popcorn. Some reserve stocks are being flown in from stateside, but it's going to be a while before we see any of them."

"Then we're screwed." Arkady tilted his chair back until it thumped against the curved bulkhead. "Once we're reduced to dunking sonars and MAD gear, our ASW air-search capability is going to fall way off."

"Well, couldn't you sort of stretch things out a little—be conservative on your drop patterns, that sort of thing?"

"A net full of holes isn't much use. I'd say let's save what we have left until we have something solid to use 'em on."

"That sounds reasonable. Make it so." From behind the cramped workstation, Amanda lifted her arms over her head and stretched out some of the kinks in her shoulders. "Frankly, I don't think the damn thing's around here anyway."

It was a quiet night aboard the big destroyer, born out of an operation that seemed to be trending toward a dead end. They were alone in Amanda's quarters, having gravitated together earlier in the evening, both to deal with a backlog of problems and for the companionship.

"Where do you think he is, then?"

"If I had any idea at all, we'd be going there. Since I don't, we aren't, and I'm sick of thinking about the subject." She leaned forward over the desktop and cupped her chin in the palm of her hand. "Divert me, Lieutenant," she said.

"Any preferences?"

"Do me a date," she challenged, watching him through half-closed eyes.

"Where away?"

"Mmmm, Everett Fleet Base, about this time of year."

"Okay." The aviator grew thoughtful. Lacing his fingers together behind his head, he stared up at the cabin overhead. "Captain, would you care to have dinner with me this evening?"

"I'd love to. What should I wear?"

"Let's see . . . that green velvet dress, the one that you're always afraid is too short for you, and your gold sandals. Not a lot of jewelry, but maybe a matching velvet ribbon around your throat. Oh, and that dress definitely calls for nylons and a garter belt. Panty hose would be too plebeian."

"Nylons and a garter belt? Is that all I should wear under it?"

Arkady gave her a sideways glance. "Surprise me. At any rate, we'll drive down into Seattle. They've got the best seafood in the world there. I think for tonight . . . the old Edgewater Inn. Not superglamorous, but it's got great attitude. It's also got this great St. Michelle Riesling for a house wine. Then an Alaskan shrimp cocktail, baked salmon with sage dressing and rice pilaf, and maybe a piece of cheesecake, afterwards."

"Yum. Then where?"

"Your choice. There's always a couple of good shows in town?"

"Could we go dancing?"

"Sure, name your poison."

"Slow, and somewhere there would be some good jazz."

"Jazz? Let's see . . ."

Amanda smiled and turned to the portable CD system on the corner of her desk. As Arkady considered, she slipped a mellow jazz instrumental into the player.

"Okay," he said after a moment. "For good jazz in Seattle, our best bet would be to do some club-hopping around Pioneer Square. They've got some neat little hole-in-the-wall clubs down there, if you know where to look."

"That'll be fun, like our first night in Honolulu."

"Yeah, we can dance some and do a little brandy and get mellow."

"Okay. I'd like that. And I think that about twelve-thirty would be right."

"Right for what?"

"For surprising you." Amanda lowered her voice seductively. "I'll be just a little bit tight after my third drink, and while you're holding me close out in a dark corner of the dance floor, I'll whisper in your ear that I've got nothing on under my dress."

"Oh . . . kay." Arkady swallowed a couple of times to get a suddenly dry throat working again. "After that, maybe a little walk to watch the city lights and to get our heads clear. And then, a moonlight drive."

"Where to?"

"I thought maybe up to Deception Pass."

"Isn't that quite a drive?"

"The freeway'll be clear that time of night. We can get out there before you know it. We'll park at the observation point at the head of that big old bridge over the Passage. We can talk and listen to a little music till the sun comes up."

"Sounds good, but you have a painful propensity for bucket seats, Mr. Arkady. Last time we did something like that, I ended up with the outline of a parking-brake lever imprinted on the back of my left thigh."

"So, we'll take a pillow for you to sit on. Don't interrupt, this is getting good. Now, just as it's getting to be dawn, we'll walk out to the middle of the bridge and watch the sun rise while the tide turns through the passage."

"Yes . . ." Amanda said dreamily. "That would work. But remember? No underwear. That could get a little cold."

"Hey, we're having a fantasy here. Flow with it."

"Good point. What's next?"

Arkady reached across the narrow desk and took up her free hand. Lifting it to his lips, he gently kissed her palm. "What's next is a little beach resort a ways farther west towards Oak Harbor. It's quiet and old-fashioned, but the cabins are nice and they have a room service that can do a pretty good breakfast in bed."

The sensual shiver rippling down her spine brought her out of her reverie. "I think it's just about time we broke this off," she said, reclaiming her hand.

"We're just getting to the good stuff."

Amanda smiled wryly. "I know. I'm well aware of your creative imagination, love. I consider it one of your more alluring features. However, I think we've teased the animals about enough for one night."

"Chicken."

"Not likely!" she replied, slipping out from behind her desk. "However, we are both going to be sane and sensible adult human beings. We're going to call it quits before we start gnawing the paint off the bulkheads."

"So be it," Arkady sighed. His chair thumped back onto all four legs. "Can I use your phone for a second? I want to get the word out to CIC and to Zero Two about securing the sonobuoy drops."

"Be my guest. In the meantime, I'm for a shower and some sleep." She paused at the door of her sleeping cabin. "Good night, Arkady, and thank you for a very nice night on the town."

"My pleasure, babe. Sweet dreams."

Amanda didn't bother to switch on the cabin light. The soft blue glow from the night-illumination panels in the overhead provided light enough to undress by. Beyond the door curtain, she could hear her Air Division Leader still on the interphone.

It was a good voice to listen to, intelligent, steady, and strong. Like its owner. As her soft cotton panties slipped down around her ankles, Amanda experienced another of those pleasurable frissons. Just for a moment, she was very tempted to abandon her good intentions.

Get thee behind me, Satan, she told herself firmly. *And you, too, Vincent Arkady.*

She went into the tiny adjoining head and stepped into the shower stall. Flipping the taps open, she nuzzled into the spray of warm water, letting herself laze under the steaming full-force flow.

Amanda rarely took advantage of the Captain's privilege of Hollywood showers and unlimited freshwater. She felt that she should set a good example by sticking to the same three-minute, wet-down-lather-and-rinse mandated by water-use restrictions. There were nights, however, when she was willing to stretch the limits. This was one of them.

After a time, the tensions of the day rinsed off of her along with the water. Amanda's head sank forward, her eyes closing against the dim lighting.

Suddenly, the shower curtain was whipped aside and another unclothed body stepped into the stall with her and covered her mouth with his.

To say that she was startled was an understatement. Then she recognized the hard-muscled body and the special texture of that kiss and it was all right. Her surprise was replaced by a strong surge of desire.

"Damn it, Arkady!" she sputtered. "What do you think you're doing?"

"Personal hygiene." He grinned back at her, standing nose-to-nose, dark hair trailing across his forehead.

"We agreed that we'd keep hands off when we were onboard ship!"

"Yeah, and I think that about now we're ready to agree that was a dumb idea." He began to nibble his way down the curve of her neck to her collarbone.

"Arkady!"

She tried to wriggle past him, but that only made things worse. Their skin grew seal slick and sweet under the water spray, and almost without conscious intent, she began to return his caresses with her fingertips and her tongue. Soon the trembling in Amanda's knees grew to the point that they threatened to buckle beneath her.

"Okay, I give, I give, you big idiot!" she gasped. "Now, let me turn this shower off before everything in here gets soaked. Let's figure out how we're going to do this."

There was a tantalizing air of the illicit about what they were doing. As they toweled off and made their preparations, they found themselves whispering and giggling like a couple of teenagers undressing in a backseat. Arkady double-checked the lock on the door and doused the office lights while Amanda prepared their bed.

Her bunk in its normal form was totally impossible. However, if she flipped its foam mattress out onto the deck of the sleeping cabin and tucked her spare bedding in around it, there might just be enough room.

This was stupid, she thought. This was incredibly stupid and risky and detrimental to good discipline and outside all common sense. But as she lay down with her damp hair spread out beneath her on the pillow and the soft sultry music from her disc player filling the cabin, she also knew that this was something that she needed very badly.

Then Arkady was beside her. There would be no subtlety this night. No jesting or small talk. They had been denied each other too long.

Sometime later, they drifted down from the peak together. Their breathing and heartbeats slowed and the delicious afterglow warmed them. They eased over to rest on their sides, neither of them willing to give up their last and deepest intimacy.

"I'm sorry," she whispered sadly, "but you just can't stay here tonight."

"I know, babe, but I don't have to go quite yet."

"No, not quite yet."

The shrill warbling of the interphone exploded in the cabin like a bomb. With the combination of a strangled curse and a startled yelp, they disentangled from each other. After several seconds of frantic floundering, Amanda managed to get up onto her knees and reach the handset at the head of her bunk.

"Yes?" she snarled with more intensity then she intended.

"Uh, Captain? This is Lieutenant Beltrain down in CIC. We just got the latest sweep updates in from Task Flag. You did want to be informed, didn't you?"

"Oh, sure, Dix. Of course. Go ahead."

"All ASW sweeps in all sectors are still negative. No solid tracks reported, no possibles being worked. All Allied Pacific Rim forces report the same. U.S. and Allied national intelligence assets report no new situational updates. Blank slate, ma'am."

"Any new instructions from Task Flag?"

"Continue current sweep patterns until oh six hundred tomorrow morning. Then stand by to deploy to expanded search zones."

"Very good. Carry on, and keep me posted."

Amanda returned the phone to its cradle with great deliberation.

"I really hope that was important?" Arkady asked.

"Not so you'd notice. Just more of the same. Nothing, nothing, and more nothing. That damn Chinese boomer must have been abducted by aliens."

Amanda dropped back down onto the mattress beside Arkady. Stretching out on her stomach, she snuggled close. They'd stolen as much time as they could from the twin taskmasters of reality and duty. Dix's phone call had shattered their mood like a brick through a plate-glass window. Still, they were satiated for the moment, and the warm darkness was a good place to talk.

"If you were a Chinese sub on the run, where would you go?" she asked,

"Okay," he said, rolling over beside her. "If I were that Red skipper, I would have burned a hole in the water after leaving Shanghai. I'd have run straight east till I was clear of Formosa and then straight south across the

Philippine Sea. I'd trust to blind luck and speed to keep me ahead of the search curve until I reached the coast of New Guinea.

"You've got a good combination of deepwater close inshore through there, which makes for a sloppy sound environment. There'll be plenty of surf and current noise, and maybe some geologic transients."

"Hmm." She nodded, her hair brushing silkily against his shoulder. "Where from there?"

"I'd work east through the Bismarck Archipelago and then out along the curve of the Solomon Islands and the New Hebrides chain. From that point, I could break out into the West Pacific basin. You've got a whole lot of empty sea miles out there to get lost in."

"No," Amanda shook her head, "that doesn't work. Let's say you do make it out into the central Pacific. Chinese naval vessels aren't set up for long-range deployment. It's not part of their doctrine. You'd be running out of food. Your power plant would be breaking down. Your crew would be going stir crazy, and there you'd be, a veritable dagger poised at the throat of Tahiti."

"Okay, babe. Then where do you think he is?"

"You were losing sight of the fact that this guy isn't just out here to hide. His job is to target Taiwan and the rebel zones in southern China. He's limited in his running room by the range of his missiles."

"Which is?"

"For the Ju Lang-2 IRBM, it's about two thousand miles. That would give you a firing arc that would extend from about Vladivostok to the north, to the Marianas to the east, to Singapore to the south. Now, given that some of his potential targets are pretty far inland from the Chinese coast, I'd tighten that up some. Say, Pusan, to Parece Vela, to Saigon. I'll bet he's still inside that arc somewhere, right now."

"The East and South China Seas and the western Philippine Sea," Arkady mused. "I hope that you aren't betting your pretty skin on that, my lady, because you'd lose. We've searched those bodies of water just about every way conceivable, short of pouring them through a strainer one bucketful at a time. He just isn't there."

"He's got to be!" Amanda coopted the lone pillow and tucked it under her chin in a carefully wadded ball. "No other place makes sense."

"Hell, that Chinese submarine would sound like . . . well, like a Chinese submarine. He'd be a sitting duck. If he was anywhere inside that arc you're projecting, we would have heard him by now and we would have killed him, just like we did the two attack boats."

Amanda shook her head again. "We only killed one of the attack boats, Arkady. The other one either committed suicide or died from a terminal overdose of ineptitude. That's all part of this, too, somehow."

Angrily, she rolled over onto her back again. "This scenario is like one of those damn visual pattern puzzles. I get the feeling that if I just look at this a little bit differently, everything will come clear."

"Maybe so, babe. But still that boomer had to have gone somewhere."

"Obviously . . ."

Amanda's voice trailed off, and Arkady felt her muscles tense. Abruptly, she sat up in the darkness.

"No," she whispered. "No, it didn't."

☆ Philippine Sea

0404 Hours Zone Time; August 24, 2006

Retainer Zero One blazed low over the night-darkened waves. It was a repeat of their previous crisis flight to Task Force 7.1, except that this journey had been instigated at Amanda Garrett's insistence. Likewise, this time the Sea Comanche carried a third passenger.

"This would be a lot more fun if one or the other of us were male," Christine Rendino grumped. She was wedged in beside Amanda in the rear cockpit, lacking the room for even a deep breath.

Amanda was in no mood for levity. "Will you be able to spot what we need, Lieutenant?"

The Intel sobered swiftly. "I can't make any guarantees, Boss Ma'am. I have a pretty good idea of what we should be looking for, and I think that Fleet Intelligence should have the assets we need to get the job done. Beyond that, I can't make any promises. You might want to give me a little more time to develop this before you beard the brass in their den."

"We may not have a little time to spare. Arkady, how long to Task Flag?"

"I've got everything wide open but the glove compartment," the aviator replied from the front cockpit. "We should be down on the flattop in another twenty minutes."

"This is damn unusual procedure, Captain," Admiral Tallman said.

Admiral Tallman and his chief of staff had been waiting for them in the briefing room on the carrier flag deck. Vince Arkady accompanied Amanda, standing behind her at parade rest, awaiting her call forward. She would need his input presently. Christine was already involved down in the carrier intelligence section, making serious medicine with her Fleet-level counterparts. Hopefully, she also would be available when the time for her input came.

"I know, sir," Amanda replied. "This is out of the ordinary. However, I believe the situation warrants it. I think I know where the Xia is."

"What?" Commander Walker came half out of his chair. "You've had a contact that you haven't reported?"

Amanda shook her head emphatically. "No, Commander, that's just the problem. We haven't. No one has. For the past six days, we've been scouring the East China Sea with the most sophisticated ASW assets available in the inventory and we haven't produced a single solid contact."

"I wouldn't quite say that, Captain," Tallman interjected. "We've accounted for both of the Hans."

"Yes, sir. We have. We were able to get fixes on both of the Red attack boats in pretty short order. But we haven't been able to even get a sniff of the larger and—theoretically—more vulnerable boomer. The reason for it is simple. It's not out here. It never has been."

"Oh, for Christ sakes!" Walker exploded. "Need we remind you, Captain, that you were the one who originally claimed to have seen the damn thing sortie!"

"Stand easy, Commander!" Tallman's voice was stern. "Go ahead, Captain. Where do you think she is?"

Amanda called up a coastal chart on the horizontal flatscreen built into the surface of the briefing table. "We saw her sortie from Shanghai, all right, but she never headed out into the open ocean."

Her finger came down on a point on the chart. "She's right here, lying on the bottom of the Yangtze estuary."

Walker didn't say a word. Admiral Tallman had reined him in with a single sideways glance. "Let's see your evidence, Captain," he said quietly.

"I don't have anything physical yet, sir, just a chain of logic. However, my intelligence officer is working the problem and should have the proofs shortly."

The Seventh Fleet C.O. nodded again. "Okay, then let's hear your logics."

Amanda paused for a moment to organize her thoughts, then began. "All along, we have been making a critical error in our projection of the Red Chinese intent. We have been assuming that we both think the same way."

"How do you mean, Captain?" Tallman prompted.

"What has been our primary assumption about the Red intent?"

"That they've been trying to break out into the open Pacific."

"Exactly, because that's what one of our subs would try to do. But we're not the Chinese. We're a blue-water navy. When we think operations, we think open ocean. The Chinese don't! They're a brown-water navy. They think coastal. All of their history, doctrine, and orientation trends that way. They would no more think of sending a major fleet unit out into the open ocean than we would of sending a carrier task force up the Mississippi River."

"Those attack boats sure seemed to be trying."

"They were decoys, Admiral. They were sacrificed to draw our attention away from the Shanghai area. The same basic tactic they've been using all along during this operation."

"That's some kind of sacrifice, Commander," Tallman mused. "Those Hans were probably the most powerful units left in the Red fleet."

"They're playing for maximum stakes here, sir. All the chips are on the table. When we interrogated the survivor off the boat we killed, he as much as said that he knew that he was on a suicide mission.

"Then there was the puzzle of what happened to the other Han." Amanda stepped back from the table and paced a couple of steps in her agitation. "We're fairly certain now that its loss off of Yaku Shima was an operational accident. But how could a handpicked submarine crew make the elementary error of running into the side of a seamount? The answer is simple.

"They didn't know it was there! They didn't have a decent set of up-to-date submarine charts for those waters, because they were outside of the Red Chinese Navy's usual zone of operations."

Amanda returned to the table and leaned in over it. "That boomer is the PRC's last roll of the dice. They would not risk it out in open water where we could get at it. It has to still be in Shanghai."

"Where?" Walker demanded. "God knows that our recon has scoured every inch of that area ever since those subs sortied, and we haven't seen a sign of anything that resembles a fleet ballistic-missile boat."

"As I said, it's on the bottom of the Yangtze. The charts indicate that there are several holes deep enough for a Xia to lie submerged in. That's a heavily polluted tidal estuary out there. A sub would be totally invisible."

"But we'd still spot the thermal plume coming off of its reactor."

"If it were on line," Amanda replied levelly. "But he's sitting on the bottom in the shallows. He doesn't need an operational reactor. He can just stick a snorkel up every couple of days to refresh his air and recharge his batteries using his auxiliary diesel."

Tallman frowned. "You're making a large degree of sense, Captain, but I'm going to need some concrete evidence on this."

"You've got it, sir."

A new voice sounded in the briefing center. Christine stood waiting in the doorway. Amanda motioned her forward. "Admiral Tallman, this is my intelligence officer, Lieutenant Rendino. Hopefully, she's been able to find what we need."

"I have, Captain. Once we knew what we were looking for, it wasn't too hard to spot."

Christine looked over at Tallman. "With your permission, sir. Your intels have some imaging ready to pipe up here."

"Carry on, Lieutenant."

"Thank you, sir." Christine claimed the briefing room's control pad from the center of the table. "I think you'll find this interesting."

Tallman gave an acknowledging nod, and Christine began her report.

"I'm sure Captain Garrett has explained our theory about where the Red boomer has been laying low. Now, the mouth of the Yangtze River is a very heavily silted and polluted tidal estuary. Lots of thermal gradients, highly opaque water quality—it's a great place to hide something if you're worried about satellite or aircraft recon. Accordingly, we had to look for peripheral indications of the sub's presence."

Using the control pad, Christine called up an admiralty chart of the Shanghai approaches. "We started with the potential hiding places. Number one is this big deep hole just east of the point where the Huangpu River empties into the main estuary."

Using the integral trackball pointer, Christine indicated the area. "Even at low tide, you've got twenty-two meters of water out there, just about enough to keep a bottomed-out Xia concealed.

"When we checked the event annex for that area, we found something interesting. A little over a month ago, three heavy antiaircraft batteries were resited to cover this stretch of the river. Two here on the mainland near Waigaoqiao and one out here on Zhongyang Sha Island. In addition, a number of light antiair gun and missile mounts were emplaced out on the end of these two long quays here at Waigaoqiao"

Christine looked around the space. "Now, Waigaoqiao is a fishing-village suburb of Shanghai. Supposedly, nothing more impressive than the local trawler fleet ever ties up at those quays. I put it to you that the Reds have deployed a heck of a lot of heavy firepower into that area just to defend their squid supply."

"What else do you have, Chris?" Amanda asked quietly.

"A smoking gun, or at least a reasonable facsimile."

"Let's see it."

Christine began to call up a series of images on the briefing center's bulkhead screens. "Here's how it works. Before we cross-decked over from the Duke, I contacted Fleet Intel here on the Enterprise to see what they might have on Waigaoqiao.

"Come to find out, a high-definition photography file was available. The thing is, until now it had not undergone a full photo analysis. Nobody had ever had a reason to really take a good long look at the area. Once we did, we began to turn up all sorts of interesting stuff."

She directed attention to the first screen. "First, over on the westernmost of the quays, nothing much seems be going on. Business as usual. The only military presence noted were the gun crews and some armed People's Police. However, over on the eastern quay, these guys are all over the place."

The monitor held the overhead image of what appeared to be a pierside security checkpoint. It was manned by a trio of tough-looking PLA troopers clad in steel helmets and camouflage, all carrying slung Type 56 assault rifles.

"We've identified them as being naval infantry," Christine continued. "The Red Chinese Marines, the best they've got."

The Intel moved on to the next screen. "This is a low-angle oblique shot of some of the buildings at the shoreward end of the pier. Circled are what appear to be several military vehicles parked undercover to protect them from direct overhead observation. The vehicles, here and here, seem to be command-and-communications vans of some kind."

"Now things get really interesting."

Her presentation had the undivided attention of everyone in the compartment. The third repeater held a view of the quay deck, cluttered with a scattering of worn fishing gear and busy with the passage of numerous Chinese seamen.

"As you can see, in spite of the increased security, the pier is still being used for fishing operations. No doubt to help maintain cover for what they're really up to. But take a look down here in the corner."

The onlookers' eyes followed Christine's pointing finger. Running down the edge of the pier, partially concealed by the jumbled stacks of sea stores and equipment, were a pair of thickly insulated cables, one half the diameter of the other.

"Those weren't there two months ago. We think one of them is a telecommunications link, while the other is a power line. Both are the kind of heavily armored cable used for underwater work.

"Both of these lines run all the way out to a building at the head of the quay. And from there . . ."

The image shifted to another oblique shot of the pier head. The cables curved down from the deck to disappear beneath the surface of the Yangtze.

"You were wrong about one thing, Captain." Christine chuckled. "They're not even using their diesel. They've just got that sucker plugged into the world's longest extension cord."

"Damnation," Admiral Tallman breathed.

"We've got to be sure," Commander Walker said slowly. "I'll admit it. This looks good. But we have got to be absolutely certain."

"A final piece of evidence, Commander. When your Fleet Intelligence officer started to get interested in this situation, he started yelling to the National Security Agency for more data flow on this area. Given the ultimate mission priority we have, we were granted real-time access to a specialized ferret satellite they had passing over Shanghai. What you are about to see can be classified as RSS. Real secret shit."

Christine changed the screen image again. "This is an electromagnetic emissions scan of the Waigaoqiao quay area. Please don't ask how we can do this from near-Earth orbit. I could tell you, but then, as the saying goes, I'd have to kill you."

It might have been a piece of modern art: clusters of intricate multicolored geometrics on a black background, some of them interconnected by yet more glowing lines. Then again, it more resembled a circuitry diagram, which, in a way, it was.

"What you are seeing here," Christine said, "is the leakage coming off every active electrical circuit within our area of interest. Let's put in the outline of the shore and the quays next, just to give us some point of reference."

She manipulated the screen control pad, calling up the appropriate graphics overlay.

"Next, we do some filtering. We eliminate all the stuff that we know should normally be out there. Boat and car ignition systems, the urban telephone and power lines, that kind of thing. Now, let's see what we have left."

What was left was a single pair of luminescent treads, running down the edge of the quay, dividing, and then extending on beyond the head of the pier into the estuary.

"The passive emission signatures on these cables verify that they are a telecommunications line and a high-tension power line. While the emissions trace is lost out in the deeper water, no cables with these specific signatures emerge from the farside of the river."

The Intel straightened and turned to face her audience. "Fa' sure, those lines have got to be going somewhere."

Amanda picked up the line of the briefing. "Admiral, the Reds know that they can't match us out in open water. They don't have the technology levels. By concealing their boat in the Yangtze estuary, they can not only keep it hidden, but they can keep it protected by the Shanghai city defenses. They also gain the advantage of a direct and secure landline communications link between their boomer and the PLA high command. It only makes sense, sir."

Admiral Tallman looked silently down at the table for a long minute. Everyone in the briefing center maintained their peace as well, giving him right of first speech. Finally, he glanced over at his chief of staff. "Well, what do you think?"

There was a new and growing tone of respect in Commander Walker's voice as he replied. "Captain Garrett makes a very strong case, sir."

"Yeah, I'm sold too. I think we've got the Xia."

Walker continued, "The question is, sir, now that we've got it, what are we going to do about it?"

"We stick to the basics, son. Find it. Fix it. Kill it. Let's assume we've got it found. Now we have to take care of the other two aspects."

Tallman looked back to the *Cunningham*'s officers. "My first thought would be a SEAL team insertion. We follow those cables out to see where they lead. Lieutenant Rendino, just how big is that deep hole you've been looking at?"

"A couple of square miles. And you're looking at strong tides, heavy currents, and zero-range visibility. It's stinkin' water for divers, sir, and that's even before you start looking at the river defenses."

"There's another point to consider as well, Admiral," Amanda added. "If the Reds even suspect that we've found their missile boat, they could order an immediate launch. Any action that we take will have to be fast and certain. We will have to make a clean kill with the first shot. We probably won't get another."

Tallman cocked an eyebrow. "Anybody have any suggestions?"

"I do, sir." Vince Arkady stepped forward to the table. "Covering that patch of water wouldn't be any problem at all for a couple of LAMPS helos. I could take my Sea Comanches in there, locate the boomer with Magnetic Abnormality Detectors, and verify the target with a dunking sonar. After that, we kill it with scatterpack V-ROCs launched from outside of the estuary mine barrier. That whole end of the operation would be a piece of cake."

"And the Reds are just going to let you waltz in there and look the place over?"

"That's the other end of the stick, sir. Chris, what all do they have covering that section of the estuary?"

"Those three heavy AA batteries that I mentioned. They have a triangular field of fire set up with one battery here, to the west of the quays, one to the east, and one across the channel here on the island. Four radar-directed hundred-millimeter mounts per battery. Their radar probably wouldn't give you too much trouble, but they'll probably have optical sights and searchlights.

"In addition, out on each of the pier heads, there's a twin-mount fifty-seven-millimeter pom-pom and an HN-5 tactical antiair missile launcher."

"No way in hell a helo could get past all that," Tallman said flatly.

"That's right, sir," Arkady replied. "Those gun batteries would have to be taken out before we could go in. And that doesn't begin to address stuff like Combat Air Patrols, the coastal defenses, the other antiaircraft batteries deployed around the city, and the gunboats on the river."

"This is building into a major operation, people."

"Yes, sir." Amanda took over the line of the conversation. "In order to successfully carry this mission off, we would have to break down the entire Shanghai defense net. It would require a full Baghdad package, a whole series of coordinated suppression and diversion strikes. We would not only need to disable their defenses, but to confuse them as to what our true intent is until it's too late."

Admiral Tallman steepled his hands on the table and stared at his interlaced fingers as if they were the most important things in the world. He held that posture silently for almost a full minute before speaking again. "Captain Garrett, do you have any idea of the scale of escalation we are talking about here?"

"Yes, sir, I do," Amanda replied quietly. "And I'm very glad that I'm not going to be the one to have to make the final decision on this."

"Me, too, Captain. Do you feel comfortable with staying away from your ship for a little while longer?"

"I have every confidence in my executive officer, sir."

"Very good. I'd like Lieutenant Rendino here to keep on working with my intelligence people for a while. I want a few more proofs on that boomer being there in the estuary.

"As for you and Lieutenant Arkady, I'd like you to talk with my planning staff. You sound like you've done some thinking about this thing. I want to start assembling a formal mission outline. We'll put a situation-and-response package together and kick it on up the line to CINCPAC. Maybe we'll get lucky and they'll tell us all to go to hell."

Tallman glanced over at his chief of staff. "Commander Walker, set it up."

"Aye, aye, sir."

The Admiral returned his gaze to Amanda Garrett. "This operation looks like your baby, Captain. What do we call it?"

"Stormdragon."

Amanda smiled in response to Tallman's raised eyebrow. "I've been reading a lot of Chinese maritime lore," she said. "The Stormdragon is a beast out of classic Chinese mythology. It lives off the coast of China and gives birth to the typhoon. It's considered to be the harbinger of all death and destruction from the sea."

☆ The White House, Washington, D.C.
1921 Hours Zone Time; August 24, 2006

As Sam Hanson entered the Oval Office, he found Benton Childress leaning against one of the window frames, looking out across the White House lawn.

"Hello, Sam," the President said without turning. "I presume you've seen the latest in from the China crisis."

"The Stormdragon mission proposal? Yes, sir, I have." Hanson didn't go to his usual chair; rather, his marine's instincts held him at parade rest beside the presidential desk.

"You're my national security adviser, Sam. Start advising."

"No, sir. I can't. Not on this one."

Now Childress did turn to face Hanson. "What do you mean, Sam?"

"I mean that the mission proposal and operational outline appear very complete and concise to me, Mr. President. I have no concrete additions or observations to make. As for whether or not this mission should be executed . . . I do not feel it as being my place to influence you either way, sir. This is a call solely for the President."

"So it is, Sam. But at least you can sit around and keep me company while I make it. Pull the ramrod out of your spine and take a seat."

Hanson obeyed. Childress returned to the desk and sank into his own chair. A single folder bearing the diagonal red slash of a confidential-materials cover lay centered on the blotter in front of him. He elected to ignore it for a moment.

"Sam, have you ever thought about running for this office?"

"Can't recall as anyone has ever asked me."

Childress smiled and removed his glasses. "Well, if the topic ever comes up, you're going to have one critical decision to make. Whether you are going to be a man damned for doing, or not doing."

Drawing a handkerchief from his suit pocket, the President slowly began to polish the lenses. "You're going to be damned no matter what, but you do get to pick the flavor of the damning."

"I guess that's something."

"But not much," Childress replied, redonning the glasses. "If I choose to do nothing about this Stormdragon affair, I could be leaving the door open for humanity's first nuclear war. Millions of people will die. A large section of the planet will be ravaged. The aftereffects will haunt us for centuries.

"On the other hand, if I authorize this strike, I could precipitate the same chain of events that I'm trying to prevent. Either way, this nation will be held responsible, as will I."

Hanson had no reply for that, and silence dominated the room for a long minute. The President drew a silver pen from a desktop holder and rolled it between his fingers. Then, abruptly, he slammed it down.

"This wasn't in the goddamned job description!" Childress said savagely. "I gave my oath of office to the people of the United States, not to the people of China. They didn't elect me! When did they become my responsibility!"

Sam Hanson settled a little deeper into his chair and met Childress's eye.

"Sir, a little while ago, you wondered if anyone had ever asked me about running for President. If anyone ever did, I'd tell them to go directly to hell. I wouldn't have your job for all the money they could print."

A brief, low chuckle escaped from the President's throat. "Thanks a lot, Sam."

Childress flipped open the cover of the folder. Reclaiming his pen, he signed the strike authorization with a single, swift scrawl of his name.

"Inform the Speaker of the House that I would like an immediate meeting with a senior congressional delegation. Then you may inform the Joint Chiefs that Stormdragon is a go."

"Very good, Mr. President."

"If I'm going to hell, Sam, it's not going to be for sitting on my ass.

☆ The World

0001 Hours Zone Time; August 26, 2006

The word came down—"Initiate Stormdragon"—and the labor began across an arc of time and space that stretched from the shores of Asia to the corridors of the Pentagon.

Meat had to be put on the bare bones of the mission outline. Intelligence had to be collected and collated: satellite, aircraft, seaborne, surface, Elint, Sigint, Imagint, Humint . . .

"Goddamn it! Will you please inquire of those paranoid sons of bitches over at Langley that if the Joint Chiefs of Staff aren't authorized to have access to that data, *who is*?"

Targeting lists had to be assessed, proposed, rejected, and assessed again. . . .

"Okay, gentlemen. We've got six major transformer stations here in the Shanghai regional power grid. Which ones do we have to kill to pull the plug on the entire east side?"

Layer upon layer of strategic, operational, and tactical planning intermeshed into a single, composite whole. Scores of flight paths for cruise missiles and aircraft alike had to be planned, plotted, and timed to the second . . .

"This is no good, Commander. You can't bring that Tomahawk stream in over that high-density residential district. You know the mission parameters. Minimize collateral risk to all civilian areas. Replot it, expedite!"

Weather, fuel loads, weaponry . . .

"Do we go with the laser-guided or do we load the GPUs? Desperate Jesus, Lieutenant! We got to start uploading ordnance in another forty-five minutes!"

Plan the perfect mission. Then plan for the mission that was not so perfect. What would happen if a carrier catapult failed with only half the strike in the air? What would happen if the Communists had a BARCAP up? What would happen if the first plane back crashed and fouled the deck?

What would happen if . . .

Stormdragon's planners struggled mightily to cover every possible eventuality, to cover every possible untoward event that could affect the outcome of the mission.

It was impossible, of course.

In the rush to prepare the strike, a single small, yet critical, planning error was made. Overlooked, it lay like a ticking time bomb within the operation plan, waiting for its moment to ignite disaster.

☆ East China Sea

2141 Hours Zone Time; August 26, 2006

There was only a single occupant in the wardroom. Christine Rendino was stretched out comfortably on the couch; her deck shoes were kicked off and she was reading a thick, garishly covered paperback.

Amanda smiled. Chris would be good company just now.

"How's the book?"

"Pretty good. The Lady Morwena is in just one hell of a mess. Lord Dalton, her dishy but distant fiancé, is off putting down the Jacobite rebellion. She's falling seriously in lust with Ian, the new head groom, and her evil uncle, the Baron FitzHurbert, has convinced the local villagers that she's a werewolf."

"That sounds like quite a yarn," Amanda replied. "I might want to borrow it."

"You're welcome. Just give me another day, or so, on it."

"It'll have to be after the operation, then."

Christine had stopped reading and had come up on one elbow. "Anything new on the op?"

"Not particularly." Amanda dropped down on the couch at Christine's feet. "We're getting updates from Seventh's planning staff, but they seem to be pretty much following our outline. It's out of our hands now."

"At least until the shooting starts."

"There will be that." Amanda kicked off her own shoes and leaned back, closing her eyes.

Christine studied Amanda for a moment, then carefully marked her place in her book with a folded page corner. Tossing the paperback onto the end table at the head of the couch, she returned her attention to her commanding officer and friend.

"Hey, Boss Ma'am, can I ask you a question?"

"Sure."

"How long have you and Arkady been lovers?"

That brought Amanda's eyes open again.

"How long have you known?"

"Well, I didn't know for sure until just now."

"Damn!"

"Oh, take it easy." Christine sat up and swung her feet down onto the deck. "It's not as if I'm going to be taking out ads or anything."

"I know, I know," Amanda said, rubbing her temples. "This was bound to happen sooner or later. Who else knows?"

"I doubt anyone. You make a pretty good bedroom commando, Skipper. I didn't think you had it in you."

"I'm serious, Chris. How obvious have we been?"

"You haven't been obvious at all. Like I said, I don't think anyone else knows. And if it weren't for the fact that I'm an instinctive snoop, I probably wouldn't have noticed anything either."

"How did you figure it out?"

"A lot of little things," Christine replied, sitting back onto the couch. "Like, for one, you aren't a nun."

"What does that mean?" Amanda demanded, settling on the couch arm.

"It means that ever since we got back to Pearl, you haven't been spending time with any of your old and available male acquaintances. And when you have gone out of an evening, you've been butter-won't-melt-in-your-mouth cryptic about it.

"Same thing with our Mr. Arkady. Big rep as a lady's man, and yet, to the public eye, he hasn't been doing any action either."

Christine shrugged her slim shoulders. "Heck, I'll play truth or dare, and even admit that I was tempted to try and toss a line in that particular pool myself. Never even got a nibble, though. For the sake of my own ego, I have to think that he's either gay or he's playing cross-my-heart-and-hope-to-die with somebody pretty special."

"How did you tie us together?"

"Mmmm, that sounds like fun."

"Chris!"

"Synchronicity. You guys were careful to never let yourselves be seen together, but you let yourselves not be seen together as well. First at Norfolk, and then back in Hawaii, the two of you developed a tendency to drop out of sight at the same time. You'll need to watch that."

"But there hasn't been anything aboard ship?"

"Well, just a couple of things. But that's only because I knew what I was looking for. You two tend to gravitate together in quiet little corners now and again. And a couple of times of late I have seen you exchanging glances that damn near make the air crackle. Jeez, I wish I could be a little fly on the bedroom wall when the two of you get back into port."

"Chris. Damn it all! This is serious." Amanda stood up again, trying to pace off her growing agitation. "Do you have any idea how much trouble I can get Arkady and myself in over this?"

"Oh, theoretically, a nice big blot on your copybooks," the blond Intel replied, her chin cupped in the palm of her hand. "Stern warnings to both of you guys from the Powers That Be. Conceivably, even the loss of your ship. And your point?"

"The point is that I shouldn't have let this happen. This affair is my responsibility, mine and Arkady's, but primarily mine. I should have been strong enough to walk away from it. But I didn't want to."

"Oh, good grief." Christine sprawled back on the couch. "Do you guys think that you are the only couple going at it hot and heavy aboard this ship? Do you know why that exercise mat happens to be stored down in the number-four ventilator room? Or what it means when a towel's hung on the outside door handle of the Enlisted Women's Showers? Men plus women equals sex. It happens. Get over it!"

"I can't just 'get over it,' Chris. And I am not just another member of this crew. I'm the captain of this ship."

"And that means that you're supposed be something other than a human being? Well, guess fuckin' what!"

"I know. I know! This job would be a lot easier if I wasn't so damned human." Amanda dropped onto the couch beside her friend. The two women sat in silence for a moment, then Christine sighed and rested her hand on Amanda's.

"Look, can you tell me one time when your relationship with Arkady has affected your judgment, or made you alter a command decision, or made you do anything that could have adversely affected the operation of this ship or the accomplishment of its missions? God's honest now."

Amanda smiled wryly. "Well, I can't actually put my finger on anything specific. But I will say that I've had to do some heavy thinking at times."

"Thinking doesn't count. Now, how many times recently has it been easier for you to keep going because you've had a shoulder to lean your head on?"

"A number."

Christine shrugged. "Hey-ho. There you go. Nature abhors a vacuum, and you've been walking around with a big empty space inside you for a long time. Filling it up doesn't make you any weaker. Just the opposite."

Amanda closed her eyes and let her head sink back. "Maybe not, Chris. I just wish that I knew where this was all taking me."

"You're just going to have to live it out and see."

☆ United States Navy Task Force 7.1
200 Miles East of the Yangtze Approaches
0010 Hours Zone Time; August 28, 2006

"CINCNAVSPECFORCE, arriving." The call over the carrier's loud speakers was nearly lost in the thundering prop wash.

With its engine pods tilted up and its huge propellers serving as lift rotors, the VC-22 Osprey eased in over the landing spot on the *Enterprise's* forward flight deck. Smoothly, it settled onto its undercarriage trucks. By the time Commander Nolan Walker had reached it, the VTOL's tailgate had lowered, allowing the sole passenger to disembark.

"Admiral MacIntyre," Walker yelled over the declining wind roar, "I'm Commander Walker, Admiral Tallman's chief of staff. The Admiral sends his compliments and welcomes you to Task Force 7.1. The Admiral also apologizes for not having you piped aboard properly. However, we are spotting the strike to launch at this time."

"Forget it, Commander," MacIntyre yelled his reply in return, handing the cranial helmet he had worn back to the Osprey's crew chief. Redonning his officer's cap, he continued, "We don't need to worry about protocol just now."

As the Osprey's engines spooled down, the operational clamor of the carrier's deck was beginning to come through: shouted orders, the wind and sea rush of the carrier's passage, the howl of the deck-edge elevators as the strike birds were lifted topside.

With warloads beneath their wings, a row of big F/A-22 Sea Raptors hunkered down along the flattop's deck edge, their plane handlers and aircraft captains paying attendance to them in the dimmed red glow of the work lights. Each was being meticulously positioned to feed into the catapults like bullets into the chamber of a gun.

"The Admiral is waiting for you up in Pri-Fly, sir."

"Very good, Commander. Let's go."

☆　　☆　　☆

"Welcome aboard, Eddie Mac." Tallman gave MacIntyre's hand a quick, solid shake. "Glad you could make it in time for the show."

"Yeah, well, that's one of the advantages of setting up a new command—you get to set your own doctrine. With me, that includes sitting in on any major op involving my people. I hope you don't mind having an observer cluttering up your decks."

MacIntyre was careful to emphasize the word "observer." NAVSPEC-FORCE had a critical role to play within Stormdragon. The *Cunningham* and her people were at the very heart of this operation; however, Seventh Fleet would be providing the guts and the muscle. This was Jake Tallman's show, and there was no time for playing any power game.

Tallman gave an acknowledging nod. "No problem. You want to take a break before we get into it?"

"No. I'm set. Let's go."

Tallman led the way back into Primary Flight Control, the aviation operations center that circled the rear of the *Enterprise*'s island structure. This was the home of the carrier's air boss and his staff, now illuminated only by ranked CRT screens and the starlight filtering in through the big observation windows that overlooked the flight deck.

Those windows were buzzing in their frames as the men entered. An SH-60 Oceanhawk was just lifting off the flight deck. With its running lights flaring, the ASW helicopter payed off to clear the carrier and climbed away to the northwest.

"The clock has started on the operation and we have initiated the Stormdragon timeline," Tallman said. "That was our Combat Search and Rescue helo launching now. She'll top off her tanks aboard the *Cunningham* and be in position off the beach when our air strike goes in over Shanghai."

"Where is the Duke currently?"

"Moving into the Yangtze approaches." Tallman nodded toward a computerized chart table that carried the graphics of the strike zone. "She's scheduled to go full stealth in about an hour, and to open fire in about two."

"Thanks."

MacIntyre stepped across to the chart tank and gazed down at the lone position hack hovering just outside the gaping dragon's jaws of the Yangtze.

"May I send a message out to her, Jake?"

"Sure. Nolan, set him up."

The Chief of Staff spoke quietly to a radio operator seated at one of the communications consoles.

"All right, sir. Go ahead."

"Thank you, Commander."

MacIntyre thought for a moment, recalling a conversation. "From CINCSPECFORCE. To Commander A. L. Garrett, C.O., USS *Cunningham*. Good luck out on the forefront of battle."

☆ USS *Cunningham*, DDG-79

14 Miles East of the Yangtze Estuary

0131 Hours Zone Time; August 28, 2006

"Any situational changes, Dix?" Amanda asked.

"Nope. Of the eight radar arrays we're tasked to take out with our first missile flight, five of them are up and radiating. We've got active bearings on them. We've also got solid GPU fixes on the other three. Two of those, the Silkworm batteries, are mobile, but the last Darkstar pass gave no indication that they were planning to go anywhere."

"Good enough." Amanda nodded. "The Reds are giving us a different reception this time, aren't they."

"I'll tell the world, Captain. You'd think they were worried about company coming."

Amanda and her TACCO studied the active Elint display currently filling the Alpha screen. The Communist garrison of Shanghai had manned their electronic ramparts. No longer concerned with drawing undue attention to the city, they had set its radar defense net fully alight. Multiple, high-powered search beams now swept the sea and sky in all directions, straining to detect the first hint of an inbound attacker.

The *Cunningham's* first task this night would be to blind those searching eyes. Ghosting along just outside of their perimeter of protection, she awaited her moment to strike.

"Any new variables to consider?"

"They've got two guard ships outside of the mine barrier. Looks like a Shanghai-class gunboat and a minesweep. I've already got a couple of flights of Harpoons dialed into the first launch template. Skriiick!" Dix descriptively drew his thumbnail across his throat.

"Okay, good enough." Amanda paused, running over her mental checklists to see if there was anything else left to be said. There wasn't.

"I've decided to hold the con on the bridge for tonight's operation. Commander Hiro will be covering things down here. Remember your mission priorities, Dix. Provide what cover you can for our helos so they can find that boomer, then take the boomer out. I'm putting you guns-free at this time. I'll trust in your judgment to do whatever it takes to get the job done."

Beltrain smiled and gave a quick nod of his head. "Okay, ma'am. We'll take 'em all down."

Amanda nodded with a smile of her own. "That we will, Dix."

She rose from the captain's chair and took a final look around the darkened Combat Information Center. At each workstation, a face was backlit by the cool glow of the monitor screens. Voices were steady. Eyes were level. There might be tension here, concern, quite probably fear. But it was controlled, buried deeply beneath multiple layers of training, self-discipline, and professionalism. This was a United States Navy war crew, and, at times like this, Amanda felt humbled that such people served at her command.

All hands were intent on their duties; none noticed the salute their captain gave them before she departed.

☆   ☆   ☆

The passageways were nearly empty and red-hued by the battle lighting. The Duke had closed up to general quarters and all hands were at stations, waiting out the final minutes to mission commit.

"Captain!"

The voice spun her around. It was Arkady.

Bulky in his flight gear, he carried his helmet under his arm. The scarlet illumination made his skin ruddy and his black hair flame.

"We've completed the hot refuel on the *Enterprise*'s CSAR helos and they've taken departure, ma'am," he said formally. "We're moving out now. I just thought you'd want to know."

There might have been a set of steel bars between them. There was a job on.

"Thank you, Lieutenant. Good hunting. Take care."

"And yourself, Captain."

He turned abruptly, breaking off the meeting of their eyes, and started back to the hangar bay. Amanda headed forward again, clenching her fists to stop the trembling of her hands. This was all part of the world she had chosen for herself. But she also knew, deep down in her heart, that she didn't have many more good-byes like this one left in her.

Reaching the bridge level, she paused at a gear locker and donned her own armor: the foam and Kevlar combat vest and the gray ballistic helmet that bore her rank stenciled on its brow. She twisted her hair up onto the back of her head and settled the helmet over it, containing her mane with the helmet's inner webbing. Stepping forward again through the light curtain, she heard the old, traditional cry.

"Captain's on the bridge!"

Four decks down and a hundred and fifty feet aft, stars glittered over the open pit of the hangar bay. Retainer Zero One was on the elevator platform, ready to be lifted topside.

Zero Two stood poised to follow as rapidly as the helipad could be cleared for her. All conceivable preflight checks had been made. With every system double-tested, the AC hands stood back against the bulkheads, awaiting the order to launch.

☆ ☆ ☆

Someone else waited as well. Christine Rendino leaned in the hatch frame, her arms crossed, an unusually somber expression on her face.

"Hey, sis, seeing me off?" Arkady said.

"Yeah," she replied quietly. "I need to tell you something."

"Like what?"

"Like this. Don't push it! You are going to be going downtown on this job. Right where all the bad boys live. If it looks too hot, or if things start to go strange on you, abort! Don't play Mr. Hero. Don't stretch the envelope. Just tell the Chinese you don't want to play and get your ass out of there."

"Aw, shucks, I didn't know you cared." Arkady grinned back.

Christine looked up, the battle lights flashing in her eyes. "This is a no-shitter, man!" she whispered fiercely. "You are staying alive for another person now! You no longer have the right to do stupid! You hear me?"

Startled by the intensity of her words, the aviator stepped back a pace.

The arch came out of the Intel's spine and a rueful humor came into her voice. "She can't tell you stuff like this, but I can. Okay?"

Arkady suddenly understood what she was saying. "I hear you, sis," he replied with a smile.

They exchanged a silent thumbs-up, putting a seal on their corners of the new pact, then the aviator moved on to his waiting mount.

Gus Grestovitch was already aboard the Sea Comanche, running his preflights. "Good morning, Mr. Grestovitch," Arkady said, lifting himself into the forward cockpit. "All ready for your moonlight tour of the mystic Yangtze."

"None of this is my idea, sir."

"You just lack imagination, son." Arkady's harness buckles clicked as he locked them down. "Let's hear that stores list one more time."

"Fuel cells, flare and chaff dispensers: full, full, and full. SQR/A1 dunking sonar pod on port-wing mount. Magnetic Abnormality Detector on starboard. Internal weapons bays, two Hellfire rounds, and two seven-round Hydra pods."

They would be doubling in brass this night. Not only would the Duke's Sea Comanches be hunting the Chinese boomer but, should a strike aircraft be downed in the Shanghai area, they would be tasked with flying cover for the Combat Search and Rescue mission.

"Check, check, and check. DTU is coming back." The aviator passed the loaded Data Transfer Unit over his shoulder to the S.O. Grestovitch, who in turn socked the cassette into the helicopter's systems access slot, downloading the mission profile into the onboard computer. Telescreens lit off, computer graphics sketching out the environs they would be operating over and the flight path they would follow.

"We're set."

"Roger D."

Arkady caught the eye of the waiting pad boss. "Take us up," he said, gesturing with a quick vertical jerk of his thumb.

The elevator moaned under its burden and Retainer Zero One was borne smoothly to deck level. The lift pad sealed off the red light of the hangar bay, leaving the helo isolated in the night.

"Ready for the engine-start checklist, Lieutenant. . . . Lieutenant? You okay, sir?"

Vince Arkady had been given a few seconds to think during the elevator ride.

"Yeah, Gus. I'm okay. I was just studying all of the different ways life can get complicated on you."

"Do fuckin' tell, sir."

On the bridge, the time hack repeater metered away the passage of seconds. A column of digital clock readouts on the CRT screen, it counted down the scheduled events on the Stormdragon time line. Amanda looked on as the uppermost hack approached zero.

Back aft, the howl of aircraft turbines became intermingled with the growling drone of rotors grabbing for lift. The lead hack zeroed out and disappeared.

"Retainer Zero One taking departure," an emotionless voice reported over the intercom.

Amanda stepped out onto the bridge wing and watched as a thundering shadow swept past the flank of her ship, momentarily hiding the stars as it climbed away into the night. Zero Two followed within five minutes.

"Communication, this is the Captain," Amanda said into the command mike. "Advise Task Flag that our helos are away on schedule and that we are proceeding to the next phase."

Lifting her thumb from the transmit key, she turned to the watch officer. "Come right to two seven zero. Close the range with the Chinese coast."

☆ Task Force 7.1

0120 Hours Zone Time; August 28, 2006

MacIntyre and Tallman had been sipping desultorily at mugs of coffee that neither particularly wanted. Now both admirals looked up sharply at the approach of Tallman's chief of staff.

"The *Cunningham* reports that her helos are in the air and that she is moving into firing position," he reported. "The Strike Boss also reports that the line of battle has been formed. We are two minutes and thirty seconds away from launch. The Strike Boss reports all boards are green. He is standing by for strike commit."

"Any word in the pipeline from D.C.?"

"Negative, sir. We are maintaining open links with both the Joint Chiefs and the National Command Authority at this time. No change in mission authorization. We are still good to go."

Tallman studied his tepid cup of coffee for a moment more before speaking.

"Very well, then. Inform the Strike Boss that he has strike commit."

Tallman set his mug on a console top. "Come on, Eddie Mac, let's go out on deck and have a look at this. It's going to be something to see."

☆   ☆   ☆

The carrier had swung to the east, screening herself with her own heli-copters and freeing her destroyer escorts to form the line of battle. Now, off to starboard, half a dozen big Spruances and Ticonderogas swept through the darkness, nose to tail, clearing their firing arcs for an objective far over the horizon.

At one time, massive gun turrets would have been indexing around; now, silo doors snapped open and launcher tubes elevated with a nasal whine of hydraulics.

Down in the Combat Information Centers, fire-control systems mur-mured cybernetically across the datalinks, apportioning targets, cycling through prelaunch checklists, counting away the seconds.

The count reached zero, and the human-born cry of "Fire" that sounded through the 1-MC circuits was a mere formality. Warning horns blared and boosters ignited. The first cruise missile flight salvoed into the night sky, each round trailing a curtain of golden flame. More flights fol-lowed, the crackling roar of their launch building and reverberating across the sky.

A mist of luminescent exhaust vapor hung low over the water and the warships were backlit in the glare of their own firepower, a shadow squadron sailing across a sun-colored sea.

For almost five full minutes, the launch raged on. It was one of those moments of piercing beauty that sometimes occur during war at sea, and all who saw it would remember. The scattering of hands topside abandoned the pretense of going about their duties to stare at the developing spectacle through narrowed eyes.

Finally, the last missile flight hit the sky. Darkness returned as their jetti-soned booster packs rained down into the sea like glowing embers. The thunder began to fade as their turbojet sustainers carried them away toward the horizon.

On the *Enterprise*'s flight deck, a new wall of sound began to grow. The first attack diamond of F/A-22s were on the carrier's catapults, the magni-fied vacuum cleaner moan of their engines reaching a crescendo as they spooled up to flight power.

Ponderously, the massive warship turned into the wind.

"Admiral, Captain Kitterage is requesting permission to launch aircraft."

"Inform the Captain that he may launch at his discretion."

Down on the steam-streaked deck, Moondog 505's canopy settled onto the cockpit rails, closing out the thunder of the night. "Set?" Digger Graves called over the ejector-seat back.

"Set," Bubbles replied laconically from the rear cockpit.

Following the directions of a wand-wielding greenshirt, 505 waddled into position at the base of number-two catapult. Below the Sea Raptor's nose, one set of flightdeck hands linked the plane's forward landing gear to the cocked catapult shuttle.

Simultaneously, checker hands verified that all ordnance safety pins had been drawn and that the fighter-bomber's wings were locked down. They also watched as Graves cycled his control surfaces: rudders, elevators, ailerons, flaps, spoilers, air brakes. They flashed Digger the thumbs-up. All go. Ready for launch.

Jet-blast deflector plates lifted into position behind the poised aircraft. Digger felt his aircraft come under tension as the catapult charged. He flared his landing lights, signaling his readiness to the cat officer, then put his throttles to mode four.

Diamond-studded flame spewed from the engine exhausts as the afterburners fired; the piercing scream of the turbofans became something beyond mere sound.

Digger took a deep, deliberate breath and settled himself deeper into his ejector seat. A night carrier launch is possibly the single most dangerous routine conducted in aviation. There is one plus to it, however: brevity. If you are going to die, it will probably happen within the first three seconds.

The cat monkey made the theatrical windmilling gesture that signaled to the rest of the deck that a plane was about to hit the sky. Dropping to one knee, he stabbed his fist forward.

The cat officer squeezed the launch trigger. Thirty tons of aircraft, explosives, and human life hurled down a hundred-and-fifty-foot track into the darkness.

The stealth bomber hovered off the end of the angled flight deck, balanced on the knife-edge between flight and not-flight. In the cockpit, Digger Graves performed a quick series of critical actions.

He had to reorient himself using the glowing HUD display, staving off the vertigo of being flung out into absolute blackness. He had to retract the landing gear and tail hook. He had to hold Moondog 505's wings level and he had to keep her nose lifted above the invisible horizon. All within a matter of a few racing heartbeats and all while recovering from the gut slug of a cat launch. To simplify his agenda, Digger didn't bother with breathing.

Somewhere in the middle of that longest second in the world, the Sea Raptor made its transition from projectile to flying machine.

The landing gear thumped into the fighter-bomber's belly and the flaps went flush with the wings as Digger finished cleaning up the aircraft. The blue glare of the afterburner flame disappeared from the rearview mirrors as he throttled back to climb power. That left only the night and the stars and the dim rogue constellation of the *Enterprise*'s deck lights dwindling away astern and below.

Digger banked the Sea Raptor toward the distant coast of China, and two protracted exhalations hissed in the plane intercom. "You know," Bubbles said for possibly the hundredth time, "I really fucking hate that part."

☆ Yangtze Approaches

0130 Hours Zone Time; August 28, 2006

"Bridge, this is the stealth bay."

"Bridge, aye."

"We're approaching radar return limits, Captain. The Reds are going to be picking us up on their screens in another couple of minutes."

"Thank you, Mr. McKelsie. It's not going to matter too much here presently."

Beyond the bridge windscreen, the coast of China showed as a band of total blackness between the obsidian of the sea and the starblaze of the sky. The bow of the *Cunningham* was a shadow dagger aimed dead-on at its heart.

Dix Beltrain's was the next voice to fill her earphones.

"Captain, we have verification from Task Flag that the touch has been executed. All cruise-missile streams are inbound and on course."

"Ordnance status?"

"All missile flights are hot. All launch cell doors are open. All systems are sequencing to fire time on target. T minus forty-one seconds and counting."

"Status on the Retainers?"

"Lieutenant Arkady reports both Retainers are at initial point, ready to move out. We are standing by for launch commit, Captain."

"Fire when ready, Mr. Beltrain."

"Very good, ma'am. All systems enabled. Five . . . four . . . three . . . two . . ."

The *Cunningham*'s deck horns squalled their flat warning. The destroyer's first round lanced into the sky, the bridge crew shielding their eyes from the yellow glare of the booster flame.

The stealth cruise missiles leveled out a meager fifty feet above the wave tops, razor-blade wings and rudderators snapping open from out of their angular fuselages. As the land-attack variant of the weapon, they had the ability to strike at a target over a thousand miles away. Tonight's mission was point-blank range for the SCM, the equivalent of firing a high-powered hunting rifle across a poker table. It did guarantee, however, that the job would get done.

The first warning the Red Chinese had of the attack was when their beach sentries spotted the light flare of the *Cunningham*'s launch on the horizon. Twelve missiles in twice that many seconds. The second warning came a quarter of a minute later as the first of the cruisers whined in over the beach.

The crews of the coastal radar stations had no chance. The inbound stealth weapons registered on the Red radar screens for only seconds before impact. Unlike the HARMs that had taken out the antenna arrays, these weapons went directly for the station control centers, guided in by the impulses of the Global Positioning Satellite System.

Just short of their objectives, the missiles pogoed, climbing steeply, then diving into their targets. The radar sites had all been hardened, either hunkered underground or heavily sandbagged. However, the half-ton, semi-armor piercing warheads of the SCMs struck with the force of Thor's hammer.

Total kill.

Inland, some Red systems operators realized what was happening as the coastal stations began to drop out of the datalink net. Shouting a warning, they fled their operations rooms, throwing themselves flat on the ground or into adjacent air raid trenches. A few survived.

One third of the SCM strike had an objective other than the radar sites. Running nose to tail up the southern channel of the Yangtze estuary, they scanned the left bank with microsecond bursts of laser light, seeking the match for a specific structural template stored in their guidance systems

They found it: the quay at Waigaoqiao that served as the power and communications head for the hidden ballistic-missile sub. One after another, the cruise missiles peeled off, streaking in toward the target.

A string of fiery detonations flashed down the length of the pier, shattering unmanned fishing boats as if they were orange crates. Amid the smoking conflagration, there came the sharper flare of an electric arc. The Communist government's link to its nuclear ace in the hole had just been severed.

Offshore and centered in a bull's-eye of spray, Retainer Zero One held low over the wave crests, her sister helo hovering a few meters away. In the Sea Comanche's cockpit, Arkady counted off the flashes of the warhead detonations.

"Ten . . . eleven . . . twelve. Twelve out and in."

The ECM threat receiver's warning tone went silent as the last radar sweep died.

Slightly to the northwest, a closer series of explosions rippled along the surface of the sea. The *Cunningham's* follow-up strike had just eliminated the guardships lurking outside of the estuary mine barrier.

"Gray Lady, this is Zero One. We have a clear board and the guardships are down. We are departing initial datum point. Zero Two, move out!"

Arkady slammed down his night-vision visor, changing his world from night black and starlight silver to multitones of softly luminescent green. The instrument readouts and navigational displays that had glowed within the HUD now were being projected directly onto the retinas of his eyes, showing the path that he must follow. Tilting his aircraft's rotors forward, he gained way down the invisible corridor that led into the mouth of the Yangtze.

It was critical that the Retainers keep precisely to their preplanned flight path. Very shortly, the airspace around them was going to become occupied by some very uncaring and dangerous neighbors. The *Cunningham's* missile salvo had been only the first shots of the engagement. Even as the Sea Comanches crossed the Shanghai defense perimeter, a second wave of cruise missiles, sixty-plus strong, crested the horizon, howling down upon the city.

It was the twenty-first-century variant of the classic time-on-target barrage: multiple weapons firing to simultaneously strike at the same objective. The missile flight paths radiated outward from their launching point in a fanlike pattern to engulf the Shanghai area, the lead Tomahawk flights bypassing the city, then hooking around to converge on the target area from all angles.

Each round had been meticulously programmed to impact at a specific one-meter-wide point at a specific instant in time. Each strike was carefully calculated to maximize the damage and shock effect to the city's defense infrastructure.

The antiaircraft guns defending the deepwater hiding hole of the Xia boomer died at precise twenty-five-second intervals. The spacing had been selected to ensure that the trailing rounds would not fratricide amid the debris clouds cast up by the initial hits.

Each big 100-millimeter mount was first smashed down into its gunpit by the overpressure wave of a half-ton warhead detonating ten feet above it. Then it was vomited back into the sky by the fiery explosion of its own ready-use ammunition magazine.

☆　　☆　　☆

Downtown, the night-duty operators in the Shanghai civil telephone exchange screamed as a cigar-shaped eighteen-foot projectile crashed through a third-floor window with a dying whine of its turbofan engine. Shedding its wings, the Tomahawk crashed through three switching banks before piling up against the rear wall of the building. The shockproof solid-state timers within the T-LAMs detonator pack patiently ticked off three minutes before firing, giving time enough for the exchange to be evacuated. When they had, the aged brick structure burst like a pricked balloon.

At the PLAAF air-defense installation west of the city, the ready-alert flight of F-7M Airguard fighters stood poised at the end of the base runway, engines idling. They had been scrambled at the beginning of the attack and now awaited final clearance to launch. It wouldn't be coming.

First, there had been a flicker of reflected moonlight over the air-defense control bunker, then the bunker had belched flame from its air vents and doors. A moment later, the control tower had been hit, folding into a spreading pool of fire.

With his air base going to hell around him, the lead pilot went to war power, kicking on his afterburner. Better to try for the sky than to die on the ground. With his flight mates following, he roared down the conflagration-lit tarmac.

Passing through one hundred knots and approaching rotation speed, the Red pilot glanced up. Something was coming in the opposite direction down the runway.

A cruise missile was streaking along the centerline, fifty feet above the deck. Firecracker flashes danced around its nose as bomblets were kicked out of its submunitions dispenser. A wave of minor explosions raced along behind it as the "runway breaker" charges shattered the tarmac.

Frantically, the Red pilot yanked back on the joystick, but his aircraft was still a critical ten miles per hour below flight speed. A landing-gear tire hooked into a smoking crater and the fighter cartwheeled and exploded. One after another, caught in the same trap of speed, time, and distance, the three other Airguards plowed into the holocaust, drawing a curtain of flame and debris down the full length of the runway.

☆   ☆   ☆

Well executed though it might have been, the cruise-missile attack did not go through perfectly. One Tomahawk went cybernetically psychotic, screaming away into the west on a beeline for Mongolia. Another, clipped by a 25-millimeter antiaircraft round, staggered off course to vaporize a tragically overcrowded apartment block. A third, tasked with taking out a torpedo-boat moorage on the Huangpu River, suffered a gyro table failure, burying itself in a Yangtze mud bank.

The forward machine guns of the Five Sixteen boat hosed a wild burst into the sky.

"Cease-fire there!" Lieutenant Zhou Shan yelled over the bridge spray shield. "Save your ammunition!"

The inexperienced bow gunner looked back from his mount, his fearful expression momentarily illuminated by a bomb flash. Shan could not fault him. There was any amount of fear abroad this night. The urge to do something to keep it at bay could become overwhelming.

Shanghai seemed ablaze from a thousand sources. The city antiaircraft batteries, blinded and cut off from central command though they might have been, still raged, spewing streams of pink and green tracers into the sky. Half a dozen major fires could be seen from the boat moorage, and every few seconds the thickening smoke over the city glowed from the flare of a new missile detonation.

"Is there word from Fleet Command yet?" Zhou demanded of his radio operator, half shouting over the rumble of the gunfire.

"No, Comrade Lieutenant," the radioman replied. "Fleet Command has gone off the air. The shore line is dead as well."

Zhou turned to face Bosun Hoong, who was leaning stolidly back against the snub mast at the rear of the cockpit.

"What do you think, Bosun?"

Hoong removed a well-smoked cigarette butt from between his lips and flipped it over the rail. "I think we have the Yankees angry with us. The Nationalists couldn't do all of this."

"I think you are right, Hoong."

Something new echoed from the sky, a deeper rumble that climbed the scale rapidly into a crackling roar as it passed invisibly across the zenith: jet engines, far more powerful than those of the cruise missiles. Equally more powerful were the two massive explosions just upriver within the Hudong shipyards. Flaming wreckage spun through the air, and all hands on the deck of the torpedo boat cowered down as the shock wave cracked over them.

"Do you wish to send a runner to Fleet Command, Lieutenant?" Hoong inquired, unfazed.

Shan hesitated only a moment more before angrily shaking his head. "Fleet Command be damned! We're getting out of here now. Start engines and prepare to cast off all lines. Signal the rest of the squadron to follow us. We'll take our chances out in the river."

"At once, Lieutenant," Hoong replied, sounding faintly pleased.

More bombs racked the shipyard area; the Huangpu River was lit blood-red by the growing fires as the Five Sixteen boat backed into the channel. As Hoong had said, it had to be the Americans, and somehow, in a way that he couldn't explain, Zhou Shan also knew that it had to be the ghost ship as well. It had returned and it was waiting for him out there in the burning night. They had affairs to conclude.

☆ Retainer Zero One

Yangtze Estuary

0140 Hours Zone Time; August 28, 2006

The pair of Sea Comanches flew below a cathedral ceiling of scintillating fire. The shells from the flak emplacements on the northern and southern banks of the great river were converging high overhead.

It was easy to read the caliber of the guns by their tracer patterns. The wavering spark streamers were issuing from the light, ultrarapid-fire ZSU-23s. The deliberate beads-on-a-string issued from the older 37-millimeter single mounts, while the more intermittent twinned rounds came from the more potent 57-millimeter doubles.

The really heavy guns, the 85- and 100-millimeter semiautos, threw no tracers at all. There was just the ground flare of the battery firing, mated to the flash of the shells detonating 25,000 feet above the Earth. Three times, Arkady also saw the inverted meteor trail of a Guideline SAM climbing into the sky.

Fortunately, none of this lethal ironmongery appeared to be coming in the direction of the Retainers. Amanda's strategy was working. No one was noticing the two rotor-winged mice creeping in under the edge of the holocaust.

"Approaching second datum point by GPU fix, Lieutenant."

"Thanks, Gus. I see it. Coming left to two nine zero on the hack."

"We're in the groove. Zero Two is following."

Arkady was careful not to nod a reply. He was "seeing" through the eyes of the Sea Comanche's Forward Looking Infra-Red Scanner. Each movement of his helmeted head was being translated into the swiveling of the camera turret beneath the helicopter's chin. Through those electronically enhanced eyes, the world was delineated in shades of heat. The darker shapes were cooler; the lighter, warmer. Open flame was revealed as a scintillating white.

There were several patches of that blatant white visible within the sweep of the FLIR, but Arkady watched for two that should be burning out over the river.

"Got 'em, Gus. Got the quays in sight. Looks like the cruisers messed 'em up pretty good."

"I ain't gonna cry over it, sir. We are now entering the search area. We are now free-fly."

"Rog." *Click.* "Retainer Zero Two, this is Zero One. We are on station. Initiate MAD search."

"Roger, Zero One. Initiating now."

The trailing Sea Comanche swung out of line angling out toward the center of the river and slowing to search speed. Arkady flared back as well, holding his altitude at fifty feet.

"Extend the stinger, Gus. Hunt's on."

"Doing it, sir. MAD is active."

Any massive body of ferrous metal, be it a deposit of iron ore, the body of an automobile, or the hull of a ship, will create a disturbance in the Earth's electromagnetic field. At close range, it can make the needle of a compass divert away from magnetic north. At greater distances, the effect can be registered on a sensitive device called a Magnetic Abnormality Detector. In the shallow waters of the littoral battlefield MAD systems became the sub hunter's best friend.

The counterpoint was that a MAD search mandated that one fly low, straight, and slow for an extended period of time.

"Can you say 'sitting duck'?" Arkady murmured. "I thought you could."

"You say something, Lieutenant."

"Negative, Gus. Stay on it."

So far, there had been no indication that the helos had been spotted. Arkady wasn't even particularly worried about radar or visual detection. But if they ran out of air strike before they found that submarine, on audio stealth, or not, somebody on the beach was bound to hear them poking around out here. If that happened, things were going to get real interesting real fast.

Off the mine barrier, the flames of the battle registered only as a wavering glow in the sky, the sounds like the rumble of summer thunder. The *Cunningham* circled slowly, awaiting the cue for her next move.

"Captain."

Amanda looked back from her position on the bridge wing. "What is it, Stewart?"

"We've just got word up from CIC," the watch officer replied. "The Retainers are on station and have commenced the search."

"Very good."

The watch officer paused in the hatchway for a moment, looking off to the southwest just as Amanda had been. "You think we can pull this off, Captain?"

"Well, I thought so when I came up with the idea."

She flipped the weather cover off the bridge wing repeater and called up the mission schedule. "We're still on the time line. The cruisers should all be in by now. From here on, it'll be up to the fast movers to keep them busy."

"The woman is driving me crazy, Bub. Feet dry at Waypoint Golf. Going tactical."

"Confirm we are on the tactical grid. Steering two nine zero true. We have acquired target-approach base leg. As far as I'm concerned, Digger, it won't be a drive, it'll be an easy-money putt."

"Thank you, ever so much, Lieutenant Zellerman."

The blackness beneath Moondog 505 subtly changed texture as the Sea Raptor crossed the coastline and headed northwest across a blacked-out Chinese landscape. As had the cruise missiles, the naval strike aircraft were fanning out to englobe their target. At staggered intervals, they would turn in toward Shanghai on a series of "wheel spoke" approach paths, no two aircraft crossing the target on the same bearing.

"I mean it, Dig. You needed to tell that woman where to get off a long time ago."

The two aviators weren't actually paying attention to the personal thread of the conversation. It was an instinctive exercise in mental stabilization, a counter to the tension load that was growing as the range to their objective shrank.

"Yeah, but then that's what I'm afraid she'll do, get off. She's sure drawn a line in the sand now, though. How we lookin' on return limits?"

"Clear sky. No tactically valid search systems active within range. Intermittent target-acquisition traces, but no locks. Shanghai zone defense is down."

"Right. GPU tracking check?"

"Ordnance and aircraft GPUs are coordinated and tracking. Looking good, Dig."

"Okay, we are approaching Waypoint Hotel. Time check?"

"On the line."

"Okay, Bub. Here we go. At Point Hotel in three . . . two . . . one . . . Coming right to zero one zero."

The stars crawled past beyond the canopy as the plane banked away to the north. Gradually, the needle nose of the big fighter bomber came to bear on a series of smoky pools of light on the horizon. The fiery beacon of a burning city.

". . . Mark, zero one zero. We're in the groove."

"I confirm that. We are on attack heading. Range to target thirty-four miles. Digger, either you get out of the Navy, or you flat out tell your wife that you're going to stay, and take whatever happens."

"Yeah." Digger Graves shifted in his parachute harness and settled deeper into Moondog 505's ejector seat.

The flames of Shanghai grew closer.

"Let's not take all night about this, Gus. This guy has got to be out here somewhere."

"So is just about every other piece of shit sunk since the Ming fucking Dynasty. The floor of this goddamn river has got to look like the bottom of a goddamn garbage can!"

"Just find us the piece that's still alive, man."

It was black magic time again in the rear cockpit of Retainer Zero One. Gus Grestovitch totally fixated on the rippling waves of green light that danced across the oscilloscope display. Half a dozen times, he had almost called out a contact. But each time something, some undefinable sense of wrongness, had stayed him. The MAD pod said maybe; his instincts said no.

Instinct, in the end, was what it was all about in this the most totally human of all endeavors. It was an edge man would always maintain over even the most sophisticated of technologies. It was why man would always remain a player, and not just a spectator, in this great game called war.

Another broad jag rolled down the oscilloscope line. Identical in appearance to the half a dozen others that had gone before . . . except for how it felt down in Gus Grestovitch's guts.

"MAD man! MAD man! Solid contact! We have a solid contact!"

"Going to hover!" The Sea Comanche check reined like a good cow pony. "What d'you have, Gus?"

"Major contact, Lieutenant. Lookin' solid. Right underneath us."

"Check it out," Arkady ordered. "We're getting tight on time."

"Aye, aye."

Swiftly, Grestovitch reconfigured the cockpit workstation, sliding the MAD pod readout onto a secondary telescreen and calling up the primary dunking sonar display.

"Dunking sonar is up. Ready to drop dome."

"Roger D. Maintaining hover. Depth by the chart is forty meters. Down dome to thirty."

"Doin' it. The dome is down."

A thin Kevlar coaxial cable began to peel off the internal reel of the lightweight SQR/AI sonar pod slung beneath the helicopter's portside snub wing. Swiftly, the sound head of the system dropped through the rotor-wash-riffled surface of the estuary.

In the rear cockpit of the helo, Grestovitch sat poised with his earphone gains turned up, ready to begin a passive audio search the second the dome reached depth. Accordingly, he nearly jumped out of his skin when a tremendous echoing crash exploded in his ears. Then, beyond the ringing, he could hear everything.

There was the humming throb of a multitude of pumps and motors. There was the clang and clatter of numerous metallic transitories. There was even the unintelligible but unmistakable murmur of human voices.

"Gus, is this guy down there?"

"I'll tell the world, sir! We just dropped our sound head right onto the sucker's deck!"

"Gray Lady, we have located the target!" The radio call electrified the Combat Information Center. "We have positive lock and positive ID!"

"Bridge, this is the Combat Information Center," Ken Hiro began to report. "Retainer Zero One has—"

"We were monitoring it, Ken," Amanda Garrett's filtered voice interrupted. "Commence your engagement sequence."

"Aye, aye, Captain. All stations, secure EMCON. Aegis systems manager, bring up your radars. Mister Beltrain, take him out."

"Yes, sir."

This was Dix's moment, his and Weapons Division. They had drilled through this a score of times as a computer simulation. Now it was time to expend the hardware.

"V-ROC and SLAM controllers, bring up your initial flights. V-ROCs, start your firing sequence."

Beltrain keyed into the air-operations circuit. "Retainer Zero One, Retainer Zero One, Vince, this is Dix on line. We're setting the datum point now. Give us a short count on your IFF."

"Gotcha, Dix. Radar beacon is up for a short count. Three . . . two . . . one . . ."

On the Alpha screen, an active radar display was overlaid on the graphics map of the Yangtze estuary and the surrounding coast. Now, well up the southern estuary channel, a target hack materialized. The Identification-Friend-or-Foe transponder aboard Arkady's Sea Comanche was interreacting with the destroyer's radar sweep.

"We have the datum point!" the Aegis systems manager announced. The Duke had fixed her enemy's position. Now all that was left was the final killing spring.

"Yeah! V-ROC systems, verify we have a full pattern set of V-ROC L's."

"Full pattern set, Mr. Beltrain. Hot birds on the rails!"

"Integrate your datum point. Stand by to fire. Vince, get your ass out of there!"

Twelve miles to the west, over the river, Arkady called back over his shoulder. "You heard the man, Gus. Up dome."

"Dome coming up, sir. This guy sounds like he's powering up to get under way."

"We're not going to let that happen. Retainer Zero Two, do you copy?"

"We copy, Zero One."

"Secure search and disengage to the east. Expedite!"

"Roger."

The Sea Comanche bobbled in hover as the sound head clicked up into its carrying mount in the sonar pod.

"Dome up, Lieutenant."

"Right."

Arkady pedal-turned the helo around the axis of its rotor head and came forward on the pitch and collective, gaining way. Retainer Zero Two blazed past a few moments later, heading for safety outside of the target zone.

"Gray Lady, Gray Lady, the Elvi has left the building. You are clear to engage!"

"V-ROCs, fire!"

Spaced at one-second intervals, four Vertical Launch Anti-Submarine Rockets blazed out of the *Cunningham's* VLS arrays, their boosters flickering balls of orange light arcing away toward their distant objective.

The face of sub hunting had changed radically during the past decades. At one time, the foe had been the great pelagic hunter-killers of the Soviet nuclear submarine force. Now, though, the threat had moved closer inshore.

Third-world states were turning to the modern diesel electric submarine as the fast, cheap road to sea power. Sophisticated and silent, these "mobile minefields" were the stingray to the nuclear submarine's shark.

A new generation of weapons had been needed to deal with this new shallow-water threat. The V-ROC L (Littoral) was one of them.

Instead of the Mark 50 torpedo carried by the standard weapon, the V-ROC L carried a throwback to an earlier age of ASW, a scatterpack of miniature depth bombs similar in design and intent to those of the World War II Hedgehog.

With their boosters burned out, each V ROC came over the peak of their parabolic trajectory. Plunging in toward their target, a laser proximity fuse gauged each round's distance from the surface of the water. At the appropriate instant, the scatterpack's bursting charge fired, dispersing the ten shaped-charge bomblets carried by the warhead bus. Ten bomblets per round, forty bomblets in all, striking the water in an interlocking pattern. A net to trap the biggest fish in the world.

East of the target area, the two Retainers had returned to a hover, reversing again to observe the weapon impact.

Through the night-vision visor, Arkady watched as the wave of impact splashes swept across the target zone.

Then came the long breath-locked moment as the bomblets sank. The submunitions were each magnetically fused to fire only on contact with a submarine hull.

Two slender columns of water jetted up from the disturbed surface of the river.

"Yeah! Gus, down dome and see if we put a hole in this guy. Gray Lady! Gray Lady! We have weapon impact and detonation! Two hits out of the pattern. We are trying to verify the kill."

"Acknowledged, Zero One," Amanda's voice came back. Any triumph she might be feeling was being tightly locked down. "Hold on station. If you've hit him, he's going to try and surface."

Gus Grestovitch cut in abruptly. "Lieutenant, massive transitory on the target bearing! Submarine blowing ballast!"

"Gray Lady! We got him! He's coming up!"

Out in the center of the target zone, a submarine's conning tower broke water. Silt-enslimed from its long concealment on the estuary floor, the Xia lifted its head sluggishly above the surface like some long-entombed dinosaur.

"There she blows! Gray Lady, we have visual confirmation of the target! We've got the boomer! I say again, we have got the boomer!"

On the *Cunningham*'s bridge, the exclamations of victory were more restrained: a fist lightly thumped on the chart table, the whispered release of a contained breath.

Amanda leaned forward in the captain's chair, holding her headset mike close to her lips. "Zero One, current status on the target?"

"On the surface and holding stable. We've hurt him, but we haven't killed him."

"Stand by, Zero One."

They'd put the barbs into their whale and they'd run it down. Now they had to drive the lance into its lungs.

"Tactical Officer."

"TACCO, aye."

"Finish the job, Dix. You know the drill. You can't miss on this one!"

"Final-phase safeties are off. All prelaunch systems are green, sir."

Dix Beltrain leaned in over the Sea SLAM operator's shoulder. "Don't commit the round. Keep the missile under manual control all the way in."

"Yes, sir."

"And remember, forward of the sail! Target only forward of the sail. If you can't drop it in right, abort the round."

"I know, sir," the systems operator replied with as much laconic forbearance as a gunner's mate first could afford with a full lieutenant.

"Okay. Shoot."

Among the arsenal of "smart weaponry" proliferating in the twenty-first century, the Sea SLAM was without doubt one of the most brilliant, because a human mind could guide it to its target.

Hurled out of its launch cell, the modified Harpoon Missile extended its cruciform fins and followed in the trajectory of the V-ROCs. Coming over the peak of the arc, the infrared imager in its nose activated, beaming a supra-eagle's-eye view of the Yangtze River environs back to its mother station aboard the *Cunningham*.

The Sea SLAM operator entered the loop. His fingers curled around a joystick and he sent steering commands back up through the datalink to the missile, guiding it to its target in exactly the same way a hobbyist might fly a radio-controlled model airplane. Only, this "model plane" carried a quarter of a ton of high explosives at the velocity of a .45-caliber bullet.

There was a further complication as well. There was a zero tolerance for failure. The SLAM round would have to be brought in on the forehull of the Chinese submarine, far enough back to smash the missile-control center and sink the boat, yet far enough forward not to directly involve any of the IRBM silos in the Xia's central launching bay.

If one of the boomer's armed Ju Lang II rounds was hit, the worst that could be expected would be a limited-yield nuclear explosion. The best would be that particles of hyper-radioactive plutonium would be sprayed throughout the Yangtze estuary, contaminating the river's mouth for the next fifty thousand years. The fate of one of the great port cities of the world lay in the hands of a twenty-year-old American seaman from Meade, Kansas.

In the crosshairs of the SLAM guidance screen, the target grew from a dark pencil stub afloat in a pale-green creek to a cigar, to a toy, to a looming black hulk all in the space of half a dozen heartbeats. With his joystick, the systems operator rode the nose of his missile down, keeping it fixed on the one exact point he had chosen just beneath the submarine's sail.

The screen flared and went to static.

☆ ☆ ☆

Upriver in the estuary, the Sea SLAM gave no warning of its arrival, its turbojet power plant leaving no flame trail behind it.

The river rose up under the forward end of the Xia's hull, lifting the
boomer's blunt nose into the air. Almost in slow motion, the submarine's
bow cap and conning tower tore away, electrical arcs dancing around the
opening wounds. Then the boomer's main hull settled back, wallowing
sluggishly like a waterlogged tree trunk. A moment more and it was gone,
sinking in its shallow water grave, the eternal Yangtze pouring in through
its breached bulkheads.

"Yes!" Vince Arkady's voice rang out of the bridge speakers. "Good shot!
Boomer is down! All the way, the boomer is down!" Somewhere behind
Amanda, a hand slapped down on the chart table and the sound-activated
intercom links sputtered for a moment as someone down in the CIC
whooped.

Amanda tilted her helmeted head back for a few moments, her eyes
closed in silent gratitude. Coming forward again, she keyed the command
mike. "Acknowledged, Retainers. Boomer is down. Disengage and return
to the ship. I say again, disengage and return to the ship."

"Retainers, wilco."

Amanda toggled across from surface-to-air to intercom. "Radio Shack,
transmit the following to Task Flag . . ."

"Admiral, signal from the *Cunningham*! 'The Stormdragon is dead. Mission
accomplished. ASW assets are withdrawing.'" Subdued cheers and a round
of applause sounded within the *Enterprise*'s Pri-Fly. Admiral Tallman's fist
stabbed the air in a victorious uppercut.

"Congratulations, Jake." MacIntyre slapped the Task Force commander
on the shoulder.

"Yeah, well, we're still doing 'so far, so good,' Eddie Mac. We still got to
count 'em all home."

Tallman turned to his air boss. "Status on the diversion strike, Commander?"

"The last bird should be making its run now, sir."

"Okay, two minutes more and we can start letting our weight down."

☆   ☆   ☆

Bubbles Zellerman stared into her targeting screen like a fortune-teller into a crystal ball. Moondog 505 had been preceded by her eleven squadron mates, all of whom had "plowed the farm" quite effectively.

Their target was the Hudong shipyards, the facility that had resurrected the Xia and its hunter-killer escorts. It was a logical target. A strike here would focus Chinese attention away from what was taking place a few miles north on the Yangtze. It would also ensure that no more nuclear-powered snakes would issue from this particular hole.

Bubbles was imaging the target through the Sea Raptor's FLIR turret. However, she could almost have done as well using visual light. Half a dozen major fires were raging within the shipyard boundaries.

Cranes, warehouses, and machine shops had been bomb-shattered and left in flames. The water gates of the main yard dry dock had been blown out and the facility flooded, and a Romeo-class conventional submarine had been lifted half out of the water and draped broken-backed across a quay. Burning oil from its ruptured tanks leaked into the Huangpu channel and spread slowly downstream, lighting off the finger piers like a string of birthday candles.

The huge, covered, graving dock was ablaze from the inside out. A score of burnthroughs flamed on its roof, and a multispectral tongue of fire, fully half the width of the river in length, roared out the open ship doors.

That holocaust had to be caused by missile fuel stacks burning off. There must have been another Chinese boomer moored in the dock. Bubbles hoped for the sake of everyone downwind that the damn fools had kept their warheads unshipped and stowed elsewhere.

"Okay, Bubbles." From up front, Digger's voice sounded totally level, totally controlled, almost uninterested. "Ten miles out from target, four miles from release point. Angle off, point nine. Verify."

"Verified. We are still in the groove."

"GPU rechecks?"

"Checked and checked. Checked and checked. Ordnance is up and safeties are off. Intervelometer setting is point five."

"Looking good, Bub. Two miles out. Enable system to drop."

Bubbles keyed a sequence on her weapons panel, unlocking the ordnance releases and freeing the fighter-bomber's fire-control system to engage the target. Flipping the safety guard up and off the manual bombing trigger on her joystick, she rested her finger against it.

"System enabled."

It became quiet in the cockpit, the only sound being the soft humming whine of the Sea Raptor's twin turbofans. There was quite a fireworks display going on outside of the canopy, however. The air below Moondog 505 scintillated with tracer streams, while above her the shell bursts of heavy antiair fire danced among the clouds like chain lightning.

Running fast at 16,000 feet, she skimmed deftly between the two threats, too high to be reached by the fire of the lighter flak and too low to be trapped within the proximity-fused destruction of the larger guns.

The fighter-bomber was cutting almost directly across the heart of urban Shanghai from south to north, the Huangpu River channel off her right wingtip. The fires of the Hudong shipyards were just coming up on their one-o'clock position. Digger and Bubbles made no effort to aim their aircraft or their weapons at the target. The bombs themselves would take care of that detail when the time came.

Moondog 505 bucked delicately twice. The light patterns on the weapons panel shifted.

"Bombs away," Bubbles reported quietly.

The weapons released by the Navy strike plane each were named with a tongue-tying acronym: JDAM/CSV (Joint Direct Attack Munitions System/Conformal Stealth Variant). Jacketed in the same radar absorbent material as their carrier aircraft, they had clung remoralike beneath its wings as it had transported them within range of their target. Now, falling free, they set out on the last leg of their journey.

Extending tail fins and glide wings, the airfoil-shaped bomb units peeled off toward their target, steered in by their integral Global Positioning Units. The same essential satellite technology that guided airliners and lost campers around the world now delivered two one-ton charges of high explosives to two specific points—said points being the exact center of the second floor of the central administration building of the Hudong shipyards, precisely fifty feet in from the northern and southern walls.

Moondog 505 was passing the target area now. Bubbles Zellerman kept the FLIR turret locked on the administrations center, recording the images for postmission bomb-damage assessment. "Three . . . and two . . . and one," she murmured.

On the screen, the southern wing of the building spewed light and smoke from its windows and collapsed in upon itself. The central bay followed a half instant later.

Not bad bombing, Bubbles thought judgmentally. *Not perfect, but not bad.*

"Ordnance is in," Digger Graves heard his backseater report. "Good run! In the pickle barrel."

"Roger. We are outta here!"

Digger rolled his hand controller to starboard and increased pressure on his right rudder pad. Moondog 505 banked away smoothly to the east in response. He came forward on the HOTAS grips as well, kicking the Sea Raptor up into super cruise mode. The g-load of the turn grew and the whisper of the turbofans grew into a rushing roar as the jet accelerated for the sound barrier.

Off the right wingtip, a last lick of firelight glinted off the surface of the Yangtze. In seconds, they would be "feet-wet" again, across the Chinese coast and clear.

Combat pilots refer to it as "catching the golden BB." The shell hadn't even been aimed at Moondog 505. It was a 100-millimeter round fired blindly into the sky over five miles away. A malfunctioning safety had kept it from detonating as it had reached its peak altitude, and it was actually plunging downward when its trajectory intersected the fighter-bomber's flight path. Its fuse cap just barely ticked the trailing edge of the Sea Raptor's portside elevator.

Fortunately, Digger Graves blacked out for only a couple of seconds. He regained awareness in a world gone insane. The wild shifting of the gravity vector told him that Moondog 505 was tumbling wildly. He wrenched at the hand controller, instinctively trying to stabilize the aircraft, only to find that he didn't have any functional control surfaces left.

The few remaining instrument displays were pulsing red or yellow crisis warnings. Orange firelight glared on the canopy, and Graves could hear the moaning and cracking of an air frame breaking up. There was no doubt in hell that their contract to fly this aircraft had just expired.

"Eject!" he screamed. "Eject, eject, eject!"

Digger reached over his head for the combined blast-curtain and ejection-seat trigger, groping for a panic-stricken moment against the g-loading until his fingers closed through the wire and plastic loops. Trying to keep his back straight and his limbs centered over the seat, he yanked the curtain down over his face.

The canopy blew off and a tornado's worth of wind poured into the cockpit, screaming and clawing. Over it, Digger heard the faint ripping thud of Bubble's ejector seat firing, and he felt the flash of heat from its rockets. Then it was his turn, and Digger lost consciousness for the second time.

Downriver, almost at the mine barrier, Vince Arkady stiffened as a piercing sound stabbed at his ears. An electronic blipping sounded in his helmet phones; shrill, penetrating, specifically pitched to be impossible to overlook or ignore. It was the herald of disaster, the Emergency Locator Beacon of a downed aircrew.

"Gray Lady, Gray Lady," Arkady was speaking over the beacon tone on the air circuit. "I'm getting an ELB out here. Are you guys reading the same?"

"Roger, we got it," Christine Rendino replied from Raven's Roost. "We have a bearing on it. Triangulating now. Okay, signal source is to your west. Back upriver."

"Can you confirm that this beacon is one of ours? Have we just lost a strike bird?"

"Stand by, Zero One. We're working it."

From the bridge Amanda had listened to the exchange, tense and silent. Now she keyed her own microphone. "CIC, try and get a skin track or a transponder burst off of that last strike aircraft. Communications, inform Task Flag that we might have a plane down."

☆   ☆   ☆

"Admiral, the *Cunningham* reports that Moondog 505 might just have gone down."

"Goddamn it!" Tallman's exclamation was explosive and bitter. "When are we due to reacquire that aircraft?"

"She should be clear of the coast now," the *Enterprise*'s air boss replied.

"Then try and reestablish commo with her," Tallman demanded. "Contact the E2D and have them try and lift a return off her radar transponder. Verify if she's still airborne or not!"

"Sir," one of the communications ratings looked up from her console, "the Hummer is now confirming that they are receiving two ELB signals on the same bearing as reported by the *Cunningham*. IFF subsignal codings match those assigned to the aircrew of Moondog 505."

"That's it," the air boss said flatly. "We lost one."

"Goddamn it to *hell!*

MacIntyre could only share in Tallman's moment of frustration and rage. This was the nightmare that had haunted every American military commander since the Korean War. An aircrew down in enemy territory. The hostiles of this world seemed to demand that the United States always play by the rules, while reserving the right to treat American POWs in whatever manner they saw fit.

MacIntyre stepped swiftly across to one of the chart boards. "Do we have a fix on those beacons yet? An exact one."

"I believe so, sir," the air boss replied, joining MacIntyre at the flatscreen display. "It's just being linked in from the Duke."

"Yeah. Jake, come take a look at this."

"What is it, Eddie Mac?" Tallman shouldered in around the screen.

"It's not as bad as it could be. Take a look at these ELB location hacks. Your aircrew is coming down over the estuary. They're going to be feetwet. Just barely, but I think we might be able to get them out of there."

"Might my ass! We are getting them out! Now!"

The first thing Digger Graves noticed was the quiet, broken only by a riffling whisper like the wind in the leaves. Then came the pain, the tearing agony in his left shoulder.

That popped his eyes open and restored full awareness. He was hanging in his harness beneath a full parachute canopy. The wind-in-the-leaves sound was the air flowing through the risers and chute gores. The pain? He wasn't so sure. The arm was still attached, and there didn't seem to be any blood, but something was sure as hell wrong with that shoulder. Maybe a dislocation from the ejection.

His next thought was for his backseater. He twisted in his harness, looking around and mentalizing an incoherent fragment of prayer that there would be another parachute in the sky.

There was. Bubbles's canopy was above him and to the right, her lesser weight giving her a reduced sink rate. Both chutes were descending into a black void some distance from the nearest fire or cluster of lights. That was just as well. Digger suspected that the locals wouldn't be any too pleased with them at the moment.

Digger tried to run a fast inventory of his escape-and-evasion gear, seeing how much had stayed with him during the bailout. Much of it had, most importantly the emergency transponder and the Combat Search and Rescue radio. The tiny check light on the transponder was already glowing, indicating that it had been triggered into action by the shock of the ejector-seat launch. His survival kit and life raft had stayed with him as well, dangling twenty feet beneath him on their lanyard.

With his right hand, he reached up and broke the inner capsule of the IR light stick on his life jacket. Producing no visible spectrum illumination, it would burn bright for several hours on a FLIR scanner.

There was a sudden tug on the gear lanyard. The darkness and the residual confusion from his blackout had made Digger misjudge his altitude. His startled curse gagged off as he hit the river.

He went deep, then his Mae West inflated and lifted him back to the surface, retching and spitting out the putrid, brackish water of the estuary. He pulled the Capwell releases of his parachute harness and tore off his helmet, looking around. A few yards away, another ghostly cloud of white nylon was collapsing into the river.

"Bub! Hey, Bub?"

There was no answer.

Clumsily, restrained by the combination of his injury and burdening equipment, he tried to swim to her. He found that he couldn't gain any ground on the drifting parachute and he paused for a second to cut loose the survival-kit lanyard. *Survival my ass,* he thought. They'd either be pulled out of here by their own CSAR people or they would end up in a Chinese prison camp.

Finally, he snagged a handful of wet nylon and drew Zellerman in to him. She still didn't move, unconscious or dead. Feverishly, Graves freed her of her chute harness and helmet and felt for a pulse at her throat. It was there, weak, but there. Fumbling one-handed, he dug out his rescue strobe and used it for a moment in flashlight mode. Bubbles was unconscious, blood streaking from her nose and from a cut on her chin, but she was alive.

He pulled her against him, her back supported against his chest, his functional arm looped around her protectively as they floated with the sluggish current.

"It's okay, Bub!" he whispered hoarsely, looking around at the hostile night. "They're coming for us."

"All Stormdragon elements, this is Task Flag. We confirm that we have a Moondog element down. We also confirm that we have two aircrew down within the Yangtze estuary. We have a valid recovery scenario. I say again, we have a valid recovery scenario. All CSAR assets commit as per Ops Plan Alpha Five. Panda Three Three, initiate rescue and recovery. Retainer elements, initiate search and top cover. *Cunningham*, assume station off the Yangtze estuary and stand by to render support as possible. All elements acknowledge."

"Panda Three Three to Task Flag. Initiating CSAR. Taking departure from holding pattern."

"Retainer elements to Task Flag. We have reversed course and are proceeding to transponder location."

Arkady might have been flying the pattern at his home air field.

"*Cunningham* to Flag. Proceeding to support station at this time." Amanda turned in the captain's chair to look aft at the watch officer. "Mr. Freeman, move us to the mouth of Beicao Hangcao channel. Assume station keeping five hundred yards off the mine barrier by GPU reckoning."

"Aye, aye, Captain."

"Combat Information Center, we have been tasked to support a search-

and–rescue operation upchannel in the estuary. Let's look sharp. We're go-ing to be all the cover our people are going to have."

Amanda was pleased with the steadiness in her own voice as she spoke. Down deep inside herself, she had flung her helmet to the deck and had screamed a denial to the gods.

"At least the damn flak's eased off," Gus Grestovitch commented from Zero One's rear cockpit.

"Yeah, that's what's got me worried."

"How come, Lieutenant?"

"Nobody's firing wild anymore. Somebody's passed the word to stop shooting. We're running out of shock effect, and the command-and-control nets are coming back up. The bad guys are bound to start paying at-tention to what's going on out here pretty soon."

"Yeah."

Retainer Zero One was flying back upriver again, retracing her previous search pattern. Only this time, the object of the search was quite different."

"Gus, you take the FLIR turret. I'm going over to low-light goggles. Keep your eyes open for the bad guys."

"Aye, aye, sir. What kind of weapons status do you want?"

"Systems hot and bays open. That'll increase our RCS, but I don't want to have to fool around if I have to fast-draw." The primary air tactical chan-nel was still saturated with transponder squeal, so Arkady dropped down to the alternate.

"Gray Lady, this is Zero One. Match my fix with the targets, please."

"Zero One," Ken Hiro's voice came back promptly. "You are on the bearing and in the ballpark. They should be in your immediate vicinity."

"Rog."

Arkady did another frequency shift to the CSAR channel.

"Moondog 505, Moondog 505, do you read? Do you read? This is Re-tainer Zero One on cover. Talk to me, guys, we're looking for you."

He lifted his thumb off the mike button. The response was mercifully swift in coming.

"Retainer Zero One, this is Moondog 505."

There was the rasp of strained breathing, but the voice was strong.

"Moondog 505, what is your status?" Arkady demanded.

"We are in the river, Retainer. Maybe a hundred and fifty yards offshore. My systems operator and I are together. She is unconscious and I am injured. Left arm isn't working so well."

"Is there any enemy activity in your area, Moondog?"

"Not that I can see, Retainer."

"What can you see? Can you give me any landmarks?"

"What looks like . . . two piers burning. Upriver. Maybe half a mile."

Okay, those had to be the quays that the Duke's cruise missiles had taken out. Arkady glanced up and spotted the same blaze. They were in the ball-park.

"Moondog 505, can you hear my rotors?"

"Affirmative, I can hear you downriver. We have flares and strobes. Shall I illuminate?"

"No. Negative, Moondog. Let's not advertise before we have to. Do you have I-R sticks lit?"

"Affirmative."

"That ought to be enough. Stand by, we'll pick up on you in a second."

Arkady eased Zero One into a hover. "Gus, surface scan with the FLIR. Forward arc. You're looking for active sources in the river."

"Searching . . . got 'em. Two active sources in close proximity."

"All right!"

"I also got enemy vehicle activity on the bank, right beyond 'em."

Five miles offshore, Panda Three Three roared through the night. The SH-60 Oceanhawk had been lurking on call below the coastal radar horizon. Now she raced for the mouth of the Yangtze at full war power.

The helicopter had been especially configured for this mission. The ASW systems console had been downloaded, along with the dunking sonar and torpedo racks. Replacing them were extended-range fuel tanks, a personnel winch, and a .50-caliber heavy machine gun mounted in the cabin door. Instead of LAMPS system operators, a team of rescue swimmers, a gunner, and a hospital corpsman grimly rode the passenger benches in the cabin.

"Panda Three Three, this is Retainer Zero One."

"Go, Zero One."

"We have a fix on the Moondogs. They are in the southern estuary channel about one click east of Waigaoqiao. We are orbiting them at this time. The recovery zone is still cool, but this state of affairs will not last. Come a-runnin'."

"We are balls to the wall, Zero One," Three Three's pilot replied. "Maintain the even strain. We'll be up with you in about eight minutes."

Nonetheless, the CSAR pilot twisted the grip throttle on the end of his collective lever a little harder, trying to nurse a few more horsepower out of his twin T-700 turboshaft engines. There was always a degree of friction between the rotor and fixed-wing factions within a carrier air group, but it was friction within a family. One of their own was in trouble now. This was not just a mission, this was a keeping of the faith.

"The air boss reports we have gunships over our aircrew, sir," Commander Walker said quietly. "They are still clear and the recovery helo is inbound."

"So far, so good, Jake," MacIntyre commented, crossing his arms and leaning back against the Pri-Fly chart table.

Tallman produced a noncommittal grunt. "Maybe, Eddie Mac. But just remember, victories come singularly. It's the fuckups that gang up on you."

In all probability, it was just a coincidence that the albatross is considered a sign of ill omen by mariners. A thousand miles west of the usual north polar–to–south polar migration route of its kind, this one had been driven off course by a summer storm. Gliding silently through the darkness on its ten-foot wingspan, it rested in the flying quasitrance that served as sleep for it on its months-long aerial odyssey.

So deeply oblivious was the great seabird that it didn't even notice the approach of the other swift-moving night flier.

There was no warning. Just a flash of white and a tremendous slam.

"What the hell?" Panda Three Three's copilot yelled, grabbing for his controllers.

"I dunno, Danny! It felt like a rotor strike!" the aircraft commander yelled back. A savage, jack-hammering vibration was racking the big helo, blurring the instrument readouts almost into illegibility.

"We got rotor damage."

"Oh, really? You think? Notify Task Flag that we're aborting! Then notify the *Cunningham* that we're coming in for an emergency recovery!"

"Skipper, we got men in the water!"

"Yeah, and sure as all shit, we're going to be joining them in about two minutes if we don't get a deck under us!" The copilot noticed some kind of matter smeared on the outside of his windscreen. Tearing open his side window, he took a swipe at it with his glove. Bringing his hand back into the cockpit, he examined it by the instrument lights. His glove was covered with blood, a single, bedraggled, white feather matted in it.

"Ah, for Christ's sake! We hit a goddamn seagull!"

The chill of the water was starting to sink inward as well. Neither Digger nor his S.O. had elected to wear anti-exposure suits on this run, and despite the mildness of the night, he was beginning to feel it.

Then there were the sounds carrying across the surface of the river. He'd heard trucks changing gears over toward shore a couple of times and had seen the flash of hooded headlights. Once, when the circling helicopters had swung clear, he'd even made out human voices.

Graves dug the waterproof SAR radio out of his sleeve pocket again. "Retainer Zero One, this is 505. The natives are starting to get a little restless down here, guys."

"We see 'em, Moondog. Don't sweat it. We're still with ya."

"Roger that, Retainer. How far out is our pickup?"

"Yeah. Moondog, we're having a little problem with that."

Already cold, Graves suddenly felt considerably colder. A good friend of his had once used that "a little problem" phrase in just that same carefully offhand manner. He'd died in the crash that had followed thirty seconds later.

Suddenly, from upstream, a searchlight lanced out across the river, a blue-white beam that wavered through the darkness like a probing sword blade.

"Shit!" Arkady tore the night vision visor up and away from his eyes as it overloaded."

"Searchlight truck on the bank, Lieutenant!"

"I see him." The Sea Comanche darted toward the source like an angry hornet. "Select Hydra pods. Four rounds. Fléchette."

"Hydra's hot, sir!"

The searchlight swiveled to target the diving helo, its glare flooding the cockpit and drowning out the Heads-Up Display. Arkady's hand flicked up to his helmet again, flipping down the sun visor. Then, bore-sighting down the light beam, he salvoed the rockets.

Four rounds were launched, but four rounds didn't arrive on target. The Hydra 70 air-to-surface rockets were carrying M255 fléchette warheads. As each round reached peak acceleration, a bursting charge exploded within it, releasing a swarm of 585 finned steel needles. A wave of more than two thousand hypervelocity projectiles swept over the searchlight vehicle, killing both it and everything else within a fifty-yard radius.

Night-blinded and a flier's instinct away from a killing bout of vertigo, Arkady pulled out of the firing run and swung back over the river.

"Well, fuck a duck, Gus. It looks like we're going to be putting in a little overtime tonight."

"No shit, sir."

On the aft monitors, the crippled Search and Rescue Seahawk could be seen settling onto the Duke's helipad.

"Air One, this is the bridge. Get that helo stricken below with all possible speed. I want that pad clear!"

"Will do, Captain."

The crisis load was building. Amanda's hand danced across the communications pad, shifting constantly between the CSAR and command channels and the ship's interphones, striving to maintain situational awareness.

"Gray Lady, Gray Lady, this is Zero One! Do you copy?" Arkady's urgent call caught her attention.

"Go, Retainer."

"How long until we get a recovery bird out here?"

"Task Flag is estimating an hour and a half to two hours, Retainer."

"Then we got problems. I don't think we have that much time. We are getting Red reaction, and I've already had to put fire in on the beach. They know that we're out here, and they're going to be swarming all over us."

"Can you keep them off the aircrew?"

"For as long as our ordnance holds out. *Ah, shit! Zero Two, pitch out! You've got ground fire on you!* Gray Lady, stand by, I'm going to be a little busy here for a minute!"

"Acknowledged, Zero One."

With great deliberation, she yanked the jack of her headset out of the communications link. She needed a few seconds to think—a few seconds out of the loop, away from the urgency and the emotion.

Her fist lifted and slammed down on the chair arm. Getting to her feet, she took two fast steps to the quartermaster's chart table. Swiftly, she began to call up the Yangtze approach block and the maps of the estuary mine barrier.

"How in the *hell* was this allowed to happen?" Admiral Tallman demanded.

"The CSAR Operations file called for the *Cunningham's* helos to back up our aircraft in case anything went wrong," his chief of staff replied. "Apparently, whoever set up the file didn't realize that the *Cunningham* only had gunships aboard."

"How long will it take to get that new angel in the air?"

"Another five minutes. They're gearing her up now."

"How about the support strike?"

"On the elevators, sir."

"Admiral," one of the radio operators interjected. "Report from Retainer Zero One. They are taking small-arms fire from the bank of the estuary."

"Goddamn it *all* to hell! Acknowledge signal to Zero One." Tallman paced off the length of Pri-Fly, seeking to vent some of his growing frustration in movement. MacIntyre could only silently empathize with him. There is possibly no worse situation in the world than to be a military commander who senses that he is falling behind the curve. To know that events are creeping out of your control in a headlong slide into bloody chaos.

"Hang in there, Jake," MacIntyre said. "You've got some good people out there working the problem."

"That's true, sir," Walker interjected. "And if we're not careful, we could have some more of those good people in the water as well. It may be necessary to cut our losses."

Tallman only grunted in reply, staring out into the darkness beyond the windscreen.

"Admiral," the communications liaison spoke up again. "Message coming in from the *Cunningham*. 'Am on station at mouth of channel through Yangtze mine barrier. Request permission to proceed upriver to recover downed pilots.'"

"My God," Walker exclaimed. "What in the hell is that woman thinking of!"

The radioman's voice continued, slightly bewildered. "There's something else as well, sir. 'Matthew, chapter eighteen, verse twelve.'"

"What's that all about?" Walker said.

"I know," MacIntyre replied slowly. *"'How think ye? If a man have an hundred sheep, and one of them be gone astray, doth he not leave the ninety and nine, and goeth into the mountains, and seeketh that which has gone astray?'"*

MacIntyre found that Jake Tallman's attention was suddenly focused totally on him.

"What do you think, Eddie Mac?"

"Jake, this is your show. I am just an observer here."

"Fine! Then make an observation! Could she pull it off? Could she get my people out of there?"

So much for being out of the loop. "I don't know if it's feasible or not, Jake," MacIntyre replied. "But I suspect that if it can be done, Amanda Garrett is the one who can do it. If you're asking my opinion, I'd say ride with her."

"Admiral," Walker interjected urgently. "If you send the *Cunningham* into that river estuary, you will be placing a multibillion-dollar warship and two hundred Navy personnel in extreme peril. We've lost one plane and two aviators. If we lose the *Cunningham* in trying to get them out, we will literally be compounding the disaster a hundredfold. Taking a risk like that isn't logical, sir."

Tallman shook his head slowly. "Nolan, you're absolutely right. It's not logical at all. But then, we're not talking about logic here, son, we're talking about the commitment we've made with our people.

"It's not logical for these kids to go out there and lay their necks out on the line purely at my command, so I can't afford to be all that logical about getting them back again.

"Make a signal to the *Cunningham*. 'Proceed with rescue operations. You are authorized to enter the Yangtze.'"

"Attention, all decks," Amanda Garrett's voice rang out of the 1-MC. The watch in the Combat Information Center instinctively looked up at the overhead speakers, awaiting the word.

"Here is the situation. We have a Navy aircrew down in the Yangtze River estuary. The helo on recovery station has been disabled, and those pilots won't last until another can be brought up. We are going to have to go upriver after them. This . . . is not going to be easy, but we are going to take care of our own. Good luck to us all."

"Ohhh, *brother*," Dix Beltrain murmured under his breath.

"Status of the SQQ-32, Mr. Beltrain," Ken Hiro asked flatly.

"System is up, sir. Diagnostic checks are green."

The mine-hunter display windowed into one corner of the Alpha screen. Within it, clear water was indicated dead ahead of the ship. But on the outer perimeters of the sweep, ominous shadowy outlines could be made out guarding the flanks of the channel.

"Stealth systems." Amanda's voice again: cool, imperturbable.

"Stealth, aye."

"Activate the deck sprays, Mr. McKelsie. That may help us if the Reds have FLIRs covering the mine passages."

"Will do."

"Very good. We're going into the passage now."

"Engines now going ahead slow, Mr. Hiro," the battle helmsman reported from his station. "Making turns for five knots."

Slowly, the mine contacts began to drift astern, out of the scan field. They were entering the single, narrow corridor that led through the barrier.

"Quartermaster," Hiro ordered. "Execute a series of GPU checks at thirty-second intervals and lock down a series of navigational datum points in the Navicom. I want us to be able to find our way back out of here if we lose the sonars."

"Aye, aye, sir." The quartermaster's reply sounded as if he were being lightly strangled.

Christine Rendino emerged from Raven's Roost and came to stand at Beltrain's side, her attention fixed on the mine-hunter display. "Fa' sure, I hate it when she does stuff like this," she whispered.

"Scared?"

The Intel nodded. "But that's only half of it. The other half is a feeling of inferiority. I'd never have the guts to try something like this in a million years."

"Yeah. I wonder if I ever will."

A building and two vehicles burned on the riverbank, with the firelight more of an interference then an aid to the two hovering helos. Retainer Zero One and Zero Two sidled downstream, covering the drifting dot that was the aircrew of Moondog 505.

Vince Arkady mentally reviewed his munitions list for the hundredth time. He still had both Hellfires on board, but only five Hydra rounds were left. There were troops and Armed People's Police out there in the straggle of boatsman's shacks and saltgrass. The two Retainers had taught them the folly of swapping shots with a Sea Comanche. Unfortunately, they had found an easier target.

"Retainer, we're getting fire from the shore again."

"Roger, Moondog. Tuck your head in. We're layin' it on 'em. Retainer Zero Two. Suppressive fire in the beach. Select target and fire. One round Hydra each."

"Roger, Zero One. On the way."

Save your powder, Hoss, Arkady thought grimly, *for the death hug's a-comin'.*

He laid the helo's thermal sights in on a reed bank along the muddy shore. He'd been seeing stealthy movement in there for the past couple of minutes, and he doubted that it was a beaver colony. The Hydra blazed and the wall of reeds shredded and flattened as if under the sweep of some gigantic scythe. Zero Two's round kicked up a haze of muddy spray farther downstream.

"How's that, old buddy?"

"That's put the fear of God back in 'em, Retainers. Thanks."

That weary voice on the other end of the CSAR circuit sounded as if it was coming from the loneliest place on Earth. Arkady groped for something valid to say under the restrictions of radio discipline, just to keep him talking.

"How's your S.O. doing, Moondog?"

"Bub's still breathing, Retainer. She's still hangin' in there."

"Glad to hear it."

"You won't be so glad to hear this, Retainer. I think we're drifting in closer to shore."

Arkady swore under his breath. "Stand by, Moondog. I'm going to see what's holding up the cab." He toggled over to the air operations channel. "Gray Lady, Gray Lady. We need an ETA on that recovery helo. Things are getting tight out here!"

"There isn't going to be a helo, Retainer," Amanda Garrett's voice came back levelly. "We are going to have to come upriver and make the recovery ourselves. We are transiting the mine barrier now. Barring delays, we should be up with you in about another forty-five minutes. You will have to hold until then."

"Roger, Gray Lady." There was nothing else to say.

"Bearing is still three hundred degrees true, Captain," the bridge helmsman announced. "The passage corridor is still trending north."

"I see it," Amanda said, peering over his shoulder into the navigation screen. "The Reds put a dogleg in the corridor to make things difficult. Watch for the turn. And watch for the shallows. We're going to start running tight on water as we get over to the far side of the channel."

"Aye, aye, ma'am."

Even a Red Chinese ship, with a port minesweeper running interference and a pilot with a marked set of mine charts at the helm, would find this tricky maneuvering. Not to mention that a Communist vessel would not have to worry about being fired on.

The windscreen wipers were hissing softly, just as they had been the last time they had penetrated into these waters. Only, this time the mist engulfing the *Cunningham* was of her own creation. High-pressure water jets on her weather decks and upper works were soaking down her decks and hazing the air around her, hopefully smothering any thermal signature that she might be leaving.

"Stealth systems."

"Stealth systems, aye."

"How does the local radar environment look, Mr. McKelsie?"

"Still sterile. We've killed 'em all, Captain. Nobody out there is looking for us."

"Acknowledged."

He was wrong, of course. The *Cunningham* was just starting to creep past the southern headland of the estuary. There would be a lot of hostile eyes out on the dark bulk of that headland. Eyes that would be alert and staring into the night for the next indication of their enemy.

Don't pay any attention to us, Amanda silently said to them. *We're just a shadow on the sea.*

They were spotted because they were a shadow on the sea. No radar detected them. No high-tech thermographic spotted their passing. But there was a sentry at his station in a bunker on the southern headlands. Ever since the start of the bombing raid on Shanghai, he had been peering warily into the night.

There was little to be seen. The only light anywhere within his field of vision was a single flickering patch of illumination low to the north-northwest. The sentry had seen the flash of man-made lightning that had given birth to it. A cruise missile hit on the radar station on Jiuduan Sha Island. Now a fire burned in the wreckage.

As the sole spark in the darkness, it had the tendency to draw the sentry's attention. Thus, he noticed instantly when the spark went out. Something moving at sea level had just occulted it. After a few moments, it reappeared as that something moved on. The sentry picked up his field phone and began to speak urgently into it.

Elsewhere in the night, gleaming steel gun barrels lifted out of camouflaged emplacements. With a predatory howl of hydraulics, they began to index across the sky.

"Bridge!" Ken Hiro's voice barked from the overhead speaker. "Channel is turning to port!"

"We see it, Ken!" Amanda dashed back behind the steering station. "Helm, come left to two six . . . make it two six five. Smartly, now!"

"Coming left to two six five, Captain!"

"Okay, we're coming around. . . . Two seven five . . . two seven zero . . . Okay, meet her! Steady as you go! Watch it! You're off-angling in the channel!"

Amanda's hands flashed to the throttles and propeller controls, trimming the propulsor pod outputs, kicking the Duke's stern over. With agonizing slowness, the Duke's position hack realigned itself between the rows of wide-set mines. Amanda and both of the hands at the helm console shared a shaky breath. Straightening, Amanda rested her hands on their shoulders for a moment.

"CIC, this is the bridge. We're around the dogleg and back in the groove. How much more of this?"

"Maybe another half a click," Christine Rendino replied. "This minefield is humongous! There must be thousands of them out there!"

"And all it takes is one," Amanda whispered under her breath.

Abruptly, the mines became the least of her worries.

Something rumbled in the distance. A few seconds later, a whispering whine began to grow in the air, building swiftly into an express-train roar that swept overhead. The roar terminated in a series of crackling thuds and a flickering glare that shredded the night.

Someone on the bridge swore as the harsh metallic light stabbed at their eyes. A row of four meteorlike balls of flame were arcing down into the river off the destroyer's starboard bow.

"Bridge! This is the CIC. Our night optics just went down! Captain, what's going on up there?"

"Starshells, Ken," she snapped into her command mike. "Someone just put a pattern of starshells over us. We're spotted, sure as anything. Lieutenant Beltrain, can we increase speed while maintaining image clarity on the mine-hunting sonar?"

"No way, Captain. We push it and we'll start to degrade from flow noise."

"Right. Bring up Sea SLAMs and Oto Melaras. Stand by to initiate counterbattery fire. There's going to be a fight."

☆ ☆ ☆

The guns were old, coastal-defense twin mounts forged over fifty years before in the Soviet Union. They had been adequately maintained, however, and their current generation of gunners had drilled for long hours for this moment. To a shouted loading cadence, hydraulic rams drove a second set of 152-millimeter illumination rounds into their chambers. Breechblocks slammed shut and the tubes lifted and traversed again.

Cannoneers fell back and pressed gloved hands over their ears. Triggers were squeezed and another shell group shrieked on their way.

Out on the headlands hooded concrete director towers perched atop the low hills, looking out over the estuary approaches. Inside them, forward observers swiveled their twin-headed panoramic range finders around, bringing them to bear on the distinctive shark's-fin silhouette revealed out in the main estuary channel. New ranges and bearings were barked into the phone lines that led back to the battery control center.

In the CIC, they couldn't hear the shells coming in. But they could see the geysers erupting out of the river on their television monitors and they could feel the thudding impact of the shock waves against their hull.

"Lieutenant Rendino, what's the word on these shore batteries?" Ken Hiro demanded.

"Four twin mounts. Eight guns in all. Six-inchers in concrete pop-up emplacements," Christine replied, rattling the facts off from her memory. "Deployed on the southern headland."

"They're only dropping four-round salvos in on us. They're holding back some of those tubes."

"No, sir," Beltrain replied. "They're alternating fire, using half of the battery at any one time to keep us illuminated. McKelsie, are we being painted?"

"Negative!" the stealth boss yelled back from his systems bay. "The EM environment is still clear. No radiation detected on any frequency."

"Sweet Jesus," Dix muttered, "they're going to kill us with antiques."

"Clarify that, mister," the Exec snapped.

"Old-fashioned iron munitions aimed by optical sights! World War–vintage stuff. In this particular tactical situation they nullify every advantage our stealth systems and ECM give us. It's an even field, sir."

"What would the old-timers do in a situation like this?"

"Go fast and zigzag like crazy!"

Ken Hiro looked back at the mine-hunter screen and at the ominous, shadowy spheres that hemmed them in. "I hope that there's an alternative to that," he said.

From his station upriver, Arkady saw the sudden glare of the starshells to the east.

"Damn, Gus, what's going on back there?"

"I dunno, sir. The Duke's Aegis system just came up, though. I'm getting a tactical display over the datalink."

That wasn't right. That really wasn't right. The *Cunningham* must have been spotted. That would be the only reason Amanda would clear away for a fight like that. Shit! Shit! Shit! This was going to hell.

His thumb moved to the channel control switch on the collective lever, on the verge of switching over to the Duke's air-operations frequency when his S.O. yelled a warning.

"Lieutenant! Surface contact on the tactical display! Proceeding downriver toward us. Speed, twenty knots. Range to this datum point, fifteen thousand yards and closing. Threat-board data annex identifies one Skin Head military surface-search radar."

"Goddamn it! Moondog 505, we have a problem. We are departing covering pattern, but we will be back. Hang in there, guys!"

"We aren't going anywhere, Retainer."

"Rog. Retainer Zero Two, this is Zero One. Depart covering pattern and form up on me. Stand by for Hellfire engagement. We got a gunboat coming in on us."

Floating in his life jacket, Digger Graves heard the rotor growl of the two covering helos begin to fade out over the broad reaches of the river. There was still sound out there in the light. The rumble of artillery, the ghost of a siren wail out toward the city.

But around the two drifting fliers, there was a momentary pocket of stillness. Graves could hear the trickling ripple of wind wavelets, and the whisper of his unconscious S.O.'s breath. Thoughts of his wife, his past, and his future tumbled disjointedly through a mind made sluggish by his growing hypothermia.

God! Was there anyone left alive in the world?

Accordingly, when someone touched his arm, Digger's heart nearly stopped.

Graves lunged forward, dragging Bubbles with him. There was something else in the water, a dark unmoving mass.

Almost without conscious volition, he went for the survival light clipped in his sleeve pocket. He snapped it on in its flashlight mode, letting the narrowest of beams leak through the fingers of his working hand.

It was someone else who had met their destiny on the great river: a coverall-clad Chinese seaman, dead, the open eye on the unshattered side of his face staring past Graves into the night. Digger switched the flash off and watched as the body merged back into the blackness. Slowly, the current carried the body off downstream, heading in the same direction as his S.O.

A prolonged shuddering shiver racked through Digger, and he held Bubbles closer.

The Five Sixteen boat and her three sisters rafted together in the shallows just below the point where the Huangpu River entered the estuary. Downstream, a battle storm raged—the lightning of starshells and the distant thunder of guns in the darkness. Closer in, they had heard the faint crackle of small-arms fire and had several times seen the meteor trail of rockets lash the shoreline.

Still they waited. Lieutenant Zhou Shan wasn't sure just what it was he was waiting for. But deep down in his belly, he knew it was coming soon.

"Radio operator. Any contact with Shanghai Fleet Command yet?"

"No answer on any naval command frequency, Comrade Lieutenant. No traffic at all except for the river patrol. They are asking for information and orders just as we are."

"There she goes," Bosun Hoong interjected from his station beside the port torpedo tube. He pointed to the north.

A pale wake streak gleamed in the darkness, a rakish shadow riding atop it. It swept by out in the deeper channel, heading downstream.

"They must be going to look into that fight out by the minefield." The bosun looked back into the torpedo boat's cockpit. "We could follow them out, Lieutenant."

"No," Shan replied flatly. "Not yet."

The first salvo had dropped long, exploding off the *Cunningham*'s starboard bow. The second dropped off her port quarter, astern. Amanda recognized what was happening: They were starting to walk their shellfire in on her ship, correcting with each salvo until they started dropping rounds right down the exhaust stacks.

Praise God that they didn't have the minefield channel preregistered. Probably no one had ever thought that an enemy would be mad enough to attempt a penetration of fortress Shanghai like this.

"CIC, how much farther until we're out of these damn mines!"

"It's got to be soon, Captain," Christine replied. "Another couple hundred yards at most."

Another blaze of light came from beyond the windscreen as the Reds renewed their illumination pattern. In the glare, she could read the growing fear in the eyes and faces of her bridge crew. Flow noise be damned, she had to get them out of this.

"Lee helm, increase speed. Make turns for ten knots."

"Aye, aye, Captain. Making turns for ten knots."

"Stealth system, fire RBOCs. Full concealment pattern."

"Stealth acknowledging. Firing full concealment pattern now!"

Out on the bow and from the forward end of the superstructure, rocket grenades ripple-fired into the sky, bursting like muddy fireworks over the Duke, obliterating the stars. The Rapid Blooming Overhead Chaff rockets would not serve any of their purposes this night. There was no radar for their metal foil packets to jam. But the grenades also produced thick clouds of multispectral chemical smoke, enough maybe to throw off the targeting of the coastal batteries' forward observers. Just for the few seconds more they needed.

"Captain, stop the ship!" Dix Beltrain's voice rang in her headset.

His demand was so totally unexpected that Amanda mentally fumbled for a moment, trying to put his urgent words into some kind of logical perspective. Her TACCO's next, even more frantic cry, however, blasted her into action.

"Captain, for Christ's sake! Ring her down!"

"All engines! Back emergency!"

On possibly any other ship in the world, it would have been too late. However, the Duke's integrated electric drive saved her. In a battle situation like this one, where sudden bursts of speed might be required, her huge Rolls-Royce/GE turbo-generator sets could be held at their maximum output. Her actual speed through the water could be controlled through the throttles of her electric motors. With no spooling-up lag, she was granted nearly instantaneous access to 100 percent of her power output.

Likewise, her reversible-pitch propellers allowed her to direct that thrust to go forward or astern with equal swiftness. As the lee helmsman shoved his throttles forward to the stops with his left hand, he also yanked the propeller controls hard back with his right.

The blades of the Duke's contra-rotating propellers pivoted in their sockets, and the water under her quarters lifted and boiled under the impact of 80,000 horsepower. The Duke shuddered to a halt in less than half her own length.

"Stop all engines! Helm, initiate station keeping on auxiliary hydrojets. Don't let her drift! Dix, what in hell is going on?"

"Watchdog, Captain." Beltrain's voice was as bleak as the tolling of a funeral bell. "Right in the middle of the channel."

"Are you sure, Dix?"

"We don't have enough definition on the SQQ to be certain, Captain. It could be somebody's old hot-water tank, for all I know. But we do have an object on the bottom in the center of the channel. It's the right size for a pressure mine, and it's sure as hell in the right place for one."

The same bleakness that had been in Dix Beltrain's voice settled around Amanda's soul. Consider a minefield as a wall that you must occasionally pass through. You must leave a passage—a doorway, as it were. And to keep the enemy from using your doorway, you needed a door.

You used a watchdog, a sophisticated naval "smart" mine fused to detonate whenever it detected the pressure changes caused by a ship's hull displacing water nearby. You deploy the watchdog in your passage channel, then you connect it by underwater cable to a land station, permitting you to arm or de-arm the mine. The door can then be opened, or shut, at your desire.

Since it had appeared that the Chinese had not used any high-tech mines anywhere else within their defensive line, Amanda had gambled that they wouldn't have one to use here. She had been wrong. The *Cunningham* was trapped.

"Zero Two, ordnance check."

"Two Hellfires. Two Hydras," Nancy Delany replied.

"Two and four here. This is going to be tight. Watch your round placement. Make 'em count."

"Roger."

The two Sea Comanches swung wide over the river to the north, moving around to flank the oncoming gunboat before it could reach the area of the two Moondog aviators.

"Gus, bring up your laser targeting. Bore-sight the FLIR and give me a screen display."

"Doin' it, sir."

Arkady shifted vision systems again, flipping the low-light goggles up on his helmet and focusing his attention on the image that snapped up on the central panel telescreen: a pale negative-image ship on a darkened river, a swirl of thermal wake trailing behind it in both the sea and air.

"Autocannon mounts forward, aft, and amidships," Arkady murmured. "Single small deckhouse. Freestanding mast. No stack."

"Looks like another one of those Shanghai gunboats, sir."

"No, Gus. No, the scale's wrong. It's too big. Way too big. That's a Hainan class. Twice the size, twice the firepower, and about four times harder to kill."

"Oh, thank you, God. Thank you ever so fucking much! Lieutenant, maybe we need to call the ship in on this one."

"The Lady's busy, Gus. She doesn't need us tugging on her shirtsleeve just now. Zero Two, follow me in! Point fire procedures! Take out the bridge and the main gun mounts!"

☆ ☆ ☆

Amanda kept her voice low and controlled. She could not, she dare not, exhibit an instant of panic or confusion now.

"Lee helm, all engines astern, dead slow."

"All engines backing astern, dead slow, ma'am."

She measured the helmsmen's voices the way a pharmacist might measure the components of a critically needed drug. Was any tremor there that might foretell a catastrophic failure under load?

"We won't have much rudder control backing at this speed, so you'll have to hold her in the center of the channel with the engines. Helm, stay on the hydrojet controls. Lateral thrust. Same orders. Keep us centered."

"Aye, aye, Captain."

"Will do, ma'am."

They both were steady. Nobody was breaking yet.

Another wavering howl. Another shell cluster impacted. Closer. The bridge deck plates rang. That had to be dealt with next.

"Tactical Officer. Initiate counterbattery fire. Oto Melara and Sea SLAM. Stealth systems, keep that smoke coming!"

"Aye, aye, ma'am. Aegis systems have shell tracks to active hostile batteries."

Up forward, she could hear the bow 76mm turret begin to traverse.

"Ken, this is the plan. I'm going to reverse us back upchannel. I don't think we've got enough swing room to turn."

"Then what, Captain?"

"That depends. Tactical Officer, could we detonate the watchdog mine with a command-guided Mark 50 torpedo?"

"I've never heard of it being tried, Captain."

"I don't give a damn whether it's been tried or not. Can it be done?"

The forward Oto Melara began to rage during the moment that Dix Beltrain paused, the high-angled gun barrel slamming abrupt three-round bursts into the sky.

"I can't see any reason that it can't."

"How much room will we need?"

"I'd like about a thousand yards."

"How much will we need?"

"Three hundred and fifty."

Out on the long reach of the foredeck, the car-length cylinder of the first Sea SLAM counterround sprang out of its launching cell. Its booster rocket blazed, illuminating from within the smoke cloud that engulfed the *Cunningham*.

"Okay, Dix, set it up. Quartermaster, back us upchannel three hundred and fifty yards by the GPUs."

Caught in the heart of her own firestorm, the Duke began to gain way astern.

At this moment, Vince Arkady's world consisted of the green tunnel of vision drilled through the darkness by the FLIR sights. With turbines firewalled and with their airspeed peaking out at a 190-plus miles per hour, he and his wingwoman went for the gunboat's flank.

Tracer fire flickered past outside the canopy, tentacles of deadly light reaching up from the river to enmesh the two diving helicopters. The Reds were chronically short of state-of-the-art technology, but they had been able to equip at least one of their gunboats with night-vision sights.

The rub was that to merely hit the target, they didn't need to work in this close. Their laser-guided Hellfire missiles had a ten-mile range, more then enough to stand out of the reach of the autocannon.

Unfortunately, the Hellfire was also designed to kill a fifty-ton main battle tank, not a four-hundred-ton surface combatant. It was not enough to simply hit the gunboat. To take it down, they would have to precision-strike at specific points aboard it.

On his own targeting screen, a glowing cross-hair spider crawled around the image of the Chinese gunboat. Gus Grestovitch was lying in the beam of the laser designator.

"Get the bridge . . . Get the bridge . . . Get the bridge . . ." Arkady chanted softly.

The cross hairs fixed on the gunboat's wheelhouse.

"Illuminating . . . got designation. Missile's hot!"

"Taking the shot," Arkady keyed the radio. "Zero One . . . missile away!"

He squeezed the initiator, fixing his eyes on the instrumentation so he wouldn't be blinded by the Hellfire's exhaust flare.

Riding the dials, Arkady started his turn away, anti–IR flares kicking out into Zero One's wake. He heard Nancy Delany call her own round away, then another sharp cry.

"We're hit! Zero One, we are hit!"

"Ah, shit!"

Arkady racked the helo through the remainder of the turn. Aimed north again, and skimming twenty feet over the river's surface, he took a split second to look out into the night again.

"Gus, try and pick up on Zero Two. Did you see a fireball out there?"

"Negative, negative. I'm not seein' nothin'!"

"Zero Two, Zero Two, talk to me! Nancy, state your status?"

"We're still in the air, Zero One," a weak return came back. "We are hit. I think a single twenty-five-millimeter round. Smoke in the cockpit and all kinds of systems failures. Nothing left but basic cockpit and engine instrumentation. Nothing will reboot. I think that one of the subsystems bays was blown right out of the aircraft."

"Can you stay in the air?'

"I have flight and engine control, and the airframe appears intact. I have no fire control and no night vision except for my low-light goggles."

"Then get out, Nancy! There's nothing more you can do here. The Duke is engaged. Head for the Task Force. You should be able to stretch your fuel far enough to reach the missile trap cruiser. If you can't, ditch as far off the coast as possible. They'll pick you up."

"Zero One, I—"

"Zero Two, the only thing you can do is to leave me one less thing to worry about! Goddamn it, Nancy, take departure now!"

"Zero Two, taking departure. My round hit, sir. I'm sorry I can't do more."

"I know, Nancy. Thanks for doing what you have."

Arkady flared Zero One around again.

"Okay, once more into the breach, ol' buddy. Let's see what we've done to this guy."

"We got a hit on him too, Lieutenant."

The image on the targeting screen panned around as the Sea Comanche completed its turn, picking up the Chinese gunboat once more. Fires were burning amidships and astern. The aft 57mm mount was clearly destroyed and its mainmast canted off center, but the 190-foot war vessel still stood resolutely downstream. It had closed to within a mile of the two drifting Moondog aviators.

"This guy is going to take a little more discouragement, Gus."

"I guess so, sir. How you want to work this?"

"We try for the wheelhouse again. Only, this time we follow the Hellfire in. We close to point-blank range, then we shove the last four Hydras right down his throat."

"Oh, man!"

"The shock effect of the Hellfire hit will throw them off long enough for us to close the range. Set us up. We're going in!"

The Sea Comanche skated in across the river, the surface glittering like hot dark oil beneath her belly. The Hainan's forward mount challenged again. Tracers arced over the canopy, descending as the Chinese gunners sought for the range.

"Illuminate!"

"Illuminating target . . . We got laser lock!"

"Taking him out!"

Arkady's finger closed on the actuator. There was a faint lurch. But there was no hot flame in the night.

"Shit, Gus, we got a misfire! Reset!" Arkady yelled, futilely crushing down on the actuator trigger again.

"Negative! She's gone! The fucker dropped off the rail! She didn't ignite!" Grestovitch's voice lifted an octave. "Lieutenant, pitch out! This isn't going to work!"

"It's got to!"

Arkady fought the rudder pedals and the collective lever, playing death tag with the twinned fire streams lashing at them, attempting to sidle out of the way while still maintaining his headlong charge toward the enemy. All he had left were the Hydra rockets. They were superb antipersonnel weapons, but they were no damn good for ship killing. Not unless you got so close that you could shove them right through the side of the hull.

They were hit.

A flash of light, a crash like they'd been broadsided by a pickup truck, and a pattern of cracks on the right side of the canopy. The Sea Comanche roared out of the far side of it, still a viable aircraft. Arkady could feel a change in the flight dynamics, but he didn't have time to sort it out now.

The image of the gunboat filled the targeting screen, overfilling it, scurrying figures of crewmen throwing themselves on the deck as a screaming, rotor-winged hunterbird dove on them. Arkady fought off the weird, deadly mindlock of target fixation and sent the Hydras on their way. The fire trails of the four 2.75-inch rockets momentarily linked the helicopter to the gunboat before vanishing within the hull. Arkady rocked hard back on the collective and sought sky.

The rockets exploded within the gunboat's engine room. Diesel oil is normally not a particularly volatile substance. But shred the tanks and fuel lines that contain it, aerosol it through the atmosphere with multiple hypervelocity impacts, ignite it by exposure to the star-temperature flame of high explosives, and it can be.

A massive chunk of the Hainan's midships weather deck blew off its framing, a massive, incandescent wound bleeding fire into the night.

"Yeah! We are living!"

"I'll take your word for it, Lieutenant."

Arkady backed off the power and circled to get back over the estuary. Twisting in his seat harness, he tried for a damage inspection. "We caught something back there. How bad are we hit?"

"The MAD pod's gone. I think the right wingtip, too."

"We're okay, Gus. I think we're okay. I got green boards."

"We gonna have to do that again, Lieutenant?"

"Hell, old buddy. We can't. The cupboard's bare."

Another voice abruptly intervened over the CSAR link.

"Retainer, Retainer, this is Moondog, do you copy?"

"Roger, Moondog, we're still out here. Just having words with a Red gunboat."

"So I see, Retainer. Thanks, guys. But we got another little problem here."

Oh, shit. "Go, Moondog. Whatcha got?"

"We're getting small-arms fire from the beach again. Not too close yet, but we need you to lay a little more nasty on these guys."

Oh shit!

"Roger, Moondog. We're on our way."

Both pilot and systems operator tuned out the darkness beyond their cockpit and refocused themselves on their job and their instrumentation. As a result, neither of them noticed the faint, chromatic blurring begin on the outside of the canopy. The rotor wash was whipping an almost microscopic spray of oily fluid through the air. The transmission pressure warning alarm would not trip for several minutes yet.

Like an enraged mountain cat, the *Cunningham* clawed back at her attackers. Her SPY-2A radars traced the incoming artillery rounds to their points of origin, and her Aegis battle management system apportioned death and destruction among the guns of the Chinese battery.

A Sea SLAM burned down out of the sky like a vengeful comet, diving full into one of the open gun pits. Its quarter-ton warhead scooped the big twin mount and the vaporizing remnants of its crew into the air. A microsecond later the wreckage was scattered farther afield as the ready-use ammunition in the adjoining bunker succumbed to its torment, the entire emplacement area erupting like a miniature volcano.

Oto Melara rounds rained down on the other battery sites. The autocannon shells were too light to damage the massive concrete fortifications themselves, but proximity-fused, they exploded overhead, raking the open mounts with hypervelocity shrapnel.

Steel found flesh, and gunners died. Their comrades maintained the loading cadence, however, hunkering down against the storm and continuing the rituals. Round in the breech! Breechblock closed! Lanyard pulled! Round on the way!

"Captain, we have reversed three five zero yards by GPU . . ."

The helmsman was interrupted by the shell howl and rippling roar of the salvo detonation. The plumes were closer now. The rounds were walking in to mate lethally with the *Cunningham*.

". . . awaiting orders, ma'am."

"Stop all engines. Hold position. Resume station keeping."

"Engines answering all stop, Captain. Station keeping on hydrojets."

Amanda slid one hand under her helmet and held the command-set earphone more tightly against her head.

"Dix, status on the torpedo?"

"System's hot and the fish is spinning up now. Targeting datum point and range safeties set. Ready to shoot. But no promises, ma'am."

"None asked. Shoot!"

"Fire one!"

From near the Duke's waterline amidships, a Barracuda torpedo sliced out of its fixed launching tube. Trailing the hair-fine filament of its guidance wire behind it, it curved away from the ship's hull.

Abruptly, the sea domed up off the *Cunningham's* starboard bow, an upheaval of shattered water far greater then any shell hit. The destroyer leaped in the water like a startled horse, the shock coming as a blow through the soles of the feet.

"Dix, what happened?"

"We lost the torpedo, Captain. It swung wide in the channel and clipped one of the contact mines."

"Reset systems and try it again! Expedite!"

"Acknowledged. Fire two!"

This time there was only the briefest of howls. Three jets of spray lifted out of the river to port.

And one to starboard.

"Captain!" one of the lookouts cried. "They've got us straddled!"

"I'm aware of that, mister. Stand easy." Amanda silently counted out seconds of running time, willing the torpedo to make the turn, willing it down into murky depths of the river. Backlit by the starshell glow, a massive, muddy column of water lifted out of the center of the channel, straight on beyond the *Cunningham's* bow.

"Yes!" Amanda leaned forward in the captain's chair. "Dix, did we get the watchdog?"

"Torpedo detonation is on target, Captain."

"Dix, did we get the mine? Do we have a clear channel?"

"Can't tell, Captain. Not yet. Bottom conditions are disturbed. We do not have clear imaging."

"Dix, we have got to get the ship out of here. . . ."

Amanda Garrett would never be able to explain just what made her do what she did at that instant. Possibly, she felt the brush of the incoming shell's shock wave. Whatever the reason, she threw her arms up in front of her face and curled forward in the captain's chair. A fragment of a second later, a wall of orange flame caved in the thermoplastic of the windscreen.

"They aren't buying it anymore, Lieutenant," Gus Grestovitch reported from the rear cockpit. "They're just shooting at us now too."

"I know." Arkady had felt two small-arms strikes on that last pass. They had been making dummy firing runs on the beach to try to keep the Chinese troops at bay. Unfortunately, the bluff was wearing thin. As he swung back over the estuary, Arkady keyed the CSAR again.

"Moondog, how you doing down there?"

"Not so good, Retainer. We're getting fired on again. That damn gunboat is drifting down on us, and I think they can see us from the beach."

Arkady glanced upstream at the flaming hulk. "Sorry about that, Moondog. It seemed like a good idea at the time."

"Yeah, well, I think we could use another one, guys."

"Coming up, Moondog."

Arkady lifted his thumb off the transmitter key. "Any brilliant notions?"

"Just one, sir."

"What is it?"

"Call the fucking ship."

"I think you're right."

As he toggled across frequencies to the command channel, Arkady looked downstream to where the starshells still rained down." As he did so, however, he saw an atypical flash of light play across the mouth of the estuary like heat lightning. That had to have been an explosion.

"Gray Lady, this is Retainer Zero One. Do you copy?"

He was answered with dead air.

"Gray Lady, this is Zero One. Do you copy?"

Arkady tasted sudden copper fear.

"Gray Lady, this is Zero One. Do you copy? . . . Amanda, Goddamn it, you answer me!"

She didn't.

Amanda straightened slowly. The burning stench of cordite hung thick in the air and soured her throat. Behind her, over the ringing in her ears, she could hear the soft, mindless wail of a human reduced to the level of a wounded animal.

She could also hear a quiet, cool voice speaking from deep in the center of her being: *You aren't hurt that badly. The ship is in trouble. Get moving! Do something!*

She found that she was on the deck beside the captain's chair, and she used it to pull herself to her feet. The bridge structure was essentially intact, but the windscreen was gone and there was systems damage: telepanels broken and electronics chassis lifted out of their bulkhead mounts.

She staggered over to the grab rail and peered out and down onto the foredeck. They had been lucky, extremely lucky.

A few feet farther forward and the Chinese 152mm round would have struck the number-three Vertical Launch System with its scores of closely ranked guided missiles. A few feet farther aft and the bridge would have been gone. A few feet to either side and it might have pierced through to the forward Oto Melara magazine.

As it was, however, it had struck the gun mount itself. The turret shell had been blown away completely, and the distorted wreck of the autocannon stood centered in the deck like some scrap-yard sculpture. The plating was torn around it, and Amanda could see a flicker of flame down between the framing.

"Damage control, this is the bridge. . . . Damage control!"

The command headset links were down. Amanda tore off her helmet and headset both and snatched one of the emergency sound-powered phones from out of its clips.

"CIC, this is the bridge!"

"Bridge, what is your status?"

"We have wounded. We need first-aid parties. The forward gun mount has been hit. Get damage control up there. Flood forward Oto Melara magazine. I say again, flood forward Oto Melara magazine."

"Acknowledged. Do you wish to shift the con to the CIC?"

"Negative. Not at this time. Have Mr. Beltrain standing by."

Amanda stumbled across to the helm console. The lee helm operator was the one producing the agonized keening as he sprawled on the deck. The helmsman was still slumped, bloody-faced, at his station. Gripping the collar of his life jacket, Amanda pulled him out of the chair, not allowing herself to care too much as she lowered him to the deck as well.

There was blood on her hands as she dropped into the helmsman's seat. She didn't know if it was hers or his. The console screens were dark, but Amanda hit the systems reset and they lit off again. Most important, the Navicom came on line, showing the path the Duke must follow to get out. Amanda verified that the ship was still aligned with the passage, then she spoke deliberately into the phone again.

"Tactical Officer. Do we have a clear channel?"

"Captain, the mine-hunter sonar is still not imaging clearly. There is no way to tell!"

"Yes, there is."

Amanda's right hand went to the main throttles and shoved them forward.

She felt the faint surge of acceleration across the small of her back, and the indicator bar of the iron log began to creep up its scale.

Amanda took the throttles to their stops. The mine-hunting sonar was irrelevant now; she had the bearing she must steer. Her left hand had gone to the helm controller, her fingers closing around the tiny spokes of the miniature ship's wheel, holding the course line.

She heard the building wail of the next incoming salvo, building into the ripping roar of their arrival. With the bridge open, the shell detonations were as loud as the word of God . . . and away beyond the Duke's stern.

For the moment, she had jerked her ship out of the enemy's gun sights. Scylla had been passed. Now came Charybdis. The Cunningham was rolling down on the datum point of the watchdog mine. Impassively, she watched as the image of her ship and the mine merged on the screen. There was nothing else to be done, except to take a deep living breath a moment later as they passed over it and swept clear of the minefield.

Another Chinese salvo dropped farther astern. Amanda became aware of the other people crowding onto the bridge, corpsmen tending to the injured and replacement hands taking over the functional workstations. A new helmsman was standing by at her shoulder.

She also became aware of the breeze flowing in through the empty windscreen frame, clearing away the stench of blood and explosives.

"Keep her in the main channel," she said. "We have some people waiting for us."

Inland, the Communist guns grated against the limits of their traversing range, no longer able to track their target. The engineers who had laid out the battery had never visualized a foe that would dare to pierce so deeply into Red territory. The men who manned them were patient, however. They would clear away their dead and wounded, and they would wait. Their enemy had passed them to gain entry to the river. They would have to pass once more to escape.

"What in the hell is the holdup on that support strike, Nolan?"

"We had to upload a new set of Mission Data Modules, sir. Those coastal-defense installations were not classified as a potentially critical target. We never visualized one of our ships having to go upriver like this."

"Admiral," the communications rating called out from his station. "Battle-damage report coming in from the *Cunningham*."

"How bad?" Tallman demanded, striding across to the communications console.

"Shell hit . . ." the radioman relayed. "Forward gun mount out . . . Casualties . . . Ship still operational . . . Clear of the minefield. Proceeding to recovery point."

"Acknowledge the message."

Jake Tallman looked as if he wanted to hit something, just once, very hard.

"Take it easy, Jake," MacIntyre said slowly, leaning back against the Pri-Fly bulkhead.

"It's going to pieces, Eddie Mac. This operation is going to pieces, and we're going to lose all those people out there, and it's my fault."

"Every operation always goes to pieces. And then we have to trust in the people we send out there to put it all back together again. Don't count Amanda Garrett out of this, Jake. The Lady has the touch."

"I get that impression. I just hope I haven't wasted it, and her."

The Pri-Fly windows buzzed softly and a booming roar leaked in from the flight deck. Twinned cones of blue-white exhaust flame climbed away from the end of the carrier's catapult as an F/A-18 Super Hornet hit the sky.

"Support strike launching now, sir," the air boss reported.

Tallman shook his head slowly. "Too late. Too damn late. By the time they can form up and get over the target, this thing is going to be over. One way or another."

Digger Graves again heard the angry slap of a rifle slug skipping off the water. He was becoming too familiar with that sound. Thanks to the light from the burning gunboat, the Communist riflemen were beginning to get their range.

The current was also drawing them closer to the bank. He had tried swimming farther back out into the channel, but burdened with a dislocated shoulder and Bub's limp form, he hadn't been able to make much headway. In growing despair, he groped for the CSAR radio.

"Retainer, we are getting down to the wire down here! We are getting fired on! Can you get these guys off of us?"

There was a long pause before the cool, steady voice Graves had come to hang on to replied. "No can do, Moondog. No ammo left."

No ammo left. That was going to be one shitty epitaph.

"Retainer. How long till pickup?"

"I don't know, Moondog. I've lost contact with my ship. I'm out of contact with everybody. No relays. We're sort of alone out here."

He wasn't going to have to make that decision about staying in the Navy after all. It took Graves a second to work up the will to lift the radio to his lips again. "I think that's it, Retainer. You'd better call it quits, man."

"Hang in there, Moondog. We're still working the problem."

"Jesus, Retainer! Don't be stupid! There's nothing more you can do! We're going to be dead here in a second anyway. There's no sense in you going out with us. Beat it!"

"I said, we are still working the problem!" the helo pilot's voice snarled back. "I am fucking well not giving up on this thing yet, and you fucking well aren't either. Stand by!"

Graves felt a hysterical laugh build up within him. Somehow he had never conceived of anyone ever having to order him to stay alive. Another bullet strike close enough to spray water in his face sobered him up abruptly. Digger Graves suddenly hoped that Retainer Zero One knew what he was talking about.

"Moondog, you still with me?"

"Still here, Retainer."

"But not for long. I'm getting you guys out of there right now."

"I thought you said you couldn't do a lift-out?"

"I can't. But I do have a dunking sonar onboard. I'm going to lower the sound head so you can grab on to it. Then I'll tow you guys back out into the center of the channel. That'll at least get you out of rifle range. Got it?"

"I'm not arguing, Retainer."

"Rajah! Stand by, we're coming in."

The noise of the circling helo began to grow. Scanning the darkened sky upstream, Graves picked up the angry-insect silhouette of a Sea Comanche, outlined against the flames of the gunboat. The sound head was lowered, and it swung pendulously fifty feet beneath its sonar pod.

"Yeah, Bub," he whispered. "Maybe he's right."

"Okay, old buddy," the voice of the Retainer said over the CSAR. "You're going to have to talk me in the last couple of feet. I can't see you once you're in under my nose."

"Roger, Retainer. Just get close."

The rotor growl was dominating now, beginning to drown out all outside noise. But Graves could see a growing number of slug strikes on the water's surface around him. The locals were apparently unhappy with the notion of losing their prey. The tracer stream of a light machine gun cut the night, not aiming at the two downed fliers but up-angled at the approaching helicopter.

The blast of the downdraft began to sheet-spray across the river's surface, and the sound head struck the water some twenty feet away. All too fast, it began to swim in his direction.

Graves had to have a hand free! He laced his left arm through the straps of Bubbles's life jacket. Ignoring the pain of his dislocated shoulder, he watched the tether approach through narrowed eyes. Waiting for the right instant, he lunged. A grunt of agony escaped him as he felt the drag on his injured limb and his fingers brushed braided Kevlar.

Ashore, someone fired a rocket-propelled grenade at the rescue attempt. The projectile struck water and exploded some fifty feet away, the concussion striking Graves in the groin and abdomen like a booted kick. He buckled over in the water, gagging, and the tether was gone, passing beyond all reach. Graves groped for the CSAR radio on its lanyard. "Back!" he screamed. "Back!"

Retainer Zero One forged ahead for another twenty feet, then went to hover. Gingerly, the helo began to reverse in Graves's direction, blindly trolling for the aviator.

A rifle slug tugged at the collar of his flight suit and seared a welt into the skin of his throat. Graves ignored it. It was now. He would do it now or he and Bubbles would die here. He grabbed for the tether again and his fist closed around it.

He pulled Bubbles to the sound head and wrapped his arms about both her and it. Every movement of his distorted shoulder was excruciating, but he forced his limb to move.

"Go! Go! Go!"

The helo nosed down and gained way, heading out into the channel. The speed was low, possibly five knots, but the drag through the water was heavy. If the pain in his shoulder had been severe before, now it was unbelievable. It tore a cry out of him and set sparks dancing in front of his eyes. He held his arms locked, however, simply because he had to.

"We still got 'em, Gus?"

"Can't tell, Lieutenant."

Arkady held focus on his flight instrumentation, not daring to let his speed and altitude drift in the slightest. He literally had two lives hanging on a thread underneath him.

The plastic canopy beside his head starred under a glancing slug impact. He could feel other faint but decisive taps ripple through the helo's airframe as well. More bullet hits. The Sea Comanche was armored against rifle-caliber fire in many critical areas, but not in all.

Almost as if answering his concern, Arkady heard a warning tone begin to sound.

"Gus, I've got my hands full. Check it out."

"Engine systems warning! Low transmission fluid pressure! We got a leak!"

"Verify it."

"We got a rise in the gearbox temperature. Shit! We got transmission fluid all over outside the canopy back here! This is for real, Lieutenant! We're going to lose it. We got maybe ten minutes at this throttle setting."

Arkady kept his hands steady on the pitch and collective. There was only one card left to him now. He had been afraid to try bringing it into play again. He had been afraid that there would still only be dead air on the other end of the radio circuit.

"Gray Lady, this is Retainer Zero One. Do you copy?"

"Retainer Zero One, this is Gray Lady. We read you."

It was her voice. Arkady suddenly found himself believing in a future again. It felt great.

"Gray Lady, what is your position?"

"We had a degree of difficulty in the minefield, Retainer. We are clear of it now and are proceeding upriver to pickup point. What is your situation?"

"Better than it was two minutes ago. We are towing the Moondogs out into the central channel with the tether of our dunking sonar. We've had shooting problems. We are having systems problems, and we need to get these guys out of the water now."

"We will be up with you in ten minutes," the weary, static-ridden, and incredibly beautiful voice replied.

"That'll be just about right."

"Lieutenant, you will wish to see this."

Zhou Shan ducked into the low deckhouse and crouched down beside the radar operator. Together they peered at the grainy sweep crawling around the circular screen of the torpedo boat's "Skin Head" search radar.

"A surface target, Comrade Lieutenant. It just appeared in Beicao Hangcao channel. Large target. Proceeding upriver at eighteen knots. Estimated range at this time, eight miles."

"Comrade Lieutenant," the radio operator spoke up from the other side of the cramped compartment. "Some of the enemy jamming has cleared. I have acquired contact with Army coastal artillery command. They are reporting that a hostile warship has forced passage of the estuary mine barrier. It, too, is reported as proceeding upriver."

Shan spoke no reply. He only returned swiftly to the cockpit. Taking up his night glasses, he braced his elbows against the rail of the bridge combing and peered downstream. The blaze that had marked the hulk of the river-patrol gunboat had abruptly gone out a few moments before, the Hainan's agony ending as it had settled beneath the river's surface.

The only light to the east came from the intermittent showers of starshells still falling out at the estuary mouth.

One of them flared exceptionally bright, and Zhou Shan momentarily made out a shadowy shape. A silhouette too sleek for any ordinary ship to have, and the narrowed outline of a tall shark's-fin mast.

"Radio Operator." Shan's voice was totally level as he spoke. The voice of a true commander. "Contact Army Artillery Command. Request they continue to fire illumination shells. We will need the target backlit when we attack."

"Bosun Hoong!" he continued more loudly. "Signal all boats to start engines!"

"Stealth systems, RCS status?" The bridge-wing repeater panel on the port side was intact and functional, and Amanda had shifted her point of operations there.

"We have no stealth capacity, Captain. The Wetball systems are grounding out and we can't isolate the shorting point. We are also reporting heavy RAM damage to the front facing of the superstructure."

"Well, it's not as if they don't know we're here. Carry on, Mr. McKelsie."

The Duke was well clear of the artillery now and was running fast through shadows again. Aboard the destroyer, the only transitory noises were the quiet clink of tools and the murmur of voices from the wheelhouse and the foredeck as the damage-control parties and rescue details went about their grim tasks. The only steady-state sounds were the moan of the turbines and the hiss of the bow cutting the river's surface. Over them, Amanda thought she could just make out helicopter rotors.

"Lieutenant! High-temperature warning light on the rotor transmission gearbox! We got almost zero fluid pressure now!"

Arkady didn't bother to comment. "Moondog, you guys still with us?"

"Still down here, Retainer." The strained voice over the CSAR was almost drowned out by the fed-back thunder of the helo.

"Almost home, Moondog. Almost home. Hang in there. The ship's almost up with us."

"Or at least I hope she is," Arkady muttered under his breath. "Gray Lady, Gray Lady. This is Zero One."

"We read you, Zero One." Amanda's voice had lifted slightly. "We have just acquired you visually. We are preparing for pickup."

"Roger, Gray Lady. Request helipad be prepared for immediate recovery following pickup."

"Do you have a problem, Retainer?" she demanded sharply.

"Not yet."

The drag and the searing agony eased away as the towing helicopter returned to a hover once more. Digger Graves clung to the sonar tether and drew down great, gasping lungsful of air. Trying to keep Bubbles's face out of the water, he had come close to drowning himself. At least out here, they weren't being shot at.

"Hey, Moondog!" This time, Retainer Zero One's voice sounded jubilant as it issued from the CSAR. "You want to see something pretty? Look downstream."

It took a moment to orient himself, and then a moment more for the shades of night to differentiate themselves. Then Graves made out the ghostly slash of a bow wave and a curved prow blotting out a growing number of stars.

He didn't realize it then, but he was becoming part of a masterpiece—the eventual masterwork of noted naval artist Wilson Garrett: *The Lost, Found*. An image frozen for posterity. The pilot clinging protectively to his wounded comrade, the helo hovering in a black sky like a guardian falcon, and the great dark ship looming out of the night before them.

"Aegis systems manager, do we have anything coming off the forward SPY-2A arrays yet?" Ken Hiro demanded from the CIC command chair.

"Negative, sir. All three forward planar arrays are nonfunctional. I'm getting an intermittent feed off of some of the cells in number two, but it's not enough to process.

"Deck teams are reporting heavy fragmentation damage on the front face of the superstructure," one of the DC officers called forward from his station to the *Cunningham*'s exec. "Look's like she's trashed, sir."

Hiro frowned. At the moment, the Duke was radar blind in her critical forward arc. She couldn't see upriver, and that was just where the threats would be coming from.

"Go to visual surface-search sweep with the Mast Mounted Sighting system," he ordered. "Cover the forward arcs. Aegis Systems Manager, do we have any alternatives?"

"Yes, sir." The S.O. looked back from her station in the command cluster. "Have the Aegis access the navigational radar and process a tactical overlay from that. The Nav set is still fully functional. Range and bearing only and no fire control, but we will be able to produce a surface-search image off of it."

"Very well, make it happen and make it fast."

She did. On the Alpha screen, the glowing details of an active radar display began to flesh out the computer-graphics chart of the estuary.

"Multiple surface contacts!" the radar operator called out. "Bearing two seven zero at ten thousand yards. Four targets! Speed, thirty-eight knots. Range is closing!"

"Get the MMS on that!" Hiro commanded, straightening. "Threat boards, what do we have on these guys!"

"Stealth systems have no data!" McKelsie called back from the Spook bay. "We lost our receptors with the SPY array."

"Signal Intelligence?"

"We have shock damage!" Over in the intelligence bay, Hiro heard a fist slam down on the top of a console chassis. "Work, you son of a bitch!" Christine Rendino snarled. "Okay . . . we are now reading four Skin Head search radars active in that arc. Given their speed and aggressive maneuvering pattern, I'd say we've got a group of Huchuan torpedo boats out there."

"I concur. Bridge, we've got a problem! . . ."

The rapid hammering of the waves faded away as the Five Sixteen boat lifted smoothly onto her hydrofoils. Lieutenant Zhou Shan felt the surge of elation that he always did at such moments. This night, however, the sensation lingered on.

All hands were at their battle stations. Bosun Hoong crouched at the base of the portside torpedo tube, his strong hand ready at the launching lever. Over the martial drumbeat of the racing engines Shan could hear the cracking of China's flag in the slipstream. Ahead awaited his nation's enemies. This was the war he had searched for.

". . . got a problem! Four hostile torpedo boats bearing two seven zero upriver. Closing the range. Attack posture. Intent is hostile."

Amanda dialed the tactical display up on the bridge-wing repeater. "I see them," she replied, holding the heavy handset of the sound-powered phone in place against her ear with a shrugged shoulder.

"Captain, this is the tactical officer cutting in. I have no fire-control designation capacity remaining in the forward arcs! Advise we maneuver to unmask the functional arrays."

"Acknowledged, Mr. Beltrain. We're doing it now. Designate targets as you bear. Stand by to fire."

"Helm," she yelled in through the open bridge-wing hatch. "Hard right rudder. Engines ahead slow. Bring her around to three five zero."

The ship began to ware about. As the Duke began to turn, Amanda snatched a set of low-light binoculars from a rack inside the hatchway. Switching them on, she lifted them to her eyes.

A mere hundred yards away, Retainer Zero One station kept low over the river. Two dots were afloat directly beneath the helo: the two downed aviators. And beyond them, upstream, were another row of pale dots: bow waves out at the limits of the binoculars' imaging.

Lieutenant Zhou Shan buried his face into the foam-rubber eyepiece of the torpedo sight, focusing the lenses on his target. The coastal guns were still hurling their illumination rounds, and now a new cluster silhouetted the enemy perfectly.

They were turning! They were coming broadside-on to give him a perfect shot! There was no mistaking that sleek, uncluttered design, that rakish mast array. It was an American—*Cunningham*! And Shan somehow knew that it was the same one that had decimated his squadron and that had killed his first crew. He felt the hand of destiny rest upon his shoulder.

"Stand by, torpedoes!"

On the *Cunningham*'s bridge, Amanda Lee Garrett was feeling the touch of destiny as well. The Red Chinese were launching a classic Jeun Ecoulle torpedo-boat attack, possibly the last one ever to be attempted. It was the equivalent of witnessing the last great cavalry charge at Omderman or the last clash of the dreadnoughts at San Bernardino straits. She was seeing the turning of a page in the history of warfare.

Historic or not, however, they threatened her ship.

"Captain, this is the tactical officer. We have designated the torpedo boats. Harpoon flights are hot. Ready to fire!"

"Shoot!"

The sound of the booster ignition startled Amanda. With her eyes narrowed and her hands pressed over her ears, she let the golden light and hot breath of the missile launch surround her.

Zhou Shan recognized his death, the four cometlike streaks of flame leaping from the foredeck of the American destroyer. Yellow fire that changed to blue as the antishipping missiles converted from rocket to jet propulsion.

He had only seconds to act. One move left to him.

The first Harpoon struck the northernmost boat of the squadron. Fused for anti-small-craft use, it detonated instantly on impact—a rifle bullet striking an eggshell filled with nitroglycerin. The hydrofoil vanished in the heart of a cataclysmic explosion.

The second boat disintegrated. The third . . . a wave of annihilation rolling down on the Five Sixteen.

"Shoot!"

The magnificent Hoong wrenched upward on the manual firing lever. The propulsive charge fired and the cold, greased length of a Type 53 torpedo lunged out of the portside tube. It seemed to hang suspended for an instant, then it plunged beneath the waves like a leaping fish returning joyfully to its home. It was the last sight Zhou Shan's eyes recorded before his world vanished into the fire.

In the CIC, the last target symbol blinked off the Alpha screen. But an instant later, a hostile torpedo hack materialized.

"Fish in the water!" Charles Foster yelled from Sonar Alley. "Torpedo data annex has identified a Type 53 in active acquisition mode. Convergent bearing! We are targeted!"

"Mister Beltrain!" Hiro barked. "Initiate Mark 50 antitorpedo program. Set range safeties to minimum and set for intercept shot!"

The Exec tore the phone handset out of its clips.

"Captain! The Reds got a torpedo off! They've got us bore-sighted! Prepping Mark 50 for antitorpedo intercept!"

"Execute intercept! Fire at will!"

She had to protect the ship. Above all else, she had to protect her ship. Then the rumble of helo rotors again shouldered past her surge of concern to register on her awareness.

"Oh, my God! Radio room! Patch me through to Zero One! Expedite!"

"Arkady! Get them out of the water! Now!" He knew which "them" Amanda was referring to, and the urgency in her voice brooked no questions or even an acknowledgment.

Swiftly he toggled over to CSAR. "Moondog! Hang on to the sound head! For Christ sakes, hang on!"

He squeezed the throttle trigger on the collective and poured power into the helo's failing rotor system. Slowly, the Sea Comanche started to lift away from the river. Arkady could feel a load come on the sonar tether. The Moondogs were coming with him.

"Lieutenant!" Gus yelped in pure terror. "The fucking gearbox is going to come apart!"

"Do fucking tell!"

Something was going on. Graves had watched the Harpoons launch from the *Cunningham* and had seen them hit. Now something else had torn past him submerged, heading out in the same direction as had the missiles. He had felt the turbulence wave of its passage and the vibration of its propulsor through the water.

Then had come the yell over the survival radio. Graves felt the tether start to slide through his fingers and the sound head shoulder up against him. Frantically, he embraced it and Bubbles both, locking his arms tight. As they lifted out of the water their full, sodden weight came onto his dislocated shoulder. Graves screamed and clung to his consciousness as tightly as he had hung on to his systems operator.

"Unit is tracking, sir," the torpedo operator reported.

Dix Beltrain, nodded, silently looking on over her shoulder. What they were attempting was still as experimental as all hell. Theoretically, the Duke's sonar system was accurate enough and her fire-control processors fast enough to steer one of her own Barracuda torpedoes into the path of the weapon that had been fired at her. Also, theoretically, the American unit would then recognize the hostile fish and score a proximity-kill with a warhead detonation.

Even if everything worked as planned, it would be the equivalent of two dynamite trucks running headlong into each other.

"Get a good hold! This is going to be close!"

Out on the bridge wing, it was as if a giant flashbulb had gone off just beneath the surface of the Yangtze. A blue-white glare, and then the river ripped itself open. There wasn't enough water over the explosion to dome.

Rather, it sprayed into the night sky in a thousand berserker jets, an ear-shattering thunderclap radiating outward from its core.

Amanda grabbed for the bridge railing as the Duke leaned away from the blast. "All stop! Initiate station keeping!" she yelled. "Hold us in the channel!"

As the destroyer rolled back on an even keel, she lifted her binoculars and feverishly swept the night. The ringing in her ears was too loud for her to focus on the sound of the Sea Comanche's rotors, but she reacquired the helo in only a few seconds.

Amanda could see a misshapen mass at the end of the sonar tether, four legs dangling. He'd done it! Arkady had gotten them out of the water before the shock wave. They all still had a chance!

Amanda was granted a single heartbeat's worth of relief. Then she saw the helo lurch in midair, a fireworks stream of sparks belching from its engine.

"Lieutenant! The rotor drive's going!"

Arkady didn't bother to try to answer over the vibration rattle and the squalling of the engine warning alarms. In the vernacular of the helicopter aviator, the Sea Comanche was "starting to lose the Jesus nut." It was entering into the first phase of a catastrophic main rotor assembly failure. Short of flying into the side of a mountain, things were suddenly as bad as they could get.

More so because of the Moondogs. Arkady could feel their weight swaying at the end of the tether.

The book said that he should be getting down out of the sky just as fast as possible, which would mean setting down right on top of the two aviators. Instead, Arkady did just what the book said not to. He firewalled his throttles, forcing the power from the turbines through the incandescent wreckage of the disintegrating transmission and up to the rotors.

Hemorrhaging, the helo staggered toward the *Cunningham.*

"Gus, stand by to jettison the sonar pod!"

No time for subtlety. No time for care. Maybe just enough time to get his charges to safety.

They were coming up on the ship with just enough altitude for the sonar head to clear the rail. Arkady had the briefest glimpse of a slender figure looking up from the bridge wing, and then they were over the foredeck.

"Gus, cut 'em loose!"

Arkady felt the sonar pod detach from beneath the snub wing, falling to the deck below. *Please God, don't let the damn thing land on the poor bastards.*

Shedding the sonar pod had gained them a scant decrease in weight and boost in maneuverability. But now the gearbox was literally going to pieces. A new volley of screaming systems alarms heralded an incipient turbine failure.

Crossing over the foredeck, Arkady kicked the tail of the dying helo around and staggered down the length of the destroyer's hull, trying for the helipad aft.

"Brace yourself, Gus! This is going to be a bitch!"

Another pedal turn and a wild side-slip to try to line up over the giant **H** in the landing area. The belated flash of the landing markers. The flicker of flame reflected in the marred canopy plastic and the shriek of metal binding on metal. The sight of the deck crew scattering away from the developing disaster. A single, sudden, panic-stricken thought.

LANDING GEAR!

"Aw, to hell with it." Arkady released the throttle trigger. Hitting the "Power Kill" switches, he let Retainer Zero One fall.

The helo hit hard and flat on her belly, then rolled onto her side. Her rotor blades exploded into flying composite fragments as they touched the deck, the fuselage floundering on the flailing stubs like a landed fish.

As the helo went still, there was a rush to open the cockpit as the crash crew moved in. Arkady released his seat harness and shoved at the canopy overhead. It didn't budge, and the aviator was suddenly very aware of the smell of hot metal and smoke. He heard crash bars start to pry into the cockpit frame.

Arkady got his feet up into the seat pan and his back braced against the top of the canopy. He heaved with adrenaline-fueled strength. The canopy tore loose, and he sprawled out onto the antiskid.

Half a dozen fire extinguishers were being emptied into the engine compartment as Arkady rolled to his feet. Joining in with the aviation hands, he helped to yank open the rear cockpit and drag his S.O. clear. Only when Gus was out and on his feet did Arkady take a second to enjoy taking a breath.

He turned to face the superstructure and the monitor camera that he knew would be there. Lifting both arms, he clasped hands over his head, sending a message to someone he knew would be watching.

On the *Cunningham's* foredeck, Digger Graves groggily lifted his head from the deck. Bubbles lay at his side, and he heard the faint whisper of a moan from her.

Damage-control hands and a first-aid team were hurrying toward them from the destroyer's deck house. Graves tried to come up on one elbow and suddenly realized that something was missing. The burning pain that had been ravaging his shoulder was almost gone. The strain of the lift or the impact of his fall had popped the dislocation back into place. The aviator goggled at his free-moving arm for a moment and murmured, "Well, I'll be a son of a bitch." Then, for the third time that night, Digger Graves passed out.

On the bridge wing, Amanda looked up from the helipad image on the repeater screen. Arkady was home. Up forward, the two rescued aviators were also being carried belowdecks. She still had to get them out, but at least they all were under her hand now. She bit her lower lip lightly and wiped away a couple of unbidden tears.

"Helm, rotate on station by hydrojet. Come about to one zero zero degrees true. Set reciprocal course downchannel."

The Duke came about within her own length, aiming her prow toward the sea, gathering herself for the dash toward freedom.

Suddenly, flickering light outlined the headlands to the south and the sound of a new volley of explosions rolled upstream from the mouth of the estuary.

"CIC, something's taking place downriver. Do you have anything on this?"

"Oh yeah, Boss Ma'am. Indeed we do!" Christine Rendino's jubilant voice responded. "We have the word from Task Flag. We have a support strike rolling in on those bad boys down on the beach! The coastal batteries are being taken out now. They are holding the door open for us!"

"And we are going through it! Lee helm, all engines ahead one third! Let's get out of here!"

"Sir, signal from the *Cunningham*! They have just cleared the Yangtze mine barrier and are taking departure from the Chinese coast. All personnel accounted for. All mission objectives completed. They are closing out the Stormdragon time line!"

"Yeah!" Admiral Tallman's fist crashed onto the console top. "Yeah!"

The tension in Pri-Fly snapped like a rubber band. Yells, cheers, and whistles made the round in the compartment, men and women alike slapping palms and exchanging embraces as they welcomed a shipload of fellow warriors back to life.

MacIntyre smiled in the semilight. "Well, Jake. I told you she could pull it off."

"That you did, Eddie Mac! Goddamn! I wish my son wasn't already married. I'd like that woman in my family!"

"I wouldn't mind it myself."

"Admiral MacIntyre." Nolan Walker handed across a sheet of hard copy. "Second message in from the *Cunningham*. Personal. Captain Garrett to CINCSPECFORCE."

"Thank you, Commander." MacIntyre couldn't help but note that even Walker had a grin on his face.

Stepping back to the bulkhead, MacIntyre held the message form up to one of the battle lights.

All sheep have been returned to the fold.

MacIntyre smiled again. Folding the paper, he slipped it into his shirt pocket.

☆ East China Sea
0534 Hours Zone Time; August 28, 2006

There was another mission waiting for the replacement CSR helo: medevac for the *Cunningham's* wounded. With the helipad still blocked by the wreckage of Retainer Zero One, the four more critical cases had to be lifted by sling stretcher up to the Oceanhawk as it hovered over the forward replenishment point.

Doc Golden had accompanied his patients topside to supervise the transfer. Now he gave the deck controller the all clear for departure.

Nodding a response, the controller passed the word to the helo pilot with a sweep of his wands. The SH-60 dipped its nose down and pulled away into the lightening sky.

Golden took a deep breath, letting it trickle out from between his lips. One more immediate job left. He picked his medical bag up from the deck and started back toward the superstructure, past his colleagues in the damage-control teams who were tending to the ship's wounds.

Up on the battered bridge, Ken Hiro slouched tiredly in the captain's chair. Things were coming back together again here as well. Electrician's mates were replacing damaged telescreens and systems modules. There was only going to be so much that the crew would be able to do, however. The Duke was going to need a long stretch in the yards before she could be pronounced fully healed.

"We've got all of the bad cases on their way, sir," Golden reported.

"How about the aircrew, Doc? I didn't see you loading them."

"We're going to be hanging on to them for a little while," Golden replied. "The docs over at Task Flag concur with me that they have no critical trauma that requires any immediate heroic treatment. Bouncing them around in a hoist basket isn't probably the best thing in the world for them either."

The physician rubbed his tired eyes. "We'll let them stabilize a little more and move 'em out after we get the helipad clear."

The Duke's exec nodded. "Good enough."

"Speaking of helicopters, what's the word on Zero Two?"

"They recovered safely aboard the *Antietam*. The Annie is en route to rendezvous with us now. We'll have Lieutenant Delany and her S.O. back aboard in time for lunch."

"Glad to hear it, sir. Especially that part about the rendezvous." Golden leaned against the side of the captain's chair and peered out at the horizon. "Things are a little bit lonely out here to suit me just now."

"Not really, Doc. The *Antietam* already has us under their Aegis screen, and straight up at about thirty thousand feet, we've got half a squadron of Super Hornets flying top cover for us. It's all over, Doc."

"Not quite. Do you know where the Captain is, Commander?"

"Wardroom."

"Thanks."

There were three of them there: the Intel, alert and radiating a near hostility, like a small and wary watchdog; the helo pilot, sprawled back on the couch, his eyes closed and his flight gear stacked on the deck at his feet; and the Captain, sitting upright in one of the lounge chairs, a mug of tea cradled forgotten in her hand.

Golden crossed the compartment and knelt down beside the chair. Taking cotton and disinfectant from his bag, he began to clean the encrusted cuts and scratches on her face and forearms.

Amanda didn't seem to notice until she felt the first sting of the alcohol-soaked swab. "I'm all right, Doctor," she said, jerking her head aside. "See to the crew. . . ."

"Don't worry, Captain. You're the last one. All wounded have been treated and have either been medevaced out to the carrier or are resting comfortably. Now, shut up, if you please, and let me do my job."

She accepted his touch and treatment then, sitting quietly as he worked. "How many wounded?" she asked after a few moments.

"Ten. All either on the bridge or in the ammunition-handling compartment under the forward Oto Melara. Four of them are serious, but in my judgment, all of them will recover."

Captain Garrett nodded again, slipping back into her state of somnolent, postmission neutrality.

"Hey, Doc." Arkady's eyes were open now, and fixed on the auburn-haired woman seated across from him. "Do you think that it might be a good idea for the Captain to have something to help her sleep?"

"Sounds like a winner to me," Golden replied, applying a bandage to a cleaned cut on Amanda's forearm.

"No . . . Lieutenant." Captain Garrett shook her head emphatically. "I'm all right. I need to stay clear for a while longer. I'm all right."

"Your choice, ma'am," Golden said judgmentally. "However, in my professional opinion, you're probably going to keel over on your own here presently."

"I know, Doc. I've been here before. I can feel it coming. I've just got to get some things cleaned up. . . . Doc, did we lose anyone?"

"One killed in action, Captain. In the ammunition-handling room."

"Who?"

"Seaman Langdon. One of the new people we took on board at Pearl."

"I never did get a chance to talk with him," she almost whispered.

Golden finished and began to stow away his first-aid materials. "Just cuts and bruises, Captain. Nothing major. But I do advise that you get some rest."

"I will, Doctor. I had to do it. . . ."

The slight rise in her voice drew the attention of them all. Arkady sat forward on the couch, and Christine Rendino took a quick step forward. Amanda Garrett's eyes refocused on the real world and she looked around at each of them.

"I couldn't leave them out there!" Her words were a plea for understanding. "I put the ship at risk. I got our people injured. I got one of them killed. But I just couldn't leave them out there. I guess it doesn't make much sense. . . ."

"It makes perfect sense to me," Golden replied quietly, "and I expect it does to Mr. Arkady here, and Miss Rendino, and just about every other man and woman aboard this ship as well."

He rocked back on his heels, thinking carefully for a moment. He was prescribing for a patient just now.

"Captain, I am not a real military officer. I can't do what you do, or make the kind of decisions you make. Nor, speaking frankly, would I want to.

However, as a doctor, I do have a certain nodding acquaintance with matters of mortality.

"Last night, it cost you one life to get two back. That's a rather tragic kind of mathematics. However, that still puts you one up on death. And anytime you can manage that, Captain, you are doing pretty damn good."

☆ Sick Bay, USS *Cunningham*

0601 Hours Zone Time: August 28, 2006

Digger Graves awoke in one of the upper berths in the cramped little ward compartment. He was bucking a massive dose of sedation, but he vaguely realized that there was something that he had to do, something that he had to say.

"Bub? Hey, Bub?"

"I'm here," a blurry voice responded from the curtained berth beneath him.

"How you doing?"

"If you must know, I feel like shit."

Unsteadily, Graves lifted his arm over the bunk-edge rail and extended it down toward Bubbles's voice. After a moment, a smaller hand clasped his with a brief, tight grip.

"We made it, Bub."

"Yeah."

"Know what else?"

"What?"

"I'm staying in."

"I knew you would."

"Yeah." The haze was closing in again, and Graves struggled to keep the words put together. Woozily, he grinned up at the overhead. "It only makes sense, Bub. . . . I mean, if I get out, where am I going to find this kind of job security again?"

"Digger."

"Yeah."

"Will you please shut the hell up."

☆ Hotel Manila, Republic of the Philippines
1818 Hours Zone Time; August 28, 2006

"This was a flagrant act of war!" The bland exactitude of the English issuing from the translator earphone did not match the pale-faced rage being displayed by Vice Premier Chang. That rage was the key point at the moment. Harrison Van Lynden stayed focused on the Chinese statesman.

"We prefer the term 'police action,' Mr. Premier," the Secretary of State replied levelly.

"We are not interested in your sophistry, Mr. Secretary," Chang nearly shouted. "Call it what you will. You admit before the world that the United States is now taking active part in this criminal aggression against the People's Republic of China!"

The crisis talks were in full session, the national delegations spaced out around the great O-shaped assembly of tables. However, this day, the majority of the diplomats were there only as the witnesses to the confrontation between the United States and Red China.

"I admit that the United States has acted on behalf of the other Pacific Rim nations gathered here at this conference. We were seeking to end the threat of the nuclear holocaust that was being held over us all."

"This was purely an internal matter of China!"

"No, Mr. Premier!" Van Lynden's hand slapped down on the white tablecloth in front of him. "The utilization of weapons of mass destruction, be they chemical, biological, or nuclear, can be the affair of no single nation in the world today. We all live on the same planet, sir!"

"And you believe that this gives you the right to conduct acts of gangsterism against my nation!"

Lucena Sagada sat quietly at Van Lynden's side, her attention focused soberly on the Secretary of State. Across the room, General Ho sat at his station beside the Vice Premier, his gaze fixed impassively on the center of the room.

"We believe that it gave us the responsibility to act on behalf of our allies who would have been caught downwind of your holocaust, Mr. Premier. No non-Chinese state here has ever interfered in China's current internal conflict. Nor has any state here had any desire to do so, until you threatened to spread your devastation beyond your own borders."

"The United States will be held responsible. I promise you that, Mr. Secretary."

Van Lynden leaned in over the table. "Mr. Premier, my government believes that the imminent threat of the Chinese civil war going nuclear has been eliminated," he stated with almost ironic calmness. "I am authorized by my president to assure you that the United States plans to initiate no further military actions against the People's Republic of China.

"However, I am also authorized to inform you that the United States now has over three hundred armed strike aircraft and an equal number of cruise missiles within range of key targets within PRC territory. We are also prepared, if necessary, to initiate a full naval blockade of the Red Chinese coast, as well as an immediate airlift of military equipment and supplies to the Nationalist and UDFC factions.

"If the People's Republic desires to expand its conflict with the United States, that will be your choice. However, Mr. Premier, I believe that your nation has enough on its plate at the moment. Anything more would not be advisable."

The stocky Chinese statesman could find no further words. Abruptly he rose to his feet, obviously intent on stalking out of the conference room, General Ho silently following suit.

"Premier Chang!" Van Lynden's voice rang like a pistol shot, freezing the man in place.

"I am also authorized to inform you of one thing further. In the event that the People's Republic should consider any further 'extraordinary actions' in this matter, be advised that a number of major military installations within PRC territory have been targeted by American ICBMs. This targeting will remain in effect until the conflict in your nation has ended . . . one way or another."

The conference was adjourned. The crisis that had brought them together had been resolved. The talks had been an aspect of that resolution, although not quite in the way Van Lynden had expected. Nonetheless, he'd call it a win. This phase, anyway.

"It's been a great pleasure working with you, sir," Lucena Sagada said, securing her final page of notes in her briefcase. "I've learned a great deal. I appreciate this opportunity."

"What in the world makes you think it's over, Lucena?"

"Isn't it?"

"For us, it's just beginning. Come on. We need to talk to some people."

The Nationalist/UDFC delegates were still seated at the master table, Secretary Ho and Professor Yi speaking quietly together. At the approach of Van Lynden and his assistant, the two Chinese rose, smiling.

"Mr. Secretary," Ho said, "the people of China can only express their thanks at the moment. Someday, perhaps, we will be able to return your assistance in kind."

"Perhaps," Van Lynden replied, coming to stand across the table from the two men.

Professor Yi nodded, a faint glitter in his aged eyes. "We were all most fortunate in this matter. Most fortunate."

"It has been my experience, gentlemen, that we usually create our own fortune . . . and that has certainly been the case here. Hasn't it?"

The faces of both Chinese diplomats subtly froze.

"What do you mean, Mr. Secretary?" Professor Yi inquired softly.

"I mean that the conference is over. The media has gone home, and now, maybe, we can do a little real statesmanship. In short, gentlemen, cut the bullshit! We know!"

"You believe that you know what, Mr. Secretary. And who constitutes 'we'?"

The list didn't include Lucena Sagada, as her puzzled expression indicated. Van Lynden's conversations on this subject had taken place on levels rarefied even for her. Now was as good a time as any to bring her into the loop.

"The 'we' are the other ministers of the Pacific Rim states. And we know that you set us up! This whole thing. This crisis. The nuclear civil war. Our intervention in Shanghai. This was all part of a plan. Yours."

"That is a remarkable statement, Mr. Secretary," Ho said. "What could prompt you to say such a thing?"

"Are you asking for evidence?" Van Lynden smiled. "We're beginning to compile it in bits and pieces. Primarily, at the moment, it's just instinct. And what we've learned from watching you operate.

"For example, I must congratulate you for conducting one of the most magnificent acts of realpolitik to be conducted in the past century. The first Chinese civil war really didn't end back in 1949, did it? You have been planning this operation, the reconquest of the mainland, for almost fifty years, haven't you? Piece by piece. Detail by meticulous detail. Planning for every eventuality. Except apparently one."

Van Lynden watched the two men like a mongoose studies cobras. "It was the atomic eventuality. How were you going to get around the Red Chinese nuclear arsenal?"

"We had made our preparations there as well, Mr. Secretary," Ho replied, the last vestige of the statesman's professional bonhomie evaporating. "We trusted in the deterrence of our own force of arms."

"No, you didn't, sir. You knew full well that the handful of bombs that you possessed would be inadequate to deter a cornered and desperate Communist government. You had to know! They were of your people! Your culture!

"Your arsenal was just large enough to guarantee that any use of atomic weapons would rapidly escalate into a full-scale nuclear exchange. One that would prove cataclysmic to the entire Pacific Rim if it occurred. One that would force the United States and the other nations here to intervene to prevent it from happening."

Van Lynden leaned in across the table. "You set us up," he said, pronouncing each word with deliberate succinctness. "This entire crisis was a Nationalist sting operation from the start. You used us to help take out the last of the Red atomic arsenal. The one remaining block on your road back to Beijing."

Professor Yi smiled as he might have at a favored student. "Rather, Mr. Secretary, think of us as encouraging your nation to make an appropriate choice. The Red dragon is dying. Soon, China shall be free again. Is this not a good thing?"

"Yes," Van Lynden said, straightening. "Yes, it is. But you took us all out on the edge to do it. 'The end justifying the means' is a line out of the dragon's book."

"Mayhap so. But it is over now."

Harrison Van Lynden chuckled. Even to Lucena Sagada, it was not a pleasant sound. "But you are wrong, gentlemen. We're going to be working together for a long, long time on a number of things."

"What do you mean?" Secretary Ho demanded sharply.

"There is an ancient tradition in your country, Mr. Ho. If one man saves another's life, then the first man becomes responsible for the second's actions. Well, guess what, gentlemen, we've just saved yours and we are now in the loop."

Van Lynden didn't give them a chance to answer. He leaned in across the table again, bracing his hands on the white cloth that covered it, his voice sinking dangerously. "Soon there are going to be any number of very critical decisions to be made about the form postrevolutionary China is going to take. Its government. Its constitution. Its borders. And we are going to be there. The United States, Japan, Korea, the Philippines . . . everyone who would have been trapped in the fallout pattern if you had miscalculated. You have invited us in, and now, by God, we are not going home until the party's over!

"Congratulations on a successful operation, gentlemen."

☆ ☆ ☆

"Good evening, my friend."

"Good evening, General," Van Lynden replied, sinking down on the concrete bench beside the Red Chinese officer. The fountain played at their backs and the first stars glinted out over Manila Bay. Looking around, the Secretary of State noted that General Ho's usual cadre of security guards were not present. Van Lynden also noted a strange air about the man. Resignation? Maybe even peace.

"Do you wish to know something funny, Mr. Secretary?" Ho said quietly.

"What, General?"

"I find that I am grateful that your nation has attacked mine."

"That is a little unusual."

"Not really. Because tonight I know that I may go to sleep with the knowledge that there will still be a China when I awake. Soon, perhaps, it will not be my China. But it will be China. Had events been allowed to run their full course . . . who could say what would have remained?"

"I don't know, General," Van Lynden replied, tugging the knot of his necktie down a couple of inches and releasing the button of his collar. "In my experience, there are usually men of good conscience on both sides of any conflict. Men such as yourself. You might have found alternatives."

Ho smiled grimly. "I think you overrate me, Mr. Secretary. As with many others, I, too, would be a desperate man with the tools of desperation at hand. For a warrior, the temptation to take one's foes down with you when you fall is strong. It is best that the temptation is gone. We shall die with the People's Republic. But our homeland will live on."

"As I said, General," Van Lynden replied slowly, "you may be able to find alternatives. I notice that you came without your security team tonight. The United States Embassy is only a short walk across the park. I can guarantee you political asylum. The new China is going to need good men and strong leaders."

"That will be a task for the new Chinese. I am of the old. Perhaps the People's Republic was not the best of states. But still, I have served it all of my life. I will die with it now—hopefully, in a battle lost before it was begun. Possibly, before the firing squad of some tribunal.

"Be that as it may, there comes a time in a man's life when he is too old to change allegiance to his beliefs just because they happen to be wrong."

"I understand."

Ho rose to his feet. "I have enjoyed our conversations, Mr. Secretary."

"As have I, General," Van Lynden replied, also getting to his feet. "Good-bye, sir."

"Good-bye."

The two men shook hands and then walked away along separate paths into the night.

☆ The White House, Washington, D.C. 1337 Hours, Zone Time; August 28, 2006

"How does it look?"

"Mr. President, according to our last set of projections, the probability of the China conflict going nuclear has been reduced to between ten and fifteen percent."

"A ten- to fifteen-percent chance that a million people could still die. That's not good enough, Sam. But I guess that it's better than it was. Maybe enough so that I won't dream about it tonight."

"Stay outside of it, sir. If you're going to command, you can't take it personally."

Ben Childress produced a brief, ironic snort of laughter. "At one and the same time, Sam, that is both good advice and the rankest kind of bullshit."

"I know, sir. I was never able to manage it either."

The two men were seated in the Oval Office, an afternoon situation briefing trailing off into a few minutes of conversation between friends.

"What else is going on out there? Has there been any indication of Red retaliation against us?"

The National Security Adviser shook his head. "The Communists appear to have their hands full. The Nationalists have taken advantage of our disruption of the air-defense net around Shanghai and are bombing the hell out of the place themselves. I doubt that the Reds are really interested in picking a fight with anyone else just now."

"That's good news."

"And here's some more. Our conflict-simulation projections indicate that our intervention may have shortened the Chinese civil war by possibly as much as a month. God knows how many people are going to live who otherwise would have died if we hadn't stepped in. And that isn't even considering the bomb."

President Childress nodded to himself. "Every little bit of positive will help, Sam. Lord knows but there are a lot of people who want to know why I took us out on the edge like this."

"How about because it was the right thing to do, sir."

"That doesn't necessarily cut it in some circles these days, Sam."

"Then use the apartment-house comparison," Hanson grunted, settling deeper into his chair.

Childress cocked an eyebrow. "The apartment-house comparison?"

"Yes, sir. Back in the good old days, the nations of the world were like individual farmsteads, scattered out across the country. Separated by time and space. If your neighbor's barn burned down, well, all that you'd see was the fire against the sky. You could get involved, or not, depending on how you felt about it.

"These days, though, the world's shrunk on us. We're all living in the same apartment house now. And if some son of a bitch is smoking in bed, we all need to be concerned about it."

"Good metaphor, Sam. What do you want for it?"

"Consider it a gift, Mr. President."

☆ 45 Miles Northwest of Amamiō Shima Island
0945 Hours Zone Time; August 30, 2006

There are few private places aboard a warship at sea. A pair of such existed aboard the *Cunningham*, atop the superstructure. Aft of the exhaust stacks and partitioned from each other by the mast array were two wedges of weather deck. If a person, or a couple, came up to these isolated spots to watch the wake, the unspoken tradition aboard the Duke was that they were to be left undisturbed.

"Morning, Captain," Arkady said, coming to lean beside Amanda at the rail. He glanced across at her questioningly, waiting, letting her set the tone for their conversation.

"Good morning, love." She was in a mood for someone closer than a subordinate just now.

"What are you thinking about so hard, babe?" he replied, taking her cue.

"All sorts of things. Past, present, and future. Yours, mine, ours."

"Such as?"

"Christine knows about us, Arkady."

"Yeah, so?"

She lifted an eyebrow. "You know about that?"

"The subject has come up between Miss Rendino and me. I repeat, so?"

"If Christine has figured it out, others are bound to eventually as well."

Arkady nodded thoughtfully, the wind of the ship's passage ruffling the dark hair beneath the edge of his aviator's baseball cap. "Definite possibility."

"So, what are we going to do?"

"Good question. One of these days, I guess we'll need to come up with an answer for that."

Amanda chuckled softly. "Maybe. Who knows. The whole thing might just resolve itself here presently."

"What do you mean?" It was Arkady's turn to cock an eyebrow.

"I've just been considering what comes next," she replied, letting her eyes trail back along the white and jade furrow the Duke had plowed in the sea. "All of my life, I've worked for one thing: having my own ship. Well, I've got her. Professionally speaking, I'm at the peak of my career right now. But it's not going to last forever. I've got a year and a half left on my tour aboard the *Cunningham*. After that, I don't know."

"Hell, babe. I don't know what you're talking about and don't think you do either. You're just getting started."

Amanda shook her head slowly. "No. Not for what I want. Back in the old Navy, it was different. After you captained a destroyer, you had a chance for a cruiser. And after a cruiser, maybe a battlewagon. Now, though, it's one combat command per customer, and the Duke's mine."

"You'll be due for another ship when you get your fourth stripe."

Amanda shook her head again. "An AOE or a tender. At best, maybe an amphib. But not a ship of the line. An aviation officer like you can get a shot at a carrier. But for a surface-warfare specialist like me, your destroyer command is it.

"There's nothing wrong in serving aboard a ship of the train, but I've already put my time in there. The next combat command that I could hope for would be as a rear admiral in command of a surface action group. I'd probably be in my early fifties at least, and that's granting I get my flag. That's another fifteen years on the beach, a whole second career. That's too long, Arkady."

"Then what are you going to do?" he prompted. There was a look in his eyes that indicated that he was suddenly intensely interested in the course this conversation was taking.

"Finish my time on the Duke. Then there are some doctrine papers I want to write. Then, I don't know. Maybe take my twenty and out. Go somewhere and raise babies and petunias while I have a few ticks left on my biological clock. I don't know."

She was leaving Arkady a massive opening just then, and she regarded her young lover steadily, wondering how he was going to fill it.

He was, too. She watched as he studied the horizon for the duration of a dozen heartbeats before replying. "I'd say that you don't have to decide anything yet. I think we have a little time left. Let's use it the best way we can."

It was as good an answer as any that she had come up with. Amanda leaned deeper into the straps of the railing and let her elbow lightly brush his in the covert caress they had developed. "Do me a date, Arkady."

"Where?"

"Japan. And I'm going to hold you to this one. We're going to be laying over there awhile to make repairs."

"Japan, huh?" the aviator smiled reminiscently. "Now, that is one place I know my way around. Let's see. Have you ever been to a real, traditional Japanese *nosan*?"

"I don't know. What is it?"

"A hot-springs resort. I know this one place, owned by the same family for the past couple of centuries or so, totally traditional. The real Japanese cuisine. The rooms are all furnished with the classic sleep-on-the-floor—style futons, the traditional bathing pools, the whole nine yards. Not many non-Japanese can get a reservation, but I might just be able to swing it."

"That sounds like fun. I . . . Wait a minute. Traditional bathing pools? You don't mean the kind where men and women . . . total strangers . . . together!"

"Fraidy-cat, babe?"

"Is that a dare, Lieutenant?"

Arkady was right—they did have a little time left.

☆ Over the Pacific

1910 Hours Zone Time; August 30, 2006

The VP-3 Orion transport, the conversion of a war-weary naval patrol plane, churned slowly to the southeast, its propellers flickering against the sky. Its eventual destination: Hawaii and Pearl Harbor.

Inboard, Admiral Elliot MacIntyre shifted position, trying to find a little comfort in the worn bucket seat. Giving it up as a lost cause, he returned his attention to the eternal backlog of paperwork in his briefcase.

A message hard copy tucked into an odd corner diverted him. It was that last one Amanda Garrett had sent him on the night of the Shanghai operation.

All sheep have been returned to the fold.

Amanda Garrett . . .

MacIntyre closed his briefcase. With the message brief still in his hand, he sank deeper into his seat. Thoughtfully, he gazed out through the small porthole at his side, studying the evening as it settled in over the sea.

GLOSSARY

Aegis   A mating of a sophisticated cybernetic battle-management system with a series of advanced planar array radars, giving a surface warship a sea- and air-control capacity out to a 250-mile radius.

The augmented SPY-2A variant deployed aboard the Cunningham-class DDG combines increased range and fire-control capacity with improved definition and simplicity of operation.

AEW (Airborne Early Warning)   The doctrine of mounting a high-powered search radar aboard an aircraft to enhance its coverage area. The Boeing AWACS is the premier example of this technology.

In Stormdragon, both the Taiwanese Air Force and the U.S. Navy also utilize variants of the Grumman E-2 Hawkeye, a venerable but still effective twin-turboprop AEW aircraft, while the *Cunningham*'s Sea Comanche helicopters can mount a padded version of the British-built Clearwater radar.

ASW (antisubmarine warfare)   The delicate and deadly art of submarine hunting.

Barracuda   The Mark 50 Barracuda is the U.S. Navy's latest-generation antisubmarine torpedo. A small, high-speed weapon utilizing multimode guidance, it is designed to be dropped from ASW aircraft, delivered to target via a V-ROC antisubmarine missile, or launched from the deck tubes of a surface warship. It is also being studied as a possible "interceptor" torpedo for use in an active antitorpedo defense system.

Black Hole System   A combination of anti-infrared technologies used to reduce the heat signature of a military vehicle.

Aboard the Cunningham-class destroyer, blowers mix cooler outside air with the ship's engine-exhaust gases before they are vented outboard, reducing the thermal plume from the turbines. Likewise, seawater is circulated through cooling jackets surrounding the ship's funnels to prevent "hot-spotting," which could provide a target for home-on-heat guided munitions.

Ching-Kuo   Produced by Taiwan's Aero Industry Development Center, the Ching-Kuo is that nation's first domestically produced combat aircraft. A light, twin-engined, air-defense and antishipping fighter, its design was inspired by the U.S.-built F-5. Its development, along with that of the rest of Taiwan's rapidly developing aerospace and armaments industry, has been spurred by Red China's continuing policy of interfering with international arms sales to the Nationalist government.

Cold Fire Launching System   A vertical-launch technology that utilizes a charge of inert gas to project a missile out of a launch cell for a midair ignition. Utilized aboard the Cunningham-class DDG to protect the RAM decking from exhaust-flame damage.

ECM (Electronic Countermeasures)   Jamming and decoy systems used to confuse and degrade search sensors and weapon-guidance systems.

Elint (Electronic Intelligence)   The collection of battlefield intelligence (target location, systems type, nationality, force strength, etc.) via the analysis of emissions produced by radars and other electronic systems.

EMCON (Emission Control)   An operational state in which a naval vessel or aircraft maintains complete radio and radar silence, rendering them undetectable to Signal Intelligence systems.

ESSM (Enhanced Sea Sparrow Missile)   Uprated follow-on to the current NATO Sea Sparrow system. A medium-range, surface-to-air system using radar guidance, it can be fired either from its own dedicated launcher or from a quad pack fitted into a cell of a Mark 41 or 42 VLS array.

F/A-18E Super Hornet   A stretched and souped-up variant of the current-model C F/A-18. The U.S. Navy's next-generation maid-of-all-work warplane, equally capable as both a fighter and bomber.

F/A-22 Sea Lightning   American naval aviation is facing two urgent needs in the immediate future. One will be a replacement for the elderly F-14 Tomcat fleet defense fighter. The other will be for the deployment of a carrier-borne stealth strike aircraft. One proposed solution has been for the development of a navalized fighter-bomber variant of Lockheed's F-22 Lightning II stealth fighter.

Fenestron   Literally "fan in tail," an advanced helicopter technology that replaces the conventional tail rotor with a ducted fan inset into the tail fin, reducing noise, vibration, and radar cross section.

GPU (Global Positioning Unit)   A mobile navigation system that utilizes radio impulses beamed down from a network of satellites in orbit around the Earth. Simple, compact, effective, and extremely accurate, this technology is finding literally hundreds of new uses in both the civil and military arenas, so much so that serious consideration has been given to a proposal to build a GPU into the stock of every rifle issued to the U.S. Armed Services.

Han Class name of Red China's first and, to date, only class of nuclear attack submarine.

Hellfire U.S.-designed antitank missile. A powerful and accurate weapon utilizing a laser guidance system, the Hellfire is finding a second niche as an anti-small-craft missile utilized by the Navy's LAMPS helicopter force.

Hsiung-Feng (Male Bee) The standard Taiwanese antiship missile. Air and sea launchable, the weapon is a copy of the superb Israeli Gabriel ASM.

LAMPS (Light Airborne Multi-Purpose System) The family of maid-of-all-work helicopters that operate off the helipads of the U.S. surface Navy. While primarily intended for ASW operations, they also perform a wide variety of secondary tasks, ranging from surface search and attack to intelligence gathering and cargo and personnel transport.

Oto Melara Super Rapid A 76mm, water-cooled autocannon produced by the Oto Melara corporation of Italy. A dual-mode weapons system with an exceptionally high rate of fire, it is capable of engaging both air and surface targets with a wide variety of different munitions types. A popular and efficient design, it serves as the primary gun armament of the Cunningham-class destroyer.

PLA People's Liberation Army. The armed forces of Communist China. Technically, the Red Chinese Air Force and Navy are not independent services, but are merely divisions of the PLA.

RAM (Radar Absorbent Material) A family of composite materials used in the creation of stealth weapons systems They work by "soaking up" incoming radar waves, converting them into thermal energy within their structure rather then reflecting them off.

RBOC (Rapid Blooming Overhead Chaff) Projector   A shipboard antimissile defense system, originally intended to protect vessels against radar-guided missiles by screening them with clouds of metal foil.

In recent years, however, additional projectiles have been developed for the system, including flare and multispectral smoke rounds that can provide protection against infrared and laser-guided munitions.

Raven's Roost   Shipboard nickname for the Intelligence Systems bay. Because of their stealth capacity, the Cunningham-class destroyers have been given an enhanced capability to perform "Raven" missions—i.e., to act as a Sigint (Signal Intelligence) and Elint (Electronic Intelligence) gathering platform.

SCM (Stealth Cruise Missile)   The follow-on to the Tomahawk sea-launched cruise missile, the SCM is a sophisticated, long-range strike weapon incorporating low radar visibility in its design. A multi-mode weapon, it can be configured for either antishipping or land attack.

SAH-66 Sea Comanche LAMPS (Light Airborne Multi-Purpose System)   The original SAH-66 Comanche was intended as an Army scout/gunship helicopter utilizing low-radar-observability technology. The SAH-66 Sea Comanche is a naval variant produced to complement the stealth capacity of the Cunningham-class guided-missile destroyer. Intended for ASW and surface search/recon operations, the Sea Comanche mounts a powerful APG 65 radar in its nose. It can also be equipped with a number of different pod-mounted sensor systems, including dunking sonars, Magnetic Abnormality Detectors, and the Shearwater AEW system. In addition, the SAH-66 can be armed with a broad spectrum of torpedoes, missiles, depth charges, and gun pods.

Sea SLAM   A ground-attack variant of the Harpoon antishipping missile. Utilizing an infrared, electro-optical targeting system developed for the Maverick air-to-surface missile, it is a sea-launched weapon, primarily intended for precision strikes against land targets.

Sigint (Signal Intelligence)   The collection of battlefield intelligence via the interception and antidecryption of enemy radio and landline communications.

Standard HARM (Homing Anti-Radiation Missile)   A derivative of the Standard surface-to-air missile. The Standard HARM is designed to seek out and destroy enemy land- and sea-based radio and radar systems by homing in on their EM emissions. The missile is equipped with a memory system that allows it to prosecute the kill even if the target transmitter is shut down.

Tomahawk Cruise Missile   A currently existent and battle-proven long-range strike weapon for use against land and sea targets. Turbojet powered and launchable from surface ships, submarines, and aircraft, the Tomahawk is undergoing a continuing evolution of systems improvements that will keep it viable for many years to come.

UDFC   The United Democratic Forces of China.

Xia   Like the majority of the other major nuclear powers, Red China has divided its strategic nuclear arsenal among a triad of different delivery systems: bomber aircraft, plus land- and sea-based ballistic missiles. The Xia-class nuclear ballistic-missile submarine makes up the seagoing leg of their triad. Resembling the early-model American Polaris SSBN, the prototype Xia carried twelve solid-fuel Ju Lang 1 IRBMs The later Block II variants had this battery stretched out to sixteen of the more potent Ju Lang II.